The Money Dragon

A Novel

Pam Chun

Aloha!
Pam Chun

SOURCEBOOKS LANDMARK™
AN IMPRINT OF SOURCEBOOKS, INC.®
NAPERVILLE, ILLINOIS

Published by Sourcebooks, Inc.
P.O. Box 4410, Naperville, Illinois 60567-4410
(630) 961-3900
Fax: (630) 961-2168
www.sourcebooks.com

Library of Congress Cataloging-in-Publication Data
Chun, Pam.
The money dragon / by Pam Chun.
    p. cm.
    ISBN 1-57071-866-0 (alk. paper)
1. Leong, L. Ah–Fiction. 2. Capitalists and financiers–Fiction. 3. Chinese Americans–Fiction. 4. Honolulu (Hawaii)–Fiction. 5. Immigrants–Fiction. 6. Merchants–Fiction. I. Title.

PS3603.H85 M66 2002
813'.6–dc21

                                                                2001054269

Printed and bound in the United States of America
        DO   10   9   8   7   6   5   4   3   2   1

The Money Dragon

The Secret of the Cover

The Red Columns contain writings from the I Ching, the Book of Changes

Red is the Chinese Good Luck color

Yellow is Imperial color of the Emperor and the Imperial Family

The Chinese Character is "Loong" which means Dragon

In the center is a Ba-Gwa, the octagon consulted in Feng Shui as a guide to enhance Ch'i

The Symbol for Yin and Yang, female and male, negative & positive, is in the center of the Ba-Gwa.

The book cover was printed on a special paper to simulate the look of aged parchment, to convey the feeling of an old history book.

The most auspicious symbols are here, but slightly out of focus, imperfect, just like the man, Lau Ah Leong.

To Ryan Courtney Leong
born the Year of the Dragon
Great-great-grandson of the Money Dragon, L. Ah Leong
Great-grandson of Lau Tat-Tung and his Phoenix, Fung-Yin

Acknowledgments

My first thank-you goes to Senator and Mrs. Hiram Fong, who gave me the initial clue: my great-grandfather's name.

I owe this story's existence to my Popo, Lau Fung-Yin, who reluctantly, then fervently, told me these tales, layer by layer, over the course of a decade. To Auntie Fannie Wong and Uncle Hanny (Stanley) Lau, and my father Kwai Wood Chun, I cherish your memories of long-ago and quieter times. I thank Grand-uncle Liu Junzuan, First grandson of Fifth wife Wong Shee, for translating his mother's written history of L. Ah Leong in China. Sincere *Mahalo* to my brothers, Lowell & Dale Chun, for their ghost stories and passion for Hawaiiana.

Deepest thanks to Thomas McCullough and George E. Ong for unraveling the legalese of immigration laws during Hawaiʻi's Territorial days. *Mahalo* to my astute readers Alberta Eckers, Terese Tse Bartholomew, John Stucky, Mela Daniel, Sharon Steckline, Cathy Mano, Elisa Kamimoto, and Patricia Wahlmann. Special thanks to Adele Horwitz for her invaluable editing. My deep appreciation to Neil Thomsen at the National Archives in San Bruno who shared his knowledge and sleuthing skills to uncover stories long forgotten. Thank you to my *ʻohana* of friends, especially Francesca De Grandis, Lewis Buzbee, Billy Hustace, and Genevieve and Paul Ong.

A giant *Mahalo* to my agent Elizabeth Pomada for her belief, energy, and gentle guidance. A sincere thanks to Michael Larsen for his overflowing well of ideas and constant encouragement.

Thank you, Dominique Raccah and Sourcebooks, for touching my life. *Mahalo hui loa* and a thousand plumeria leis to Peter Lynch, whose enthusiastic support brought this book to light. A special thank-you to my extraordinary editor, Hillel Black, for his insight and kindness.

And last, but first in my heart, thank you to Fred Joyce III, who never complained when my thoughts dwelled in another world.

My fondest love and *Aloha* belongs to my son, Ryan Courtney Leong. He inspired me to pursue the voices of our ancestors. Their struggles gave us our future.

Table of Contents

Part IV

Part V

Foreword

by former U.S. Senator Hiram. L. Fong,

Hawai'i 1959–1977

I knew L. Ah Leong. To all his customers he was "Lau Faat Leong," one of the most successful merchants of Chinese ancestry in Hawai'i's history.

As a child I frequently accompanied my mother to shop at his retail store on the north side of King Street, between Kekaulike and Maunakea Streets. The store was always jammed with boxes and boxes of groceries and usually crowded with customers. On many occasions, I have marveled seeing him talking on the telephone, selling grocery, and collecting money simultaneously.

In those days, there was much racial profiling in Hawai'i. That Lau Ah Leong succeeded so well is a testimony of his shrewdness, hard work, perseverance, and strong Confucian values.

When he came from China, kings and queens ruled the Hawaiian nation. He survived political and economic turmoil when powerful businessmen overthrew Hawai'i's monarchy. He stood up against the Territorial government of the United States after the islands were annexed. Despite the odds, L. Ah Leong's wholesale and retail mercantile empires spread throughout the Hawaiian Islands.

I have known Pam Chun since she was a child in Honolulu and a classmate of my daughter's. A few years ago, my wife Ellyn mentioned that I knew her great-grandfather, L. Ah Leong. We were surprised that she had never heard his name before. Thus, Pam began her search, a long and difficult process to research and discover the great-grandfather she had never known.

This is the fictionalized account, the story of a legendary man. This is also the story of conscientious Chinese businessmen who survived adverse laws and discrimination, and their families who were forced to merge cultures and traditions.

There is a Chinese saying, "When you drink the water, remember its source."

We have come a long way from our source.

Our children and our children's children must remember this past.

The Lau Family Tree

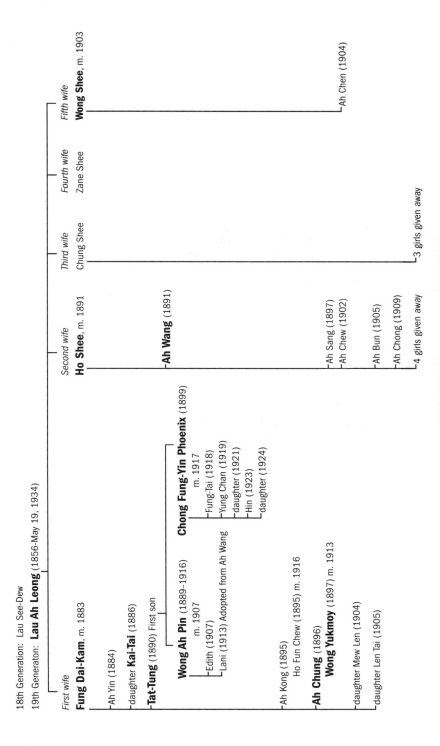

PART I

Chapter One
China: 1917

The first time I heard L. Ah Leong's name, I was swinging upside down from the lychee tree. Papa, home from his stores in Singapore, beguiled Mama with tales of his fellow travelers. What did I care about a rich Chinese merchant in Hawai'i, a barbarian port? I wanted stories–of sword-wielding pirates roving the South China Straits, of emperors bewitched by tiger demons, of ghosts rising from graves on moonlit nights.

"Where is this Hawai'i?" I asked.

Papa grabbed at the ribbons in my hair. He teased, "If you sail toward the sunrise, the moon will turn full three times before you get to Hawai'i, the Sandalwood Mountains." I thumped his shoulders with my thick braids and laughed so hard when he caught them that I fell out of the tree.

How was I to know that ten years later, when I turned eighteen, L. Ah Leong would pluck me from the ship where my baby and I were imprisoned by Immigration? That I would make love to his First son under the Hawaiian moon, flee from his First wife, and refuse his last, loving, dying wish?

ॐ

The next time I heard L. Ah Leong's name, Papa was dead.

"Lau Tat-Tung is the husband for your First daughter," Matchmaker Tsay insisted with a tap of her fan at Mama. "First son of L. Ah Leong, richest merchant in Hawai'i."

"Too far away," Mama disagreed. She fluttered like a sparrow and frowned at the thought of losing me, her eldest daughter.

"Think how lucky for Phoenix to have a millionaire father-in-law with a Five-Star Name, a title awarded only to titans who possess great power, wealth, and honor. They call him the Merchant Prince of Hawai'i. So famous he doesn't use his surname. I can count on one hand the men who have the prestige and fortune to receive the honorable Five-Star Name from the Governor of Kwang Tung Province. Remember when Ah Leong returned two years ago? How we were all invited to his three-day banquet to celebrate his new estate? His chefs served two thousand people a day.

"Tat-Tung is his First son from his First wife." Matchmaker Tsay raised her fan to the number one position to emphasize her point. "An excellent match for Phoenix, born the year of the Rat. Tat-Tung is a Dragon like his father, a natural leader of men: strong, creative, and smart."

"Short-tempered and stubborn," countered Mama.

Matchmaker Tsay shook her head and clucked "tsk tsk." Her wrinkled fingers thumbed through the tissue-thin pages of the red-edged Chinese almanac. "See? Dragon stubbornness is only on the outside. Inside, he is soft-hearted, honest, and sensitive. He will appreciate the strong-willed energy of the Rat. Too bad his first wife left him a daughter. Besides, Hawai'i follows American laws. Phoenix will be his only wife." She reminded Mama that besides his home and business in Hawai'i, Tat-Tung's father had built three estates, all larger than ours, in the mountainous Chinese village of Kew Boy.

From the next room, Grandfather and I peered through the crack of the open door and watched Matchmaker Tsay and Mama consult the almanac for a propitious meeting date. Matchmaker Tsay's heavily powdered forehead crinkled into miniature crevices. Mama shrugged her narrow shoulders.

I slid back in my chair and turned to Grandfather for support. His sharp-eyed, usually serene visage, known and respected throughout

China and Singapore by shrewd businessmen, drooped with despair. I was in tears. This meeting had gone far too smoothly. Mama had five daughters and one son. According to Chinese tradition, my baby brother, Grandfather's only male heir, would inherit the family estate and business. As a well-bred Chinese daughter, my duty was to marry well. Sons from four wealthy families vied for me, but they were Second, Third, and Fourth sons. Not worth marrying, I huffed to Mama. I refused to be subservient to their First brother and his wives, nor would I put up with concubines. Mama warned in that case, either I marry this American or become a Buddhist nun like my auntie.

৵৵

A few days later, Mama scrutinized Tat-Tung and weighed what she saw with Matchmaker Tsay's words about the eldest son of Hawai'i's famous Merchant Prince. Tall, with large dark eyes that spoke of many lifetimes, thick black hair, and a smooth tanned complexion, he stood proudly in a Western-style suit, yet gestured with the humble manners of a Confucian scholar.

From my hiding place in the carved balcony above the parlor, I wondered if he thought of his dead wife, then blushed at my naiveté. What did he learn from a father who had lived with five wives and an impressive parade of young servant girls, all in the same house? Some of Tat-Tung's mothers, brothers, and sisters now lived on his father's estate, five miles north.

When he entered, his broad shoulders moved as if he was used to walking where the open air is kissed by ocean breezes. His eyes were bold and kind, his gaze observant and thoughtful. An interesting challenge, I hummed to myself. He had been educated in Hawai'i and China. Perhaps his Chinese breeding had tempered any crude American ways.

Mama signaled the servant to serve the jasmine tea and almond cakes. Like a swallow fluttering her feathers protectively in her nest, she leaned back and gazed searchingly at this Hawai'i-born Chinese. Would he take care of her eldest daughter? her almond eyes asked. She took a breath, then gazed directly at him.

He answered her questions like an educated man with new ideas. Discreetly, he glanced past her. A dozen carved chairs were formally arranged with carved side tables inset with marble. Thickly woven Tientsin rugs muted footsteps and voices to a refined tone. He turned back to Mama and accepted the tea she offered. Other men would clumsily grab the tiny cups; he used one hand with the other to balance. I had chosen tender, flaky almond cakes. He passed that test too; he ate them neatly, confidently, without a flurry of crumbs falling into his lap.

Of all my suitors, Grandmother and Mama thought Tat-Tung, an experienced businessman almost thirty years old, would make the most mature husband. Anyone less worldly could not handle me; I was seventeen, almost too old to marry.

"You have too much fight for a young man. Older is better," Grandfather decided. "Your beauty outshines the fabled Moon Maiden, but you're too sassy."

"It's not my fault," I teased back. I reminded him that he had slipped me into another village for tutoring to avoid the provincial village gossip. For what does a girl need to read and write? other families criticized. He told them to mind their own business. After all, I was the one who ran the family estate when he was in Singapore, now that Papa was dead. Since we Hakka Chinese did not believe in foot binding like the Punti, I was free to race my cousins and climb the camphor wood trees behind our house. Punti Chinese had settled in the rich broad plains of South China eight hundred years before our Hakka ancestors arrived. The Punti couldn't understand our dialect. Even worse, they were appalled that we Hakka didn't bind our little girls' feet.

Too many girls, the other families told Mama; she should have drowned them at birth. "Give them away, now that you have a son." Mama waved away their advice. Her girls would take care of her. They would not forget their family.

After Tat-Tung left, Mama asked me what I thought about this Hawai'i businessman. I tossed my braids and said, "Not bad. I'll marry him." Mama caressed my cheek, her fingers soft and trembling. When she lifted my chin, my tears overflowed like the spring floods.

"Oh no, what have I done?" I choked. This man offered me an uncommon life, the prestige of being his only wife, the First daughter-in-law of L. Ah Leong, the legendary Merchant Prince of Hawai'i. But at what price?

Grandfather Chong and my late father, Chong Kook-Jai, owned a prosperous grocery and restaurant business serving silver mines and rubber plantations in Singapore, operated shoe factories, and dealt in pewter and rubber. In Singapore, then a Strait Settlement, the miners thought only of the riches they would find, not of the backbreaking work and malaria. The Chong businesses prospered since we dealt only with Chinese we knew, who believed to default a debt would be a loss of face; one must start off the New Year with a clean slate, without debts against their family name.

Every two years, Grandfather and Papa returned. Mama ran down the path when she heard the cheer from the village watchtower announcing their approach. When the men approached she clasped her trembling hands, her heart racing, bursting, overflowing with anticipation. Then Mama would have another baby or two. Papa would buy more rice paddies and enlarge the house.

In 1908, an epidemic swept through the Mei Hsien district when the men were home from Singapore. Chinese herbs were no match against cholera. Western doctors would not come to our village in the mountains. Every day the gravediggers wheeled through the village.

"Why didn't I die instead of my only son?" Grandfather cried from his sickbed. I hurried to him with a pan of cool water to soothe his forehead. The damp towels sizzled with fever—still he burned. I turned to Mama and Grandmother for help, but they wailed, prostrate at Papa's death bed. We had no time to bury him with the formal rituals. Only thirty-nine years old, he had been lucky in all aspects of his life. Now he lay in the graveyard he had just completed to honor his parents when their time came.

I was only ten when Papa died. From a sedan chair carried by two men, dressed in cotton pants and tunic, I supervised the farmers and paid the workers, a task Papa gave me when I was five. When hungry and murderous robbers swept through the village, I hid the rice in secret wall panels and concealed my family in rooms under the floorboards beneath the beds. I clasped Mama tight to keep her from crying out when bandits shattered the doors and windows to splinters.

When debts and rent money had to be collected from faraway villages, I hiked with my older cousin and uncle over high mountains laced with narrow foot paths. We crossed gorges that fell away to mist as in ancient brush paintings. When I was twelve, my uncle fell ill on one of these trips. I stayed to comfort him. My cousin left us his down coat and continued on for help. The cold crept under my skin. When the still night was so black I thought I had gone blind, my uncle died. I cowered next to his body under the heavy coats, hidden from the bandits who prowled the roads at night. Save me, Kwan Yin Goddess of Mercy, save me, I chanted over and over. I wept when, as a misty purple dawn crept across the skies, I heard the beat of my cousins' running feet and their cries, "Phoenix! Phoenix!"

When the tigers poured down from the hills, I called everyone into the house and locked our heavy doors. I peeked out the windows and watched the hungry beasts stalk the streets. A tiger pounced on a villager who waited too long to run to safety. Tiger jaws nipped his head off with a crunch and chewed on what was left.

Now I could leave all the sadness of my life behind. Tat-Tung offered me a comfortable life as the wife of the modern, sophisticated, American First son of L. Ah Leong, the great Merchant Prince of China and Hawai'i.

"Yes, I will marry him," I promised Mama.

☙☜

I grabbed the sides of the sedan chair when my wedding procession of gift-bearing porters and musicians crested the mountain peak. "This is my home, my husband's house?" I exclaimed. I parted my beaded veil for a better look.

I squeezed my eyes shut and thanked Grandfather. For a month, he had negotiated the auspicious gift exchanges through Matchmaker Tsay. Loud chatter had filled the parlors as aunts, cousins, and servants embroidered endless afternoons so red wedding coverlets and my new wardrobe as a married woman danced with propitious flowers and birds.

My future husband and his father traveled back and forth between their great mercantile businesses and estates in both Hawai'i and China. L. Ah Leong had great face, as recognized by the honor of his Five-Star Name. What I saw before me was evidence of this family's great honor, wealth, and power.

Ming Yang Tong, L. Ah Leong's largest estate in China, commanded the base of a towering hill, enfolding it within its walled borders. As we got closer, the sun flared off the windows of its two hundred rooms. Glazed tiles glistened from dozens of rooftops. Within its high perimeter walls, *Ming Yang Tong* was a complete city with mature orchards, vegetable gardens, and livestock. Its two hundred rice paddies stretched in sensuous green bands far beyond the horizon.

That first day stretched endlessly with ceremonies, prayers, and banquets. But when night fell, blacker than the night my uncle died on the mountain path, Tat-Tung led me through the maze of high-ceilinged parlors and sitting rooms, up a stone stairway, to the heart of *Ming Yang Tong*. He had picked the best of the 118 bedrooms: coolest in the summer, warmest in the winter. He fumbled with the heavy brass latch of our room, then proudly eased open the door. He led me in, his eyes waiting, watching my response.

Dozens of fat yellow candles flickered in the large airy bed chamber. Their glow bounced off the tall ceilings and across the whitewashed walls. I turned slowly. I approved his arrangement of my tall wardrobes and the carved bed sent by Mama, but didn't know how to tell him. This was the first time I was alone with my husband. I was used to taking charge. Now I was supposed to be demure.

Confidently, he opened my trunks and removed the thickly quilted bedding. I knelt next to him, our heads close but not touching.

I felt his breath, languorous as the summer breeze that caresses the ripening rice. I looked deep in his eyes and shivered happily at the pleasures they promised.

"Here," I whispered. I fingered the silky covers and showed him which layers I wanted on our marriage bed.

❦❦

Eight months later, on a warm morning when spring enticed all the birds to twitter and court, Tat-Tung surprised me in my favorite spot: under the *pak-lan* tree in the garden.

I jumped, startled by the shower of white petals.

"Phoenix, I thought you were playing mah-jongg with my father's wives." He laughed and released the shivering branch. He wore a burgundy mandarin gown fastened with jade buttons carved to resemble peonies, an auspicious flower.

"You're always busy working on your father's accounts, so you never know what I really do," I answered coyly. I turned back to my book and added, "Or you're playing the moonharp all day with the other rich men." He looked like an elegant Confucian scholar when his head tipped in concentration over the lacquered case of the butterfly-shaped moonharp painted with auspicious bats, vases, and symbolic Buddha's knots. The first time I heard his fingers ripple over the strings, I saw his soul. Sometimes it was as lilting as a waterfall dancing down a spring mountain, sometimes as sorrowful as the moaning winter winds, sometimes as dark and turbulent as a midsummer typhoon.

He raised an eyebrow. "But only when you're embroidering in your private parlor, talking fashion and jewelry with your aunties and cousins."

I tossed my head and continued to read. He stepped out in the sharp China sun and lit a cigarette, a habit of the young sons of the wealthy, and contemplated how I had changed. He said that he liked the way I pulled my hair back into a sleek bun fastened with jade and gold pins, a perfect frame for a dainty oval face, red rosebud lips, and skin that glowed like the full moon. I blushed. He traced his fingers along the designs of my colorful cotton tunic.

"How the light shimmers around you like a protective cocoon," he added and seated himself contemplatively at my side.

I reached up to his brow and touched his hair, short and parted in the Western style. His Westernness protected me, a shield against the confusion of living without an emperor. I wiggled the tip of his ear lobe with my finger and whispered, just in case one of his mothers might be passing through the hallway, "My American husband, do I please you?" I needed no answer. I knew each time he cried out, his taut body shimmered with sweat, when our bodies entwined under the China moon. I sensed something bothered him now. After a few seconds, he took a deep breath as if he dreaded what he had to say.

After the death of Yuan Shi-ka'i, presidential dictator of the Republic of China, warlords terrorized the country. No one could keep track of their constant battles to command districts and provinces. Without a strong emperor or president, China plunged into chaos.

At first, he thought we were safe at *Ming Yang Tong*, guarded by his men. Then he heard fleeing villagers report that warlords targeted the largest landowners. The poor needed only the flimsiest excuse now to find a way over the high stone wall surrounding our estate, the largest in the province. They would tear down our thick doors and raid our stores of food. But worse, they captured the rich, slit their throats, and sliced their children into bloody ribbons. "Phoenix, I've ordered my men to pack our things." He apologized that he had to leave my furniture behind. We would join his father and the rest of his family in Hawai'i.

My book tumbled. The thin-tissue pages fell open on the stepping stones at my feet. "No, I won't go." I shook my head and leaned away.

"We have no choice." His voice was tender, stung by my refusal.

I held my hand up. "No, my husband, not now," I pleaded.

He frowned. "So, you've been seduced by the opulence of *Ming Yang Tong*—leisurely days of embroidery and mah-jongg, meals prepared by our chefs, and being carried aloft on sedan chairs." This time, his voice was firm, uncompromising. The Confucian ethic demanded obedience to one's husband. Without it, family harmony would be lost. He squared his shoulders. The power of his authority stilled the air. He repeated slowly, "I insist."

I lifted my chin, proud but shy. "I'm pregnant."

His laughter, relieved and joyful, echoed off the garden walls. "We definitely can't stay. My child must be born in Hawai'i."

"Mama won't even let me walk home anymore. How can I cross the ocean to Hawai'i?"

He put his arms around my shoulders, enveloping me in the crisp clean smell of his elegant gown and the lingering scent of anise from his cigarette.

☜☞

Mama and my grandparents visited for the last time. When Ah Chen, the thirteen-year-old son of Ah Leong's Fifth wife, yelled that visitors approached, I jumped up from the carved *huanghuali* chair in the parlor and dashed through three pavilions to see. Ah Chen had just pulled open the heavy front door. In the distance, my family's three sedan chairs crossed the Five Arch Bridge that L. Ah Leong had built connecting the town of Kew Boy to his estate, then followed the grass river bank to the high stone wall surrounding *Ming Yang Tong*. Ah Chen unlocked the iron gates and flung them open. Above the three sedan chairs, sunlight sparkled off the boughs of the lychee, loongan, starfruit, and tangerine orchards surrounding the house.

Grandfather, in a tunic with carved jade and gold buttons, stepped from the first chair. He hugged me, not waiting for my formal bow. Grandmother and Mama followed, in dark blue and teal tunics accented with gold earrings and solid jade bracelets.

During those weeks of tearful packing, I wanted to show Mama and my grandparents how happy I had been at Ah Leong's fabled estate. Our family quarters overlooked the central courtyard–so easy to find. When afternoons steamed hot and lazy, Tat-Tung used to guide me through the maze of bedrooms and formal reception parlors in the other wings, dazzling me with their treasures. I thought I could do the same for my family. But I forgot which way to turn and which staircase led to which wing. Halls stretched to longer halls and identical doors. Stairways led up to balconies, down to courtyards, up to bedrooms, and down to sitting rooms.

"Ai-yah," I gasped when I opened a door to what I thought was the Fifth parlor. "There should be a dozen rosewood chairs here and a marble-topped table there. Was the furniture rearranged? And where are the pictures of my husband's family in Hawai'i? They were displayed in the lacquered cabinets along the walls." I panicked. Where was I? How would I find my way back?

Steps, quick and sure, approached from the sitting room to the left. A skinny thirteen-year old boy tugged at my sleeve.

"Phoenix, you must ask me to help you."

"I apologize for disturbing you, Ah Chen." I bowed uncomfortably. Every time I saw him, I remembered that he was born the year Tat-Tung had married his first wife. The brothers' resemblance was strong, stamping them with their father's indelible mark: a strong square face, soul-searching eyes, and a determined set to the jaw. I always wondered how Ah Chen thought I compared to my husband's first wife, Wong Pin.

"No, no, it is I who disturb your visit with your family," he replied.

I sighed, frustrated and confused.

He grinned. "This place is too big." He bowed to the others. "Grandmother, Grandfather, and Mama," he exclaimed. "I am sorry to interrupt Phoenix's excellent tour. Remember me? I am Eighth son Ah Chen, Lau Ah Leong's Fifth wife's only son."

With an adolescent wink, he insisted, "May I accompany you through our father's new house?" He led us through luxuriously carpeted and furnished parlors and sitting rooms, through storage rooms with banquet tables and benches to seat two thousand, through a separate kitchen building with woks so large I could use them as beds, through a building used solely for storing firewood.

Grandfather's eyes lit up when Ah Chen opened the doors to Ah Leong's third and smallest house, a retreat for quiet contemplation and study for his descendants. Grandfather approached the rosewood desk in the library where an ink stone and bamboo brush stand stood ready for a scholar's hand. He extended an elegant forefinger, touched the rolls of expensive rice paper, and sighed. When Ah Chen told him that no one slept in the eighteen furnished bedrooms here, Grandfather whispered wistfully, "I would live here."

※※

All this time, Tat-Tung's ten-year-old daughter, Edith, glowered in the background. Since the day we met, I had offered to teach her embroidery with the ladies. Edith refused. She was tall for her age with a small nose and melting dark eyes like her father's. She would grow up to be a beauty if only she could find something pleasurable to erase her perpetual scowl. I invited her to walk along the river outside the high stone wall to feed the swans and geese since she especially loved watching the undulating movements of the swans as they lowered their heads to eat. Instead, Edith complained about me to her father.

Lies, lies, I agonized, but said nothing in my defense.

The dawn after my family said their good-byes, my husband, Edith, and I boarded the narrow hand-poled boat that would take us to Swatow. Ten hours later, we arrived at Tat-Tung's three-story hotel managed by a Lau cousin. Tat-Tung searched for passage to Hawai'i. He found no ships. In 1918, America was at war.

A month later, my husband received a message from Ah Chen.

Dear First brother,

Flee! Bandits head to Swatow now to kidnap you and your family. They say our father will pay millions to get his First-born American son and family back alive. Tell father we are safe for now. Tell him to not return until China's civil war is over. Go now! Farewell from your Eighth brother, Ah Chen

I threw our clothes back into our trunks. "Where will we go?" I wailed. I didn't care if my tears fell in angry stains on his suits. "If the walls of your father's house can't protect us, where can we go?"

"There will be ships in Hong Kong," Tat-Tung promised. But in Hong Kong, thousands fought for the same escape route.

He badgered the shipping offices of his business associates. He received the same news everywhere; few ships crossed the Pacific now. One must be patient.

No matter how many times we sponged off, our clothes clung to our bodies. By the end of the day, we stank with perspiration and the rub of close body contact. The extra weight of pregnancy, the heat, and the humidity pressed down on me. Most of the time, I lay exhausted in our flat, nauseated by the pungent, ripe odors of teeming crowds, their foods, and their debris.

Three months later, our daughter was born. Our treasure, Tat-Tung gasped when he held her for the first time and inhaled her milk-sweet scent. She had rosy cheeks, a gentle disposition, and eyes like her father: round as ripe loquat, deep as pools of dark raw sugar. She rarely cried. Instead, she watched Tat-Tung's face, concentrating on the movement of his lips and the sparkle in his eyes. The Kowloon fortune teller said she had the eyes of an old soul; she would capture the hearts of many. So I named her for one of the four mythical Chinese creatures magically reborn from the ashes of its own funeral pyre with energy, hope, and promise. Her name was Fung-Tai, the phoenix whose beauty and good luck entice others to follow her, for Chinese prefer boys and we wished for a son.

Two weeks later, Tat-Tung ordered our *amah*, our servant, to pack up our belongings. A ship was leaving for Hawai'i. We couldn't wait until the baby was older. With civil war in China, and America at war, who knew when the next ship would leave?

I thought I could manage by myself when my husband said we could not bring the *amah* he had hired in Hong Kong. The ship heaved to and fro, sliding me and baby Fung-Tai from one side of the cabin to the other. When I bathed her, the wash pan slid across the floor. The bath water flew up with each sway of the ship. "Wait, wait!" I cried. My body was so light that I, too, rolled with each pitch of the ship. My milk stopped. Baby Fung-Tai wailed. Even worse, I knew nothing of diapers: when to change them and how to wash them. Luckily, a wispy-haired man said Fung-Tai reminded him of the granddaughter he had left behind. He offered to gather cloth to make her diapers.

Edith pinched and slapped the baby when she thought I wasn't looking. I said nothing to Tat-Tung. It's not her fault, I reminded myself. If anything happened to me, how would I want someone to treat my own baby?

Since our first-class suite had no adjoining bathroom, I had to leave my baby alone if I had to go. So I placed her in the middle of the bed surrounded by pillows, and propped chairs along the side of the bed. One time, the ship rolled as if the seas meant to turn us upside down. I returned to everything–chairs, pillows, bedding–strewn on the floor. I tore through the jumble. When I found my baby asleep in the middle of the bedspread, I collapsed, clutching her in my arms. My heart beat so loudly I thought it would explode through my chest and wake her. What have I gotten into? I cried. And where was my husband? Probably on deck walking with Edith, listening to her lies, I moaned.

Early one morning, just as dawn turned bright with the rising sun, Tat-Tung hurried us up to the deck. We heard cheers and beheld dozens of yachts flying towards us like flocks of elegant white birds.

"O'ahu!" Tat-Tung pointed out. "See Diamond Head, the mountain on the tip of the island? A lookout there signals that a ship is in sight. The whistle at The Hawaiian Electric Company blasts so loud the whole town can hear." Caught up in his excitement, I wrapped my arms tight around my baby.

"Silly woman," Edith muttered under her breath, thinking no one could hear. "So stupid."

All of Honolulu, it seemed, had turned out to greet us. Dark-skinned boys bobbed in the sea below and flashed white crescent smiles. They motioned to the passengers to throw coins into the water, then dove after the money. Within seconds, they popped to the surface with bright coins in their teeth. Cheers erupted from the crowds.

Statuesque bronze-skinned women glided along the docks and called out in melodious musical words over the music of the Royal Hawaiian Band. Garlands of flowers in a myriad of colors cascaded from their arms like colorful waterfalls.

"Flower leis," Tat-Tung explained. "They're given in *Aloha*, a Hawaiian word that means I love you, hello, and good-bye."

How would I ever learn all this? There was more bewilderment when Immigration told Tat-Tung I could not be released for three weeks. They had too many Chinese to interview, check, and document.

Three weeks! "Your child and I will be dead by then," I protested. "I need a milk-nurse before the baby starves to death."

"I'll get help."

"When?"

"You will be off this ship today." Tat-Tung took out his papers and quickly double-checked that they were in order. He pocketed them. Then he hugged me with baby Fung-Tai between us. I traced the sharp crease of his crisp white collar with my finger tips, feeling the strong hot pulse at his neck. I held my finger there at his heartbeat, wishing his speedy return.

"How?"

"I'll get my father." He picked up baby Fung-Tai and tickled her cheeks. Her eyes never left his, even when he handed her back to me.

The crowds of departing passengers pushed towards the gangway. How I envied them, mostly Caucasian or Hawai'i-born Chinese with their papers in order. I tugged on his sleeve.

"How can your father get us off? He's Chinese, and Chinese are second-class citizens in the United States." The other women passengers had told me how difficult it was for Chinese to travel. When Tat-Tung's father came to Hawai'i, Hawaiian kings and queens ruled the island nation. Now that Hawai'i was a United States Territory, the American Immigration Department enforced the Chinese Exclusion Act of 1882. The Chinese passengers described how even Hawai'i-born Chinese could be denied reentry, depending on the inspectors. Because of the

Chinese Exclusion Laws, the government demanded that each Chinese had to have a special identification card for the Hawaiian Islands with their picture. In addition, witnesses living in Hawai'i were required to testify under oath on their behalf upon each exit and reentry to the Islands. Immigration could even prevent Chinese from leaving Hawai'i if they felt they did not have a good reason for traveling abroad.

"Tell your father we wait desperately for him to save us," I whispered. I gave him the paper upon which I had written our names in delicate calligraphy, Lau Fung-Yin and Lau Fung-Tai. "I changed my name to Fung-Yin, the Brilliant Phoenix. All the girls in this family will be as beautiful, strong, and resilient as the Chinese Phoenix."

He pressed my fingers to his lips. Then he grabbed Edith's hand. They threaded a path through the Chinese crowding the deck of the SS *Nanking*. Edith flung me a scornful look. She clung to her father and pranced down the gangplank to the dock. He maneuvered past the guards and walked through the Immigration station, an imposing tile-roofed building.

I sat on a deserted deck chair and watched the docks until Fung-Tai cried again for food. "Poor baby," I whispered, "my milk is gone. I only have rice water to feed you." She wailed louder, pursing her lips as if sucking a phantom breast. Only then did I return to my cabin to wait for Tat-Tung's return.

How I longed to flee this ship, my prison for three weeks. I had paced the small confines of my cabin for most of the journey, afraid that the other Chinese passengers my age, students going away to school, would laugh at how young I was—how naive and stupid to be eighteen years old, married, and a mother. I washed and put on a dark blue *cheong-sam* with red bias around the neck and hem. I had made the elaborate matching mandarin button sets myself while sitting in the carpeted parlor of *Ming Yang Tong*. If Tat-Tung were to return, he should come soon before the Immigration Office closed for the evening. Fung-Tai could not last another day without milk. I pushed our trunks closer to the door.

When Fung-Tai fell asleep, I carried her up on deck and watched the docks and the streets. Compared to China, Honolulu was clean, orderly, lush. Even the sea was bluer here than in Hong Kong. I saw coconut trees with heavy long fingers of green growing only from the top. Over the din of men unloading the ship, I heard chattering birds playing in the flowering trees. Was it the brightness of the sun or fervent hope that made everything look so lively, so colorful?

I paced the deck while Fung-Tai bobbed her head sleepily. The Chinese were the only passengers left waiting to be screened by Immigration. Although many had valid reasons to enter Hawai'i, they were still anxious. Even a Christian minister and his wife had to wait for their interview so they could disembark. There were wives joining husbands, sons returning home, and professors returning to the University, all stuck here because they were Chinese.

From them, I learned what my new life would be like in Hawai'i. Free education was guaranteed for all children and great fortunes could be made. Not like China where the whole village used to pool their resources to educate one man to take the civil service exam and bring honor to the village. They pointed out men studying papers detailing complete family histories. These were the "paper sons," claiming to be children of legitimate merchants, teachers, ministers, and other exempt classes. Their "fathers" were really uncles or brothers, or other sojourners who found having "sons" a profitable business. How daring they were to brave this deception; even those with legitimate papers were terrified of the Immigration interviews. The Inspectors separated husbands from wives, children from parents. After the standard questions of birth and names, they asked detailed questions about the number of rooms and doors and windows in one's house, the number of chickens or dogs a certain person owned, then fed wrong answers to other family members to confirm or deny. Any blunder was grounds for deportation.

The grandfather who had helped me with Fung-Tai's diapers said Hawai'i was like China, where everything was available for a price.

Nearly all the Immigration Inspectors could be bribed to approve an entry into Hawai'i. He himself had the required cash: $1,350. The Chinese network had the names of the cooperative inspectors, secretaries, and Chinese interpreters. With the Inspector-in-Charge himself one of the biggest perpetrators, $1,350 was the entry fee for those who could afford it.

I paced the deck of the ship. The air cooled. Activity on the dock had stopped. People went home for dinner. Soon the sun would grow larger and brilliant orange as it neared the horizon.

I stood alone at the rail with my baby feeling the trade winds caress us with sadness and longing. The fresh breeze blew in from the sea and seagulls called plaintively as they swooped for the scraps thrown out by the galley crew.

The number of porters decreased from the dozens of that morning to a small handful milling around barefoot or dozing in the lazy afternoon. A few lei sellers remained with their baskets of flowers to accost the visitors who came late. The crew returned draped with leis. When they walked by, the heady fragrance of these tropical flowers overwhelmed me with their exquisite scents. The men let me touch the delicate petals and stamens: bright red, deep yellow, delicate purple. I could not imagine the variety of exotic flowers that grew here.

Then I saw in the distance a cloud of dust galloping towards the wharf. In its midst, two horses raced, hot breath snorting like demons, hooves churning the streets into billows of dust that grew until it arrived at the dock with a "Whoa, Screech!"

My husband and a fat, bald man dressed in a worn Chinese shirt and pants jumped from the wagon. White-skinned uniformed officers met them, and all hurried into the Immigration station. Out they came. Two tall officers talked intently to the older Chinese. He nodded and waved them towards the boat with authority.

"That must be your grandfather L. Ah Leong," I told my baby. "See how he orders the white men to get us? And how they bend their heads to him? See? He is looking for us now."

All four charged up the gangplank. When Tat-Tung introduced his sixty-two-year-old father, I bowed and said my formal greetings in the Hakka dialect, a musical cadence more like the Mandarin spoken in northern China and unintelligible to the Cantonese-speaking Punti.

Ah Leong waved magnanimously. "I have come for my First daughter-in-law and her child."

I bowed again and again. "Thank you, thank you, thank you." I fought back my tears. "You have rescued us."

"Nothing to fear. I have taken care of everything. You've come home now." He peered at baby Fung-Tai. "So, this is the baby who is starving to death. When your father came to get me, the Immigration officer was already at my store telling me about my grandchild who would not stop crying. They were afraid you would die. And then they would have been responsible." His laugh bellowed across the docks. Then he turned and waved for us to follow.

He wasn't much taller than me. But he was powerfully built with muscular shoulders, strong square hands, piercing eyes, and a determined jaw. No one could tell from his rough work clothes, the clothes of the common laborer, that he was the millionaire merchant whose business empire straddled China and Hawai'i, whose touch guaranteed money would flow like the waves across the Pacific. Tat-Tung had said that his father had so much face, such a prestigious reputation among his peers, that he didn't care what others thought about the way he looked or the way he ran his businesses. There was no mistake in the way he carried himself and commanded respect, that he was the businessman whose reputation was so sterling that the Chinese, who believed in auspicious signs, called him the Money Dragon.

I walked down the gangplank steadied by Tat-Tung's arm. "*Fi de, fi de*. Hurry up, hurry up," he speeded the porters trailing behind with our trunks and baggage. We followed the cleared path commanded by his father.

From my seat behind the men, I swayed with the roll of the carriage and watched Hawai'i unfold. The farther away I rode from the ship, the better I felt. The sky was brilliant blue, the trees and grass lush and thick. Flowers, massed in profusion, were everywhere. The extravagance of blossoms was a luxury, for in China nothing is grown that is not edible or of commercial value.

Thank you, Goddess Kwan Yin, for my father-in-law's generosity, I prayed through my tears. He wielded his power and influence over the white officials. They bent to his command and released me. I praised the music of his horses, "clop-a clop-a clop-a," as they carried me to my new life of freedom under his protection, the powerful Money Dragon of Hawai'i.

How could I have guessed that one day I would climb out the window of L. Ah Leong's house to escape?

Chapter Two

Honolulu Beginnings: 1918

Most people were home for dinner at this time of the day. L. Ah Leong scoffed with a nod at the empty sidewalks. But at his store, his sons were still taking orders and tallying profits in their pads. I stared up at him and marveled. Those legends about his success must be true.

"The L. Ah Leong store is better than home," he chuckled. He leapt off his wagon in the middle of the street.

I heard men shout, "Ah Leong, you back already? What's your new daughter-in-law like?" They hailed my husband and surrounded our wagon so all I could see were tanned Chinese faces, curious and kind.

"Ah, a dainty sparrow," Ah Leong answered with a flourish of his hands and a nod in my direction. "Skin as fair as lotus petals."

"Not like your wife, Dai-Kam?" One of the men drew himself up on his toes, squared his shoulders, and rippled the muscles of his arms.

"Someone who can load the delivery wagons faster than your sons?" grinned the other. "Who can belt you across the store with one swipe of her fist?"

"Tat-Tung doesn't need a woman like his mother." Ah Leong waved away the insults in disgust. "My son's a gentleman. A scholar. His wife is refined."

"You need grandsons, not a frail flower."

Ah Leong puffed his chest. "Her baby has such powerful lungs that Immigration came, in person, to ask me to please take them home. No interview. They could come back in a couple months when they feel better."

His friends gasped. No interview? No demeaning questions to confirm her identity? Immigration never made exceptions.

An elder businessman put his hands on the shoulders of his companions and shook his head. "Tat-Tung's smart. He has chosen well. After all, he will carry on his father's legacy." He gestured with a sweep of his hand towards a building beyond my vision. "I remember when you started your business, Ah Leong. Who would have guessed you'd be the largest merchant today?"

"You see?" Ah Leong shook his finger in the faces of his friend's companions. "Even L. Ah Low remembers. My empire exists because I had the vision. And you," he thundered, waving his hands at the Chinese clustered around him, "would never have been in business."

These men, comrades from the days when they were all queue-wearing subjects of the Monarchy, elbowed each other. "Business! All he thinks of is business."

Ah Leong raised his voice. "Every can of meat, every sack of rice, every vegetable is in my store because I said, 'Okay, you go there!' I hired the workmen. I told them where to put the shelves, how high, how deep. I hired the store cook, trained my sons, brought in the workers. You see the sign above my store? It's there because of me. Those big English letters spell L. Ah Leong Store. My name! My store!" He waved his thick arms in a possessive arc.

Ah Leong and his friends continued their jocular teasing until he motioned them away.

"How do they think I got the energy to do this?" he snorted to my husband. He stood in the street, hands on his hips, and watched his friends' backs fade into the sunset, their footsteps on the wooden sidewalk growing fainter and fainter. He growled, "Because I have been to the land of the dead."

For a long time I wondered what my father-in-law meant. It took me years to sort the legend from the lies, to fit the pieces together. Now, only I know the true story of L. Ah Leong, the Money Dragon.

PART II

Chapter Three

The Dragon Awakens: China 1871

With each breath of hot wind through the gorge, the wooden bridge creaked with a life of its own. The slit boards yawned.

Balance! The boy gripped the rope sides of the narrow bridge and swore at the top-heavy load strapped to his back. He glanced down unwillingly, imagining the hundreds who had fallen—now unhappy ghosts grabbing for his soul.

The hot wind slammed the bridge. The boy Ah Leong sank to his knees and slipped from the ropes that bound him to the crates as if he were a human mule. The wind flung the crates first, then tossed him head first into the river.

He jolted in midair—his sleeve snagged on a rusty nail. Above, the safety of the bridge swayed beyond the grasp of his fingers. Below, the waters swirled in muddy eddies: thick, brown, and opaque.

"Help!" he screamed, arms outstretched. His anguish bounced from the rocks and slammed against the water.

But the villagers of Jiaoling squinted in the bright sun and turned away with a shrug. So many of these old bridges crisscross this region of steep mountains and cascading waterfalls. What was another beggar? Let the boy drown. The muddy waters will swallow him. Let the village further down bother about his body when it surfaced. Yes, he is better dead.

No! He grabbed at the air. His sleeve tore loose from the nail. He bellowed when the river reached up to grab him.

He gasped for air but the water pulled him back and clasped him tight. He did not come up again.

☞☜

"Dreaming, Ah Leong? Only five years you've been here. It's happening as I told you." Ah Leong's partner, Ahuna, sat at the wooden table in the shade of their Kapaʻau general store composing letters for their customers, translating in his own grandiose words the simple longings of the men who worked the sweltering cane fields of Kohala on the Big Island of Hawaiʻi. The year was 1881. Sunlight scattered through the dusty windows to cast a sepia tone throughout the well-stocked general store and coffee shop. He enclosed in each letter the money men trusted him to send home. Ahuna dabbed his tapered bamboo brush on the ink stone with a soft tap-tap and looked up at his twenty-five-year-old protégé. In dusty work pants and faded blue cotton Chinese top, Ah Leong's mentor exuded fatherly concern.

"In partnership with you," acknowledged Ah Leong. He gripped the weathered door of their Kapaʻau general store. If life was better now, why was he fighting this emptiness? As a beggar among hundreds of desperate men, women, and children in the maze of shops and warehouses that crammed the Chinese river port of Jiaoling, he had bartered his strength for lodging and rice. Sometimes he trudged endless hours over steep paths, some too narrow for the hundred pounds of charcoal or lumber on his back. At night, he removed his only shirt and trousers, washed and mended them for the next day, and slept naked and cold on charitable bedding. Now he traded with plantation workers in Hawaiʻi, making twice their ten dollars a month wage.

Ha! He had risen far above those who thought he would be better off dead. They would grovel at his feet when he returned as the richest man in Kwang Tung Province. He envisioned his victorious return in the dazzling finery of a Chinese scholar. But Chinese measured wealth in sons and wives. Only a dozen Chinese women, all old and married, were in Kohala. Bah! His father had foolishly believed he was blessed by the gods when Ah Leong was born.

In 1856, his mother had wrapped her squalling newborn in yards of red cotton. She laid out offerings in translucent tea cups at the temple of Kwan Yin, the benevolent Bodhisattva. She beseeched the goddess to give her son the name Lau Fat Leong, meaning Good Buddha: a prosperous name, a name of integrity. She chanted and swayed. When she shook the bamboo fortune sticks, one numbered sliver sprung from the cylinder and landed at her feet. Ah! she gasped. She asked the temple monks to record Lau Fat Leong, first Lau son of the nineteenth generation, born in the village of Kew Boy in the Year of the Dragon.

Ah Leong's father repaid her devotion nine years later by gambling away their rice fields and home. He abandoned her and his daughter and fled on foot with his only son to northern Fukien Province. There they begged in the marketplaces, amazing villagers with their martial arts. They created thunder claps with their huge hands. Stocky legs flowed through powerful leaps. Grace and speed. Intense concentration and discipline. Tremendous inner strength propelled their bodies into the air. They had needed these traits to survive.

"You know you had to prove yourself. For five years you slaved in my stores in Swatow. Now, as a merchant you make a fortune," Ahuna harrumphed. He scratched his sun-baked neck and continued his task.

"For what? I'm alone."

"Sometimes, alone is better than family. These letters speak of loneliness, too. Mothers, fathers, wives, and children miss them," Ahuna answered. He lowered his voice. "I have not seen my wife in five years." He finished his client's letter and checked it off in his account book. "But my store in Swatow advises me that a Hong Kong businessman arrives tomorrow with two nieces."

Ah Leong turned to Ahuna, his breath caught in his heart.

When the Chinese bachelors gathered at night they passed on the mythical legends: the power of rhinoceros horns, bulls' balls, and live snake eggs to build and maintain the male *yang* and absorb the power of the female *yin*. The First Emperor, Shihuangdi, believed that one of the paths to strength and longevity lay in frequent and prolonged sex without climax, reabsorbing the essential essence into his body so it would nourish his brain. The Emperor boasted of sex with twelve hundred women and became a god for his endurance. The bachelors groaned. Even one wife was a status symbol in Hawai'i where out of eighteen thousand Chinese men, fewer than one thousand were married.

Sons. Wives. Loneliness obsessed Ah Leong.

That night, he slipped out into the solitary comfort of darkness. He ran along barely visible footpaths until they disappeared completely. Then he parted the tangled vines and entered the moist jungle where distant waterfalls cascaded from lava rock cliffs to pierce mirrored pools. Moonlight struggled to penetrate the soft darkness, but Ah Leong knew the way. He dug his toes into the melted bark of fallen trees, relishing the rich scents of decay and life.

In a clearing where the air vibrated with legendary voices, he repeated his nightly rituals and prayers. When he lifted his arms in salutation, the spirits whispered their presence. "You are back," the wind hissed.

Slowly, Ah Leong bent his knees, weight shifting to the right and back. His arms parted the air as if it were thick, gooey, heavy. His muscles glowed with a silver sheen. Sinews carved by a lifetime of rigorous discipline flowed through each movement with such grace it seemed time had stopped.

He stood suspended, meditating on the messages he heard, then leaped explosively into the air. He whipped through the mist. He pulled power out of the jungle's humid breath and the humus-rich earth. Upon his command, energy rushed through his body as if fired by lightning bolts, just as it had many years ago when he had drowned in the river near Jiaoling and had brought himself back to life. Deadly Dragon Awakens, the masters called that rare power. Then he spread his arms, threw back his head, and inhaled long and deep, at one with the jungle night.

☞☞

The clipper ship stood tall and graceful in the bay. Sharp, lean, and quick. Her dark hull reflected the faces of the local boys who swam up and marveled at the tall masts rigged with the orderly maze of sheets. When Ahuna climbed aboard, her captain squinted across the deck and nodded discreetly towards Fung, the Chinese businessman Ahuna had come to meet.

The man towered seven feet tall, with a thick beard so wiry it defied the salty breeze that played upon the open deck. He held aloft a huge water gourd and emptied it down his throat. Then he dipped the empty gourd into a water barrel and, leaning over the rail, splashed the next scoop over his head. Water and sweat streamed from the end of his queue.

When the giant straightened, Ahuna saw that Fung had eyebrows that bunched across the top of his eyes in a single, fierce line. His scowl revealed blackened teeth and a breath powerful enough to repel the attacking Huns. Calf-high leather boots in the East Indian style encased mammoth legs that paced possessively, impatiently, across the wooden deck.

Fung whipped off his shirt in the tropical heat to expose a massive chest—bare, smooth, and polished like sinewy marble. He tossed his damp shirt to a small Chinese attendant who bobbed and scurried away.

Ahuna approached with wide, firm steps and bowed. "I am Ahuna, elder merchant of Kohala, spokesman for the Hakka Chinese on the island of Hawai'i." He bowed again, eyes fixed on Fung. "Also known as Lau Kong-Yin, the merchant from Swatow."

Fung scowled but nodded recognition.

"We are hospitable people here and toast your august presence." Ahuna lifted a yellowed bottle and two whiskey glasses from a woven bag. "'Okolehao," he offered, "from pineapples." Local farmers had tried to grow pineapples with mediocre success. So far, its chief value was as a potent liquor.

Fung was hot and thirsty. He had debts to collect in these primitive islands and here was the first civilized man he had met. He lifted the murky glass offered him and sniffed. He blinked at the potent fumes and motioned Ahuna to drink first.

Ahuna lifted his glass, downed the shot, and burped loudly with a satisfied "Aaah!"

It was Fung's turn. The liquor burned a searing path down his throat. When it landed, circles of heat radiated through his muscles. His great eyebrows lifted, his Mongol nostrils flared, and his ears turned crimson. He guzzled the rest.

Ahuna refilled their glasses and the men sat, eyes cautious and wary. But with each drink, they grew more boisterous. Ahuna slapped Fung's shoulders and Fung stamped his feet. Soon the giant's eyes softened and his laughter reverberated like colossal prayer bells.

Ahuna asked what Fung's business was in Hawai'i.

Fung said he had debts to collect. Then he leaned forward and motioned with a quick nod to the two women standing near the stern of the boat in view of their guarding uncle. "Two nieces. Promised my brother I'd find them husbands. "

"You," Fung thumped Ahuna's chest. "You need a wife."

Ahuna held out both hands in protest. "No, no. I have a wife in China."

Fung threw back his head and bellowed, "One is not enough. Show your wealth. Take another. My nieces are young and strong," he gestured with a muscled arm.

The taller girl stared at Ahuna with an imperious glare, exuding an air of defiance. Fung Dai-Kam's eyes were exotically round as ripe loquat. Seventeen years old and a husky six feet tall, she had stamina and energy–a woman who could work hard and provide many sons. Cotton cords held thick braids pulled back from velvety olive skin.

Her younger sister, a petite, slender girl, dropped her eyes to the hem of her trousers and turned her back. Ahuna raised an appraising eyebrow. But the woman he chose was not for him.

He looked again at the older girl. She had a voluptuous allure, hinting that something else was in her breeding besides the Chinese; it gleamed with red highlights in her hair when she walked in full sunlight. Her full lips and figure could not hide behind her plain tunic and trousers. She would banish Ah Leong's loneliness.

Ahuna turned to Fung and nodded towards the girls. "Your older niece suits my young friend."

"You choose Dai-Kam?" Fung threw back his head. His laughter reverberated through the harbor and cannonballed up the mountains. "Is he tall and powerful like an ox?"

"No. He is short and muscular like the prize horses of the Mongol plains. Brawny and powerful. Lean with no excess fat."

"Is he as smart as the Monkey King?" Fung challenged.

"He is cagey and shrewd like the Emperor's advisors."

Fung's eyes narrowed in thought. "This man, is he family?"

"No. I saw him die. But he brought himself back to life. Almost killed me, too."

Fung stroked his wiry beard and flexed his chest. He leaned forward and pondered Ahuna's words. "Tell me of this man you value so much you would give him a woman you could have yourself."

Ahuna poured the last of the 'okolehao into their glasses and motioned Fung to drink. Then he sat back and told of how Ah Leong fell from the rickety bridge.

"I was sorry to see him drown. The boy could do the work of two men and had a clever tongue. When his body washed up on the rocks, I picked my way down to retrieve it before the scavenging beggars got to him. When I bent to pull him up the bank, an iron grip grabbed my ankle and flung me upwards. My feet flew over my head. I thought I was dreaming when I saw the 'dead' boy roll over with the ease of a panther. He sprang to his feet, crouched low for attack. His skin was blue. His watery eyes shimmered, still and wary."

"But he was dead!" exclaimed Fung.

Ahuna raised his left eyebrow with a glint. "After I assured the boy that I was an honest merchant, he motioned me up. I was breathless, unable to move. He bent down and pulled me to my feet as easily as he would have tossed a leaf to the wind. Then he spread his arms and threw back his head so the sun fell fully on his face and body. Whoosh! The breath of life entered his body. He flew in the air and whipped his arms and legs with reborn energy. The force threw me backwards.

Sunlight blazed on the water he flung from his body. The winds swirled around him. The flush of life transformed his face and body." He added in a low, hushed voice, "This man is magic."

Fung gasped, awed by Ahuna's tale.

"See how my hands tremble to think of it again? Never before have I seen anyone return from the dead." Ahuna lifted his glass and sucked the last drop. "He knew Deadly Dragon Awakens—I thought that power was only legend." Then he turned away, his jaw trembling.

Fung's eyebrows arched. "You took him in?"

Ahuna traded spices, teas, silks, and export porcelains to the Europeans. So when the word spread like the wind that overseas Chinese were sending money home, he packed dried ducks, preserved eggs, medicinal herbs, and other goods for the *wah kiu*, the overseas Chinese in *Gum Sahn Yun*, the Gold Mountains of California, and *Tan Heung Shan*, the Sandalwood Mountains of Hawai'i. The boy worked like a demon.

In 1876, the two joined the men pacing the wooden deck as the SS *City of Peking* plowed east to San Francisco. For three months, they fanned themselves when the heat of the Pacific rose in the doldrums, then groaned when the clipper pitched and rolled in the open ocean. Most of the men on board were contract laborers dreaming of gold nuggets plucked off the streets of San Francisco. Ah Leong and Ahuna ignored these dreams and stayed on the clipper when it followed the trade winds to Kohala on the northern tip of Hawai'i.

In the 1870s, the lush, fertile valleys of Kohala whispered promises in the softness of the days and nights. Chinese brought the secrets of sugar production here from Canton and hired fellow Chinese for the backbreaking work in the cane fields and sugar mills. Their community of plantations, stores, and farms thrived in the rich agricultural area of cool breezes and tropical rains.

"Bleaaah!" the Chinese screamed when they tasted poi. They wanted rice. Only another Chinese understood what these homesick Chinese wanted and spoke to them in the soothing cadences of their dialect.

In Hawai'i, with so few Chinese and nearly all of them men, names were shortened to reflect their casual familiarity. Lau Kong-Yin became Ahuna. He changed Lau Fat Leong to Ah Leong. Ahuna taught Ah Leong the art of roasting and brewing the freshest coffee beans from the fertile Kona coast where moist air, clear sunshine, and porous volcanic soil produced the richest coffees.

Five years later, he chose Ah Leong's wife.

❧❧

Four days after Ahuna met her uncle, Fung Dai-Kam handed Ah Leong the red paper her mother had given her when she left Hong Kong. "Choose the man you want to marry," her mother had told her.

It was not the traditional way. But when Dai-Kam overheard Uncle Fung tell her father about the Chinese in Hawai'i, she knew there was more to life than sewing tiny stitches into intricate patterns for the rich ladies, staring at the ships that sailed out of Hong Kong harbor for exotic ports while she remained trapped without a dowry and future, or bumping elbows against her parents and sister in the single room they called home in Wan Chai.

Waving her arms, she chased Fung down the rickety wooden stairs when he left. "Take me! Take me!"

Uncle Fung whirled at the sound of his niece's loud shout, unmistakably clear above the din of the crowded alleys. Surprised by her gumption, he frowned. "I already asked your parents. Your mother needs you," he said bluntly.

"So I can go blind stitching her fancy patterns? Take me and my sister to *Tan Heung Shan*, Hawai'i, with you."

Fung raised an eyebrow. Her tone and stance were commanding him, not asking a favor. He turned to continue on his way.

She grabbed his shoulder and held him fast. "Uncle Fung," she pleaded, "I am young and strong. I want adventure. I do not care if the man you find for me is poor." She squared her shoulders and clenched her fists. "I will make him rich."

Uncle Fung could feel the fiery energy of his niece, who unfortunately took after the determined, hot-tempered, broad-shouldered male Fungs. So unlike her sister, demure and slim. He narrowed his fierce eyes and grunted.

Dai-Kam tossed her head, a glint in her eyes. "Sell us if you want to. Make a profit. But to someone who wants a wife, not a whore."

He threw back his head and bellowed. "Bah! Don't insult me. Sell you? I should pay the man who dares to take you!"

☙☙

From her place of honor, Dai-Kam observed their guests, Chinese, Caucasian, and Hawaiian, toast her husband at their wedding banquet. Plaques engraved with proverbs surrounded the doors and windows of the simple wood building embellished with scrollwork linking the beams and posts. The Chinese men pressed closer. They shoved red envelopes with "marriage money" in her hands and stared wistfully, reluctant to leave her side.

Here in Kohala, the salt-sweet breeze stirred the dust of the rural roads in her footsteps. When she paused to take a breath, the land stretched expansively green down to water so brilliantly blue at midday that the sight hurt her eyes. The ocean crashed against rugged lava coasts. White waves pounded her ears with hypnotic cadences, day and night.

Every day, she stretched her arms into the sun when she hung out their clothes behind their rented cottage in Kapa'au. She felt the kiss of constant winds through the channel between the islands of Hawai'i and Maui. The humidity made her cotton blouse cling to her arms and breasts. The sun that dried their clothes so quickly swept her tawny skin with a sprinkling of chestnut freckles.

But the men who worked the fields turned dark and wrinkled like dried dates. Their hands were rough and cracked, sometimes slashed by the razor edge of cane leaves. Their words were foreign: "Pidgin English," Ah Leong told her.

Her husband was unlike these laborers. His hands were worn hard and smooth like the wooden counter at his Kapa'au store. And unlike the weary trudge of the plantation workers, he moved with strength and grace, as if he strode on resilient Tientsin carpets instead of grass paths. His cajoling words, so unlike the brusque Hong Kong manner of speech, could beguile her to do anything he wished. His friends weren't surprised when he abandoned his solo visits to the jungle.

But he repeated his father's failure. Ah Leong and his partners went bankrupt.

❧❧

1884

To Lau Kong-Yin, Kohala, Island of Hawai'i

Ahuna,

Thank you for referring me to your friend, L. Ah Low of Honolulu, O'ahu. He gives me work in his store as stock boy and store cook. Dai-Kam cooks for his large family. She takes our first-born, a strong son, with her. We save money by eating all our meals at our respective jobs. We live in an upstairs flat on the corner of Queen and Punchbowl Streets, across the street from 'Iolani Palace, home of the Hawaiian King and Queen. The local people call this place Kaka'ako. Every morning when I get up, the first things I see outside my window are the headstones in the graveyard of Kawaiaha'o Church. This is where I go if I fail again. (signed) Ah Leong

❧❧

The scream of a thousand mynah birds startled Ah Leong awake. He flung his arms over Dai-Kam. She stirred. "The babies?" she murmured instinctively.

"Asleep," he assured her. He stroked her dark tresses cascaded across the pillows, and bent his cheek to catch the short breaths that came just before she wakened. In the distance, dogs barked. Earlier than usual, he noted suspiciously. He sat up and looked past the poinciana trees bobbing in the morning trade wind, to the black and gold gates surrounding 'Iolani Palace.

Two years ago in 1887, the Hawaiian League, an armed political group of Caucasian businessmen, had forced King Kalakaua to accept a "Bayonet Constitution" that seriously curtailed his powers. Since then, the traffic to and from the Palace had increased: royal carriages departed and returned, the Caucasian and Hawaiian delegates of the new "Bayonet Constitution" convened, and the Royal Palace Guards increased their patrols. Nothing seemed amiss this last morning of July in 1889.

Ah Leong dug back into the warm curve of Dai-Kam's side. He liked this Kaka'ako area where the local folk lived in wooden cottages, dark green with white trim, "missionary green" they joked. For good luck, his neighbors planted hedges of ti plants from the forests. In the morning, when palm fronds rustled in the trade winds, backyard roosters announced the beginning of another day in the Hawaiian Kingdom. Mothers cooed lullabies in English, Hawaiian, or Chinese, while dogs rolled in the dirt road. Young children played chase in the dirt streets. The ladies gossiped on their front stoops and talked-story between endless washing and cooking. On Sundays, he and his neighbors sat on their doorsteps to listen to the choir from Kawaiaha'o Church across the street. In 1820, Hawaiian converts had built this coral-block church for the first Congregationalist mission to Hawai'i on the site named for the sacred spring that once bubbled up in that spot for Ha'o, the long-ago queen of O'ahu.

"Those babies!" Dai-Kam moaned when she heard her girls' wakening cries. She flung an arm over her face. "Ah Yin!" she barked.

Her son tumbled out of his cot with his eyes closed and patted his sisters cradled in drawers by his bed. "Sssh! Mama still sleeping! Go back to sleep," he whispered. The three-year-old shook her head. The one-year-old babbled back.

Ah Leong pulled on his trousers and carefully looped the closures on his work shirt. He watched his five-year-old son attempt to lull his sisters back to sleep and avoid their mother's wrath. "Ah Yin," he called, his voice low so only they could hear. "Be my good boy."

Ah Yin lifted his head and stared yearningly when his father slipped down the wooden stairs to the street.

The hushed march of many footsteps approached. Ah Leong slid into the shadows. One hundred and fifty young Hawaiians led by Robert Wilcox, a Hawaiian educated at a military academy in Turin, Italy, stepped in cadence towards the front gate of 'Iolani Palace.

Ah Leong's heart fell. He had heard the rumors that the Hawaiians were determined to take back their government from the sugar planters and restore the Hawaiian monarchy to full power. Wilcox led the militant pro-monarchy faction. They would be slaughtered if they tried to retake the Palace from the well-armed, well-funded Americans. But the Hawaiians marched through the palace gates tipped with gold, up the sun-sparkled walk, and through the etched glass doors. There were no gunshots, no cries, no sounds of battle.

The young shopkeeper sighed with relief. As the trade winds blew away the early morning showers and the sun dried the dew on the koa trees overhead, his customers tromped in off the dirt road and huddled in the coolness of his store to prolong the start of the day. He poured a full measure of dark Kona beans in the wooden grinder and vigorously cranked the iron handle until the air was heady with the rich aroma.

At first, the talk was that this counter-coup by the young Hawaiian loyalists against the Bayonet Constitution had succeeded. Enterprising businessmen such as Claus Spreckels, the sugar baron, had taken advantage of the naiveté and inexperience of the Hawaiian government to grab enormous land concessions at absurdly low prices. Concerned about keeping competitive in the sugar industry and shocked at what they considered the excesses of the monarchy, the Americans pressured the United States to annex Hawai'i.

But King Kalakaua defied the Americans. He revived the Hawaiian culture and encouraged celebrations rekindling the traditions of hula and music that the missionaries had banned as sinful pleasures. The hypnotic beats of drums and powerful chants echoed through the islands as the Hawaiians reached back to their ancient past, to the time when the land and power were theirs.

Meanwhile, the prosperous sugar plantations sought more power and control. Flush with land, commerce, and prestige, the Americans married into the royal family and increased their stranglehold on the islands. The leaders of these *Kamaʻaina* cartels, descended either from early missionaries or from annexationist businessmen, capitalized on vast land and political bases acquired by their ancestors. They controlled Hawaiʻi's economy now. Only the presence of the Hawaiian monarchy kept them from absolute power.

Throughout the morning, Ah Leong glimpsed men running behind buildings next to the Palace. Some carried guns. Others carried boxes of dynamite. One carried a bag of nails.

At the first splintering explosion, Ah Leong ran out the door. He whipped around the corner and up the stairs to his flat. He grabbed Ah Yin from the steps where he sat startled by the sharp blasts.

Around him, neighbors screamed for their children. When the Japanese grandfather next door tripped on his cane, his daughter dropped her wet laundry, scooped up his skinny body and ran with him to their cottage.

Four young Hawaiians scrambled down from the branches of the banyan tree they had climbed for a view of the palace grounds. "*Auwe*, they're blowing up the Palace!" they screamed. "Here they come."

Ah Leong barricaded the doors with the kitchen table and stools. Dai-Kam slammed the windows shut. "The guns come," she whimpered. She crushed Ah Yin and her babies to her chest.

Ah Leong curved his body around them like a protective cocoon, hushed his wife's tears, and calmed her terror. He, who had defied death, was not afraid. But the nauseating smell of gunpowder and blood filtered in through the closed windows and doors as the fighting spread from the Palace to their doorstep.

If Wilcox and his Hawaiians were defeated, all hope to regain full power for the Hawaiian monarchy would die. The American businessmen, backed by their private armed soldiers called the Honolulu Rifles, planned to depose King Kalakaua and claim the Hawaiian nation for America. These sugar barons were enticed by a lucrative treaty to eliminate sugar tariffs that made Hawaiian sugar cheaper, and thus highly profitable.

Ah Leong and Dai-Kam clutched each other until the guns were silent, then crawled to the front door and cracked it open. They choked on the thick gunsmoke and gasped for air. In the evening twilight, they stumbled over bodies ripped by homemade bombs of dynamite and twenty-penny nails.

Dai-Kam gagged and turned her head. Shadows, weeping softly to avoid the patrols of the Honolulu Rifles that had surprised the Hawaiian loyalists, spirited away the injured and dead Hawaiians. Only bloody pools remained to stain the soil, the blood of the Hawaiians soaking the land that once was theirs.

The coup failed. The Hawaiians surrendered. The Americans reported seven of Wilcox's men were killed and twelve wounded. Wilcox was arrested but later acquitted because no Hawaiian jury would convict him.

⚘⚘

Ah Leong rubbed Dai-Kam's arm. The heat of her skin pressed tight against him on their narrow bed. His was a sensuous touch–firm, strong, insistent.

"Ah Yin is fidgeting and the baby is crying himself to sleep," she hissed. She sighed and closed her eyes.

The year was 1891. Robert Wilcox had risen to the status of a folk-hero for his valiant but ineffective insurrection against the Bayonet Constitution three years ago. Since then, Dai-Kam had given birth to another son, Tat-Tung.

Ah Leong cupped her breasts, round and heavy like bountiful pomelos. "I'll wait," he sighed. He peered over the edge of the bed at Ah Yin's cot and saw the glimmer of his son's blinking eyes. Wide awake. He looked at the three drawers next to Ah Yin. The two girls, now three and five, were sound asleep. His newborn son, Tat-Tung, sucked hungrily on his fist.

Meanwhile, he felt his wife's breaths grow heavier. She would fall asleep before him, as she did every night since their fourth child was born.

He rolled on his back and closed his eyes. And as always, his thoughts reverted to his business. The previous year, he had applied in writing to the Minister of the Interior of the Kingdom of Hawai'i, C. N. Spencer, to be admitted as a citizen of the Kingdom of Hawai'i. Compared to China's four thousand–year-old civilization, this was a young nation. King Kamehameha the Great had united all the islands only a hundred years before. Nevertheless, Ah Leong was proud of his Naturalization Certificate that listed as his guarantors L. Ah Low, Lewis J. Levey, J. F. Morgan, and M. Phillips and Company. He held out the document to his friends, pointed out the names of his prestigious guarantors, and boasted that he now waved to King Kalakaua as one of his legal subjects, Naturalized Citizen No. 131 of the Hawaiian Kingdom.

He dreamed of the day he would revenge his family's loss of face. Yes, he would return to China and build estates grander than the house his father lost so those who let him drown would speak his name with awe.

King Kalakaua left for San Francisco on November 1890, beleaguered by the political turmoil at home, his power diminished by the American businessmen. Once he was celebrated as Hawai'i's Merry Monarch. Now his spirits sunk, wearied with the Americans' increasing demands for more land and power. Two months later, Kalakauas' boat sailed into Honolulu Harbor draped in black. "The king is dead!" the Hawaiians wailed. They stripped the city's festive decorations celebrating the King's return and pounded their heads on the mourning stones of their hidden *heiaus*, the temples of their ancestors.

Now Ah Leong ran out each time Queen Lili'uokalani, King Kalakaua's sister and successor, rode past on her royal carriage. She had the political power and support that could return real power to the monarchy. But the Americans grew more militant. The Queen's radiant smile faded and she looked exhausted, beleaguered, much like his wife's wilted expression when he came home from work.

As he drifted asleep, his thoughts lingered on the inventory list Ahuna had sent him. It included one servant girl. His eyes popped open. He smiled. Then fell sound asleep.

❧❧

The following week, Ah Leong bounded up the stairs to their flat. "Dai-Kam, we have been married ten years. You need a servant to do the housework and be *amah* to our children," he exclaimed. He plopped on the bed where his wife sat nursing the baby, then stood up again, too excited to be still.

Her dark eyes met his eager smile. She shifted Tat-Tung to her other breast. "What kind of servant?"

"Ahuna has contracted for laborers through his store in China. I bought the contract of a sixteen-year-old. She works for me now. She will do whatever you say."

Dai-Kam laughed at how the tiny hands of her son grasped at her bountiful nipples. She pursed her lips, then smiled. "Aaah, I will keep her busy."

Dai-Kam brightened with her new freedom and power. She didn't care that this plump girl looked like a sagging pear or wore her sparse hair in a dowdy bun. Or that she barely spoke. Or that she turned away, head obediently bowed, when her mistress gave her orders. Her pinch-faced servant had to cook, scrub, and hang clothes until Dai-Kam was satisfied.

Ah Leong comforted his twenty-seven-year-old wife further. He would let her rest at night since she had just given birth.

Five months later, Dai-Kam shrieked, "My servant is pregnant." She flung her wood-chopping ax over her head and chased after her husband.

"In China, men have many wives," Ah Leong answered with an authoritative wave. "Didn't I tell you she is my Second wife?" With a single bound he leapt to the opposite side of the room, keeping the small eating table between them.

Dai-Kam stretched to her full height, steeled her shoulders back, and yelled so loud the entire neighborhood could hear. "You don't need another wife. You have me."

"I can afford it," he shouted back.

She hefted her ax and swung.

"Ho Shee is my Second wife. I bought her to help you," he bellowed in defense. He leapt far beyond her reach. "You said you needed help with the children."

"I am more than enough woman for you. I give you four babies and you're busy making more!" She drew her height over him and swung again.

Vociferous screams thundered out their open windows.

The neighborhood men shook their heads; it would take more than a blow from Dai-Kam to knock out Ah Leong. Their wives tsk-tsk-tsked at the yelping and Ah Leong's howls. The men bet that within an hour, Ah Leong would charm Dai-Kam as he always did, cajoling her to accept his rascally ways.

Chapter Four

The Kaka'ako Store: Honolulu 1900

Ah Leong slapped his palms on the money counter with a solid whack. "That's right, Ching. I'm taking ten one hundred–pound bags of rice." He leaned forward with a grin, relishing the surprise on the rice merchant's face.

Ching tipped back his bamboo hat and scratched his dusty black hair. Frustration wrinkled his tanned brow. His ebony eyes squinted into sad commas. "That's half my shipment," he complained. "I won't have enough for my customers in Chinatown."

Ah Leong reached into his money box and held out five bills. "Cash," he offered, waving them seductively. He glanced past Ching and spied plumes of black smoke rise over Chinatown. An acrid smell like burning wet garbage wafted in with the early morning trade wind. "You can't go there anyway. The fire department is burning the buildings at Beretania Street and Nu'uanu Avenue. Five deaths in Chinatown yesterday—bubonic plague." Another controlled burn to get rid of the rats and fleas which meant more business for him.

Ching shuddered. He looked furtively at the evacuees milling about the small Kaka'ako store. Some chatted with Dai-Kam as she wrapped their parcels with brown paper and loopy knots. "I remember when you had no customers," he grumbled. He shoved the money Ah Leong handed him deep in his baggy trousers.

"And everyone said I'd go broke when I opened this store." Ah Leong added, waving his arms in a grand sweep. "Everyone said Chinese did business only with Chinese, Japanese only with Japanese, and Hawaiians only with Hawaiians. Even you said I had to be in Chinatown with my own kind, not out here in Kakaʻako with the *haoles*, Hawaiians, and Japanese." That was ten years ago when King Kalakaua was still alive.

In 1893, pro-annexation Americans, with the help of the U.S. Marines from the visiting gunship USS *Boston*, arrested Queen Liliʻuokalani. They imprisoned her in ʻIolani Palace. Outraged, newly elected U.S. President Grover Cleveland ordered the Queen restored to her throne.

But the new Provisional Government declared that the Kingdom of Hawaiʻi would now be the Republic of Hawaii headed by Sanford B. Dole.

Against the wishes of the Hawaiian people, President McKinley signed the authorization to annex the islands in 1898 and Hawaiʻi became a U.S. Territory.

Now it was January 1900, the beginning of a new century in Hawaiʻi.

"You lucky your store is next to Kawaiahaʻo Church, Ah Leong," muttered Ching. "How did you know they'd set up evacuation camps here?" He shrugged. "You're doing more business than anyone else."

"Tell that to your friends in Chinatown, Ching," Dai-Kam shouted as the rice merchant walked out the door. She threw back her shoulders and turned to the next customer with a broad smile. Although she had been in Hawaiʻi for twenty years, Dai-Kam preferred to wear the high-necked Chinese tunic and skirt even to work in the store, and still wore her thick hair in a sleek bun. She felt more comfortable in figure-hugging Chinese attire than the loose muʻumuʻus other women wore. Besides, her full figure reminded her forty-four-year-old husband of all that his thirty-six-year-old First wife meant to him: the caress of her thick sweet curtains of hair, their tumultuous nights, and many sons. She overheard the local men swear that she was so voluptuous and tall that she had to be part Hawaiian, especially with her dark eyes, deep as pools of raw brown sugar.

Since the discovery of bubonic plague, their storefront bustled from dawn to sunset. As soon as a case of plague was discovered, the fire department incinerated the house and contents. The occupants were sent to the quarantine camps next to Kawaiahaʻo Church across from the Lau's store.

Evacuees from the makeshift camps stumbled in as soon as they smelled brewing coffee. Many were unable to sleep surrounded by new sounds: unfamiliar belches, strange snores, and invasive voices. Mothers with chunky-faced babies strapped to their backs came to buy fish and vegetables. Others needed fruits, bananas, and poi, staples once delivered to their homes each morning by Chinese peddlers laden with fresh foods bouncing from wooden poles across their shoulders.

Ah Leong cheered each evacuee with a steaming mug of coffee. He asked where they had come from and offered, "You need something, you ask me. When other stores close, we stay open. So convenient. My wife and I cry many tears for you."

Dai-Kam nodded proudly in agreement. The store's success proved that her $200 dowry had been invested wisely.

Between customers, she sewed muʻumuʻus and shirts at the second-hand trundle machine in the back of the store. As needed, she could unload, stock, and deliver, even slinging hundred pound sacks of rice under each arm. On demand, she loaded orders in her wheelbarrow and charged through town, sweat dripping from her brow.

"Yes, yes," Dai-Kam answered when Ah Leong nodded at the empty corner he had just cleared for the new rice. She was eight months pregnant but she slipped easily from behind the counter and walked energetically out to Ching's wagon. On the way, she stopped a Chinese elder shaking Ching's hand. She pointed to the quarantine camps and then to the store, eyes lit, arms waving. Then she yanked the rice merchant towards his wagon.

The new visitor entered the store. He exuded the scent of a freshly pressed white shirt and Borax. "Hey, Ah Leong! Have time for an old friend?" He flashed a crooked-tooth smile.

"L. Ah Low," Ah Leong exclaimed, happy to see the old merchant who had given him and Dai-Kam jobs in Honolulu after they went bankrupt in Kohala. He tucked the nub of a pencil behind his ear and pulled the ragged hem of his mended work shirt taut over a stocky belly.

"Ching said he sold almost all his rice to you," Ah Low exclaimed. His sharp eyes peered from the leathery folds of his face at the stocks of merchandise piled unevenly in every cranny of Ah Leong's crammed store. Ah Low had rebuilt his own business after the 1886 Chinatown fire, but his sons ran his stores now. He sighed that he was glad to be free of the long work days, but missed the camaraderie of old friends.

"Too bad, that fire. Accident, they said," Ah Leong commiserated. The prosperity in Chinatown, that community of familiar faces, herbal smells, and dialects, had been destroyed in the 1886 fire. Although the Chinese rebuilt, renewed anti-Chinese sentiment by the plantation owners inflamed old hurts and dangerous emotions.

Ah Low scoffed, "Caused by 'a wok in a restaurant' the fire chief claimed. He said 'the Chinese build shoddy buildings too close together.'" Ah Low lowered his voice and leaned forward. "They wanted to run us back to China. We worked hard to get here. Earned our right to do business."

"I don't know why they want us out." Ah Leong shook his head. "No one else will live in that 'A'ala swampland. All the mosquitoes from Nu'uanu breed there. You can smell the foul stench at low tide. At high tide, Chinatown floods right there where Nu'uanu River meets the ocean." The Chinese did not mind living in these ramshackle wooden buildings crammed so tight sunlight never reached the ground. These were temporary quarters, a substitute village of bakeries, tailors, cobblers, and apartments. After they fulfilled their five-year contracts, they planned to return to China rich with their American dollars.

Ah Low nodded and patted his protégé on the shoulder. Ah Leong never followed popular opinion. Instead, he observed, analyzed, and questioned to formulate his own ideas. Ah Low enjoyed taking the time to explain things to him. "For decades, way before you came, more Hawaiians than Chinese lived in that area. When the Chinese moved there for cheap housing, the *haoles* claimed that the Hawaiians were up against 'unfair competition' from the Chinese."

Ah Leong laughed. "Hawaiians and Chinese get along better than anybody else. My First wife and I both speak fluent Hawaiian, and see how many Hawaiian customers we have."

Ah Low gestured with a crooked finger. "I read in their *haole* newspaper that they say Chinatown is 'dirty, overcrowded, rat-infested, and often diseased.' All they see are narrow alleys and underground cellars that remind them of a warren of burrowing animals. They say the Chinese are a strange yellow race who wear pigtails, talk an outlandish lingo in high falsetto voices, are reputed to eat shark fins and rats, and make medicine out of toads and spiders. They say Chinatown is a vicious place, the haunt of gambling, opium smoking, and lotteries."

Ah Leong shook his fist. "They know nothing!"

Ah Low agreed so vigorously, his skinny white queue fluttered like a leaf. "With our own people we can tell jokes and make everybody laugh with us. We remember favorite folk tales and pretend we are in China. Smell foods of our childhood. Hear news of our village, families, and friends. No need to explain too much."

The old merchant leaned closer and whispered under his breath. "What bothers me is the way they talk. *Pake* they call us. *Pake* meant 'respectful Chinese' in Hawaiian. Now they say it with a snarl."

✼✼

Outside, Dai-Kam picked up the last two sacks of rice, one under each arm, and stepped into the shade of the store.

Ching waved to her, stared nervously at the smoke billowing from Chinatown, and headed home. "Haw!" he yelled. His horse whinnied and clomped down the street with ten rice bags, each stenciled with a red rose, in the half-empty wagon.

Ah Leong glanced up at the sound of Ching's command, the neighing of his horse, and the jangle of the harness. Then he turned and stared at the corner where his wife had stacked the new rice. He narrowed his eyes. He demanded, "Dai-Kam, what did you unload?"

Sweat beaded from his wife's forehead and trickled down her neck. Despite her pregnant girth, she stepped nimbly around him, each arm curled around a hundred pounds of rice, and flung the bags on top of eight identical bags stenciled with a blue rose. She straightened her back, relieved to be done with her task, and fanned her face with her hand.

Ah Leong flung his fists in the air. "That's the wrong rice!"

She waved off his blustering rage. "That's what we always get," she retorted and stomped towards him.

"No, no, no. That's the junk rice. I paid for the red rose grade. Take it out! Catch Ching. Tell him to come back." His stubby finger wiggled in the direction of the wagon disappearing down the street.

Dai-Kam pulled herself up and straightened her shoulders. Her ripe belly swelled upward. "Take it out? I just carried it in. A thousand pounds."

"Out!" he commanded. "I don't want it."

Before he could react, she whipped back her arm and smacked him across his chest.

"Oooof!" Ah Leong's breath collapsed. The force flung him up onto the stack of rice still warm from sitting in the hot sun. He lay too stunned to move if he was alive, certain he was dead.

☞☜

It was a little after nine in the morning when the fire department put the first torches to the frame structure behind Kaumakapili Church in Chinatown. The fire chief had calculated that with a northeast wind, the fire would eat its way back towards Kukui Street, destroying the contaminated homes, rats, and fleas.

But an hour later, the wind shifted east. Embers flew to the dry roofs of Chinatown's closely packed buildings, then lodged in the Waikiki tower of Kaumakapili Church. Flames transformed the church towers into twin torches fifty feet high. Sparks and embers jumped to the dry wooden rooftops of Chinatown.

Half a mile away, the Laus heard the fire roar.

Dai-Kam grumbled, "Where are those fire trucks?"

At that minute, flames engulfed Fire Engine Number One on Maunakea Street. The other Chinatown firehouse had already burnt down to the ground. Chinatown was a growing mass of hot white flames flaring against the sky. The uncontrolled fire took an animalistic life of its own. It drew its breath from the brisk wind and blew devastation down on those trying to subdue it.

The Laus and their evacuee neighbors crowded in front of the store to watch the growing panorama of towering flames, billowing black smoke, and flying embers. They shrieked "*Ai-yah! Auwe!*" when the fire fighters set off dynamite at Kekaulike and King Streets and the reverberations echoed back from the Koʻolau Mountains. They choked on the black air and stared, unbelieving, as strong winds whipped the flames toward the wharves, obliterating everything in its path.

❧❧

A spry figure approached Ah Leong as he shoved the bins he stacked on the sidewalk back into his cramped nook of a store. It was the hour of twilight after the golden sun fell into the sea. Neither day nor night, this time of the day seemed breathless, suspended between reality and dreams. After a month of daily rains, the acrid smell of incinerated wood lingered in the trade winds. The oppressive stench added to the depressing sight of thirty-eight blackened acres, the site of last month's Chinatown fire, stretching down to the sea.

Ah Leong straightened when he saw his visitor. "Yuen Gnew-Nam! I haven't seen you since before the fire," he exclaimed.

Brushing his hands off on his trousers, he stepped forward and asked if he could assist Yuen before he put everything away. Days were slower now. Customers tried to bargain his prices down, if they could. How could he blame them? Especially with the horrific losses they suffered.

The Chinese suspected the new Territorial government used the bubonic plague to break the strength and wealth of the Chinese. The Caucasian-run newspapers refuted that even the homes of quarantined Caucasians in the wealthiest areas had been burned during the plague.

Whole blocks, whole neighborhoods were not cremated, countered the Chinese. The Great Chinatown Fire had eliminated Chinatown and killed Chinese trade: three million dollars lost in the inferno.

The visitor held up a fine-boned hand in friendly refusal. "Time for close?" Yuen asked, stroking his wispy beard. Unlike most of the Chinese in Hawai'i who were tan, sturdy people from South China's Pearl River delta, this man, wiry and long-limbed, had the high-cheekboned, elegant features of a Northern Chinese, especially with his fair complexion. The smell of smoke still clung to his blue work shirt and trousers although they had been soaked in Borax, sun dried, and ironed.

"Yes," answered Ah Leong. "Since the fire, the Board of Health says all businesses must close early."

Yuen waited while Ah Leong checked his depleting stock and did his final calculations. When the merchant was done, he tossed his notebook and nub of a pencil in the old wooden box under the counter.

"You lose everything in the fire?" Ah Leong inquired. He grabbed two porcelain teacups from the shelf, wiped off the dust and ash with the inside hem of his work shirt, and set them out on the counter in the waning light of sunset. These were sturdy cups, a splash of eggshell blue defiantly bright amidst the oppressive dust.

"My twenty-five-year laundry business is gone," Yuen answered. His shoulders visibly slumped.

"Your wife and children?" Ah Leong asked. He turned up the gas on the burner he used to boil water for his coffee-drinking customers and added a hefty pinch of tea from a pewter canister into a porcelain teapot as blue as the teacups.

"Staying on my brother's taro farm in Manoa. My eldest daughter Sun-Mui takes care of them all."

Sun-Mui had herded her bound-foot mother, brothers, and sisters to safety despite the screams of frantic neighbors fleeing the fire. Yuen stayed in his laundry to beat out the flames. But the water pressure dropped and the bucket brigades were harmless swats against the inferno. When the flames towered higher than the buildings around him, he fled with the others. In his dreams, he heard the screams of wives searching for husbands, of lost children wailing. All had been gripped with panic when they were trapped between lines of armed citizens who corralled them like contaminated criminals.

"Aaah, these people," Ah Leong gestured to the crowded makeshift camps on the grounds of Kawaiaha'o Church, "are too crowded. No privacy. It's better you stay with family." The merchant turned off the gas and poured the bubbling water into the teapot.

Through the ash-streaked window, the men stared at the tents where families huddled, single men congregated around kerosene lamps to ponder their future, and mothers argued how to keep their children fed. Yuen's asthmatic wife could never survive in such an unprotected place. Especially a bound-foot woman like Lum Shee. She was a slender shadow, black hair pulled back from a pale, oval face. Not at all like Dai-Kam, Ah Leong mused, rubbing his bruised chest. He poured two cups of steaming tea and offered one with both hands and a nod to his friend.

Yuen accepted with a grateful bow and sat on the wooden crate the merchant offered. Although Yuen was Punti, he spoke Ah Leong's Hakka dialect. Both men were about forty-five years old now, and had arrived in the 1870s when Hawai'i was a small community. It was easy to keep track of fellow Chinese then.

Ah Leong balanced on another crate and sipped his tea. His brow creased as he thought of the horrific past week and the devastation that remained. "Yuen, soot and ash still cling to the trade winds here. Who knows if the plague is still with us, or who among the homeless carry the seeds of death? You hear the cries. You see the blank stares. Why have you left the safe valley of Manoa to come all the way down to this burned-out city? Why not stay where the air is clean like the dew on a spring morning and the mountain streams are safe to drink?"

"I came to help. These people are not used to living under the open sky. They suffer from black smoke in their lungs and eyes. You hear their cough? How it sounds like they breathe water instead of air? Sometimes their breath is dry like twigs scraping on glass." He added that he had brought his herbs, then bent his head to inhale the fragrance of the strong black tea Ah Leong brewed only for his closest friends.

"How did you learn this healing?" Ah Leong asked, staring at Yuen.

He himself had coughed up puffs of black soot for days after working on the bucket brigade. When he was the privileged son of a landowner, long before his father had gambled away their lands and reduced them to beggars, he had awakened from a nap in the woods where he often practiced with his martial arts masters. He lay still as if sleeping, his eyes half open. Mesmerized, he watched his masters practice the powerful magic of herbs, conjure spirits to do their bidding, and return the breath of life to things that were dead. Dishes such as simmered baby bear paws, hearts of golden chickens, and fragrant rice from the delta appeared in porcelain bowls as thin as poppy petals when Master Sung clapped his hands like thunder. As his disciples ate, Master Sung explained the properties of each herb and dish.

Even in Hawai'i, the men in the tea houses talked of the tonics and pills that could rejuvenate old men and women and restore the balance of one's *ch'i*. *Ch'i*, the cosmic energy and breath of all things, was in a constant flux between the complementary forces of *yin* and *yang*, dark and light, masculine and feminine, earth and heaven. It required learning and study, secrets handed down from father to son, from master to disciple, for many generations to master the flow of *ch'i* within one's body. Few learned herbalists brought their art to the remote country of Hawai'i.

Yuen sipped his tea, eyes closed in focused concentration. Then he cradled the empty tea cup in his hands. "My people came from the north, from the ancient capital of Chang-An near the junction of the Wei and Yellow rivers in northern China. A thousand years we studied, traveled thousands of miles through hundreds of villages before we settled in Chuck Hum village, Heung Shan district, twenty-two generations ago."

"Myself, I am only nineteen generations from Kew Boy village. Your family has a great history," Ah Leong acknowledged. "I am honored that we are both from the same province." Ah Leong's people, the Hakka or "guest people," had migrated to Kwang Tung Province eight hundred years after the Punti from which Yuen descended. Because of their late arrival, the Hakka were forced to live in the inhospitable mountains. The Punti, who farmed the fertile delta lands and lush flat plains, looked down on the struggling Hakka and ridiculed their clothes and incomprehensible dialect.

"Yuens were welcomed everywhere for the cures we brought. My father showed me how to collect the herbs and prepare them. This knowledge he passed to me, as his father passed it to him, from generation to generation."

Ah Leong harrumphed. "A laundry is no business for an herbalist trained in the secrets of your ancestors."

Yuen stroked his beard with delicate fingers. "Before I came here, I raised chickens in New Zealand for nine years. But they did not want Chinese to settle there, only to work. When I came back to my village, I married, then came to Hawai'i alone. I sent for Lum Shee and my daughter Sun-Mui after nine years. The laundry business was the only job I was allowed to do."

Yuen paused, eyes closed, then huffed as if inhaling a bad memory. "I do no more laundry. The fire was my sign." He shook his head to erase the wasted days and nights of boiling vats and hot irons.

Yuen looked at Ah Leong, beyond the present, and far back into the past. The fading sun threw its glow into the sinking twilight, coloring the sky with red-purple splashes. "You know all life and natural phenomena are created by the five basic elements: wood, fire, earth, metal, and water. Their constant interplay, combined with those of yin and yang, explain all change and activity in nature."

In the mist of his memory, Ah Leong recalled these teachings from his masters when he was a child and the mystic lessons that he had practiced in the solitude of the Hawaiian jungles many years ago through his twenties and thirties. The teachings of the universe had been his. He had known these powers.

"These forces interact in patterns according to their natural relation-ships. Each force is produced or destroyed by another. In the great fire that destroyed Chinatown, wood burnt and fed fire. Fire produced ash which will generate earth. Earth is the source of metal which can liquefy into substances that flow like water. With water, wood grows. Such is life: an endless cycle."

Ah Leong refilled each teacup and nodded for Yuen to continue. He leaned forward to catch each word, his eyes glimmering eagerly. "This fire has changed and renewed the land it devastated. Not a single life was lost. A good sign. A fire that burns down to the ground so cleanly burns away all evil."

"A pure start," Ah Leong murmured. He searched Yuen's cloudy eyes to read the hidden meanings. "Yuen, if I were to build on that ground…" He paused, calculating the possibilities.

"It would be blessed and clean. Like a phoenix rising from the ashes of its funeral pyre." Yuen's eyes twinkled. He picked up his teacup and toasted Ah Leong's future.

Chapter Five

Rising from the Ashes: 1903

Dai-Kam walked to their new store during the busy mid-morning hour. After her husband's lunch break, she would return home. By then, the servants her husband called "wives" would have her midday meal prepared and she would gossip with them at leisure.

Three years after the Great Chinatown Fire of 1900, the streets of the rebuilding Chinatown vibrated with grinding saws. She stopped and watched sinewy men, bronze and barechested in the tropical morning, fling their hammers in rhythmic pounding. Pidgin English, the polyglot language of the locals, conveyed the plans and designs to the builders of the new community. Lumber, smelling fresh from the mill, framed the skeletons of the buildings. Chinese, Japanese, and Hawaiians traversed the streets and buildings to check on the progress of their new homes and businesses. Whole families hauled up beams and slapped on coats of paint to protect the wood from the life-giving but wood-rotting rains.

Dai-Kam herself was an awesome sight, all six feet of her packed voluptuously in a dark blue Chinese tunic and skirt. Her skin was tanned a healthy tawny glow, setting off large round eyes and sensuous lips.

She turned down King Street, fresh-scented with sawdust. Red brick and masonry facades distinguished the new Chinatown. Businesses dominated the first level: open store fronts for the general stores, splayed window displays with central entrances for the restaurants, herbal shops, barber shops, and offices. From the living quarters and offices on the second story, the regular rhythm of shuttered windows looked out onto the main streets. Incised Neoclassical and oriental motifs ornamented the doors and windows. Colors were clean and bright: red, green, yellow, and blue. Canvas canopies shaded the sidewalks of the stores now open for business.

The new L. Ah Leong store at 11 North King Street was located across from Oʻahu Fish Market, where 150-pound aku, iridescent ulua, sweet ʻamaʻama, and mahimahi were hauled in before sunrise by the fishing boats and sold alongside the octopus, squid, and colorful reef fish caught by the hand-thrown nets of the dawn fishermen. The smell of the sea mingled with the aroma of fresh sawdust.

Ah Leong credited some of his business's growth to Ching Mook, husband of Dai-Kam's younger sister. Both sisters had married within a week of Uncle Fung's arrival in Hawaiʻi. Ching Mook, an educated scholar in Kaimuki who provided well for Dai-Kam's sister, had parked his new hack in front of the newly opened L. Ah Leong Store. The word spread. No one had seen such a fine muscled horse and elegant carriage before. They shone like the radiance of new gold. People flocked to see for themselves, then shopped at L. Ah Leong's, the busiest retail operation in Honolulu.

Other Chinese businesses—butchers, restaurants, barbers, and fish markets—opened near his store. Chinatown prospered and Ah Leong's fortune grew.

Dai-Kam stepped back on the dirt road, placed her hands on her hips, and inspected their new storefront: a haphazard stock of goods stacked from floor to ceiling. Her husband had jammed every inch: enticing piles of fresh vegetables carted in that morning from the country, tins of imported goods from China, Chinese-made garments, as well as the shirts and muʻumuʻus she herself had sewn. He stocked the familiar Asian fruits that the Chinese farmers now grew: pomelo, loongan, kumquat, and lychee.

Stacks of feed, rice, and beans impeded sidewalk traffic. Pedestrians were forced to stop, look, and wiggle between the stacks and bins.

When she worked with her husband, Dai-Kam gossiped with friends she had cultivated over the past twenty-three years. She boasted about her own household of four sons and two daughters. Sometimes she watched her husband and marveled how he could carry on so many conversations at the same time. How easily money flowed into his hands. Still wearing a queue in the style of most Chinese men, in common Chinese work shirt and blue cotton trousers, he made shrewd housewives and tightfisted bachelor men feel that he offered them his best bargains.

She never mentioned the three sons and four daughters from Ah Leong's other women, except in anger. She had threatened to move out every time he brought home another servant girl but Ah Leong cleverly beguiled her. Didn't she command greater prestige as his First wife and acknowledged mother of all his sons? Didn't she receive the best prices when shopping anywhere in Chinatown? And at mah-jongg, no one dared to argue with her. As for his other "wives," didn't they cook, clean, and care for all the children including her own? And every night he always returned to her bed, to his First wife.

She saw her husband wave to his old partner, Ahuna from Kohala, and point up to his new sign painted in red and gold: L. Ah Leong Store.

Ahuna waved his hands in approval, then strode across the street to join him. They shook hands and slapped shoulders with the heartiness of old friends.

"Come in. Look around," Ah Leong coaxed with the enthusiasm of a rising businessman.

"How many years I have not seen you!" Ahuna exclaimed. "Now this! You make me proud." He turned and saw Dai-Kam approach. "Dai-Kam, you have done well. Ah Leong tells me you work side by side with him to build this business." He congratulated them both.

"I thought you would want a larger space," said Ahuna with an energetic wave of his arms. He approved of the extensive array of labeled cans, stenciled boxes, sealed crocks, open bins, and stacks of rice, feed, and grains.

"It's bigger than that nook we had in Kaka'ako. Mr. Morgan advised me to keep the size manageable. I do import and export business now. Sell retail and wholesale. Small retail businesses can't buy in volume to get wholesale prices, so they buy from me. My wholesale business covers three islands: O'ahu, Maui, and Hawai'i. Mr. Levey from the main bank on Fort Street gave me the names of businesses too small for the *haoles* to deal with. Wholesale trade balances my retail." Ah Leong beamed.

"I heard you have dealings on nearly every island. Everyone I know buys from you. They say 'No order too small or too big for L. Ah Leong.' You've come a long way since we were partners in Kohala."

"You taught me well, Ahuna."

"You have learned from far wiser men. How do you know so many *haoles*?" Ahuna asked. He himself had dealt mainly with Hakka Chinese in all the decades of his business in Hawai'i.

"When I was in Kaka'ako, I saw them riding to the Palace all the time. On Sundays, they drove by in their carriages with their families to go to church. I nodded whenever they passed. Pretty soon they nodded back. I talked to them at the government offices. They have so much money, so much influence."

Ah Leong's strategy at that time had been to protect his merchant status among the Caucasians and the Hawaiians in a time of anti-Chinese sentiment. His friendships had paid off. Not only was he well-known among the American businessmen, but his Hawaiian citizenship gave him the privilege of being one of the one hundred Chinese men allowed to vote.

"I watched how they did business. I talked to them to find out how they thought. I knew I could do the same thing they did. Some of them are rich and have important titles. But inside, they are men like me. Mr. Levey, Mr. Morgan, and Mr. Phillips sponsored me for citizenship. See the horse-drawn wagon I got from Mr. Phillips? I deliver, too." Ah Leong pointed to the docile horses and worn cart tied in front of the store. Paint peeled from the weathered sides, but the cart was deep and sturdy.

Ahuna had seen Ah Leong instinctively vary his speech and stance to relax new customers and create a disarming affinity. Able to chat glibly with the Caucasian businessmen, he was known to a network not accessible by most Chinese. White society was especially impressed when Ah Leong gave the Catholic brothers his huge tract of land at River Street to build St. Louis College. But at the core, Ah Leong's values were traditional Confucian Chinese.

"Last time you said you had two wives?" inquired Ahuna.

"Now four."

Dai-Kam opened her mouth and turned to her husband. She gripped her fists and seethed, eyes blazing.

"And sons?"

"Only seven, so far. Third wife has only daughters. Fourth wife has no children. Six girls born so far–a waste of rice," Ah Leong muttered waving his hand to dismiss the thought.

Ahuna pulled Ah Leong out to the street, just out of Dai-Kam's earshot. "Americans educate girls," Ahuna reminded him. "What does Dai-Kam say about that?" he asked lowering his voice.

Ah Leong shrugged.

"I hear now that Hawai'i is annexed we must follow the laws of the United States," Ahuna reminded him. Americans had laws about marriage, educating children, registering births–more laws than the locals could keep track of.

Ah Leong slapped Ahuna on the back. "My household's harmonious," he insisted. Dai-Kam yelled at him for days each time he brought home a new wife, even threatened to leave. But as a traditional Chinese patriarch, he would have his way. Confucian ethics demanded each wife's obedience for the preservation of family harmony. After all, he acknowledged her as the mother of all his sons. And he needed her.

He had needed her money to start the store. Even more, he needed her energy to keep it going. She was worth two clerks–able to load and deliver without complaint. Plus, no one besides himself could out-bargain her when it came to negotiating a profitable deal. Ah Leong rubbed his chest absently. Of course, when she got mad he paid the price.

He turned to his friend and gestured to his modest belly, "You, Ahuna, you look like you're eating well." The older merchant wore a collared shirt and slacks like the city men. But Ahuna looked weathered, with deep furrows in his tanned face and thinning hair bleached brown by the sun.

"I sold my Kohala store to two plantation workers," Ahuna answered. "My stores in China need me and I have children to enjoy," he confided, smiling with anticipation.

"Many sons, I hope?"

"Yes, many sons. Not as many as you..."

"You must catch up." Ah Leong squeezed his mentor's shoulders. "Someday I will return to China in imperial splendor and build a great new house reflecting my glory. Many wives, many sons, and many grandsons will bear my name in China and Hawai'i." He threw his hands up in a grand flourish.

Ahuna turned to his friend in surprise. "I thought you had settled here for good. You, your business, your family, have greater opportunities here than in the village. You have been established here a long time. You have connections and networks among the Chinese and non-Chinese."

"China will grovel at my feet when I return," Ah Leong growled. "Ahuna, they tore the pillows and blankets from our beds and wore the clothes off the backs of my mother and father." He smirked with the vision of his triumphant return, the returning beggar now a man of tremendous honor and face. He would get his revenge.

When Ah Leong turned to talk to a customer bargaining for a better price on local rice, Ahuna stepped out onto the dirt road to watch. Ah Leong never missed a syllable, able to charm two customers at once, negotiating with wholesale or retail customers simultaneously while giving orders to his workers. He easily slipped from Chinese to Pidgin English to Hawaiian, speaking the language of trade, that communication that links all groups. He treated everyone, rich or poor, with the same enthusiastic energy.

"Ahuna!" Dai-Kam caught up to her husband's first partner before he could disappear down the street. Together, they walked down the wooden sidewalk.

"You are like my father, Ahuna. Always, I can talk to you and you will advise. You know Ah Leong. He always had girls on the side. A month or two later they're gone. He told you he calls three of them his 'wives,'" Dai-Kam confided. "Second wife came before King Kalakaua died. She's twenty-eight. Third wife is young, not even twenty years old. She's given him two girls. And Fourth wife is even younger. I don't know how he gets them from China. Didn't Americans stop Chinese immigration?" She anxiously turned the thick jade bracelets that circled her wrists. She added, "At mah-jongg, my sister said her husband Ching Mook told her that the American law says men can have only one wife. I told Ah Leong to get rid of the others before he gets into trouble."

She couldn't bear to mention the pain that tore through her body when she heard Ah Leong's intimate laughter taunting her through the thin wooden walls, his climactic cry, and the creaking springs as his body relaxed. She had given up crying a long time ago. Resentment and rage took its place.

"These other women flatter him, but you are his legal wife," Ahuna said. Twenty years ago, Ahuna was captivated by the determination of her wide-eyed innocence. Now he saw tiny lines in the once flawless complexion and the worry of her set jaw. "You are his First wife, mother of his first-born son. I remember how difficult it was to get him to leave your bedroom in Kohala. He had starry eyes."

"Times change," she answered pensively. His energy and drive, so overwhelming when she was a young bride, had once intimidated her. At work, she admired how he charmed each person who came to their store, how he sensed their needs and found ways to pull business in his direction. He was always thinking of new ways to expand, to make their business bigger, stronger, more profitable. She saw how men listened to him. Especially white businessmen. They seemed surprised at his energetic enthusiasm, his keen business sense, and his nose for profit. Her jealousy grew with each new woman he brought home. She felt herself changing, drawing hard boundaries around their personal lives, boundaries that he was always pushing.

"It's the old way of the rich Chinese. They believe they are entitled to as many wives and families as they can afford. Extravagance demonstrates their wealth. It enhances their image, improves their face. But the American government believes in rights. You are his First wife married Chinese style, and his First wife in Hawai'i," Ahuna reassured her. "You are his legal wife." He held out his arm like a Western gentleman and walked her back to her husband's store amidst the whistles of the workmen.

Her jealousy never subsided. Years later, Tat-Tung lamented to his wife, "Phoenix, my mother's jealousy was so great, she even resented me, her son." The neglect and anger Dai-Kam inflicted in childhood tormented him, yet she possessed a power he could not escape.

Chapter Six

Tat-Tung's Early Years: June 1903

Tat-Tung ran up the slippery steps to the covered lanai. He kicked off his shoes and added them to the line of footwear at the front door—two dozen pairs of worn straw slippers and shoes for three mothers and a dozen children. The design of their Victorian home had been adapted for Hawaiian living by a wide verandah circling gracefully around the exterior. Fine scrolled woodwork lent an airy feeling to the pillars and framed a view of growing Honolulu, if one had time to enjoy it. Tat-Tung didn't, judging by the clatter of stoneware bowls and porcelain platters on the dinner table inside. Quickly, he opened the screen door and greeted his mother, aunties, brothers, and sisters.

Without acknowledging him, his mother, Dai-Kam, continued her gossip across the dinner table with his father's Second wife, Auntie Ho Shee. His father's Third wife, Auntie Chung Shee, picked what she could for her two daughters and stayed out of the line of flying chopsticks. Each mother sat with their own children positioned close to her so she could grab the choicest morsels for her favorites. His brothers and sisters were too engrossed by the smells of fresh chicken, duck, pork, and vegetables to give him more than a glance over the rim of their rice bowls. With so many chopsticks dancing in and out of the dishes, they maneuvered hastily to get enough to eat.

Tat-Tung placed his books on his bed, washed his face and hands at the faucet in the back of the house, and returned to the one empty seat. He dumped the last of the rice and green beans in his bowl, then glared at his brothers and sisters. They hadn't even left him bones to suck on. He slumped, tired and hungry. His day at Saint Louis College had started with an hour of Palmer penmanship practice at seven. Because of L. Ah Leong's magnanimous gift, a large parcel of land on River Street when the Catholic fathers wanted to build a private boys' school, St. Louis welcomed the opportunity to educate his sons. The Chinese saw merit in the strict discipline of the Catholics, whose moral teachings and high educational standards complemented Confucian beliefs. So Ah Leong sent all his sons, in home-sewn trousers of bleached rice bags, to the Catholic all-boys' school for their Western education.

Mother and Auntie Ho Shee, both pregnant, leaned back in their koa wood chairs while Auntie Chung Shee lifted the youngest children down from their seats.

His mother rested, eyes closed, and fanned herself after the ordeal of presiding over the daily dinner for wives and children. When she grew tired of listening to the hungry click of Tat-Tung's chopsticks scraping the bottom of his bowl, she opened her eyes. "Here's three cents for saimin," she said and dismissed him.

☙❧

"*Ah Bahk*, saimin, please."

The wiry cook, his white apron splattered with the day's soup stock, looked up. Raindrops tapped louder now on the tin roof of his saimin stall in continuous rhythm with the whoosh of swaying branches above. Mynah birds scolded the rain. Who was calling him the courteous title of "Ah Bahk," meaning uncle? Most Honolulu people were home with their families at dinner time. His own family had joined him in the back of his store for noodles and vegetables.

"Home from school so late, Tat-Tung?" the cook exclaimed. He got up from the warm circle of his wife and children. "Your head's all wet. Sit. Sit. Saimin is all you eat again for dinner? A scholar needs to feed his body as well as his mind." His straw sandals shuffled noisily across the wooden floor. He welcomed Tat-Tung with a wide gap-toothed grin and eyes lilting up to his temples.

Tat-Tung envied the teasing of these parents with their children, their noisy banter, and the warm chatter that bound them together. Not like his family. As far back as he could remember, his mother favored Auntie Ho Shee's children, not her own. At first, he craved the attention she gave to his half-brothers and half-sisters. One day, when they all held out their hands for the hard candies she brought home after long afternoons of mah-jongg, she turned to her two eldest sons and barked, "Too old." She slapped their outstretched palms and waved them away.

Ah Yin and Tat-Tung stood frozen, turning red while the others laughed at their misery. Ah Yin was six years older than Tat-Tung, and Tat-Tung was less than a year older than Ah Wang, Auntie Ho Shee's eldest son. Not that much difference in age.

"I give you extra *char siu*," the cook said. He filled a large bowl with masses of crinkly noodles and ladled chicken broth up to the edge of the bowl, fragrant with the steam of chicken, shrimp, and mushrooms. Green onions and slices of *char siu*, a glistening red roast pork, floated on the top like an armada of little boats.

"*Do-jei*, thank you, *Ah Bahk*. You're so kind."

The cook puffed proudly. "I'm proud to feed L. Ah Leong's First son."

Yes, with Ah Yin gone, he was considered the First son.

After their sons received a Western education, affluent Chinese sent them back to their village for a Chinese education under the tutelage of clan scholars. Eldest brother Ah Yin never got to China. After another contentious argument with Dai-Kam, he walked out on his wife and two daughters and jumped a steamer for a distant port. Before he left, he accused his mother of making his life torture. He vowed never to return.

The patter on the tin roof was steady now, signaling that the drifting showers had moved on. The rain would leave behind the clean smell of washed wooden buildings, leaves and flowers bobbing with the weight of water drops and puddles glistening on the rough roads. Brave souls emerged from the cover of awnings and scurried across the streets of downtown Honolulu.

The year was 1903. Hawai'i had changed for the Chinese. Hawai'i had become a United States Territory five years before when President McKinley signed the authorization to annex Hawai'i. Two years later, Chinatown was burnt to the ground. The rich American sugar planters who now sold Hawai'i-grown sugarcane without tariffs had became more powerful by developing the pineapple industry.

The Chinese in the rebuilding Chinatown distrusted the territorial government. The Chinese Exclusion Laws of this new government from the Mainland intruded into their personal lives and dictated what they could do, even when and where they could travel outside Hawai'i. His father said when he came to Hawai'i in the 1870s, there were more Chinese men than Caucasian men. The Caucasians needed the Chinese labor for the sugarcane, but were afraid their growing numbers would give them power. So they passed the Exclusion Laws to control the Chinese.

Even in these modern times, his father was old-fashioned when it came to family. Ah Leong followed the strict dictates of culture and tradition to mold and sculpt his family's life in Hawai'i. Cherished sons were educated. Unwanted daughters were given away. Now that Tat-Tung had taken Ah Yin's place as First son, he was expected to carry on the legacy of Ah Leong's business empire.

Chinese expected their sons to marry well, to produce grandsons to perpetuate the clan name. Since marriage was a momentous family decision, Tat-Tung and his buddies knew their parents would arrange marriages for them soon. The boys shared the facts of life with great zeal; the sexual *jing* of women was supposed to mature at age fourteen and the *jing* of men matured at sixteen. Tat-Tung would soon find out for himself. Last night, he overheard his father tell his mother that he was returning to China with his two eldest sons: thirteen-year-old Tat-Tung and Auntie Ho Shee's twelve-year-old Ah Wang. His mother argued against it but Ah Leong stubbornly held his ground. Then he lowered his voice and murmured words Tat-Tung couldn't understand. Ah Leong left Dai-Kam's room an hour later.

When Tat-Tung got up in the morning, he saw his father stride out of Auntie Chung Shee's room, slippers flapping in the quiet of the rustling trade winds. *Baba* chuckled when he saw his son, then entered Dai-Kam's bedroom and locked the door.

ॐॐ

"A successful merchant always has business on his mind, Tat-Tung. Here we see who has the choicest vegetables, meats, and eggs," Ah Leong said in a low voice.

He kept his son close to his side as he shopped, bargained, and argued. Sunday market day was his time to meet old friends, discuss the latest political scandals, gossip about friends and enemies, and exchange jokes from home.

Vendors hailed them. A deal with the well-known merchant would justify their trip to the city and feed their family for a month.

Ah Leong wove through the pulsating tide of people with his son, teaching by example how to build the valuable relationships that made up his business network.

"Do not confront directly. Be subtle," he advised. "Those with greater face will treat you with respect and honor your word as a peer." They picked from baskets of bok choy, all varieties of squash, fresh taro with leafy green heads, bunches of bananas just chopped from the tree, live chickens and ducks in bamboo cages, tilapia splashing in buckets, and the prized barnacles called *opihi*, popped that morning from the lava rocks washed by the tides.

They stopped near Choy Sum, the second store from the corner of Hotel and Maunakea Streets. Yuen the herbalist, plainly dressed in a blue cotton shirt and trousers, sat regally on a wooden crate. True to his word, he never went back to the laundry business. Since the fire, he stayed on in Chinatown as a healer, overwhelmingly popular with the reverent crowd surrounding him. His eyes were milky, skimmed with an opaque cloud. Now that his sight had failed, he propped a rough staff of monkeypod wood behind his seat.

Tat-Tung hung back when Ah Leong barged right up to the front of the crowd. His father's boldness embarrassed him; in moments like this, Tat-Tung pretended to be alone, not with *Baba*. His father chatted with familiar joviality. The herbalist nodded and chuckled, a twinkle in his cloudy eyes. Yuen deftly wrote his prescription on a piece of paper and handed it to Ah Leong, who thanked his friend and, with the same movement, slipped a generous roll of silver into Yuen's hands.

"Hey, Tat-Tung," Ah Leong bellowed across the packed sidewalk. He searched impatiently through the crowd.

Tat-Tung sighed with embarrassment but walked quickly to his father's side. If he didn't, he would receive a knuckle on his skull, even more embarrassing.

Ah Leong shoved his son in front of Yuen, his square hands proudly on his son's shoulders.

Tat-Tung bowed.

Yuen lifted the boy's face and lightly touched his high smooth forehead. Through his dimmed sight he saw Dai-Kam's large round eyes, shimmering and guarded. His fingers traced a handsome face of sorrow and depth–strong pride, great loyalty, and a good heart.

The boy averted his eyes in respect and awe. The herbalist's touch felt magical, like the passing of a feather.

"We have the highest respect for our scholars. Now you go to China. You will study Lao Tzu and the teachings of Confucius," Yuen said.

"And Bing-Fa, the philosophical strategies of warfare," added Ah Leong.

"Your father is one of the best merchants in Chinatown. You will learn the secrets of his success. Ask him how he uses Bing-Fa." Yuen turned to Ah Leong. "You take good care of your son," he ordered. He tapped the merchant firmly on the chest with his forefinger. "This son will watch out for you and give you the best advice."

He tilted his head to Tat-Tung and added, "And good luck to you."

Ah Leong thanked Yuen with a short bow and motioned his son to follow. Yuen called out his parting words with a wave, "Remember, the best herbs grow in Sichuan. They are most potent." He turned to his next patient. Ah Leong looked back at the queue of customers waiting for Yuen and chuckled his approval.

҉҉

At noon, the close of market day, Ah Leong and his son joined the boisterous crowd in the upstairs Chinese restaurant a block from the Oʻahu Fish Market. The men met here for lunch and talked of old times in China, new deals to be made in Hawaiʻi, and the business of trade between the two.

The fans churned indolently, swirling the aroma of freshly steamed foods out wide windows ornamented with red and gold fretwork. From the streets, the cacophony of loud Chinese voices would be heard for the rest of the afternoon. The men ate and gossiped, building their business, political, and social ties. Here, they were free from the strain of the work week, when they adapted to the ways of the Americans. They sauntered to the tables of their friends, joked, and laughed with others along the way. Now and then, they yelled a jocular insult across the room to an acquaintance, which was picked up and elaborated on by others.

Ah Leong and son sat at one of these crowded tables. Waiters brought tray after tray of shrimp, beef, pork, and tofu dumplings, delicate rolled rice noodles, and platters of seafood noodles. This was one of the best tables, positioned with a view of every man coming and going, where the diners could see and be seen.

Shrewd in the manipulation of information and people, Ah Leong maneuvered through the politics and gossip of the other merchants. He was considered an old-timer from the days of the monarchy by both the ruling government officials and the Chinese, many who dealt with him through investments and his wholesale and retail operations. Some considered his many wives, children, and businesses indicative of his wealth and powerful face. His support of any new business venture, noted by everyone in Chinatown, substantiated its worth.

Ah Leong waved over C.K. Ai, an old friend, and asked about his business. Ai said it was doing very well, thanks to his benevolence, then acknowledged his cronies at the table. Ah Leong waved for another teacup and pair of chopsticks to be brought for his friend.

"I have nothing to do with your success, Ai. Hawai'i needed milled rice and lumber. You started the right business and had the faith to come back stronger than before," complimented Ah Leong.

Ai waved off the praise as he pulled out a chair, "All of us worked hard to pay back our debts after the Chinatown fire. I feel for our friends who declared bankruptcy after that catastrophe. They returned to menial labor to pay back every cent they owed."

Ah Leong shook his head in admiration. "The law said they didn't have to." The other men nodded knowingly, proud of the reputations their fellow Chinese upheld. Integrity was important. Their word was their bond. A sterling character, one's good face, reflected upon both family and business, and marked one whose life was in harmony with society and the cosmic energy.

When C. K. Ai and C. M. Kai conceived the idea of opening a lumber and rice-milling business in Honolulu, they figured that with the growing population of Asians the rice mill would be profitable. The lumber business was a gamble. The men didn't have the $60,000 they needed, and hoped to obtain the capital by selling shares to their friends. L. Ah Leong, known for his shrewd conservative business sense, visited C. K. Ai and subscribed to ten shares of their corporation at $100 a share. When the other Chinese heard that Ah Leong had put so much money into this new venture, they followed his lead. Ai lost everything when the Great Chinatown Fire of 1900 destroyed his business. Instead of declaring bankruptcy, Ai rebuilt his lumber empire, now the largest in the Territory, from scratch. His faith in the community and their support, despite their own three million dollar loss, made him one of their most successful businessmen.

"And you, Ah Leong, how is business?" asked Ai.

"Not bad," Ah Leong answered modestly. To be boastful would be indiscreet and tempt bad luck. "I leave for China next week with my two eldest sons. All my sons will have village brides."

The men turned to Tat-Tung and aaah'd. They thought of their villages and long-ago families. They thrust red *li-see* envelopes towards Tat-Tung.

The young man's eyes lit up. He glanced at his father for approval.

"No need, no need," protested Ah Leong, more in good manners than humility. He motioned the *li-see*, the traditional red envelopes stuffed with silver dollars, back with quick gestures of dismissal.

"For Tat-Tung's trip," argued his friends. They pressed the *li-see* in his son's hands as Ah Leong feigned refusal. "For good luck, to study harder and bring back a healthy fertile bride," they insisted. They threw their heads back with raucous laughter. Other tables turned to see who was causing the ruckus, then waved when they recognized the rowdy merchants pushing and roaring at their own coarse jokes.

The young man blushed and thanked his father's compatriots.

The men continued their talk of family and business. They smoked their cigars, sipped dark *bow-lei* tea, and ordered more plates of *dim sum*. Ah Leong spun his web, as all successful Chinese businessmen do, tied by affiliations and camaraderie, knotted by marriages and business deals. Together, all succeeded. Endorsement and support by Ah Leong, the Money Dragon, guaranteed success.

When Tat-Tung and his father left the tea house late that afternoon, Yuen the herbalist was still on his wooden crate in front of Choy Sum. He leaned forward to consult with an elderly woman. He held her pulse to feel the flow and blockages of her *ch'i*. Then the herbalist turned and winked at him.

Tat-Tung caught the sparkles from those cloudy eyes and grinned.

Chapter Seven

The Laus of Kew Boy Village: 1903

When Tat-Tung sailed to China for the first time in 1903, he saw for himself the mountainous lands that dominated his father's dreams and obsessive yearnings. His father said they would learn to speak, think, and act like "real" Chinese. Tat-Tung and Ah Wang shrugged. At thirteen and twelve years old, all they cared about at the beginning of their adventure was their exuberant send-off at Honolulu Harbor.

"We have to say good-bye to *Baba* and my brothers 'Hawaiian style,'" Ah Leong's First daughter Kai-Tai insisted. With broad powerful shoulders, the legacy of her mother, she commandeered her three mothers and dozen siblings through the crowds towards the lei sellers. Even the dockside streets overflowed with departing passengers and well-wishers.

Caught up in the excitement of "Boat Day," Ah Leong's First, Second, and Third wives joined the friends and relatives buying flower leis for the departing passengers of the SS *Siberia*.

"Look. Picked from my yard this morning," offered Napua Akana. She held out a dozen leis of *lokelani*, *'awapuhi melemele*, *pakalana*, and gardenias. "See the dew? And the aroma! Aaah, sweet and lasting–like the love you send with your men."

"Buy them all, Mother. Tat-Tung and Ah Wang have never gone on a boat before," Kai-Tai ordered.

Dai-Kam shrewdly surveyed the flowers. Confident that Napua reciprocated for the quality service she received at the L. Ah Leong Store, Dai-Kam picked a dozen of the freshest and draped them over her left arm. She ordered Second wife Ho Shee to pay, then followed her First daughter to the boat. Ho Shee emptied her wallet into her palm, counted out Napua's coins, then ran to catch up.

Ah Leong shouldered his way to the gangplank. "Hey, hey, hey," he bellowed. He cut a swath through the crying, hugging, and kissing crowd–wide enough for himself, Tat-Tung, and Ah Wang to walk abreast. Kai-Tai steered her mothers and brothers in his wake.

When the SS *Siberia* pulled away from the dock to the heartrending refrain of "Aloha Oe," the Lau women on the dock waved to their three men stacked to their ears with leis.

Ah Leong waved good-bye to his First wife Dai-Kam, the passion of his youth with the strength of a broad-backed ox. Second wife Ho Shee, the obedient docile one, moved her hands with short motions, back and forth, back and forth. He could read no expression in her blank, pinched face.

Third wife Chung Shee's fingers fluttered sadly. She feared Dai-Kam or Ho Shee would send her away if they knew how much she loved their husband, how she longed for his nightly visits. So she never complained when the other wives treated her with disdain and gave her the filthiest cleaning and back-breaking chores. She obeyed with sweetness and a gentle spirit.

She was already asleep when he came to her bed the night before after the store closed. He had lifted her cotton shift and gazed at her unblemished porcelain skin, drinking in the radiance of her nakedness. He cupped her slight breasts. She had awakened and arched her back as he ran his hands down her body as if to absorb her youthful heat. "Aaah, come. Let me make you cry out," she had whispered.

He had sighed with anticipation when she draped his body with her long dark hair. He remembered how she had gasped the first time he had undressed her. Despite her virgin modesty, she reached out for him then as she did now. How could he have guessed that this gentle village girl who moved with the grace of an agile seabird was capable of so much passion? Even more exciting to him was that she never closed her eyes, the way his other wives did, when he was upon her. She watched every tremor of his body with delight. "More," she would cry, "more." And as always, they ignited the night until they finally rolled apart, satiated and consumed, when the rooster crowed at dawn.

☙❧

The two Lau sons, too homesick to wave good-bye to their mothers and sisters, had crammed their hands in their pockets and choked back tears when the SS *Siberia* pulled away from the dock. They did as their father instructed and threw one of their leis into the churning waves. He had pointed to where their leis bobbed and drifted back to shore exulting, "Look, you'll return."

Honolulu Harbor could not compare to Hong Kong, to the whistles and horns of steamers, square-sailed junks, and tugs that crisscrossed the waterways day and night. The thick humid air throbbed with the pungent scent of exotic spices and foreign lands.

In Hong Kong, the boys encountered the crisp efficiency of the British officers, white-uniformed men who briskly stamped their passports and waved them through with a respectful nod to their father. They gazed with bewilderment at the Chinese who, in Hong Kong it seemed, came in all sizes, shades, and mixtures–from light-skinned Eurasians to hearty, bushy-browed Huns. And the colorful clothes: Malaysians in deep-colored sarongs, Burmese in *longyis* printed in the geometric patterns of their villages, Thais wrapped in the intricate ties of their *panung*, Indian women in gold-threaded saris, and dark-skinned Punjabis with their magnificent turbans.

They boarded the train to Swatow. China unfolded. Outdoor toilets called outhouses perched over the banks of enormous fish ponds where giant carp swarmed. Barefoot children and parents bent over rice fields planting their hopes for a good harvest. Occasionally, they caught the stare of a man walking the rice paddies with his water buffalo.

At Swatow, they boarded a barge pulled upstream by two donkeys on shore. At another city, they hopped on a carriage. People yelled, "Who are you? Where are you from? Where are you going?" Barefoot children chased after them as if they were emperors. Squatting on stoops, old men and women with wizened visages studied the boys' faces as elders do when they look for linkages in the faces of the young. The Hawai'i boys stared back, unable to believe that these were kinsmen who shared a common ancestry.

Weathered stone homes stained with centuries of black mold loomed forbidding and cold compared to the airy wooden cottages and mansions of Hawai'i. Unlike the cool tradewinds at home, the air hung with the stillness that forebodes oven-like temperatures.

Ah Leong timed their arrival in Kew Boy to the cool of morning when dew clung to the short grasses that grew along their path and the rice paddies resembled picturesque green steps dotted with water buffaloes and herders. For the occasion, they dressed as upper-class Chinese in clothes called *Woo Ping*–black satin skullcaps, the long banker's coats of *dai fong chau* silk, and black pigskin-soled satin shoes in reverse appliqué.

He pointed out an old man, awkwardly attired in a newly tailored black tunic and trousers, strutting pompously through the parted crowd. "My father," he warned his sons.

Lau See-Dew's skinny queue was pulled back from a wrinkled face from which two little eyes surveyed the gathering crowd. The old man's arms pumped at his side with each proud step. He delivered his welcoming speech, an oration he had practiced daily for three weeks to the pigs in his backyard. For years, the old man gestured, he and his wife scoured the countryside like miserable peasants, gathering grains of rice to eat. They sold their only daughter in marriage to the Wong family. Now, due to the success of their scholar son, Lau See-Dew had much face in the community. His only son, the returning Lau Fat Leong, had donated a large sum of money to the Governor of Kwang Tung and received a Five-Star Name in recognition of his prestigious wealth and honor in both Hawai'i and China. In Hawai'i, he was so famous he didn't even need to use his surname; everyone knew the flourishing merchant Ah Leong.

The whole village should be proud of their returning clansmen, he concluded with a vigorous nod of his wrinkled head and a grandiose sweep of his scrawny arms in huge circles. "See his big belly," he puffed. "See how prosperous he has become."

Ah Leong looked down at the village men who scrambled to help him unload. Their words made him laugh: Look, it is Lau's son. The one who drowned. He returns! A miracle.

He knew they remembered how shamefully they threw him out of his own house. In revenge, he would remind them, often. "See how they stand aside to let us pass through the crowds," he boasted to his sons.

❧❧

Ah Leong motioned his sons into the bedroom they shared. Tat-Tung and Ah Wang, just back from a tour of Kew Boy with Grandfather Lau See-Dew, cheeks flushed from the fawning attention of the villagers, hurried to their room.

Ah Leong closed the door. He crossed his arms and nodded for them to sit on Tat-Tung's bed before he spoke. In front of his parents' small stone cottage he would build a new house worthy of a wealthy merchant, a house that all his families in Hawai'i could return to whenever they wished, a house that would establish his presence on ancestral soil. Their lessons in Chinese literature, history, and music would begin the next day. Their private tutors would instruct them in this very room. He lifted an eyebrow. The boys nodded

Meanwhile, he had an important chore for them. "I put these trunks under your bed, Tat-Tung," Ah Leong said. He lifted the coverlet and pointed out five bronze-banded trunks under the bed. His First son nodded. "It is your responsibility to sit here and guard them, day and night." Tat-Tung nodded again. Ah Leong turned to Ah Wang. "You, Ah Wang, come and check with him often. If he has to go, you take his place. Always, one of you sits here."

Ah Leong opened the first box. Thousands of Chinese silver dollars, each as big around as an American baseball, were stacked to the lid. "You are thirteen. This is your responsibility, Tat-Tung," Ah Leong repeated softly.

❧❧

First, Ah Leong built a new temple for the village.

Next, he ordered a new village gate carved of stone with the Lau family name on the tall columns that flanked the road, so all who entered had to pass under it.

Third, Ah Leong built his first house in China. He named it *Nam Shun Lau*, the Story of the Southern Breeze. The village air billowed a dusty brown with the daily roll of supply carts laden with building materials. Men hauled in quarried stones for the walls, glazed red tiles for the roofs, and bronze bars for the windows. Workmen balanced like delicate cranes on bamboo scaffolding two stories high to construct the forty-eight bedrooms, three atrium courtyards, eight special storage rooms, a high-ceilinged kitchen, and Ah Leong's vault.

Tat-Tung verified the bills, contracted for workers, and paid in silver. When his father purchased the rice farms around the estate, Tat-Tung audited their production before negotiating as low a price as he could.

In one atrium courtyard, his father ordered rock formations, "Earth bones," hauled by a team of horses all the way from Kweilin. Single drops of water had shaped these unusually convoluted rocks, one drip at a time, over endless centuries.

From their bedroom window, Ah Wang and Tat-Tung watched the workmen position the Earth bones. *Baba* had the geomancer decide each precious rock's auspicious placement. "See this shape?" the boys pointed out, "these are the jagged mountains from deep in the interior of China, the mystical mountains from the paintings of the masters." They envisioned secret kingdoms, miniature villages, and magical places in the contorted rocks.

"I can't wait to play there," Ah Wang exclaimed.

"Yes," his brother grimaced. "When the house is completed, *Baba* will lock his silver in his vault and we'll be free." He waved longingly at the boys who came every day to his window.

The first day the village boys came they yelled, "We live in your house." Tat-Tung shook his head and shrugged that he didn't understand. "Your house, the house your grandfather gambled away. He lost it to our father and uncles," they shouted.

The next day, the boys brought him a cricket in a cylindrical wicker cage to keep him company. He held the cage between his palms, wondering how long the cricket would sing if it knew it would never ever be free.

Every day after that, whenever he signaled that his tutors were gone, the village boys gathered inquisitively at his window. They asked him about Hawai'i, a place as foreign to them as China was to him. "Our father says you are rich. He and our uncles say you are too young to have so much money. He says you are too smart," prodded the eldest, a boy five years older.

Tat-Tung didn't know what to make of their questions. The boys seemed friendly. He sensed that their families didn't welcome *Baba's* return. But he was lonely, with only Ah Wang as his confidante.

☜☞

L. Ah Leong waved down a rickshaw and motioned Tat-Tung up. He barked out his destination to the leather-skinned coolie. Then he leaned back and pointed out the sights of the port city they were visiting as they headed to one of the herbal shops tucked in the alleys. The familiar sea scents reminded him of a long-ago time, after his father wrested him from a pampered childhood and turned him into a beggar pleading for work in exchange for rice.

"Food and sex. Confucius teaches that these are indispensable for life!" Ah Leong chortled with gusto. His son blushed, but his eyes glistened with interest. "Food and sex are the strongest natural instincts, the fundamental indicators of health, and the best way to attain longevity. So, now you know why I am here." First wife Dai-Kam oversaw his home and families in Hawai'i. To ensure Confucian harmony and to further display his abundant wealth, he needed a Fifth wife to take care of his family's home, lands, farms, and needs in China.

His sister's mother-in-law had picked a prospective candidate. A poor widow with buck teeth, Wong Tat Chan had hoped her first husband would rescue her from her family's poverty. Since his death last summer, she had toiled in the fields until her young hands became raw. She knew she wasn't pretty and her body was bony from wanting rice when there was none. But as Lau Ah Leong's wife, known by her "wife name" of Wong Shee, she would always have rice to eat.

Tat-Tung's eyes grew bigger. Another wife for *Baba*? Another auntie for him?

Inspired by his son's rapt attention, Ah Leong continued. Chinese categorize their foods with the same classifications that distinguish curative herbs in Chinese herbal medicine: the Four Energies and Five Flavors. After consuming a meal rich in hot foods such as lamb, ginger, peanuts, or chili, a knowledgeable chef prevented excess heat by serving cool deserts such as lychee, watermelon, or papaya. A trained Chinese cook struck a fine balance not only in flavor, aroma, texture, and color, but in the energies and essences they imparted to the body upon digestion. After a Chinese banquet, guests felt hungry an hour later because of this quality and balance; the food mixed well in the stomach, digested easily, and was distributed rapidly throughout the system.

A healthy sex life was the other secret of longevity. As they rode through the unmarked back streets, Ah Leong told his son how one of the most potent aphrodisiacs was discovered. "Long ago, a goat herder noticed that his billy goats could mount their mates many times. Again and again. He was fired with curiosity! He jumped over rocks and ran through meadows to observe them. Was it the water? The grass? An insect bite? He noticed that they ate from a certain patch of weeds. Thus, our esteemed Chinese herbalists discovered one of the strongest herbs known for male potency: *yin yang hue*, or 'horny goat weed.'"

At a shop lined with thousands of tiny drawers and hundreds of bottles, Ah Leong gave young Su the herbalist, son of old Ma the herbalist, his prescription from Yuen.

Tat-Tung inspected the dusty bottles that young Su, a gangly thirty-year-old bachelor, brought out for his father. He cleaned a label with his finger to read the calligraphy.

"We have a scholar who wants to know why this works," Su

acknowledged to Ah Leong, tipping his head towards the boy. He lifted an eyebrow at Tat-Tung appraisingly. "Your sexual *jing* matures in two years. You won't need this for many decades. However, your father wants to make sure your new mother will produce an heir to watch over his lands and homes here."

Tat-Tung put the bottles down quickly.

"My son is naturally curious. You know these young men," Ah Leong harrumphed.

"Of course, he wants scientific proof that these medicines work." Su tapped his temple with his forefinger. "Western scientists are studying Chinese medicines to find out what our ancestors have always known." Su turned to Tat-Tung and said, "I have something to show you." He hustled to the back of his shop and rummaged through stacks of dusty magazines under his desk. He waved a magazine and returned. "A former English teacher sends me Western science magazines," he said, ruffling through the pages to find the pictures he wanted. Tat-Tung shifted uncomfortably as Su peered at father and son over the rims of his round wire spectacles and explained.

"So you see, sperm count and semen density increase substantially during the first few hours after the horny goat weed is taken. The herb expands the capillaries as well as the major vessels of the circulatory system permitting the hormone-enriched blood to penetrate the body's most sensitive tissues. By flooding the brain with hormone rich blood, you are sensitive to the well-placed touch and the pleasing scent of your woman..."

Ah Leong harrumphed Su to stop.

Tat-Tung learned that the best Chinese herbs grew naturally in China. The craggy mountains and deep valleys of Sichuan were the richest sources of potent wild herbs. The strongest herbs, such as ginseng, depleted the soil; after the herb was pulled, nothing ever grew there again.

Tat-Tung tugged on Su's wide silk sleeves. How could he recognize these herbs in the wild? Could he grow them in Hawai'i? Would their potency be the same? Before the boy left, Su had searched through his dusty desk and handed Tat-Tung his prized text on Chinese herbs.

❦❦

Ah Leong's money flowed like the rivers that swelled their banks in the spring. He invited friends and relatives from Kew Boy and the neighboring villages to a banquet on the meadow behind the Great Ancestral Hall to celebrate his Three Happinesses. He thanked the gods and his ancestors for his business success and good luck, the completion of the Lau family's new ancestral home in China, and his marriage to Fifth wife Wong Shee. In lieu of tables and chairs, his guests lounged on the bamboo-braided sheets usually used for drying rice in the sun.

Tat-Tung and Ah Wang followed the powerful Wu Shu movements of the lion dancers through the streets, jumped at the hundreds of firecrackers thrown at their feet, and clapped with the clash of gongs.

At the end of the day, two thousand guests staggered home with commemorative rice bowls and chopsticks and all the leftover food.

Tat-Tung invited his new friends, the boys who had kept him company while he guarded his father's silver, to his new house. The next day they reciprocated; they asked if he would come to the house his grandfather had gambled away.

Tat-Tung believed his friends' elders when they said he was grownup enough to join their sons in their private parlors. He told Ah Wang later that opium wasn't bad; all the rich young men indulged. Servant girls had padded into the ornately furnished parlor bearing trays of sweets and tea. His companions, most between fifteen and eighteen years old, played the erhu, zither, and moonharp all afternoon. Everyone applauded when Tat-Tung displayed his virtuosity on the moonharp. They praised his singing. To celebrate their friendship, the eldest boy, the one who had told Tat-Tung he was too smart, brought out an opium pipe. They all smoked to their friendship.

Tat-Tung said the village boys gave him just a little bit, enough for him to feel serene and balanced.

"Is it bad?" Ah Wang asked.

"Not if it chases away my loneliness. But don't tell *Baba*," his brother cautioned. He and his brother knew about opium hidden in the regular mercantile shipments from China to Hawai'i. In Honolulu, the Chinese merchants repacked the opium in Prince Albert tins. Some was sold to clients, some included in regular orders to the plantations. Opium created the fortune of many Hawai'i merchants. The locals whispered their names and ignored what was unpleasant, preferring only to see their prosperous facade.

Tat-Tung sought opium's comfort and the camaraderie it brought with his new friends. Unlike his family in Hawai'i, especially his mother who scorned and belittled him, the village boys praised him. They plied him with food, drink, and opium. He yearned for the sharp burning in his throat that preceded descent into the shimmering world of dreams.

☙☙

"Next year's banquet will be greater!" Ah Leong's bellow echoed through the great dining hall of his new house. He threw his head back and laughed at the shocked faces of his family. Everyone–sons, new wife, parents, sister, and husband–stared up from their rice bowls.

Tat-Tung put down his chopsticks. "Why another banquet, *Baba*? Grandfather told me that the governor of Kwang Tung was so astounded by your munificence he was going to give you another honor. You must have fed all the people in China!"

Ah Leong rubbed at an imaginary spot in the glistening arm of his carved chair, then surveyed the prosperous scene before him: his growing family, mounded platters of expensive food, and new furniture from the workshops of Hong Kong. He leaned back. "Next year, we celebrate your wedding, Tat-Tung, to Wong Pin."

Tat-Tung dropped his chopsticks. "*Baba*, I am only fourteen years old!" He had seen Wong Pin's parents, a scholarly family in a nearby village, and heard of their daughter. She was fair and as dainty as a swallow. She reputedly made lace fit for an emperor's court. He didn't want a wife, yet.

Ah Leong straightened his shoulders and nodded imperiously. "How lucky. I had to wait until I was twenty-five before I could afford a wife."

For the next nine months, Tat-Tung studied Su's book and tried to remember what his schoolmates had told him about the male *jing*. His friends bolstered his spirits with music and opium. At night, he clicked open the case of his moonharp. Melodies, luscious yet delicate, rose from his fingertips. He released the landscapes of his soul: pain, joy, rejection, fear, uncertainty, and hope.

Ah Leong listened to the intricately woven lyrics that fluttered like butterflies through the parlors of his great new house. He leaned back on his polished high-backed chair and congratulated himself on how well he had molded his heir.

Ah Wang was despondent. Not only would he lose his older brother and best friend to a girl, but his father announced that he was choosing village brides for all his sons. Ah Wang would be next.

True to his prediction, Ah Leong celebrated with an even greater banquet to honor Eighth son Ah Chen, born nine months after he married his Fifth wife, and the wedding of his First son, Tat-Tung.

His chefs prepared a three-day banquet for two thousand guests. On the first day, the colorful banners of province and district officials proclaimed the presence of noble guests. The second day's banquet was reserved for the families of the bride and groom. On the third day, all the villagers and their relatives dined. As before, the guests took home the leftover food as well as the commemorative rice bowls, cups, and chopsticks.

Before he returned to Hawai'i, Ah Leong supervised the construction of a concrete bridge in Jiaoling across the river where he had once dangled, a beggar boy not worth saving. In the middle of the bridge, he embedded a large plaque so all who crossed would thank him. It read simply, "Lau Fat Leong personally spent $5,000 to build this bridge in 1904."

Chapter Eight
The Many Wives of L. Ah Leong: 1905

Dai-Kam stood ramrod straight, proud and regal, the children lined up beside her, when she welcomed her husband home. She had run the L. Ah Leong Store while he had been in China the last two years. She had greeted each customer, stocked the shelves, and locked up each night.

L. Ah Low, who had employed her as a housekeeper and her husband in his store when they moved to Honolulu from Kohala twenty-five years ago, stopped by once a day and advised her if she had questions. He read her the weekly letters of instruction from her husband. L. Ah Low's crooked-tooth smile had fallen when he read with wavering bobs of his skinny white queue that Ah Leong had married a wife in China "to take care of their farms and house," a new ancestral home in his village with forty-eight bedrooms. She had heard, not from him, that he had a new son.

When her husband returned, Second wife Ho Shee would fight her for his bed, to keep a claim on her status.

She didn't have to worry about Chung Shee.

In fact, the first time Third wife Chung Shee was alone with Ah Leong, she begged to move out. She pleaded with him when he wrapped his body around hers and clenched her braids. Her almond eyes reflected her sadness. "Please, my love," she wept, "I want you to myself, to be closer to you. I want to love you without your other wives listening to our bed." During the day she didn't dare complain. She remembered when Fourth wife, younger than she, died childless after eight years. No one even remembered her name now.

After a week of Chung Shee's weeping, Ah Leong kicked out one of his tenants. Chung Shee moved into the apartment above the L. Ah Leong Store. The youthful blush returned to her full sweet face. Her three little girls ran up and down the stairs which made up their new playground. They bounced their balls from the staircase and skipped through the alley, bobbing glistening black pigtails woven with colorful ribbons. When First mother Dai-Kam strode towards the store, they scampered upstairs as quickly as their bare feet could run and hid under their bed. Chung Shee shook her head at them. But all three sat as still as statues.

After work, Ah Leong ran upstairs. He knew Chung Shee waited naked in her bed, her jet black hair flowing in waves upon the sheets, her skin smelling of fresh silk.

His first two wives didn't mind his absence in the least. Nine months after he returned from China they were both nursing newborn babies, Dai-Kam's eighth and Ho Shee's seventh.

The September after Ah Leong's newest son and daughter were born to his first two wives, the wind shifted. The Kona winds blew in from the ocean carrying chills and fevers. The changing temperatures gave people a hacking cough.

"What's this?" Ah Leong cried when he found Chung Shee hiding tissues stained with red spittle. He ran downstairs to get Yuen, the blind herbalist who sat outside the second store from the corner of Hotel and Maunakea Streets.

Yuen placed his hands on Chung Shee's forehead, tapped her vital spots, and listened to her difficult breathing.

"Kind healer Yuen, it is nothing, just a passing weakness," Chung Shee rasped. Her gentle voice trembled to hide her fear.

The blind herbalist waved his hands over her body, unblocked the flow of her *ch'i*, and willed life and energy back into her body.

Ah Leong searched the apothecary shops for the herbs Yuen

requested. *Tian nan xing* was a poison when fresh but a potent healer when dried. Yuen mixed it with beef bile to neutralize its toxins. *Jie geng* diluted the accumulation of phlegm, and *xuan fu hua* stopped the cough and nausea. Yuen wrapped the herbs in a cheesecloth pouch which he simmered in glazed pottery bowls suspended in boiling water. When Ah Leong told him the color of his tonics matched the piece of amber Yuen held out to him, the blind herbalist strained the drugs and coaxed the sick woman to drink. Within days, healthy color returned to Chung Shee's face.

"Ah Leong," Yuen told his friend when they listened to her sleep easily at last, "this disease has been with her a long time, long before the Kona winds came. I can't save her." He placed his fingers on Ah Leong's arm and felt his disbelieving reaction. At least the end would be swift now.

When Chung Shee slid her limbs against Ah Leong's body at night, she was more ardent than before. Long after he thought he was exhausted, her tender fingers renewed his passion until he thought he would explode a thousand times. "Oh, to spend a lifetime with you," he gasped. "I will be young forever."

She laughed softly in his neck. "You will be mine forever." She drew her protector tight against her breasts. "Promise?"

He groaned, exhausted and spent. "Yes, yours forever," he promised.

She closed her eyes and wished she could always feel his warmth, his passionate energy.

One day when Yuen came to prepare her daily tonics, the merchant ran up from his store to thank him for saving his wife's life. Yuen turned his cloudy eyes to Ah Leong.

"My friend, remember that Chinese saying 'Just before death comes the brightness.' She is close to death but has made peace with herself. With this peace comes a renewed energy that she gives to you. No, she is dying as I told you. She will last another week." Ah Leong pressed a roll of silver into Yuen's reluctant hands and thanked him for being so humble.

The next week, Chung Shee died in the apartment above the L. Ah Leong store, her little girls and Yuen at her side.

❧❧

Ah Leong winced with each wet plop of dirt on Chung Shee's coffin. Behind him, the black-veiled mourners wailed loudly in mounting crescendo. When the grave was half filled, the wails stopped so suddenly that the silence startled the merchant. Ah Leong turned, nodded, and watched the four ladies walk towards the front gates of Manoa Cemetery.

The rituals of mourning and burial were important as acknowledgment of one's position in society. As his Third wife, unrecognized under American law, Chung Shee was an unattached spirit with no one to mourn her, no one to pay homage to her memory other than her little girls and Ah Leong. His other wives, Dai-Kam and Ho Shee, refused to sit the overnight vigil with Chung Shee's body. She had no son to lead her funeral cortege so there was no use hiring the gong beaters, the musicians, or the men to carry the titles of her ancestors. Since no one would walk behind her coffin besides her daughters and husband, Ah Leong had hired Akana Mortuary to bury her in Manoa Cemetery to the accompaniment of four old Chinese ladies, professional mourners, who would let Chung Shee's spirit know she would be missed although her funeral was pitifully simple.

Chung Shee. The love and passion of his maturity. He was only fifty. Would he find another wife so sweet and compliant, so forgiving?

The workmen patted the grave flat and shouldered their spades. Ah Leong watched them leave. He was alone.

He tipped his head back and inhaled the mountain breeze that whisked through Manoa valley. He flexed his body, bent his knees in the moves he had learned long ago from his masters. Deadly Dragon Awakens. Long ago, those moves had brought him back to life. But he had never learned how to bring back another from the land of the spirits. He moved his arms slowly to the right with rhythmic strong motions like a crane in its ritual mating dance. The air shivered with a silence that no bird dared to violate. He leapt up into the air. Sun sparkled off the sheen of his face.

When he landed, he dropped to his knees. "Chung Shee, I cannot." He hung his head. "I cannot bring you back. I don't know how," he whispered.

☜☞

Ah Leong ran his fingers over the few cotton tunics in Chung Shee's wardrobe, remembering the last time she wore each. How their pale colors made her long black hair seem to glow. He winced at the frayed collars and cuffs. He had only noticed how Chung Shee radiated youth and beauty, never how worn her clothes had become.

He refused to let Dai-Kam have the apartment cleaned out and rented. So it remained as it was when his Third wife was alive. Occasionally, he came here to think, as he did on this late afternoon.

He turned at the sound of the tap-tapping up the stairs. The front door opened and Yuen entered. "Ah Leong? The air is cool as if the shades are drawn and not a single light bulb glows."

"I need no lights to remember."

"I cannot heal a grieving heart, my friend."

"Your presence is healing enough." Ah Leong thanked his blind friend for worrying about him. And when pressed, he confided what he had done to bury his grief. He told how he had walked through the classy department stores on Fort Street and the downtown grocery stores that catered to the rich whites. He visited Caucasian businessmen he had known since the time of the Monarchy. He sounded new business plans off his mentor, L. Ah Low. At his own store, he tried to please each customer with cheerful energy. The housewives who thought him charismatic before were now convinced that he was irresistible.

Yuen nodded. It was good for Ah Leong to bury his grief in his business.

Ah Leong read him the letter he had written to his Second son, Ah Wang, ordering him to return home; it was time he put his education to use. Besides, now that his sons were old enough to assume responsibilities at the L. Ah Leong Store, he had other plans.

☜☞

Ah Leong leaned forward from his vantage point on shore to catch a first glimpse of Ah Wang among the passengers disembarking from the SS *China* at Honolulu Harbor. Chung Shee had been dead six months. At the bottom of the gangplank, uniformed agents directed the Chinese passengers towards the Immigration station where they disappeared from view.

He turned and strode through the wood-framed glass door at Immigration. The male receptionist, a junior grade officer seated beneath the sepia portrait of President Theodore Roosevelt, looked up from the black Underwood typewriter that clacked with each awkward jab of his two-finger typing. He nodded when Ah Leong said he was expected.

The merchant looked back at the lines of Chinese filing in for processing. How enviously they looked up at him—their mouths agape, shoulders hunched, shuffling hesitantly as agents directed them into lines. They fumbled with their documents and looked around with dull bewilderment.

Ah Leong walked through a hall of identical varnished doors and opened the one marked Private Interviews. He sat back with casual familiarity on one of the spindleback wooden chairs in the waiting room decorated in institutional beige. He tipped his head with a slow exhale on his cigar. Had he looked that stupid when he came thirty years ago? Not he. Even when he was young he never lacked confidence.

He tapped his worn shoes off by the heel and stretched his bare feet. They were creased with character, callused by honest labor, a healthy broad foot tanned as dark brown as a Hawaiian's. "Luau feet," the local folk called them.

George Curry, Immigration Inspector, opened his office door and greeted the stocky merchant. They exchanged the pleasantries of acquaintances who have known each other for a long time, before Territorial days, before the days of the Republic, back to the leisurely days of the Monarchy. Ah Leong advised him that C. K. Ai was the other witness for his son and his wife. In that case, Curry said, they would interview Ah Wang before the others.

Ai cracked open the door. "This room, eh?"

"Ai! Thanks for coming," Ah Leong waved him in without getting up.

Ai's lumber business had rocketed upwards with the economic growth of Hawai'i. Ai, a church-going family man who traveled to China often on business and philanthropic missions, had just ended four years as president of Honolulu's United Chinese Society, the parent organization of the family, trade, professional, regional, and cultural associations that community-minded Chinese supported.

Since his return from China, Ah Leong had also been busy. He and Dai-Kam had purchased land along Beretania Street. Now, after eight children and thirty years in Hawai'i, she had gone to see their new house in China. His Fifth wife and Tat-Tung's new wife would take care of her.

When Dai-Kam arrived in Kew Boy, she gave Ah Wang his father's letter. He and his wife returned today.

"Ah Wang? I thought Tat-Tung would take over your business."

"I'll teach Ah Wang how to manage the store on King Street. Next year, I bring Tat-Tung back. He's studying in China. Wong Shee says he plays the moonharp like an imperial musician; the nightingales fly from the trees to sing to his melodies. And he has exhausted the knowledge of his private tutors." He smiled smugly. "A scholar and a gentleman." All the pleasures he was once entitled to and denied, his favorite son enjoyed.

"I remember how he listened and observed everything," Ai said. He recalled how Ah Leong coached the bright-eyed son who accompanied his father to market each Sunday. "His mind works quickly, like yours, eh?" He elbowed his friend.

Ah Leong modestly shook a callused hand to protest the compliment. "My businesses will grow quickly if I turn the finances over to him."

"Ah, so frustrating, these taxes," Ai shook his head slowly in agreement. "This American government creates more new taxes to cripple us. Taxes eat profits. They take time to track and prepare. Each year lawmakers think of new taxes for Chinese to pay or business licenses only Chinese must buy. What are they afraid of?"

"Second-class citizens, that's what we are. Remember when you and I first came? They thought the Chinese would overrun Hawai'i. They said Chinese belonged on the sugar plantations when we tried to open our own businesses. Then they passed the law that said all businesses had to keep accounts in English, Hawaiian, or some European language. That law was aimed at us. The same year, they tried to limit us from working anywhere except in the rice and sugar fields."

Ai gestured with his hands, "Then the new American government said Hawai'i was their land. Not for Asians. What's that they said? It was the 'white race against the yellow race, and nothing but annexation could save the Islands.'"

Ah Leong added loudly, "Then they annex Hawai'i and the 1882 Chinese Exclusion Laws extend to Hawai'i." This meant that each time Chinese wished to travel, they had to apply for reentry back into the United States before they left.

"Now they interrogate us like criminals."

"And I have to ask you to come as a witness when the inspector knows my son Ah Wang perfectly well." Ah Leong's voice rose loud and gruff.

"Hush, my friend. They might hear," Ai cautioned.

"Always we are afraid they hear," Ah Leong grumbled.

Ah Leong scoffed at the Exclusion Laws. He had taken advantage of his long history in Hawai'i from the days of the Hawaiian Monarchy, through the turmoil under the Provisional Government and the Republic of Hawai'i, and as a Territory of the United States. Now he was fifty-one. He had made it his business to know the Immigration officers and the men who held the real power in Hawai'i. He expected them to make exceptions for him.

☙❧

A few days later, on April 12, 1907, on an afternoon when customers darted in and out of the L. Ah Leong store to dodge the intermittent showers, the hard tap-tap of the sheriff's shoes slammed on the wood floor. Ah Wang quickly weighed out Mrs. Chang's dried shrimp and mushrooms and tied her packages in brown paper with a neat knot of red string. He kept his head down when the Portuguese officer served the warrant to his father. By the time Ah Leong bellowed in protest, the sheriff had already run halfway down King Street towards the courthouse.

Ah Leong stood in the middle of the store by the stacks of flattened preserved fish and crunched the paper the Portuguese had forced in his hands. He whipped off his merchant's apron, threw it to Ah Wang behind the sales counter, and charged through the congested Honolulu sidewalks.

"Out of the way, out of the way," he commanded. He maneuvered through the crowds, swatting the air with the clenched document. "Hey!" he shouted when his body glanced the manapua vendors balancing hot pans of Chinese pork buns hanging from poles across their shoulders.

C. K. Ai spied Ah Leong's powerful strides and massive shoulders bearing straight for the front gate of his lumber yard. He tucked his clipboard under his arm.

Ah Leong shook the warrant in his hands and muttered to his friend.

"This way!" Ai grabbed Ah Leong and motioned him through the lumber yard to the back room where machine parts mingled with receipt books in haphazard stacks. He pulled out a stool and motioned Ah Leong to sit. Shaking his head as he read Ah Leong's document, he thought of the government's new campaign to keep the Chinese on the plantations where they would not present a commercial threat. Territorial laws already required higher license fees for "alien" tradesmen and skilled and semiskilled workers. Other government bills were being proposed to raise rental fees for Asians, forbid their purchase of materials and supplies, and double their license fees.

"I was going about my own business, like any other merchant, and the sheriff walks into my store this morning and hands me that." He pointed a stubby finger at the warrant in Ai's hands. "I am charged with Unlawful Cohabitation it says. What does that mean? Then the sheriff says I have to appear in person in the U.S. District Court tomorrow. Tomorrow is Saturday. My peak day," Ah Leong growled. "They're trying to destroy me."

"What will you do?"

"What can I do? These *haoles*—they do business with me. Now they arrest me." Ah Leong paced, picked up handfuls of nails and bolts, and jiggled them as if testing for weight—his habit as a merchant. "My Hawaiian customers told me that when their people first saw Westerners, they could not believe that such pale-skinned men existed. Since *hao* means 'breath of life' and *ole* means the 'absence of,' they called them *haole*. These breathless, lifeless people cause nothing but trouble."

Ai took a deep breath to compose his response and frowned. "Your business is legitimate, Ah Leong. You have earned the right to do business. You pay the taxes. To the *haoles*, Unlawful Cohabitation means you live with more than one wife. All at the same time. In the same house. It is not Christian, having more than one wife. This is what offends them," he said. He put down the warrant and handed Ah Leong a cigar.

"I am not Christian. I am Chinese."

"My friend, I am Chinese and a Christian. For you, this is a matter of lifestyle. Chinese style, you can have as many wives as you can afford. But you are not in China. We do not live under the Hawaiian monarchy any more. You must act like an American now. Did they not say anything to you before this?"

"Not one word! They know Dai-Kam is my wife. Sometimes *haoles* ask who are the other ladies in my house. I say 'my children's Aunties,' but they never said, 'We're going to arrest you!'" Ah Leong lit his cigar and waved it with a grandiose gesture. "I am Chinese with a Five-Star name..."

"Yes, in China. Here, you cannot fight the *haoles*. They control Hawai'i. We have no chance in these American courts. They say our children who are born here are nonresidents. We are nothing. Our words do not count. We cannot testify."

Ah Leong bellowed that a man could spend his whole life in this country, work seven days a week from dawn to midnight, raise his children to respect their elders, and still he would lose. Didn't he smile and talk sweetly to the *haoles?* Didn't they bargain and barter with him? Yet they cared not for him, only for the taxes he paid.

Ai said his friends told him that in the Mainland, it was even worse. In California, a Chinese could not testify against a white man, no matter what lies they said. He heard that bosses kept the Chinese in chicken coops like animals. They forced them to work in their gold mines, then kept the pay they promised them. There they died.

"Still, it is better for us in Hawai'i." Ai got up and paced thoughtfully. "Ah Leong, you have plenty face. They cannot do much against you, otherwise all the Chinese will revolt against the Americans. You remember the protest meeting at the Chinese Theater in 1894 when they added extra taxes only to Chinese-owned businesses?"

"Hah! Thousands of Chinese arrived soaking wet. The police pushed us off the sidewalk, tried to start fights. We had to sit in seats puddled with rain. Not a good night," Ah Leong answered, puffing on his cigar.

"But the government backed off on the Chinese tax laws. You see?"

☞☜

On Saturday, Ah Leong walked alone to the United States Court of the Territory of Hawai'i. Those who had heard about the sheriff's visit gossiped idly in the street in front of the L. Ah Leong Store. Inside, Ah Wang waited anxiously for his father's return.

District Attorney Brock asked Ah Leong if he had brought an attorney since he was being charged with Unlawful Cohabitation, a federal offense.

"No," Ah Leong answered loudly. The confident look on his face rang with defiance. After his discussion with Ai, he decided that an attorney would not make any difference. He was a Chinese in a white man's court. He would take care of his business as he had always done, by himself.

Brock motioned the Chinese interpreter to read, "The Grand Jurors of the United States charge that L. Ah Leong, on the 30th day of May, in the year 1905, in this District and within the jurisdiction of this court did unlawfully cohabit with more than one woman: Fung Dai-Kam, Ho Shee, and Chung Shee, against the peace and dignity of the United States."

Brock turned to Ah Leong for his defense.

"But Chung Shee is dead," Ah Leong argued. "She died last year."

"The charge is dated May 5, 1905, when she was alive. Mr. Lau, you have heard the indictment against you in Chinese. Shall we repeat it in English?"

"No."

"How do you plead?"

Ah Leong glared.

"If you plead guilty, you avoid a jury trial."

The merchant looked at the sea of white faces in the courtroom. He recognized many. "I was married, Chinese style to all three women. We lived together. Yes, yes, yes! In the same house. I had children by them all! At the same time!"

"Order in the court! Order in the court!" Judge Sanford B. Dole slammed his gavel to control the outraged shouts from the galley. "Return for sentencing in five days," he ordered Ah Leong. The merchant stomped out, jaw clenched in a smirk.

Dole, first and only president of the Republic of Hawai'i, a bearded man with deep creases steamed from the sun and pale eyes like the full moon, traced his lineage from the first missionaries to Hawai'i. He had tremendous interest in the local people, spoke Hawaiian fluently, and had devoted his law practice to defending their interests. But as President of the Republic of Hawai'i, he defied President Cleveland's order to restore the throne to Queen Lili'uokalani. After the United States successfully annexed Hawai'i under McKinley, Dole had returned to the bench where he had sat before his friends overthrew the Monarchy. Once, he had championed Chinese citizenship and their rights to homestead. Now he fought to ensure a Constitution that protected Caucasian rights and privileges, that protected the interests of his associates and plantation-owning friends.

L. Ah Leong strode out of the courtroom to an isolated spot–a grove of trees protecting a circle of sunlight on the stiff grass. He threw back his head and held out his arms, the sun full on his face and body. He took a deep breath. He gripped his muscular hands into fists of iron. He narrowed his eyes and focused his mind against the Americans.

☙☙

Five days later, Ah Leong walked the short distance from his store to the United States District Court. For his first appearance he had worn Western clothes so the Americans would think kindly of him. Today, he wore his old work shirt and pants, the shabby clothes of a hard-working merchant.

Judge Sanford B. Dole asked Ah Leong if he had anything to say before he pronounced the sentence of his Court.

Ah Leong said, "No."

Judge Dole pronounced Ah Leong guilty of Unlawful Cohabitation. The Court fined him $300 and the costs of the prosecution amounting to $22.75.

Instead of going home that night, Ah Leong slipped into Chung Shee's apartment as if she still waited naked in her bed, her skin smelling of fresh silk. He sat cross-legged on her bed and closed his eyes with his arms circling slowly over his head, as if to gather up her essence. He willed her alive. But all he had left was her sweet, sweet memory.

☙☙

First wife Dai-Kam had left for China with her three youngest children in January 1907, three months before her husband's indictment.

Now that Second wife Ho Shee was the only wife left in Honolulu, she did two things after L. Ah Leong's trial. First, she gave Third wife Chung Shee's daughters away. Second, she went to the government offices to get a marriage license to L. Ah Leong in accordance with the new American laws.

Unwittingly, she sowed the seeds for more trouble than Ah Leong could ever imagine and gave him the premise to rip apart the empire that he and his First wife had built.

PART III

Chapter Nine

Captive Wives: 1907

Once Matchmaker Tsay sent our family's acceptance, the L. Ah Leong family in Kew Boy delivered one hundred wedding cakes packed in red lacquer boxes, eight cakes per layer. All my aunties, cousins, and sisters came to my house when they heard of this wondrous presentation which represented only a part of the six betrothal ceremonies. How the ladies fussed over these shiny boxes festooned with red ribbons inscribed with the characters for "Double Happiness." Mama and Grandmother sent word to all my boy cousins and uncles to help us distribute these cakes to our relatives and friends so they would know of my impending marriage.

The boys in my village were shocked. Since Mama had only girls, Grandfather used to dress me as a boy and take me to village meetings and temple ceremonies. "My grandson," he explained. Only men were allowed at these gatherings. I used to lower my voice and play games with the other village boys. I even caught, barbecued, and ate rats with them. Some of my favorite playmates came to my house to express their sorrow. "Ah! We didn't know you were a girl," they exclaimed when I greeted them in embroidered tunic and pants, my long hair braided in intricate knots and festooned with jades and gold.

After my engagement to Tat-Tung, the mother of his First wife, Wong Pin, came to my family home.

"Phoenix," she wept, dabbing her eyes on a handkerchief she pulled from the sleeve of her elegant tunic. I bowed respectfully, touched by her thoughtfulness.

I was seventeen years old then, naive and innocent. "I'm sorry to hear about your daughter," I murmured. Tat-Tung's first wife had gone to Hawai'i ten years ago when she was eighteen, and died of consumption last year in Hawai'i. I ushered Wong Pin's mother and two sisters into our parlor and called for tea and cakes to be served. All three were dressed in fine cotton tunics and dainty trousers embroidered with birds and flowers in brilliant colors. Excellent needlework. The girls had hair black as soot while their mother had turned pure white. All were fair and dainty. How generous of her to congratulate me, I thought.

"I wish you the happiness Wong Pin never found," the older woman said, her voice soft and sad. "But I warn you. Be careful." I dropped my eyes, shocked and frightened. I wish I had been bold enough then to ask, Why?

☙☙

When she entered the Immigration office in 1907, Wong Pin swayed awkwardly as if she treaded on rose petals. She steadied herself at the table between herself and the Immigration inspectors, clasped her hands around her uncomfortably pregnant belly, and dropped her eyes to her feet.

Tong Kau, Immigration's Chinese interpreter, motioned her to sit. When she did, her skirt fell in embroidered panels over the tips of her flowered slippers. Her brocade tunic was a rich dark blue edged with green. Tong asked in her Hakka dialect, "What is your name?"

"Wong Pin," she replied. She still felt the roll of the sea. Even now, the chair moved up and down beneath her and the inspectors swayed like the smokestacks of the steam ship she had just taken across the Pacific.

She answered that she was eighteen, born in Moon Tin in Chungking, and had never been in the United States before. Her father was dead. Her mother lived with her four brothers and two sisters in China. She had married Lau Tat-Tung on December 4, 1904, according to Chinese custom. She was his first and only wife. He had left for Honolulu four months ago, in August, on the steamer SS *Korea*.

"Why did he refuse to let you come with him?" asked Tong Kau. Under the Chinese Exclusion Laws, Wong Pin could have entered

Hawai'i with her merchant husband as long as he proved they had been married for at least a year and had continuously lived together.

"He wanted to, but the American Counsel in Canton refused to let me accompany him. They told my husband to get a paper from the government of the Hawaiian Islands. Only then could I come."

Wong Pin handed him the marriage certificate Tat-Tung had sent. Kau translated the document for Inspector George Curry, then escorted her out one door while Curry brought in her husband.

As mandated by the *Treaty, Laws, and Regulations Governing the Admissions of Chinese from the U.S. Department of Commerce*, Inspector Curry interrogated Tat-Tung even though the inspector himself knew the answers to the questions, the same questions he had asked the seventeen-year-old merchant four months ago when he returned from China.

Keep alert, Ah Leong had warned his sons. He advised that the only way to ensure the interviews would be conducted fairly was to answer all questions exactly: the ages, birthdates, and full names of all twenty siblings and their mothers, including the sailing dates of each and every time they had gone to and from the Islands. Listen for the devious questions—and their insinuations. Despite the many times Tat-Tung had gone through the interviews, and the thick files on each member of the Lau family that the officers reviewed prior to every interview, Immigration still attempted tricks and entrapment. This time, halfway through the interrogation, Inspector Curry asked, "Where were you born?"

"Punchbowl and Queen Streets," answered Tat-Tung, in the home where the inspector knew all of L. Ah Leong's American children had been born.

"In Hong Kong?"

"No, Honolulu."

"Born here or in China?"

"Born here." Tat-Tung gritted his teeth to keep from snapping at the Inspector.

He satisfied the rest of Curry's questions: he had gone to China in 1903 and returned in August 1907; while he was in China he went to school; he married Wong Pin in his village on December 5, 1904, in the Chinese custom. He was here today because he received a letter from his mother, who was still in China, that Wong Pin would arrive on the *Nippon Maru.*

"Why didn't you bring your wife then?"

"My mother refused to let her come." Meanwhile, his father demanded his presence in Hawai'i.

"Is that what you told your wife?"

"I told her I did not have the right papers. I would arrange her passage when I went back to Hawai'i."

"Your wife says that you and she went to the American Consulate. That they refused to let her come."

"No."

"If your mother refused to let your wife come before, why is she allowing her to come now?"

"I wrote her a letter and she changed her mind." His calm, level gaze hid his true feelings: his pain when his mother forced him to return without his wife, his shame when Wong Pin cried at being abandoned, and the angry threats he had used against Dai-Kam. Since he controlled the finances of the L. Ah Leong businesses now, he had threatened to withhold Dai-Kam's generous allowance if she held his wife captive.

☞☜

"Wong Pin," Tat-Tung called. He repeated, "Wong Pin, I've come for you." He touched her shoulder.

She lifted her head and her lilting almond eyes opened wide. The chair still swayed and bobbed beneath her. Who was this person who called her name? she wondered. A familiar Chinese face. No queue. He wore a Western suit like the Inspectors. His manner was commanding, self-assured, and confident.

"Come," the stranger coaxed, his hand outstretched to support her. "Tell me where your trunks are and I'll put them in the delivery wagon." His touch lingered on her pregnant belly.

"Tat-Tung? Husband?" It was him. She hung her head.

He put his arms around her and whispered the endearments she thought she would never hear from his lips again. And when her tears fell like the spring rains, he wiped her eyes with the anise-scented handkerchief from the front breast pocket of his suit. He had to get back to work or his father would complain all afternoon, he said. She shuddered. If his father was anything like his mother, she would not survive.

The last time she saw him, he had driven away without a backward glance. She had clung to the portals of the great gates of the Lau estate in China and stood there for a long time. When the dust from his carriage settled on the road, she knew he would never return.

Night and day, his mother had ordered cleaning, cooking, and sewing. Wong Pin wasn't used to manual labor; her mother had taught her useful arts such as singing, music, and embroidery. She was shocked to find herself on her knees doing the chores her servants had done.

When Dai-Kam received Tat-Tung's letter, she stormed through the house until she found Wong Pin scouring pots in the kitchen with Ah Leong's Fifth wife. "You, leave now! Out of my sight. Your selfish husband dares to take my money." Dai-Kam put her hands on her hips and turned to Fifth wife. "This daughter-in-law is so clumsy and slow I have to get rid of her. I'm tired of trying to teach her how to cook and run a household properly." She waved a husky arm at the young woman's belly. "Look at her, so fat with her baby. Go. I don't want to be your nursemaid when it comes." She raised her fist and Wong Pin didn't wait to see if it would come down on her.

The scornful looks of the others while she packed didn't bother her. Even when she huddled in the dark women's quarters on the ship, she hadn't minded it too much after she got over being seasick. Every day she prayed that her baby would wait until she arrived in Hawai'i to be born. Her wish had been granted. And now she was safe with her husband, far from his monstrous mother.

She held tight to Tat-Tung with one arm. With the other, she clutched a padded silk bag close to her body where she could feel its weight. These treasures comforted her, her jewelry and the gold-encrusted hair combs that sparked the envy of every woman who saw them. She felt she was of little value, but her treasures were of infinite quality.

Her husband pushed from behind to help her up to the seat of the wagon. The porter returned doubled over from the weight of the carved trunk that held her dowry of silk bedding and clothes. Another ride, but it would be a short one to her new home.

After being cooped up in the boat for the long voyage, the daylight hurt her eyes. Rain fell lightly, then more intensely as the horses trotted the short distance to Queen and Punchbowl Streets. Tat-Tung held an umbrella over her head. At the sight of the paper and bamboo umbrella, just like those she used in China, she smiled.

"My husband, I long to sing for you again when you play your moonharp." She smiled sweetly at him. She had been astounded at how well their voices harmonized, and how he created poetic worlds with his music, landscapes of flowing rivers and tumbling waterfalls. His hair was cut in the Western style now, and parted to the side. She had never seen him dressed like the foreigners in the streets of the European and American sections of China. Also, he didn't smell Chinese anymore. He smelled Western. A faint fragrance, like anise, lingered on his clothes. In time, she hoped she would look and smell Western like him.

By the time Tat-Tung stopped the cart at the Lau family houses on the corner of Queen and Punchbowl Streets, the rain had washed away the humiliating and brutal memories of China and the dizzy recollections of her journey. He held out his hand to help her down. When his warm fingers clasped hers, she felt blessed to be in Hawai'i, the fragrant Sandalwood Mountains.

And she was, until her mother-in-law Dai-Kam returned to curse her to death.

❧❧

Three years later, the formidable Dai-Kam lowered herself in the stiff arrowback chair and faced the same two Immigration inspectors who had interviewed her daughter-in-law, Wong Pin. She adjusted her indigo Chinese tunic, then nodded that they could begin.

Inspector Curry signaled the stenographer who began to write, *Case of Fung Dai-Kam and Children of L. Ah Leong*. Tong Kau administered the oath.

Dai-Kam testified that she was forty-two years old and had lived in the Hawaiian Islands for twenty-four years. She returned to China in January 1907. She had married Lau Ah Leong in Kohala when she was seventeen years old and had eight children by him, which she named with their ages and marital status. She was the first and lawful wife of the fifty-four-year-old merchant.

"Has your husband any other wives?" Tong Kau asked.

"Yes, but not lawful wives."

"Are you sure you are the first wife?"

"Yes."

"Has your husband any other wives in the Hawaiian Islands?"

"Ho Shee, aged thirty-five, came eighteen years ago. She is Second wife."

"How many more wives does your husband have?"

"Third wife Chung Shee died here in 1907."

"How many more?"

"Wong Shee, age thirty-one, lives in China. He married her seven years ago to take care of his new house there."

"Hasn't your husband any other wives whom he sent to China several years ago?" Tong Kau asked. Dai-Kam said no. These women did not count. Ah Leong had five boys and four girls by his Second wife, three girls by his Third wife, and one boy by his Fifth wife. Most of his daughters, useless eaters of rice, had been given away.

When summoned, Ah Leong sauntered into Curry's and Kau's office as witness for his wife, two sons, and one daughter.

"Name them," requested Curry.

"My wife is Fung Dai-Kam, and the children are Lau Ah Kong, Lau Ah Chung, and Lau....daughter."

"You forgot the name of your own daughter?"

"Yes."

"Lau Len-Tai?"

"I forget," Ah Leong shrugged. "I always call her *Ah Moy*, little sister."

"How old is Dai-Kam?"

The merchant frowned and shook his head.

"Well, fifteen or sixty-five?"

"Thirty-seven, I think."

❦❦

DECISION: January 7, 1910. Cases of Fung Dai-Kam, wife of citizen; Lau Kong, Lau Chong, and Lau Len-Tai, Hawaiian-born.

Applicants are identified by Lau Fat Leong (L. Ah Leong). Dai-Kam and Ah Leong, according to their statements, were married at Kohala on the Island of Hawaii, Hawaiian Islands, a number of years ago. It also appears to be established beyond any doubt that neither Dai-Kam nor L. Ah Leong had at that time or ever had before that time, a spouse. It therefore appears that there was no impediment to their marriage. They have lived together since that time as husband and wife. Dai-Kam has been held out to the community as the wife of Lau Fat Leong (L. Ah Leong). There has been no divorce between these people.

The status of L. Ah Leong has, in previous investigation by this office, been established as that of a naturalized citizen. Since the above named Dai-Kam appears beyond any doubt to be his lawful wife, I recommend her admission.

From the records of this office, the Hawaiian Birth certificates presented, and from statements now made, I am of the opinion that the other three applicants were born in the Hawaiian Islands, and I therefore recommend their landing. I might add in the case of Dai-Kam, that she has lived in the Hawaiian Islands for more than twenty years, returning to China recently, early in 1907. (signed) George Curry, Chinese Inspector

❦❦

Ah Leong snapped the reins of the carriage and drove away from the Immigration station with his wife and children at his side.

"You see how much has changed in the last three years? Chinatown has grown up around us," he boasted with a grandiose sweep of his arm at their buildings and lands.

Dai-Kam congratulated his foresight when he showed her the improvements and quoted the increased rents. Two-story neoclassical brick buildings replaced the crowded wooden shanties typical of Chinatown prior to the 1900 fire. In those days, Chinese bachelors lived six to a room. Garbage collections had been virtually nonexistent, the water supply questionable, and sanitation spotty. No one else would live in this mosquito-infested swampland off Nu'uanu River, only the Chinese sojourners who dreamed of retiring to China after fulfilling their five-year contracts.

But now, continuous facades of splayed display windows with a central entry opened out at the street level. Some, like the L. Ah Leong Store, had open shop fronts. Airy second-story windows, some arched, sported bright spinach-green shutters and white trim. Families lived in these second-story apartments. Along the roof lines, highly articulated parapet and cornice details added elegant oriental touches. Not only were the buildings of a uniform height, the sidewalks were flat and even. The new streets were graded for proper drainage and wide enough for two fully loaded buggies to pass with plenty of room, even with the trolley tracks planned for the middle.

Dai-Kam knew her husband owed her his success but would never admit it. She thought back to the early days of Hawai'i when the ladies dissected every detail of life they gleaned through the gossip at the mah-jongg tables. Mrs. L. Ah Low's prophetic words were, "Have to look out for yourself, ladies, that's what I say. Chinese ladies are nothing without their husbands. You need security. American laws say you own half of your husband's possessions. Buy land."

The ladies were aghast. In China, everything belonged to the husbands.

Mrs. L. Ah Low raised her voice in triumph. "See? That's why I tell you to get your husbands to buy land in both your names. Half is yours."

Long before she left for China, Dai-Kam had told Ah Leong that the lands that stretched from their store to the wharf would be a good bargain. She cajoled him with visions of bungalows for those escaping the plantations. Every week, didn't new families ask them where they could find a home and a place to open a business?

Definitely not, he had argued. He had negotiated a good deal when he purchased Queen Kapiʻolani's land and house on Punchbowl Street where they lived. He needed his capital to expand his business and he was thinking of building in China.

"Then Mrs. L. Ah Low's husband will buy it all and make a huge profit in rents. He'll have greater face than you," she had pointed out.

Ah Leong fumed. He asked his friends about the possibility of land values rising in Honolulu. "Meet me downtown tomorrow at the First Circuit Territorial offices to sign some papers. We're buying the Buckle estate at Kamakela," he ordered one evening when he rolled into bed. Dai-Kam threw back her head in a throaty laugh and wrapped her body around his.

After that, whenever she heard about lands for sale, she told her husband. They purchased all the land along Beretania Street and all the land between their store and the waterfront and over to River Street. Before she left for China in 1907, Dai-Kam could stand on the crowded sidewalk outside their store facing Honolulu Harbor and survey their holdings: as far as she could see to her left, to the harbor in front of her and to Nuʻuanu River on her right.

When the Catholic fathers asked for donations to build St. Louis College, Ah Leong gave them his large waterfront parcel on River Street for their school, earning greater respect and face from the Caucasian community.

Now Ah Leong guided the horses through the street and paused to show her his latest addition to the L. Ah Leong store.

Dai-Kam gasped. She stood and pointed to the highest point of the building where the words L. AH LEONG BLOCK 1909 glistened from the highest cornice. "Everyone can see it," she yelled. Gold outlined the red letters against a green background. Red for good luck. Gold for prosperity and longevity. Green for wealth. The words shone from the articulated parapet erected above the corner building at King and Kekaulike Streets.

Ah Leong puffed his shoulders back. "It's made of brick. It will last forever." He continued her tour of the L. Ah Leong Block along King Street, up Kekaulike Street, down Hotel Street, and back on Maunakea Street. He had constructed the buildings in harmonious groupings in brick, with a regular rhythm of second-story window openings. Revenue-producing storefronts lined the street level. Bright overhead canopies protected the sidewalk and shoppers from the heat of the sun and the tropical showers, creating an inviting ambiance.

She held her head high and waved to their friends and customers. Everyone now knew: Dai-Kam had returned.

❧❧

"On our estate in China, mangoes and lychees swell to sweet and juicy perfection," Dai-Kam sighed for the hundredth time to the ladies at her mah-jongg party. "Whenever I stepped outside my front door, the fruits dropped into my open palms." Clack! Clack! She jubilantly flashed a victorious smile and displayed her winning hand.

"Aaah," her friends sighed for the hundredth time. Dai-Kam always won. They settled their bets and settled in for the next round.

Dai-Kam threw back her shoulders and tossed her head with pride. "My husband's servant, he calls her Fifth wife Wong Shee, knows how to treat me with the respect I deserve as First wife. Her illiterate brother fixes anything that needs to be repaired and oversees our rice fields that stretch far past the horizon. Tat-Tung's wife, Wong Pin, cleaned my room and my night pots every day until she got pregnant and useless." She looked out across the parlor, to one of the tables relegated to the less-skillful players, and smiled triumphantly at pinch-faced Second wife Ho Shee shrinking in her chair. Yes, she had heard every word.

Dai-Kam turned to her companions. "Did I tell you about the bridge I built in China?"

When she first arrived in her husband's village, she was shocked that farmers and villagers had to walk for miles out of their way to cross the river to get to the weekly market. So she built a rest pavilion and red stone bridge over the river, shortening the route to market by hours. Using the revenue from forty rice paddies she had purchased, she offered free tea to market bound travelers from April through October. Every day, her relatives filled the gigantic stone container in the center of the pavilion with boiling water and fresh tea leaves. A plaque on the bridge honored her benevolence. Everyone in the province bowed when she passed and hailed her kindness.

Second wife Ho Shee seethed with each retelling. In Dai-Kam's absence, she had had to oversee Ah Leong's Honolulu household, the meals, her own children, as well as the families of Lau sons, their wives, and grandchildren. With Dai-Kam's return, she was relegated to her old subservient position.

But in China, she would rank over Fifth wife Wong Shee. Six days after Dai-Kam returned to Honolulu, Second wife Ho Shee packed up all her belongings, including the marriage license to L. Ah Leong that she had obtained in 1907 without his knowledge. She left for China on the SS *Korea* with her youngest son and daughter with no intention of ever returning to Hawai'i.

Chapter Ten

The Rise of *Ming Yang Tong*: 1910

The rumbling noise Ah Wang heard all morning came from his stomach, not the wagons in the street. Before he could run back to see what the store cook had made for lunch, he heard his father bellow, "What's this?" He wheeled around just in time to see the United States Marshal shove a tan envelope in Ah Leong's hands.

Ah Leong ripped open the official red seal, glared at Ah Wang with a look that meant stay, then stormed up the stairs to Tat-Tung's office.

Ah Wang returned to the money counter. Better here than in his brother's shoes. His older brother would handle *Baba's* problem as he took care of everyone's. He remembered the pain when their father returned to Hawai'i and left the two boys alone in China with Auntie Wong Shee, *Baba's* Fifth wife. Ah Wang had cried, homesick for Mother, for Auntie Ho Shee, for his brothers and sisters. He didn't want to speak only Chinese and live in China, even if he had his own bedroom. Tat-Tung had taken care of him, even helped him with his studies when the tutors called him Numbskull.

He didn't know that Tat-Tung was lonely, too. After all, his older brother had a wife, and the estate and *Baba's* businesses to run. Only when Tat-Tung stumbled home one day, eyes bloodshot, serenely smiling, did Ah Wang realize something was wrong.

"Look at me," Tat-Tung had slurred, drunk with the devil opium. The drug devoured his strength but he couldn't resist, so firmly he had fallen. "The tail of the dragon will destroy you. I thought it would kill the pain but it makes my head scream." He had been at another party with his friends, playing music, singing, and reciting poetry. As usual, the servant girls brought trays of sweets, teas, and the ubiquitous opium pipe. His village friends had made snide comments when they thought he slept under opium's spell. But he heard. Now he knew his so-called friends had tricked him, a jealous scheme to destroy his family name. He grabbed Ah Wang's tunic. "Don't be like me. Never, never touch opium. Promise!" He screamed and sweated through an agonizing withdrawal.

The following month, Ah Wang collapsed in a rigid ball with a belly that felt like burning knives. Tat-Tung probed his brother's stiff abdomen. Ah, he frowned, his herbs could not cure appendicitis. Although weak from his bout with opium, he ran from village to village to find the Western doctor who knew how to cut out his brother's infected appendix.

"Twice, you saved my life," Ah Wang cried the next day when he woke up, amazed to be alive.

☞☜

"Read this," Ah Leong growled over the swift clack-clack-clack of his son's abacus. Tat-Tung's fingers continued to fly across the beads, adding up the sums affirming the profitability of the Lau empire.

"Hey, this is more important." His father waved the paper impatiently in his son's face and flung it on his desk. Receipts and invoices flew up and resettled in disarray.

Tat-Tung's fingers stopped their flight after the last row of figures. Unruffled, he picked up the official-looking document. *The United States versus L. Ah Leong,* he read aloud. He shifted to the left to feel the direct rays of the sun relax his cramped shoulders, flexed his arms, and rolled his head from side to side to loosen his neck. Today he wore a crisply pressed white cotton shirt, pleated tropical weight slacks, and a loosened silk tie. He frowned, reached for a cigarette, and reread. Anise scented smoke floated up and out the window, pushed gently by the rotating overhead fan. His face had a warm, tan hue despite the tiresome days spent calculating the store's accounts.

Ah Leong paced slowly around the room, tapping books and invoices with his right index finger.

"*Baba*, here. Sit down." Tat-Tung got up and offered his chair. Ah Leong motioned him away and turned his back to pace.

His son walked to the bright uncurtained window and reread the document. "The U.S. Government has indicted you for Bigamy. It is a crime against the United States to take a second wife while your first wife is alive."

"Humph! They already convicted me in 1907 for Unlawful Cohabitation. I paid their $300 fine."

"This time, the Grand Jury says you married Fung Dai-Kam in 1886 and married Ho Shee in 1907."

"They're wrong! I married your mother in 1881! I married Ho Shee ten years later."

"It says Ho Shee went to the government office to get a marriage license after you were convicted for Unlawful Cohabitation. They question why you have two wives on record."

"Marriage license? What marriage license?" He flung his fists up in the air. "No wonder she left for China with no return papers. She couldn't wait to leave me in trouble with the government. Ingrate! I bartered dearly for her from Ahuna. I gave her a job, children, and a home. What kind of future would she have had otherwise?"

"Auntie Ho Shee is in China and we don't have this marriage license. Why did she get it? Who told her to do this?"

"Humph!" Ah Leong crossed his arms and growled, "Why should the Americans care what happened before they came?"

Tat-Tung placed the warrant on his desk and rubbed his chin. "Under the Hawaiian Monarchy, people followed traditional customs. We have an American government now that says we must follow new rules. According to American laws, you can have only one wife and you must have a marriage license to prove you are married." Leaning forward, he suggested that his father talk to an attorney to find out what his options were.

"A waste of money."

"Not if you get the right advice. Let the laws work for you."

"What do they expect us to do, turn back time? Change the past? In those days, it was up to the man how many wives he wanted. In the days of King Kalakaua and Queen Lili'uokalani, I knew everyone in government. They knew me, they knew my family, they knew my business. Now we have these Americans from the Mainland who don't understand Hawai'i."

"You have no choice. They could throw you in prison. Talk to your brother-in-law, Ching Mook. I'll go with you. You have to appear tomorrow."

"No. Let them come get me." Ah Leong thumped back down the stairs.

Tat-Tung picked up his forgotten cigarette and watched the curls of smoke rise languidly to the ceiling lamp. These Americans didn't care about the local people or consider the cultural past of the country they had annexed. They had trapped his father between their new laws and the old traditions of the Hawaiians and the Chinese.

He tried to figure out why the Americans singled out his father. Didn't his classmates from St. Louis College say that their business professors at the University of Hawai'i cited L. Ah Leong as Hawai'i's role model? The professors used Ah Leong's business in their case studies and assigned their students to observe the famous merchant. Tat-Tung peered out the window. There were two dozen college students today standing in front of O'ahu Fish Market, spying on the L. Ah Leong store. Sometimes their customers complained about the students taking notes and eavesdropping on dealings with his father.

Under the grand edifice of the L. AH LEONG BLOCK, their business boomed with the explosive growth of the community and flourishing opportunities in the young Territory of Hawai'i. The economy had skyrocketed with a fledgling tourist industry, pineapple, and of course, sugarcane. In Chinatown, the liveliest section of Honolulu, the L. Ah Leong Store was open seven days a week from six in the morning to ten at night. When Tat-Tung wasn't negotiating with suppliers or assisting customers, he was buried behind stacks of accounts and ledger books in the upstairs office. But when he heard the frenzy of customers outnumbering clerks he clamored down the narrow wooden stairs and grabbed an order book to assist his father and Ah Wang.

In the early morning when dew moistened the lips of the blossoms, Ah Leong's sons pulled back the wooden doors that opened the store-front to the street. They hauled bins of rice and feed out onto the side-walk and stacked them as thickly as they dared. Farmers brought fresh mangoes and bananas, heavy-scented from the country. Buyers came on foot, followed by wives or sons pushing carts. Bigger buyers arrived by horse-drawn wagon.

When daylight broke, shoppers checked out the imports from Asia and vegetables fresh from the country. Dried herbs and crates of pre-served vegetables packed in straw, warmed by the sun, enticed all to buy. The cacophony of tongues was a rhythmic mix of English, Portuguese, Japanese, Chinese, and Hawaiian.

On boat days, Tat-Tung's brothers, Ah Wang and Ah Chung, met the inbound steamers and hauled back the crates stamped with huge block lettering in English and Chinese. Ah Leong paid his sons ten dollars a week. But it was older brother Tat-Tung's orders they respected, not their father's.

L. Ah Leong gloried in this hub of mercantile activity. His world was simple in purpose and complex in texture, driven by goals for wealth, power, and status. As the Territory developed, as his family and fortunes expanded, these linkages grew more complicated. Everything was in order; he had his wives, sons, and businesses. His elder sons worked for him and their wives produced many grandchildren. His retail and whole-sale businesses were expanding. His investments and real estate appreci-ated in value. His two horse-drawn wagons carried goods to stores and homes throughout Honolulu serving all who did business with him.

His fellow Chinese now wore the short sleeve shirt and slacks in the Western style. But Ah Leong was comfortable in his coarse Chinese work clothes. People do business with me, not my clothes, he boasted. But he showed he wasn't too old-fashioned—he cut off his queue.

Ah Leong's success threatened his American peers. How ironic, Tat-Tung mused. His father's goals for wealth, success, and prestige were focused on China, not America. Every Chinese New Year when the monsoons flooded his village, his father sent large donations through the Red Cross to buy rice to make *jook*, the hearty Chinese rice soup, for the victims. During famines, droughts, and earthquakes, he sent hundreds of dollars to aid the needy. He contributed extravagantly not only to his ancestral village and district, but to his province as well.

China was his homeland, where the names of nineteen generations of Lau men were carved in stone in the Ancestral Temple. Generations of Laus were buried in the mountain cemeteries of Kew Boy Village in China. He had honored his ancestors when he returned to his ancestral lands and built the new temple and village gate upon his triumphant return in 1903. He returned his family's honor and face when he built his conspicuously large house in Kew Boy. Its forty-eight bedrooms meant that Ah Leong would fill it with wives and married sons and children, an achievement possible only for the wealthy. The Chinese would regard his great house, his many wives, and numerous sons as blessings bestowed upon a man with great face, a man who had achieved harmony in his life according to the revered teachings of Confucius.

His businesses in Hawai'i were merely his means to that end.

After the trial, his father would return to his homeland to lick his wounds. The Chinese appeared acquiescent and compliant. But like many of the old settlers, his father had a long memory.

Tat-Tung could hear his loud voice above the din downstairs, bargaining loudly. The slam of the money drawer indicated that a sale was concluded. The flurry of activity meant that until tomorrow, he had more important matters on his mind.

⚘⚘

When Mr. Lau Ah Leong did not appear before the District Court of the United States of America to answer his Bigamy indictment, U.S.

Attorney F. L. Davis issued a bench warrant for U.S. Marshal Edwin Hendry to apprehend the defendant.

The Marshal found Ah Leong at his warehouse where, by the light of a single bulb, he reviewed the handwritten packing slips and inventory lists for shipments to Maui and Hilo. Ah Leong growled at the Marshal. Still wearing his worn work shirt and neatly patched trousers, he stormed to the court house where he squared his shoulders and faced the judge.

Hendry addressed Judge Robertson. "In obedience to the Warrant, I have the body of the said L. Ah Leong before the Honorable District Court of the United States in and for the Territory of Hawai'i, this twenty-first day of March, 1910."

The Judge asked Ah Leong what he had to say in his defense.

"I have nothing further to say that I have not already told Judge Dole," retorted Ah Leong. He looked around at the white faces packing the courthouse. These were not his people. He did not care what they thought.

❧❧

"Tat-Tung," Ah Leong bellowed up to his First son. It was ten o'clock. Dinner smells had been wafting from the store's kitchen for the past hour. Hungry and excited, Ah Leong stormed up the staircase.

Tat-Tung looked up from the voluminous receipts and accounts he checked, balanced, paid, and collected. To the Western eye, Ah Leong ran a single store in Chinatown, a convenient and humble cover. Only Tat-Tung and Ah Leong knew the extent of their empire—the real estate, the businesses and homes in China and Hawai'i, the founders stock in many Hawai'i companies, the wholesale network throughout three of the Hawaiian islands.

"I'm going back to China. Short rest," his father panted in eager breaths. He handed his son a small square of paper. "I'll take this much money. You handle the rest if I need more." He smiled as if the past few months had not been an aggravating ordeal.

Chinatown buzzed with heated anger. Why did the government concern itself with Chinese matters? As late as the 1870s, the Hawaiian

Supreme Court had recognized the legality of polygamous marriages. Few outside the Chinese community concerned themselves with the marriage arrangements of the Chinese; it was their private life. Impassioned views about Ah Leong's indictment and conviction were discussed in the *dim sum* houses and across mah-jongg tables. What could Chinese, who had married during the Monarchy when the marriage laws of the Hawaiians and Chinese allowed for multiple spouses, do when their nation was unlawfully seized by the Americans? Whose laws were really valid? They felt the Americans resented L. Ah Leong, a Chinese who dared to build his fortune right under their noses.

Ah Leong feigned disinterest in the local debate. All he wanted now was to arrange this trip to China. His contacts in China and Hong Kong said there were opportunities on a Chinese railroad system, export fish markets, hotels, and more paddy fields in Canton.

"I'll come back with the accounting. You keep track. Don't tell anyone," he ordered.

"What's this?" Tat-Tung raised his eyebrows and peered at his father's figures spotlighted by the single cone of light from the ceiling lamp. He crossed his arms and leaned back waiting for the explanation of the one unexpected item: a new estate.

"Look." Ah Leong whipped out a drawing from his pocket. "You know the property across the river, the one with paddy fields down the Dragon mountain? The *feng shui* is propitious for my new house. See the *ch'i*? Calm flowing water to the south brings wealth. Four main doors, one facing each of the cardinal directions: north, east, west, and south. Ten separate outdoor toilets—one for each son and his family. One hundred and eighteen bedrooms for all my wives, sons, grandchildren, and great-grandchildren to come. The greatest estate in all of Canton."

"One hundred and eighteen bedrooms?"

"An auspicious number."

"We don't all go back at the same time."

"I can afford it," his father roared. "Gee Sook Tong will sell me his land."

"It's too far from Kew Boy village."

"Across a small stream," Ah Leong insisted. He caught his son's dis-approving glare. "I'll build a bridge from Kew Boy to the new house."

Tat-Tung took the map his father held out. He studied the layout of the village area, its many rivers and forbidding mountains. He pointed to an area on the same side of the river as the village. "Build on this hill instead. It's on higher land so we don't need to worry about the spring floods."

His father harrumphed. The family who owned it turned down his offer; they planned to build their own house there. "But Gee Sook Tong will sell me all this land." He pointed back to the land across the river near the Dragon Mountain. His eyes lit up. "See how big the area? I asked him, 'How much?' He said 'You are a rich man. I will ask a high price.'"

Tat-Tung cocked his head expectantly. He had seen his father bar-gain down to the bone. His reputation as a scrooge was well deserved.

"He wanted 1,500 Chinese silver dollars for the area of each paddy capable of producing two baskets of rice. They never thought I would accept their price. I said, 'Okay, I will buy it all.'"

His son jolted up, too stunned to speak. He leaned forward on the high-backed koa wood chair he used during the sixteen-hour work days and stared at the agreement his father handed him. "At that inflated price?"

"Yes, that is too much to pay. But I am a rich man. I told him I would give him the full amount, not one penny less," Ah Leong declared with a proud nod.

Tat-Tung mentally calculated this sum against the cash flow of the store. "You can have this much," he said, recalculating. "Your business has needs. Taxes are due."

"Hah! The government wants taxes and taxes and more taxes. How do they expect anyone to make a profit?"

"They'll throw you in jail if you don't pay." Tat-Tung lit a cigarette. The exhaled smoke curled up to the ceiling in the dim light. "While I was in China, the books were neglected. I had to rewrite them so the tax man wouldn't come after you. We had to cut inventories and ask our suppliers to extend credit."

"That was *my* money they wanted. The government did nothing to earn it."

Tat-Tung took a deep breath. "We'll pay the taxes. You have enough trouble with your wives."

"I have no problem with my wives. The Americans do. Bigamy, hah! $500 they fined me. Plus $20.35 in court costs! They thought that staggering sum would break me. They thought the Chinese were weak and easily intimidated. I didn't give them the pleasure of watching me locked in a futile battle against them. I didn't even contest the charges. You should have seen their rigid Christian faces. I drown my anger with glory."

"You tell me your plans for China, *Baba*, and I'll show you what your store needs." Tat-Tung reached down and pulled out his private ledger books from the hidden compartment under his desk.

The store cook brought up their evening dinner and the planning continued. The two men negotiated sums of money and projected cash flow. Tat-Tung worked up his business forecast and his father strategized to take as much money as he could.

On the date his ship sailed to China, Ah Leong boarded with a Chinese guard, a Hakka kinsman trained in the martial arts. The merchant had offered to pay for his trip back to his village, a three hour walk from Ah Leong's Kew Boy, in return for his services. The Hakka consented. He carried only a staff and sheathed sword. Other weapons were so cleverly concealed in his tunic that he moved as silently as a warm wind.

☜☞

News of Ah Leong's arrival had been the talk of Kwang Tung Province for weeks. Villagers crowded the path of his horse-drawn carriage when it thundered through Kew Boy's new village gates with the Lau family name on the tall columns that flanked the road, down the main street past the Great Ancestral Hall, and past the temple he had built.

The entourage of porters approached the arched portals bearing the name of his estate carved in large bold strokes. They continued the triumphant procession up to the front door where the household and staff stood at attention. Fifth wife Wong Shee and her son, Lau Ah Chen, rushed down to the carriage to greet him with deep bows. Second wife Ho Shee and her children bowed from the top steps. Wong Shee's brother and his two sons who maintained the grounds touched their heads to the ground, then ran forward to unload their master's trunks.

Ah Leong stood up on his carriage and surveyed his prosperous view. The estate was surrounded with uniform green tiers of bountiful rice paddies, a picturesque scene of water buffaloes and farmers planting, weeding, and harvesting. Twice a year, his wives claimed two baskets of rice per paddy from each tenant farmer. He would never again be hungry, poor, and invisible. He threw his head back and laughed—loud and hearty.

He pointed to Gee Sook Tong in the crowd. "Come to my house," he bellowed so everyone there marveled at how his voice could be heard as far as the Dragon mountain. "And bring your five strongest sons."

In China, his infamy in Hawai'i earned him the reputation as someone the Americans feared for his defiance. Twice, the Americans convicted him: once for unlawful cohabitation and once for having many wives. Twice, Ah Leong paid the fines and walked away, his businesses bigger and stronger than before. The Chinese agreed that he was blessed with unchallengeable wealth, prestige, and power. His fortunes had blossomed a thousandfold and his many wives produced many sons.

The next day, Gee Sook Tong and his sons hurried to Ah Leong's house. They bowed. Their knees trembled in anticipation. Ah Leong flung open five trunks filled to the brim with silver. Gee Sook Tong burrowed his arms in the Chinese dollars, eyes greedy, seeing his land turn to silver.

That same day, Ah Leong ordered Second wife Ho Shee to walk with him to the hill across the river, to the land he had just purchased.

Up to now, she quivered whenever she passed his rooms, terrified of the moment she would have to face him alone. Tucked in the trunk in her bedroom was the letter Dai-Kam had sent about his Bigamy conviction, and the warning that her betrayal had cost Ah Leong time and money.

Ho Shee wrung her hands when Ah Leong laid out the map of the land. She nodded obediently when he said that he would have a manager build the house who would come to her when decisions had to be made. He expected her to oversee the construction so his new house would be exactly what he wanted. She promised that it would be as he wished.

Ah Leong had no qualms about assigning Ho Shee this task. Dai-Kam was his stormy passion and workmate, Chung Shee the heartbreaking love of his maturity, and Wong Shee the guardian of his estates, lands, and family in China. Ho Shee had always been the obedient, docile wife who bent to his and Dai-Kam's imperious demands. She had erred grievously. She could restore harmony in their relationship by fulfilling her responsibilities as Second wife. If she failed, she would lose her position and jeopardize the future of her five sons.

To emphasize his point, Ah Leong requested the tutor for his Eighth son Ah Chen, son of Fifth wife Wong Shee, to recite the Confucian classics after dinner to Ho Shee and her youngest son Henry. Confucius taught that social order prevailed when each individual knew their exact position in relationship to others, and their corresponding responsibilities. Subordination had a three-level hierarchy: the young to the elders, female to the male, and people to the established authority. In addition there were the Five Human Relationships: between ruler and subject, father and son, husband and wife, elder brother and younger brother, and friend and friend.

And so Ah Leong's will prevailed. His new estate, *Ming Yang Tong*, "The Shining House beyond the Bridge," extended across the base of one of the largest hills. The main house was faced with white marble. Three atrium patios opened to the sky with two wings of rooms extending from each. Lychee, loongan, starfruit, pomelo, tangerine, and pak-lan trees flourished in patios large enough to butcher cows for the major celebrations. A room built just for the chopping of wood supplied the kitchen. Fresh drinking water bubbled from the spring at the base of the hill.

Glazed red tiles covered its roof, caught the rays of the sun, and radiated it back like a beacon across the tiers of paddy fields. The side of the house against the Dragon mountain was three levels high with bronze-barred windows to let the sunlight spill safely into two hundred furnished rooms. The front of the house showcased the formal parlors. Four massive double doors, one on each side of the house, faced the four cardinal points: north, south, east, and west.

The villagers were astonished at the lavish extravagance when the workmen built ten stone buildings: one outdoor toilet for each son and his family.

He built a small house to the west of the main house. It had eighteen bedrooms, fully stocked libraries, and four comfortable parlors. Ah Leong envisioned his descendants would stay at this retreat when they came to China to study.

Around it all, he built a carved stone wall five feet high and an outer moat stocked with swans and geese.

He built a large stone bridge across the river to his first house in Kew Boy. He named this bridge *Tai Fong Chew*, "The Arched Path over Water." Then he built another bridge named *Loong Woon*, "The Dragon's Claws," to get to the next largest village. In all, he built ten stone bridges in the vicinity of his estates. On each he embedded a plaque with his name, the date of completion, and that each had cost him personally $5,000 apiece.

Tat-Tung was right. China embraced Ah Leong with the exuberance of a mother welcoming her triumphant son. With the infamous trials behind him, Ah Leong enjoyed new notoriety and even greater fame. He purchased more rice paddies and store buildings in nearby towns. He invested in fish markets and built a short railroad from Chieuchow to Swatow. He bought three thousand out of the five thousand offered shares in the great Chinese railroad that ran one hundred thousand miles from Kowloon to Kwangchou to Hankow to Peking.

Then he returned home to his beloved L. Ah Leong Store with a list of approved brides for Third son Ah Kong, now fifteen, and fourteen-year-old Fourth son Ah Chung. Twenty-year-old First son Tat-Tung and his wife Wong Pin had a daughter, now three. Nineteen-year-old Second son Ah Wang and his wife had a year-old son and were expecting a second. He looked forward to filling his large new estate with grandsons.

When he returned in 1915 to see his completed house, Ho Shee hired a dozen chefs for the welcoming banquet. Ah Leong invited everyone in the village to celebrate another Triple Happiness. He thanked the gods and the ancestors for his wealth and success, the marriage of his First wife's Third son Ah Kong, and the completion of his estate, *Ming Yang Tong*. So many guests and party-crashers came to his three-day celebration that they overflowed the tables; they had to run home to get their own mats to sit on. L. Ah Leong welcomed them all and ordered more food. A parade of district governors, province governors, and Five-Star dignitaries waving red and gold banners heaped honors upon the merchant. They cheered at the puppet players and the Chinese orchestra that performed in the gardens.

The celebrations were so extravagant that the village of Kew Boy passed on the legends of L. Ah Leong until the Communists swept through in 1950 and fired on his doors.

Chapter Eleven

Tales of the L. Ah Leong Compound: 1918

The L. Ah Leong Store.

The words cascaded from my tongue like a waterfall. I practiced as I unpacked my trunks and folded my clothes in the small bureau I shared with my husband, Tat-Tung. For this task I wore a loose tunic and trousers to keep cool in this balmy heat.

Tat-Tung rested on our bed, legs crossed, the newspaper propped on his chest with baby Fung-Tai, fed and asleep, in the crook of his arm. He had unbuttoned the top buttons of his Western-style, short-sleeved shirt. He looked up from his paper and flashed a cocky smile at my precise pronunciation. "My beautiful Phoenix. I look forward to showing you the L. Ah Leong Store in the heart of Honolulu's Chinatown. You can get all your food and clothes from its shelves."

Compared to the two hundred rooms of *Ming Yang Tong*, Ah Leong's estate in China where we first lived, our cottage behind his towering Queen Anne Victorian in Hawai'i was a quaint shack. But at least we were off that boat. Just yesterday, I thought baby Fung-Tai and I would perish before we were released. My baby had wailed day and night when my milk dried up on the long passage across the Pacific. But my father-in-law, L. Ah Leong, rescued us from the grip of death. He raced his horses through the streets of Honolulu and carried us to our new home, far from the clutches of Immigration.

Ah Leong had not been back to China for three years, not since he gave the extravagant party that celebrated and blessed the completion of *Ming Yang Tong* and Third son Ah Kong's wedding. He didn't return for my wedding to First son Tat-Tung. But I was his twenty-seven-year old-son's second wife, and a mature eighteen years old. My husband said that he and his father couldn't both leave the L. Ah Leong Store for long periods. And his father preferred to work, to watch his profits grow, buy lands, and keep tabs of the pulse of Hawai'i's growing economy now that Chinese had left the plantations and come to town seeking better jobs and business opportunities.

I closed my eyes and tried to imagine what the biggest retail and wholesale business in the Hawaiian Islands looked like. "It must be bigger than the glittering emporiums in Hong Kong," I declared, remembering the months we spent in that cosmopolitan port.

He shook his head. "No, it's different."

"In what way?"

"You'll see," he answered mysteriously.

I happily doubled the size and magnificence of the L. Ah Leong Store. I envisioned shelves piled to the ceiling with the latest food and fashion, adding smartly dressed clerks assisting a steady stream of customers. My father-in-law was the wealthiest person in Hawai'i if his store was even half as big as his estate, *Ming Yang Tong*.

"I'll take you on a tour of Honolulu. You'll see for yourself," Tat-Tung promised.

He borrowed the store's horse and carriage; it wasn't appropriate for his wife, First daughter-in-law of the noted L. Ah Leong, to walk through downtown Honolulu. He pointed out whole tracts of land that his parents owned on either side of King, Punchbowl, Hotel, Maunakea, Kekaulike, and Beretania Streets. He explained that years ago, his parents anticipated that demand for houses and land would increase as the population grew. Single-story, wood-frame buildings lined the hard-packed dirt streets. Thick dark grass and a profusion of flowering bushes bordered the roads. Overhead, monkeypod and banyan trees offered shade and a concert of brilliantly feathered birds.

"What kind of Chinese are here?" I asked. "What village are they from?" My husband explained that most were Punti, from the Heungshan District, the west Pearl River delta of southern Canton. No wonder I did not understand them.

Tat-Tung explained that the Chinese here lived in three worlds: their village in China, the Chinese community in Hawai'i, and the Island society at large. They strove for prestige in each.

In Hawai'i, clubs became the new villages. Chinese joined surname associations called *tongs*, since everyone with the same surname are considered related even though they come from different districts and speak different dialects. Our surnames distinguished our links in a long history of illustrious clans.

Chinese also joined associations and *tongs* for their district in China. These clubs helped migrants and the elderly, and sent money to China during droughts, floods, earthquakes, and famines. The Laus belonged to Lung Kong Kung Shaw, the Society of the Four Families, an organization dating back to the period of the Three Kingdoms, 220 A.D., when the three powerful kings, Lau Pei, Quon Yu, and Chong Fei became sworn brothers. Ah Leong was one of the society's cofounders in Honolulu, and one of its two Hakka officers. The others were Punti from Heungshan.

I was surprised that my father-in-law was considered a skinflint in Hawai'i despite his impressive donations in China. Tat-Tung described the last time Chinatown had a drive for China's famine relief. When the fundraiser's representative walked into Ah Leong's store and began his eloquent speech, Ah Leong grabbed his broom and chased him off yelling, "Heungshan, Heungshan! You send all your money to Heungshan. I'm from Mei Hsien. Why should I give to you?"

"May I see where you work?" I asked.

My husband nodded and snapped the reins. We passed graceful stone buildings with oversized eaves and upscale department stores featuring American fashions. Tat-Tung pointed out many companies his father had cofounded or owned stocks in. I bowed my head to the men who called out to my husband by name. He, too, was as famous as his father.

We stopped across the street from a noisy open-air fish market. Sweet-smelling fish, fresh from the sea that morning, lay on beds of ti-leaves and seaweed. Gargantuan Samoan crabs, each over a yard wide from claw to claw, struggled out of their tubs. In the market and along the wooden sidewalk, barefoot locals mixed with well-dressed matrons, all speaking different languages.

"There," Tat-Tung pointed across the street, "is where I work."

I whirled eagerly. "Where?" The brick building across the street had many storefronts crowded side by side.

My husband pointed out one of these awnings: L. AH LEONG STORE. Below the awning, shoppers had to worm their way past pungent bins of dried vegetables and bags of feed crowding the wooden sidewalk. Inside, boxes and dusty cans were stacked from floor to ceiling on cramped shelves. A single fan suspended from the ceiling churned the warm air blowing in from the street. The walls were dusty green and the floor was well-worn unswept wood.

"Where?" I grabbed Tat-Tung's sleeve. This could not be it. We had stores like this in my village back in China.

I had anticipated a gigantic American market commensurate with L. Ah Leong's great face and reputation as one of the most successful Chinese in Hawai'i. After living in his sumptuous estate in China, I expected his main store to display the same impeccable elegance. Wong Shee kept *Ming Yang Tong* and his other two homes so clean that their floor tiles gleamed by candlelight. Even our lush courtyards in China were bigger than the dusty storefront before me. Was this was our family business? This disappointing filthy village storefront? How could it support Ah Leong's many wives, sons, and grandsons? How could we live off this little store?

At the front counter, L. Ah Leong loudly ordered his sons and workers to their places and whipped order slips in their faces. At the same time, his fingers whizzed across the abacus so quickly they became a blur. He smiled and cajoled his customers. "Ah, Mr. Wong, the dried ducks arrived this morning from China. I saved one for you.

No other store gets ducks this meaty, this tasty. Why, the scent alone takes you back to your mother's kitchen. Mrs. Freitas, what is your wish today? Just tell me, and I'll find it for you. I'll get you anything you want, except Mr. Freitas." His customers laughed, swept up in his glib banter.

"That junky place?" I choked. "Look how the dirt flies in through the open door." Where was the glittering emporium? The well-ordered shelves? The latest fashions? Disappointment shattered my heart.

I wanted to scream, "Take me back to Hong Kong!"

❦❦

I made my husband's tea each morning before the dawn bathed the Ko'olaus in bright purple-pinks.

At the L. Ah Leong store, the store's cook was already preparing *jook*, the hearty rice gruel for the men. Whap whap whap, whap whap. His cleaver rebounded against the monkeypod chopping block in fierce rhythms. The store was waking up.

As mynah birds started their pre-dawn chatter, Tat-Tung joined the Lau men on their walk to work. Bye-bye, I called each morning in the dark, Bye-bye, Bye-bye. I clutched baby Fung-Tai to my chest as we waved from the porch. When their backs melted into the dawn, I stepped back to my new home.

Ah Leong and Dai-Kam lived in a grand Victorian mansion graced by tall palm trees and lush flowering bushes. The main parlor was decorated with an eclectic arrangement of polished Hawaiian koa wood tables, Chinese lacquered chairs, embroidered runners, cloisonné vases, and rice-paper scrolls. Their auspicious designs included flowers and motifs such as flying bats with outstretched wings holding coins, signifying that wealth had arrived. Windows were flung open to the wide verandah to welcome the cooling trade winds. The main kitchen was the heart of the complex where we daughters-in-law shared the cooking and cleaning. The dining room in the main house seated the entire family. Dai-Kam controlled all menus and meals.

On the same property, land willed to Queen Kapi'olani by Bernice

Pauahi Bishop in 1886, the Lau sons lived within earshot of the main house. Their tropical bungalows, furnished with hand-me-down furniture, were set off the ground on wooden lattice foundations so the tradewinds could play against, around, and under. Each house had cozy front porches for reading, sewing, and visiting. Each house was painted white to reflect the heat, trimmed in red for good luck, and built close enough so that conversations would drift out the screened windows to be interpreted, misinterpreted, and passed along.

The Confucian doctrines of filial piety and preference for sons gave housing priority to sons and families in order of birth. Tat-Tung and I shared the bungalow closest to the main house with Dai-Kam's Third son, Ah Kong, and his wife. Dai-Kam's Fourth son, Ah Chung, general stock boy and delivery man at the L. Ah Leong Store, enjoyed the privacy of his own bungalow because his wife was Dai-Kam's favorite.

Ah Leong's Second wife Ho Shee's five sons ranked next in the hierarchy and lived in the back houses. Ho Shee's eldest son, Ah Wang, managed the daily operations at the L. Ah Leong Store.

In my first letter home to Mama, Grandmother, and Grandfather, I described how work drove Ah Leong's life. His success was a measure of his wealth, prestige, power, and face. With increased wealth and face, he could attract more business and negotiate better deals and investments. Great face meant greater influence in the general community. He conceded the home front to his First wife.

But at the L. Ah Leong Store, he depended on my husband to deal with the finances and laws of the American government. Only Tat-Tung had the calm logical mind of an analyst and the two-culture education to guide his decisions. He understood American laws, accounting, and taxes. He knew Sun Tzu's *Art of War* that governed the Chinese way of business as well as the Confucian and Taoist philosophies that governed our lives. I felt that with my knowledge of healing, herbal medicines, and Buddhist doctrines, I complemented his Western upbringing.

"Sadly," I confided in my letter, "I do not see much of Tat-Tung. He leaves for work before dawn and comes home at midnight."

I didn't see how Ah Leong expected his sons to work 112 hours per week. From the ships from Hong Kong and San Francisco they unloaded goods with wooden handcarts or packed on the backs of sturdy porters, then manually loaded the heavy crates and baskets onto their horse wagon. From the wharves, they drove to the L. Ah Leong warehouse. After uncrating, they carted the goods to the storefront where they stacked bins, barrels, and bags from floor to ceiling. Then they sold, loaded, and delivered.

"Go ahead, tell the police," Ah Leong dared anyone who complained about his congested sidewalks. The police took the complaints but tossed them when the accusers disappeared around the corner. Some tried to complain to Chang Apana, one of the most infamous police officers who walked the beat of downtown Honolulu. Plaintiffs fared no better at police headquarters where Ah Leong carried even greater clout with the Chief of Police.

I hung my head when I overheard other Chinese mutter, "Where's his pride, dressed like a poor peasant?" Everyone else tried to present a prosperous image to influence friends and family. Except for his big shot clothes, his *Woo Ping* reserved for trips home to China, Ah Leong's entire wardrobe came from his store's stock–faded Chinese workshirts, mended trousers, and scuffed old shoes.

Tat-Tung told me that his father believed he was acting honestly. In Hawai'i, he defied the image of the successful millionaire, not drawing attention to himself with fancy clothes or superior airs. In China, our ancestral homeland, he indulged in imposing estates, lavish family celebrations, and exorbitant shows of spending and philanthropy. Chinese understood the importance of great face and family honor. That's why he maintained three impressive homes in his ancestral village.

﹌﹌

The next month, I could not stop my tears from staining the thin blue paper of my letter. My brush shook angrily when I described how I was treated. The women in the family were flattering and friendly at first, I wrote Mama. Dai-Kam had welcomed me by placing two heavy jade bracelets around my wrists. She insisted I call her Mother, as her own sons and daughters did.

Two weeks later, I was suspicious about the way Mother and the other ladies in the family cast side-long glances when they thought I wasn't looking. I felt imprisoned by my bungalow's walls, the regimented meals we ladies were required to cook, and the dreary loneliness of my empty house while I waited for my husband to come home.

One warm night, I bundled baby Fung-Tai to my chest. "Wouldn't your father be pleased to see us waiting for him?" I crooned. I nuzzled her milk-sweet cheeks. She gurgled happily. I slipped soft Chinese slippers on my bare feet and tiptoed past Ah Leong's house, beneath the open window of Mother's lighted parlor where she gossiped nightly with her favorites, her First daughter Kai-Tai and Fourth daughter-in-law Yukmoy.

Their loud voices froze my steps.

"Mother," complained Yukmoy, wife of Dai-Kam's youngest son Ah Chung, "Tat-Tung rests upstairs in his quiet office all day while my husband drives all over town making deliveries, carrying those heavy loads. And Ah Leong always asks Tat-Tung's advice. It's always 'Tat-Tung says this,' and 'Tat-Tung says that.' Tat-Tung is getting too powerful. I don't tell you this for myself or my husband," she suggested sweetly, "but for your own protection. You know how much your Fourth son Ah Chung and I worry about your happiness."

After thirty-seven years of Ah Leong's "wives" and servant girls, fifty-four-year-old Dai-Kam worried about protecting her status. Women needed youth and beauty to maintain a man's attention. Men like her husband needed only money and power.

Against the lace curtains, I saw Yukmoy's shadow when she arched her dainty white neck and stretched her slim body. "You can't trust Ah Leong." She held up two bejeweled fingers and lamented that he still had two other wives alive, not to mention the servant girls that came and went. "Your ungrateful eldest son, Ah Yin, abandoned you, his wife, and his daughters. Now that Ah Yin has run away to San Francisco, Ah

Leong calls Tat-Tung his First son. Huh! You can't trust Tat-Tung either–he tells you nothing. As for Ah Chung and myself," she added, looking down at the new shoes that Dai-Kam had bought for her at the upscale American store on Bishop Street, "we only wish to honor you."

I gagged when Mother cooed and thanked Yukmoy. I ran back to my own house, my sanctuary from the lies that burned my ears and prickled my skin. How could I hope to fight back? Yukmoy had made it a point to tell me that Mother personally chose her for her youngest son. Every night while I washed greasy dinner plates, Yukmoy flashed her presents from Dai-Kam, gold rings and jade bracelets, on her way to the parlor to "rest" with Mother.

Second wife Ho Shee's eldest son, Ah Wang, outranked Yukmoy's husband. But Ah Wang and his wife were too busy with their babies which came in rapid-fire succession, which is how my husband ended up raising Ah Wang's daughter.

The day Ah Wang's wife gave birth to her third baby in five years, Tat-Tung raced home early. His brother's house was quiet except for the babbling of Ah Wang's first two children. He picked up the baby basket. Empty. He barged into Ah Wang's bedroom.

"The baby! Where's the baby?" he demanded.

Ah Wang's wife barely opened her eyes. "Too late. I never saw it," she answered.

"Dead? Is it dead?"

"I told Ah Wang to get rid of it if it was a girl." She dismissed him with a weary hand, not even rising from her bed. "*Baba* only wants grandsons."

Tat-Tung stormed out, tracked down his brother, and took him back to the midwife's house. My husband went from house to house to find the country family she had given the baby to.

"Imagine, wasting three days looking for someone else's daughter," Yukmoy giggled in my face. She delighted in recounting my husband's perceived faults whenever there was a gathering of women to side with her. She knew I struggled to raise all three girls: my husband's eleven-year-old, Edith; Ah Wang's five-year-old, Lani; and my own daughter, Fung-Tai. "He said one could not give away their own 'flesh and blood.' It was his half-brother's girl, not really that close," Yukmoy concluded. She sniffed with an arched toss of her head. "Your husband's a fool."

My husband loved children so much that he ignored these cruel words. But I burned with shame.

Now I understood how my husband's First wife, Wong Pin, although she had greater status as the wife of the First son, had been no match for his family. Poor Wong Pin. Had their abuse caused her death?

"Beware! Be careful. Be strong. The Laus are wild people," Wong Pin's mother had warned me before I married. I should have heeded the tragic pain in her face. When tears came to Wong Pin's mother's eyes, I had clasped her cold hands to my heart. She wept, "My daughter was so smart, an excellent wife. I told her not to be scared. Their lies frightened her." The American doctors shook their heads when Wong Pin refused to respond to their medicines. She drifted away from Tat-Tung, their daughter Edith, and life.

Although I saw how they were, I had been taught that the family comes first over the individual; maintain harmony by respecting the family hierarchy. If you are kind and good, you will receive kindness and goodness back, my mother said. I wish her words worked for me.

☞☞

The first time Dai-Kam ordered me to chop wood for the cooking fire, I walked out to the backyard and confronted the huge stack of logs. My fitted tunic bound my fine-boned arms so I could barely lift the giant ax. I took a deep breath and aimed. My high collar chaffed. Again and again I chopped. My hands stung and burned.

In the kitchen, the other women sniggered.

Dai-Kam strode out, broad shoulders thrown majestically back. "Good for nothing," she yelled. I squinted up at her towering figure. With a single swipe, she split the biggest log clean through with one stroke, not a drop of sweat on her high forehead.

"What good is such a dainty wife," Yukmoy cackled, "when in Hawai'i a woman must work?"

In my heart, I resented them. They think I'm too stupid to fight back, I muttered. I flung the split wood into the fire. So what if Yukmoy has already been here four years? So what if Kai-Tai, a gigantic monster like her mother, has lived here all her life? I'll keep their taunting and harassment to myself. If I fought back, Tat-Tung would look bad for marrying a disobedient wife.

In the solitude of my bungalow, I plucked the splinters from my once soft palms. The images of home returned. In China, my family was considered rich because we never needed to buy rice. But we worked hard. Every day, at the first light of dawn, workers came for the breakfast that Grandmother had prepared hours before. Mama walked to the fields with the workers to supervise. Grandmother cooked the rice and salt cabbage that our servants put in big wooden buckets hanging in balance from a wooden bar. Then I lifted this bar across my shoulders and carried the mid-morning meal all the way out to the fields.

For my husband's sake, I kept silent. He had enough to worry about with his father's business. Each week, I went to the temple and gave offerings to Kwan Yin, the Goddess of Love and Mercy. I prayed for the strength to be strong and kind to my family. I imagined the rituals performed by the monks at the temple at home. I repeated the prayers the Buddhist nuns taught me for power and knowledge, peace and contentment.

"See how she tries to outdo us? She prays every week," Yukmoy complained to Mother.

"Yes," I muttered to myself, "I pray for your tongue!"

⁊⁊

A year later, I was pregnant with my second child. Each day I grew more homesick. I wanted my mother. I wanted my maids. I wanted to go home. I missed the scent of the camphor trees behind our family home, the trees my sisters and I used to climb to the delight of Grandfather who called us his little monkeys. In those carefree days before marriage and children, servants washed my waist-length hair and braided it with ornate ribbons and jade pins. On festive days, I joined Mama and my sisters to visit cousins, wearing our new outfits fashionably handmade, ate sweets, and played mah-jongg. How I missed the way everyone vied to do my family favors because we were wealthy and carried much face.

Here, I wore loose cotton tunics to do my chores and bound my hair back like a common servant. Every morning after breakfast, I made rice water for baby Fung-Tai because I still had no milk to give her, hand-washed two buckets of diapers and cleaned my house, then rushed to the main house to clean Mother's room, make her bed, and clean her night pots.

And while I scrubbed, washed, and chopped, Mother and Yukmoy scoffed, "Who pays attention to girls? Men want sons."

I felt no one in this family loved me or my daughter. Only my husband. Tat-Tung brought home fresh fruits to keep my skin milky. He watched for new books from China, knowing I missed the well-stocked library at his father's estate. I coveted the traditional tales of deities like Madame White Snake and the Monkey King. I devoured courtly tales of long-ago emperors and empresses, of beautiful peasant girls turned into shimmering stars because of forbidden love.

When I smiled at the simple pleasures he offered, he whispered that I was beautiful, with skin as soft and pure as undyed silk. He held my chaffed, splintered hands to his cheek and said they felt like clouds.

One afternoon, I cried alone in my mismatched parlor. These cheap chairs had stuffing that popped through the seats, scuffed legs, and holes too big to be mended. The end tables were scarred, their tops marred with water rings. In China, Mama would have been embarrassed to give such trash to our servants. But Tat-Tung could not afford to buy new furniture with the pittance that Ah Leong paid his sons. My father-in-law said he became a beggar after his father lost the family fortune, so his sons should be grateful with the sixty dollars a month he paid them.

I scrubbed and cleaned these castoffs, hoping to buff the shine of pride into them. Useless, I grumbled. They looked as pitiful as before. I felt sorry for myself. But for my husband's good name and my children's sake, I kept up the appearance of obedience.

I could imagine my mother-in-law's screams, "You too high class for my furniture? Mine not good enough for you?" And Yukmoy would snigger that no one else complained, only me.

❧❧

Back at Ah Leong's estate in China, whenever I became homesick I would ask pinch-faced Ho Shee, L. Ah Leong's Second wife, for permission to go home for a visit. She never answered me. Instead, she scurried down the shadows of the hallways. Wong Shee, L. Ah Leong's Fifth wife, would rush into the room. She told me that I could do anything I wanted to since this was my house.

"I only want to be polite and let you know where I am going," I explained.

"Go home and enjoy yourself. I'll take care of everything here. I'll call the men to carry you," Wong Shee insisted.

I could easily walk the three *tongs*, a three-hour walk over the mountain pass, down the valley and up again to my mother's house, but Tat-Tung insisted his two men carry me wherever I wished to go. I did not mind but the men huffed and struggled when they got to the narrow peaks. I clung to the sides of the chair when it swayed precariously. At one steep passage, the men put down the chair. The oldest bowed repeatedly with his cap twisting in his hands, gray beard shaking.

He begged, "Oh, Madame Lau, please do you mind to get down so we can walk over this mountain? Please do not say anything to the Master." I walked easily over the steep mountain passes and hopped back in when we came to safer ground.

I was so absorbed in these memories that I did not hear the insistent tapping.

"Phoenix, open up." Dai-Kam's First daughter Kai-Tai gestured urgently through the screen door.

Mother and Yukmoy had gone out. Kai-Tai usually completed their inseparable threesome. Why was she here? I jumped up and apologized for not hearing her knock.

Kai-Tai stepped in and frowned when she saw my parlor. She sat and brushed an imaginary crease from her turquoise tunic. Around her neck and sleeves were appliquéd black clouds edged in silver. She lifted her eyes and smiled like a majestic princess.

I whipped off my faded apron and offered her tea. Silently, I despaired that every cup had a chip or crack.

She offered to help, but I insisted on serving her. She talked of pleasantries, then paused. "I know how you feel. Mother doesn't like my brother and it is not easy for you."

My hands flew to my mouth. I dropped my eyes quickly. I mumbled, "I don't understand." I was so lonely in this place with no one to talk to except my husband. Could I trust Kai-Tai? Why would she tell me this?

"My mother has worked hard all her life and thinks only of herself now."

"Treats us like servants," I sniffed.

"That's how she was treated when she was a young woman. She plays favorites, pitting one against the other. Tat-Tung was always too smart for her. You're smart too. We know nothing about reading and writing, about Chinese medicines and proper prayers, like you. Mother can only make her mark." She was surprised to see Dai-Kam sign deeds of sale with a simple X.

How could education be something to fear when it brought pleasure to one's mind and heart? I shook my head. Grandfather had sent me to study with the Buddhist nuns in the next town because education was considered inappropriate for a young girl. After all, I was expected to marry well. The Buddhist nuns taught me to read and write. I learned the Confucian doctrines and read literature from the Ming dynasty. I smiled when I remembered how the other girls would rush outside to play. Not I. I would ask the Buddhist nuns to tell story after story. I never tired of listening to them.

Kai-Tai stood up and went to the window to look down the gravel path from the main house. When she was sure that no one approached, she returned to her seat and leaned forward. Her voice was husky.

"My brother loves you and his children dearly. He gives you all the love he never received as a child." She lifted an eyebrow when I coughed to hide the tears in my eyes. She handed me her handkerchief. "He keeps the store from failure. Other businesses fail quickly in Chinatown. People think it's so easy: open a store and wait for customers to come. They don't know how to make a profit. He's the smart one in the family. My father and mother are lucky to have him manage the finances. My father knows it. My mother will never admit it. All of us, his brothers and sisters, respect him."

Looking up with a rueful smile, she added, "Look at me. I'm lucky to be here. Ten sisters have been given away out of the dozen girls from my father. Dead, Mother called them. I was the first-born girl. I could have been dead a long time ago."

Kai-Tai said that when my husband's first wife died, Yukmoy stole all of Wong Pin's exquisite gold and jade jewelry. Then she went through her drawers and grabbed all the doilies and lace runners that the dead woman had made.

From the back bedroom, I heard bare footsteps on the hardwood floor. A door creaked open. My daughter padded in and buried her sleepy head in my lap. Kai-Tai cooed, "My favorite!" and lifted Fung-Tai to her lap. She rocked my roly-poly, nine-month-old baby in her arms crooning how much she was like her daddy.

"Your husband endured loneliness and neglect," Kai-Tai continued. "My father was obsessed then, as he is now, with business. Mother worked side by side with him, then fought him over his women. Her own children were a burden, especially her first two sons. I used to hide when she beat them. They stood there and took it, like little men. My eldest brother, Ah Yin, ran away. Tat-Tung is considered the First son now. My father depends on him. Mother resents their bond."

I dabbed at my eyes with her handkerchief. I felt trapped.

"There are others who are jealous," Kai-Tai said. She lowered her eyes, dark pools like her mother's. Almost in tears, she admitted that her heart ached for Tat-Tung. "He's a good man, soft-hearted and gentle. I intercede for him whenever I can and temper our sister-in-law Yukmoy's advice to Mother."

We heard the crunch of footsteps in the driveway accompanied by Mother's booming voice and Yukmoy's laughter. Before Kai-Tai left, she placed her callused hand on my arm in reassuring support. Then she slipped into the main house as if she had been sitting there all afternoon waiting for their return.

On the hard wooden armchair in the late afternoon heat, I snuggled my daughter in my lap and contemplated the plight of young wives. We marry with dreams and hope for the life that we are promised we would have. How many of us attain that happiness that marriage and family should bring? Instead of admitting defeat or fighting back, we pretend. When we have daughters-in-law ourselves, we become the all-powerful matriarch and overwhelm everyone else in the same way.

There is another way, I resolved. I can change the pattern, stop the cycle of domination. This family judges me according to whether I do what they want. If I don't meet their unrealistic expectations, they say I'm stupid. So many times I wanted to scream what I thought. To maintain family harmony and my husband's honor, I kept peace in my heart.

I closed my eyes and made a vow. I would be patient and kind to Dai-Kam, Ah Leong, and their families. I did this for my children and their future.

I clasped Fung-Tai's tiny hands in mine. I prayed for love and mercy. Goddess Kwan Yin, give me strength, I begged. My husband loves me and the children. How many women have this much?

I leaned back and made up my mind. Let them think I am innocent to the biases and intrigues of the household. I appear naive and helpless. Let them believe what they will. I will have my freedom.

Chapter Twelve

Escape: 1919

Each night, when the trade winds blew the air sweet with the white scent of plumerias, I boiled Tat-Tung's bathwater over the gasoline stove. I stoked the fire and listened warily to each sound, for legends say that keen ears can hear the old Hawaiian spirits marching their ancient paths. Ah Leong walked home from work with his sons in this dark hour.

My husband sighed when he lowered his lean body into the steaming water. He soaked, eyes closed sensuously, head leaning back. I ran my fingers down his cheek and felt his waning strength.

Each week I prepared special herbs to adjust his *ch'i*, weakened from the opium the villagers had given him when he was young. I placed the herbs in a little water and steamed it for hours in a glazed pottery bowl to extract the concentrated essence known as medicine dew. These herbal broths, secret recipes passed down from my grandfather when I was a young girl, were strong and powerful.

While Tat-Tung and I sipped tea in the quiet darkness, our girls ate the treats he brought for them: sliced watermelon, succulent lychee, or juicy mangoes.

But jealous eyes never slept. Yukmoy complained to Mother that Tat-Tung brought special food home for me every night and that I never shared with anyone. Hah! I could never do that since my children never got enough during the family meals.

"Here, here," Mother and Yukmoy grabbed the best morsels for themselves and Yukmoy's children. Their chopsticks snatched the tenderest and juiciest pieces. I took what I could for my girls without breaching the fine manners I had been taught. The other children jostled and grabbed like ill-bred urchins. We had all prepared this food together but Mother protected her favorites.

My husband's first child, Wong Ping's daughter Edith, who had sassed me and pinched Fung-Tai when I wasn't looking, now insisted on sitting to my right with her half-sister in her lap.

Our adopted daughter Lani, Ah Wang's second daughter, cowered on my left, afraid of the daily errands that Mother sent her on. With our growing horse and carriage traffic, the streets she had to cross were wide and frightening. I never knew when she would disappear on one of Mother's tasks.

After each meal, Edith scooped Fung-Tai in her arms and called to Lani who slid off her chair to the floor in a breathless second.

"Look at those girls," Mother pointed out when they escaped. "Always sticking together."

I envied them. I had to clear piles of greasy dishes and scrub down the kitchen before I could leave. Every scrap, crumb, and drip had to be swept up to foil the armies of ants and cockroaches that invaded our homes nightly.

Our two bedrooms were our only sanctuary. There was a double bed in each, worn wooden dressers with peeled varnish, mismatched chairs, chipped mirrors, and assorted hand-me-downs from the main house. I brightened these rooms with a red silk coverlet and tasseled wall hangings with fanciful scenes of China brought from home in my wedding chest. I arranged lace runners over the dressers and silver hair combs and brushes from Singapore on the mirrored vanity. I wished I had the carved marriage bed and tall wardrobe Mama had given me for my wedding, but we had fled Kew Boy Village one step ahead of the warlords and bandits.

"What do you want to eat today?" I asked the children when we returned from lunch at the main house. With hands over our mouths to keep our laughter secret, we left when no one was looking. We bought saimin at ten cents a bowl or moon cakes at five cents each.

In the afternoons when the other children took naps, I closed my doors so the others thought we were sleeping, too. Edith unhinged the latch on the wooden screen of her bedroom window and lowered it onto the floor. She drew up a chair and swung one leg, then the other, out the window. When she landed on the ground outside, she called to Lani. Lani followed her sister's example. When both girls were ready, I leaned out and handed them baby Fung-Tai. I hiked up my tunic and jumped out the window.

The Japanese dentist next door watched for us each afternoon. He laughed at our antics when we tumbled out one by one. I spoke only Chinese then, so I did not know if he talked to us in Japanese, English, or Hawaiian. I waved. He waved back.

Off we went to movies in the local theater, window shopping downtown, or exploring. If we had money, we took the trolley to Kapi'olani Park to look for goldfish in the lily ponds or follow the horses parading along the paths. In the valley of Manoa, we listened to the plaintive calls of wild peacocks and the chittering of mynah birds in the tropical forest.

A ride on the trestle towards Diamond Head took us through the ten thousand coconut trees of Waikiki, across its taro patches graced with heart-shaped leaves, past flooded rice paddies patrolled by ducks. Here, bent in half like little stick figures, the Chinese rice farmers weeded and planted the seedlings in paddies mirrored like silver plates. On the beach, members of the royal family lived in surf-front estates with wide lanais and pristine views of rhythmic white waves.

If we didn't return in time for dinner, Ah Kong's wife told the others that the girls and I were still sleeping. See, their bedroom doors are closed, she pointed out. We weren't missed.

Mother bought toys for all her grandchildren except our girls. So we made up our own. Leaves became tea sets. Rocks created faraway palaces. When the weather was nice, my girls took their make-believe games out on our front steps, away from the cousins who bit and hit. Sometimes they played quietly. Other days, they ran noisily up and down the wooden stairs.

But when they heard the crunch of their grandmother's steps on the path that curved between her house and ours, they grabbed their toys and scrambled up the steps. Their bare feet thumped across the wooden porch. They scampered through the front door and slammed it shut. BANG. Then I knew Mother was coming.

Our bungalow was our sanctuary, but it couldn't protect us from jealous barbs and sanctimonious gossip. If my husband bought me something I needed, like a pair of shoes or a comb for my hair, Fourth daughter-in-law Yukmoy told Mother, "She's so selfish, she must make him get her everything new." Her words stung like a cold slap.

"Don't buy me anything," I told my husband. The hurt in his eyes pained me. He knew the $100 a month he now brought home was never enough. I held my hand to his heart, feeling its anxious beating. I said, "There are many things we need but I don't want to hear your mother scold us anymore." Living with his mother had already killed one wife.

He knew how I felt, but we couldn't complain. I was supposed to be deferential to my mother-in-law, as my husband was to his father. To keep harmony, we had to keep mindful of our duty. To maintain my husband's honor and his good face within the family, it behooved me to respect Mother's demands, whether or not I felt they were fair. My feelings were not important compared to family honor.

One day, Dai-Kam's maidenly First daughter told me that Mother was completely redecorating the main house. Did I need anything? She squared her husky shoulders and offered to help me move anything I needed. The secondhand dealer was coming that afternoon for the old furniture. I could live with our mismatched parlor, but our three girls now slept on one bed while Tat-Tung and I slept on the other. I ran to the main house. "Mother, how much do you want for Kai-Tai's broken-down bed?" I asked. I counted out the seven dollars she asked for.

Then, Edith, Lani, and I moved the bed ourselves. We struggled with it down the stairs of the main house, pushed it up the stairs to our bungalow, and dragged it across the wooden floors to their bedroom.

Edith's eyes sparkled–a bed of her own. To celebrate, we walked to Chinatown to tell Tat-Tung. He was so pleased he gave us three dollars to buy new sheets.

"Mama," Edith asked on the way home, "will you teach me how to make my own bed?"

"Of course," I promised.

Edith took the package of new linens from my arms and promised to carry things for me now that I was pregnant. We almost had to run to keep up with her. When we got close to home she raced ahead.

"Go ahead, Lani, catch Edith," I urged. Fung-Tai was getting heavier. I looked forward to putting her down. As I climbed up the front stairs, I heard screams.

"Mama! Mama!" A pale Edith leaned against the bedroom door. Her bed was gone.

I ran to the main house. I heard Yukmoy's laughter as soon as I threw open the front door. She sat in the parlor, the juice of fresh pineapple dripping from her lips. She arched her plucked eyebrows and pointed at my frustrated face. "Mother sent the secondhand dealer to pick up Kai-Tai's broken bed. Too bad!"

I stumbled back to my bungalow, curled up on my bed, and cried. I felt helpless and abandoned by the family that was supposed to be mine.

How could she sell what was ours? I repeated over and over. As long as we lived here, our lives were not our own. If we stood up to Mother, we were labeled disobedient and disloyal.

Stop it, I told myself. You can do better than this.

I ran my fingers over the tear-stained faces of my children and resolved that we would never go back to the main house to eat. I got up from the bed and locked the doors to our rooms.

❧❧

The girls and I hopped out of the window the next morning after the sun steamed away the morning showers.

I looked for a clean, quiet area, friendly neighbors, and a big house with the right *feng shui*. It had to have the proper elements around it to promote the beneficial flow of that vital cosmic energy force, *ch'i*. I considered each home's orientation to the water, the mountains, and the surrounding buildings. Was it in harmony with the trees and the turn of the road? I studied what way the rooms faced and how the rooms flowed one to the other.

A woman pointed out a quiet street next to the Queen's Hospital. Someone she knew, a happy family, was moving.

Ah, I thought, this home will be filled with their love and joy. I didn't want a house that had seen tragedy, for anger and fear cling to the walls of a house forever, ensnaring all who breathe the air and dust left behind.

The rambling house on Circle Lane had four bedrooms. Low-growing palms and lush ferns graced the entry. The front porch was five steps up from the street–a covered, columned porch large enough for children to play in. A heavy koa wood rocking chair sat to the left of the screened front door. I could rock my babies on my lap while watching the children at play.

A towering hibiscus hedge enclosed a grassy side yard. The hedge was thick enough so the children could not get through, but allowed them to watch the activity in the lane. A healthy mango tree, straight and even, shaded the yard.

I almost cried when I saw the most important room, the kitchen. It had enough space for our whole family to chop and cook together. It even had a kitchen table where we could eat without bumping elbows and knees. Behind the kitchen sink, a breezy window looked out on the backyard and the high cinder block wall of the Queen's Hospital. The kitchen's entrance from the side yard had easy access for the milkman, the ice man, and the delivery boy who would bring our groceries.

The Morgado family preferred to sell the house completely furnished since they were moving to the Kahuku area, to a sugar plantation job that offered them free housing. The double Victorian parlor was decorated in the old Hawaiian style with solid koa wood tables and chairs and overstuffed furniture. Tall windows framed by burgundy velvet draperies accented the high ceilings. Round black push-button switches controlled electric lights–brass and etched crystal chandeliers and wall sconces.

"Mrs. Lau, you will be happy here," Mr. Morgado said when I handed him a cash deposit. "There's plenty room for the babies that will come. But, let me caution you." He paused. Creases deepened in his sun-weathered forehead. "When you move," he said enunciating slowly, "don't let your mother-in-law know."

Why? I asked. What did he know?

He was from an old-time Portuguese family. Everyone in Hawai'i knew everyone else. "If Mrs. L. Ah Leong knows you are moving out she will scold you. Poison will come out of her mouth. When your husband's First wife Wong Pin moved out, Mrs. Lau cursed her. She chased after her First daughter-in-law and tore at her hair. She yanked out her hair combs. *Auwe!* Wong Pin screamed when her braided coils unraveled. Her hair flew up and covered her face. You know that sign for bad luck. Soon afterwards, your husband's wife died."

I felt my mother-in-law's tentacles reach out and curl around my neck.

Chapter Thirteen

Circle Lane: 1919

Tat-Tung whipped open the door of our tiny bungalow behind Ah Leong and Dai-Kam's grand Victorian, kicked off his shoes, and slammed the front door. Wham! He sat in silence in the moonlit parlor, his palms held tensely in front of his face, tapping his finger tips. I could feel his tension as if it were an iced sword between us.

"Your bathwater is hot. Will you come now before it gets cold?" I asked. I wiped my hands on the threadbare hand towel and approached him.

"Did you tell my father about Fourth brother Ah Chung?" he demanded, his voice like a seething volley from the darkness.

Indignant, I replied that I never talked to his father unless spoken to.

"Those liars."

"What do you mean?"

"You know Ah Chung takes things, like preserved ducks, cans of abalone, packages of the large dried mushrooms, shoes for his boys... He hides them under his regular deliveries and drops them home on his routes."

I bowed my head, embarrassed for my husband. Ah Chung's faults reflected badly on all his brothers.

"Ah Wang works downstairs and sees Ah Chung sneak around. But you know Ah Wang, he never likes to confront anyone. So he told *Baba*. My father laid a trap for Ah Chung. Caught him taking home half the canned hams from yesterday's shipment. *Baba* fired him. That was yesterday. Today, my mother accused you of tattling on her innocent Fourth son."

"How would I know what Ah Chung does at the store?" I cried in defense. "I'm pregnant with three girls at home. I see Yukmoy getting presents and extra food but I thought your mother bought them for her." Her children wore new clothes while mine made do with hand-me-downs. And when the scent of sweet cakes fresh from the oven wafted in the breeze, we knew Mother and Yukmoy were enjoying their private afternoon teas while my children's stomachs growled with hunger.

My husband's voice softened. "Mother scolded that I should teach you manners. I told her that Ah Chung was stupid enough to get himself caught."

I turned away from the doorway and poured the water for his bath. He peeled off his shirt and trousers and climbed in. "Aaah," he sighed. He closed his eyes and leaned his head back to soak. His wet skin glowed like polished alabaster. His legs parted and relaxed.

I knelt behind him and dropped my blouse. Cradling his head between my breasts, I massaged his head, his neck, his arms, his chest, plunging my arms deeper and deeper in the water. I felt for his meridian points and gently pressed to relieve the tension of his body. He moaned as he felt his *ch'i* flowing. I caressed him, dissolving our problems in the warmth of the bath and the dimness of the dark room.

❧❧

When he put on his night robe and came to bed, I buried my face against him, smelling the clean scent of soap and sun-dried freshness.

I confided how the girls and I had looked for a house away from his parents and family, where we could be on our own. I described how we cleverly outwitted his family in our search and found exactly what we needed. After I consulted the Chinese almanac for the auspicious day, a new gas stove would be installed. We would have our own ice box.

"And you know what else?" I sat up in bed, an arm on either side of him. "There's a telephone."

"A telephone," he repeated, moving a strand of loosened black hair out of my face with the faintest touch of his fingers. Whenever someone called for any of the Laus, they had to call Mrs. Moy's tailor shop. Then Mother had to run across the street and upstairs to tailor Moy's to answer the call.

"I put it in your name," I emphasized, tapping him in the chest with my finger.

"I don't need one." He stared at the ceiling, calculating the repercussions of this extravagance.

"You're head of the family. You need a telephone in your own name."

"A new house. A telephone. How much does this cost?"

"Don't worry. I paid cash." Out of his pay at the L. Ah Leong store of $100 a month, I gave him $40 to spend and saved $60.

He said nothing more. He rolled over to face me. He ran his fingers down my cheek and the curve of my neck.

"After the new stove is installed, I'll call you. Bring your father's delivery wagon and pick us up here," I whispered in his ear. "We'll be packed and ready to go."

He chuckled and slipped my cotton nightdress over my head.

❧❦

The next day, I opened my wedding chest and picked out a shimmering jade green tunic, one that reminded me of the leisurely days when we lived at Ah Leong's estate in China. I dressed our three girls in their best clothes. Then I strapped baby Fung Tai to my chest and walked to the L. Ah Leong Store.

"*Baba*," I called when I saw him at the front counter with his cronies, a trio of arguing merchants. I hoped I had chosen the right time, when he was least busy.

Ah Leong, dressed in blue Chinese workshirt and mended trousers, glanced up and pointed at the stairs to the upstairs office. "What? Tat-Tung is working." He turned back to his friends.

"I came to see you, *Baba*." Ah Leong nodded as if he welcomed the visit of four beautiful ladies. He motioned Ah Wang to take his place at the money counter and walked with us to where the sidewalk was less crowded. I did not see his Fourth son, Ah Chung, who had caused so much trouble.

I looked him straight in the face, then respectfully lowered my eyes. "*Baba*, I need your help."

He grunted and nodded, tilting his head to one side as if I were a comrade imparting important trade information.

"*Baba*, I have much to thank you for. I know you paid my fare to come to Hawai'i. You saved my life and the life of my daughter. I will always be grateful."

"You are my First son's wife."

"Thank you, *Baba*. I try to bring honor to your family. But I cannot live in your house anymore." How could I explain that his wife and daughter-in-law tormented us day and night? That they spied on us, eavesdropped on every conversation, and lied to him? That my children feared his wife, their cousins beat and bit them, and they were denied what others enjoyed? "We must move, *Baba*."

He narrowed his eyes and appraised my words without surprise. He looked back at his store and thought for a long time as many expressions flitted across his face, even the look of a once-frightened child. He looked down at me and nodded. "I have other houses. On Beretania Street I have many cottages. You choose. Tell my Third son Ah Kong to give you the one you want."

"No, no, no. I didn't mean to ask for another house."

"No apologies. I give you any house you want." He waved grandly, generously.

"*Baba*, you are so kind." I didn't want to tell him that I had already bought a house. And I didn't want him to lose face.

"See? You have no problem. I understand." He smiled as if he had concluded a profitable deal. "Any house you want, you move in for free." He patted the girls' heads and said he had to get back to work.

❧❧

"What do we do now, Tat-Tung? Your father wants me to choose one of his cottages on Beretania Street." I stuck my head into the steam rising like billowing clouds from his bath and inhaled its clean scent. "Shall we move to Beretania Street instead of the house on Circle Lane?"

"No," he answered in a sad, low voice.

"We could save money if we lived in his cottage rent-free."

My husband slid under the water and rose back up with his hair slicked back. His skin glistened in the dim light. He sighed.

"My first wife accepted *Baba*'s offer." He sighed again and slowly sank under the water as if to blot out the memory. He rose again with both anger and sorrow in his eyes. "She died there. I never want to see those cottages again."

☞☞

The next afternoon, I hopped out of the bedroom window with our three girls and took the trolley to Manoa Cemetery. At the entrance, I bought a package of incense and a bouquet of white gingers weighted with rocks and newspapers in a gallon can. These I handed to Edith. She walked us to her mother's grave. Her hands trembled when she placed the gingers in front of the modest lonely marker.

We bowed our heads while the burning incense spiraled our prayers to heaven.

"Wong Pin, please watch over your daughter. Protect your husband," I prayed. "I cannot fight the Laus alone. I need your help."

☞☞

On the auspicious day, the monks from the Kwan Yin temple came to bless the Circle Lane house and our family. The gas stove was installed and delivered.

The very next time Mother, Fourth daughter-in-law Yukmoy, and First daughter Kai-Tai left to go shopping, I ran to tailor Moy's to call Tat-Tung. "Come *now*," I said.

He ran downstairs, but the L. Ah Leong Store delivery wagon was out on deliveries. He hailed a taxi. We didn't have much to take, just our clothes and the trunks I had brought from China. We left behind the shabby furniture Mother had allowed us to use. We unloaded our belongings and hurried up the stairs of our new front porch.

I ran my fingers over the shiny gas stove. I would never chop wood again. I opened the ice box and checked where the ice man would place the block of ice when he made his delivery. The girls ran from room to room, their bare feet echoing through the large rooms. We sat in each of the chairs pretending animated conversation, then laughed at our own silliness. This was our house, our very own place. I planned to build a little alcove in the kitchen to place my figures of Buddha and Kwan Yin. I could light my daily incense and thank the gods for watching over my family and giving us peace.

The girls inspected each corner of the yard and peeked through the hibiscus hedge that surrounded their play area. They would enjoy a chop suey mix of playmates—Hawaiian, Caucasian, Japanese, Chinese, and Portuguese.

When Tat-Tung returned to the store, I finished unpacking our clothes. At dinnertime, the girls ran to where I stood in the middle of my empty kitchen. "I don't know what you're going to eat. I don't have any money left to buy food. We're stuck now!" I warned, shaking my empty hands.

My husband's adopted daughter Lani hugged my legs. "Mama, I don't have anything to eat, but I feel so happy. I'm not scared of anybody any more." I knelt down and wiped her tears with my fingertips. Yes, it would be difficult living away from the protection of L. Ah Leong. But we were safe, happy, and free.

❦❦

Mother stormed through our empty bungalow and yanked open every drawer to see what we had taken. Yukmoy followed, complaining about our ungratefulness.

I didn't care. I walked back to Ah Leong's house and handed Dai-Kam one of the jade bracelets she had given me for marrying her son.

The next time I saw Yukmoy, I peered down at the circle of jade on her arm and sniffed, "That's my *old* bracelet. Mother gave it to you."

Yukmoy protested, "No, no, no. I bought it from her."

I tossed my head and retorted, "You don't fool me." I flaunted two new jade bracelets that I had made in the latest style. I showed them that I could afford my own jewels.

Chapter Fourteen

The Stolen Can of Curried Chicken: 1919

My husband said I taught everyone a lesson. I was an exemplary wife, mother, and First daughter-in-law who stood up to his mother to protect my family. Even at work, his brothers regarded him with greater deference.

He complained that now he had to take a taxi home because Circle Lane was much further from work than our bungalow behind his parents. But instead of whispered greetings when he walked through his front door, he was greeted with laughter and happy welcomes. His children had others to play with and spoke Pidgin English as fluidly as Chinese. My neighbors invited me to quilt with them on their front porch. For each child, I planned to make Hawaiian quilts, hand-stitched in flowing patterns.

However, our tranquillity did not extend to the store. A month after we moved to Circle Lane, my husband was engrossed in tallying receipts when he heard his father bellow, "Get down here." He leaped down the wooden stairs. The store seemed to vibrate with a din of voices–loud, gruff, cajoling, urgent–negotiating and ordering in a fusion of languages. Customers pointed and yelled. His father and brothers scribbled in their sales books. To an outsider, this was chaos. To Ah Leong, this was business.

Ah Leong whirled angrily. "What were you doing upstairs, sleeping?" Everyone stared.

Tat-Tung paled.

"Look at all these customers. You should be working down here," his sixty-two-year-old father thundered. He threw him an order book. What could be more important than these customers? Accounting was a nuisance. All he cared about was the money he held in his hands.

That night, Tat-Tung returned to his office to tally the accounts he had abandoned earlier. His body ached. His father's cruel and insensitive words had cut deep into his heart. His head echoed with a cacophony of orders and accounts shouting for attention.

He jerked up from his books. It was so quiet he could hear the cockroaches scurrying across the floor downstairs. What time was it? Midnight. The store cook must have served dinner.

He clicked off his light and slowly walked down, each step as tired as the next. The wok in the back kitchen was empty. Everyone had eaten, locked up, and left. In the dead of night, the dark store took on an oppressive atmosphere. He stared at the untidy stacks of goods, the bins overflowing with feed and grains, the narrow aisles squeezed between the shelves. For all his life he would be trapped here, suffocating under his father's hand. When his father died, he would take his place, designated to lead the business, to dictate to his brothers and all their sons as was done to him.

From six in the morning to ten at night, he worked without a break, without assistance. If his brothers refused to go to Maui or Hilo to pick up their shipments or deliver to their wholesale accounts, Tat-Tung was the one Ah Leong asked to mediate and give the order; when Tat-Tung commanded, his brothers obeyed. If conflicts arose with customers or shippers, Ah Leong turned to my husband for solutions. His First son was his confidant, the giver of solid, thoughtful advice.

Tat-Tung surveyed the shelves. He picked out a single can of curried chicken and plopped the contents into the wok. He turned up the gas. The aromatic scent of curry layered with spices wafted through the room, reminding him of how much he denied his hungry spirit. He slumped, alone and exhausted, and rubbed his tired eyes.

Business consumed his father twenty-four hours a day. He ran it lean, turning every penny back into inventory and expansion. When the family got together for Chinese New Year's, the Moon Festival, Ching Ming memorials, weddings, and birthdays, Ah Leong's conversations reverted to the store, investments, profits, and growth. Other merchants complained about the store's unfair hours and delivery that ran late into the night and all day Sunday.

The burden fell on Tat-Tung to sort out the activity. Sixteen hours a day, seven days a week, he tuned out the noise of the business downstairs to concentrate–manually tallying the credit accounts, receipts, and payments; segregating the taxes to collect and pay; balancing the payables and receivables; and accounting for the leases, rents, and other accounts. Money and inventory moved so fast that it took organization and tight financial management to keep a business strong, especially one as diversified as his. His back ached from the endless hours of sorting the confusion of receipts and invoices that came up in boxes from the sales floor. No one else could figure them out.

❧❧

He walked home because no taxi worked in the dead of night when even the streets lights were off.

I lay waiting; I never slept soundly when Tat-Tung wasn't home. I boiled hot water for his bath and massaged his tired shoulders as he soaked away the humiliation and hassles of the day. I felt his shoulder muscles knotted in tight fists and his *ch'i* drained of vitality. That morning, we both fell asleep exhausted, dreamless.

After a short nap, he got up and went back to the store. But within an hour, I heard his steps on the front porch.

Heart pounding with foreboding, I ran to the front door. When I saw his face, I knew. I put my hands up to him but he walked past me and slumped in his high-backed reading chair.

He needed time. Men have their pride and will not talk until they are ready. In the meantime, they have uncomfortable feelings to sort out.

I invited him to have breakfast with the children. But he sat absent-mindedly silent. Despite his gloom, he couldn't stop the children from running to greet him.

As he held Fung-Tai, a tear rolled down his cheek and nestled in the soft curls of her hair. He had so much love for his family. We were all he had. I turned away and called the girls into the kitchen for breakfast.

Soon we heard him click open the delicately inlaid case of his moon-harp and tune the strings. The sorrowful melodies he learned as a young man in China, the only expression of his deep sadness and inner turmoil, floated through the house on Circle Lane.

I held the girls' hands and told them to close their eyes and listen with me, to hear what China was like. I envisioned Tat-Tung playing not in our parlor on Circle Lane, but in the atrium at his father's grand estate in China, *Ming Yang Tong*. I described the sun-ripe scents of tangerines and lychee bursting from the trees around us in the spring of our love. Above, clouds billowed in a turquoise sky, pushed by the hot breeze. His eyes were half-closed in concentration, his teasing expression now relaxed and his lips pursed as if for a kiss. Sadness flowed out from fingers leaving tranquillity in his heart.

I tiptoed to the parlor. After a while, he told me what had happened and the hurtful accusations of his father.

☞☜

"I was the last one to arrive at the store," Tat-Tung said. "I had never been late before, but then, last night I had been the last to leave. The delivery men were already headed out with their full loads for the day and the horses were dancing with anticipation. My brothers moved faster than usual, avoiding *Baba* who yelled louder than normal. The workers were preparing the wholesale orders in double time and loading them into the waiting carriages. Everyone was in a terrible mood. I stopped Ah Wang as he carried the bins to stack on the sidewalk.

"'What's wrong?' I asked.

"'Robbery,' Ah Wang answered. He was shaken. How could that be? I was here until past midnight. I asked what was stolen. 'A can of chicken. *Baba's* berating every person here for wasting his goods. Says his store cook feeds everyone plenty,' Ah Wang muttered, keeping his head down.

"I looked up to see my father waving the empty can he had plucked from the garbage. 'Who is it? Who dares to steal from me? Ungrateful sons? Thankless workers? Hey! Who opened this, ate my goods?'

"'*Baba*,' I shouted. I walked up to him as he roused himself to greater fury. 'I did it.' My brothers turned, speechless. I stared at each of them and slowly turned back to my father. 'Last night you all left. I was still working. You left me no food. Forgot about me upstairs. I opened one can of curried chicken for my dinner.'

"'My cook feeds you,' he yelled.

"'No, you all ate and left. Didn't even come up to see if I was still alive. You think I can work with you all day and go back upstairs and finish just like that? You think it's easy keeping track of your books? You throw everything in a box and I have to sort out what you sold, for how much, how much you paid, how much you collected, what is retail, what is wholesale, and the taxes. When I'm not here you don't pay the taxes and the tax man comes to throw you in jail.'

"'Taxes not necessary. Cuts my profit,' he scoffed.

"'You have no idea how much work is involved.' I said.

"'Hah! You do nothing upstairs. All you do is sleep.' He threw the can at me.

"I felt the lies and jealousy of my mother and Yukmoy in my father's words. He's getting old and believes the insidious lies of the women who cater to him. I said, '*Baba*, you don't want me to do anything but work. Not even eat. You treat me worse than a dog. If you think it's so easy, hire someone else.'"

My husband buried his head in his hands. Sorrow cracked his voice.

"I turned and walked out," he gasped. "It was against everything I believed in or had been taught. But if my father thinks all I do is sleep at work, I will not be there." He paused. The air shimmered with silence. "I told him I quit," he repeated in disbelief.

I closed my eyes and turned away. I could imagine the uproar–his brothers gasping, the workers' eyes opened wide, jaws agape. Father and son, both born the year of the Dragon. Stubborn and shrewd. Perhaps that is what doomed their relationship. Fiery tempers spewed fire from their veins. Too much alike. Today was the turning point. Uncharacteristically, he had defied his filial responsibility as First son.

"You rest," I whispered. I rose from my chair and returned to the kitchen. I mixed herbs with water in my pottery bowl to steam special tonics to restore the yin and yang balance of his *ch'i*, to rejuvenate his body and spirit.

☜☞

Early that evening, long before the store's normal closing time, Ah Leong walked up Circle Lane calling, "Tat-Tung, Tat-Tung."

I glanced quickly at my husband. He folded his newspaper, rose from his high-backed reading chair, and walked to the door.

"My son, how are you? Rested? Good, good." Ah Leong smiled through the screen door. For the children he brought a large tin of English butter cookies. "My granddaughters are growing so big. Look, *Gung Gung* brought you some treats. You ate all your dinner? Ah, Phoenix, you're looking well. I'm sure this time you'll give me a grandson."

The girls hid behind their father and peeked suspiciously at Ah Leong. Normally, their *Gung Gung*, their grandfather, ignored them. Now he was at their house, offering them presents.

I welcomed Ah Leong into the parlor and hustled the children out. They must stay in the kitchen and not bother their father and grandfather the rest of the evening, I warned. I opened the cupboards to get tea and almond cakes for the men. They poured themselves whiskey instead.

"Tat-Tung, we missed you today at work. Everybody asked, 'Where's your First son?' I told everyone you needed to rest. I work you too hard." Ah Leong was a master at smoothing over hurt feelings and building up egos when he felt like it. He laughed as businessmen do when creating a congenial mood.

After the general description of the day, Ah Leong lowered his voice. "I need your advice. What did we agree on these contracts?" he asked. He handed Tat-Tung a large stack of papers. Later, he asked about shipments and price negotiations. They worked for an hour or so. Ah Leong took extra care to express appreciation for his son's help.

"Well, we'll see you tomorrow then?"

Both men pushed back their chairs and walked to the door.

"I quit, *Baba.*"

"Aaah, well," Ah Leong answered. This was not an answer he would accept. "I know you work hard. You rest." He paused and sighed. "I want to go back to China next month. I haven't been back in four years, not since we finished building *Ming Yang Tong.* You know you're the only one who can run the business for me while I'm gone." He bid us a gracious good-bye.

Tat-Tung leaned against the heavy rail of the porch. Long after his father disappeared in the darkness, he stared out at the stars sparkling over the still Honolulu night, the faint smell of anise rising from his cigarette.

The two Dragons were head to head. Each night for two weeks, Ah Leong walked down Circle Lane calling for his First son. Each night the two went through the finances and problems at the store. Each night Tat-Tung refused to return to work.

The third week, Ah Leong quit coming.

Dai-Kam scolded Ah Leong all day, every day. "You throw all your money in the cash box. Who's going to sort it out now? Are you so weak you can't force your son to work?" She flung the charge accounts in his face; they were all mixed up. She accused Ah Leong of losing money. "You can't leave for China now, not until Tat-Tung comes back."

Her husband's face steamed a blotched red. He bellowed, "I don't need him anymore." He hired a regular bookkeeper, a Japanese woman.

The fourth week, Ah Leong returned to Circle Lane. The men negotiated at the kitchen table over whiskey shots in teacups. Ah Leong offered his First son double salary, $200 a month, to work six days a week, not seven like the others.

From then on, Tat-Tung came home from work tired but fulfilled, his honor restored. The delivery boy gossiped that L. Ah Leong was afraid of making his First son angry. The brothers turned to Tat-Tung whenever their father gave an order and deferred to his judgment even more, responding to his commands and decisions over their father's.

Tat-Tung was surprised that the store cook called him to dinner each night before the others. When he wished, lunch was brought up to him in his office, always with ample servings.

Later, out of earshot of their father, Ah Wang confided that Ah Leong almost passed out when he got the Japanese bookkeeper's bill. She charged $500 for the week, and would only work Monday through Friday.

Chapter Fifteen

Ah Leong's Power over Immigration: 1919

Ah Leong stormed through the busy streets of Honolulu, eyes riveted straight ahead, and growled at the hails of his friends. He stomped up to the office of his First son without saying a word to his other sons and workers.

The stormy look on his father's face told Tat-Tung that the Immigration interview had not gone well. He leaned back on his chair, his starched white shirt starkly crisp in the late afternoon light, and took a deep breath to prepare himself. Through the open windows he heard the "clop-a, clop-a, clop-a" of the horses along King Street, the churning of the delivery wagon wheels, and an occasional "ha-oo-ga" of one of those new horseless carriages that sped down the streets of Honolulu at up to twenty-five miles an hour.

Ah Leong paced the tiny office. "I have a First Class cabin booked for July 5 on the *Shinyo Maru*," he grumbled. "Immigration wouldn't give me a passport." He threw down the packet that contained his Form 430, *Application of Chinese for Preinvestigation of Status*, his Citizen Identification #1932, his record of naturalization, a dollar bill, and a photograph of himself.

"What reason did you give?"

"Pleasure."

"And what did Inspector Farmer say to that?"

"That wasn't a good reason to travel." Ah Leong smarted from Inspector Farmer's insinuation that his real purpose was business. Ah

Leong insisted it was pleasure. The Inspector retorted that since Ah Leong had no real reason for traveling abroad, under the present regulations he would not approve his application. The merchant had jumped to his feet, indignant.

"You may appeal," Farmer snapped. He walked out and closed the door, leaving Ah Leong facing his empty chair.

Tat-Tung knew his father distrusted the American government. Despite their contributions to the economy and stable cultural lifestyle of the islands, the Chinese were still singled out through laws like the Chinese Exclusion Act. In turn, the Chinese considered the abrupt and confrontational methods of the Immigration Service rude and disrespectful, so they felt no need to tell the truth, especially when it came to private matters.

Ah Leong huffed impatiently. "Fifth wife Wong Shee writes that warlords threaten to take over my stores and markets unless I pay for their protection. These bandits grew bolder! I need to exert the power of my Five-Star Name. I have the protection of the Governor of Kwang Tung."

But those glory days were gone. In 1910, Dr. Sun Yat Sen founded branches of the Chinese revolutionary organization, Tung Ming Hum, in Hilo, Hawai'i, and the island of Maui. The goal of this organization, which eventually became the Kuomintang, was to unify China as one nation. Thousands of dollars were raised by the Chinese in Hawai'i who clung to China as their homeland. Meanwhile, militarist Yuan Shi-ka'i came out of retirement to defend the Chinese emperor from the revolutionaries led by Sun. When the six-year-old Manchu emperor relinquished his throne in 1912, Yuan Shi-ka'i, not Sun Yat-Sen, became president of the Republic of China. Instead of heeding the wishes of the revolutionists, Yuan became a ruthless dictator. After his death in 1916, China broke up into hundreds of small units controlled by politicians, militarists, and warlords who fought for power and control.

In the smoky tea houses and ornate meeting rooms of the family associations and benevolent societies in Hawai'i, news of sweeping raids on their villages by warlords and bandits outraged kinsmen. Some supported the Kuomintang with money and arguments. Others sought to restore the Ming dynasty to Peking. Associations sent thousands of dollars to support the various political groups, and the two Chinese newspapers, *Hawai'i Chinese News* and *United Chinese News*, took opposing stands.

Tat-Tung frowned at the mention of bandits. The memory of his hurried escape from China in 1918 still brought back the panic of Hong Kong, Phoenix's anguished tears, and the hungry wails of their baby. His father had already sold a good portion of his China land not only to pay off the warlords, but for capital to expand his Hawai'i business. It was only since the Great Mahele, during the time of King Kamehameha III, that land, once under the sole conservatorship of the king, could be purchased.

"I have been here forty years," Ah Leong fumed, "a naturalized citizen of the Hawaiian Kingdom since 1890. I am a citizen of America. How can they deny me the right to travel? Citizen is citizen."

"Not if we're Chinese. I am native born, but Immigration considers me a nonresident," Tat-Tung reflected. He rested his elbows on the armrests of his chair and tapped his fingertips. Of course, maybe they could use this racial bias to their advantage.

"They'll listen to a *haole*. They'll jump to the wishes of an influential Caucasian they respect. Let's see who we can use." Tat-Tung sat up and thought through the most powerful men in his father's social circle.

"*Baba*, ask your friends at the Chamber of Commerce to help you. The Immigration Service will not deny Mr. Dillingham, Mr. Lewis, and Mr. Denison. You know what power they hold."

Ah Leong paced the floor, barely aware of the cacophony of the business beneath them. Turning to his son, he leaned forward with his weight on his knuckles and chuckled conspiratorially, "How humble Farmer will be to get a letter on my behalf from the richest American businessmen."

His son agreed. "You have been in business here almost forty years. How many can boast that? You have clout. Have your *haole* friends help you."

His father's bravado returned. He knew how business was done in Hawai'i: by word of mouth and on the strength of friendships. His son's education had paid off; he thought like a Caucasian and a Chinese. The best of both worlds were in his head. Grabbing the documents returned rudely by Inspector Farmer, he pounded back down the stairs.

Tat-Tung took a deep breath and turned back to his accounts. Life went smoother when his father was negotiating a promising deal or celebrating a victory. In this case, his father would enjoy using his influence to negotiate a favorable letter to the Immigration Service from his prominent white associates. It was the way of life here. Power was not only in the quality and quantity of influence one had but who these contacts were. His father had been here long enough and was shrewd enough to know the ones who controlled government and commerce.

☜☞

Richard Halsey, the Inspector-in-Charge of the Immigration Service, received a letter from the all-white Chamber of Commerce of Honolulu headed by Walter F. Dillingham, A. Lewis, Jr., and George P. Denison.

Dear Sir:

Mr. L. Ah Leong at 116 North King Street, this city, desires to leave the territory at the earliest convenience for China, and in his behalf I hereby desire to make formal application for the issuance to him of a passport.

Mr. Lau is a merchant in Honolulu and has been for about 37 years. He is an American citizen, having been naturalized under the Hawaiian Kingdom and carries "Record of Naturalization" executed and issued to him by the Minister of the Interior.

Mr. Lau has been a particularly active man in business and finds it necessary, in the interest of his business, to make a trip to China, and prays that his passport may be issued which will permit his leaving Honolulu at the earliest opportunity so that the interests which he has in China, and the interests which he has here may be continued and maintained in the same degree of efficiency.

May I express the hope that favorable action be given this

application so that Mr. L. Ah Leong's arrangements to leave may be executed.

Very truly yours,

(signed) Raymond C. Brown, Secretary

Chamber of Commerce of Honolulu

A month later, L. Ah Leong appeared a second time before Immigration Inspector Farmer. Farmer ran through the preliminary questions then asked, "Did you apply for a Form 430 certificate in March of this year?"

"Yes."

"And your application was not considered because you did not show a sufficient reason for traveling to China. What is the purpose in your going to China now?"

Ah Leong opened his eyes wide and declared innocently, "I have some stores at Swatow. I am going to start a new company there and I want to buy goods in Hong Kong to send to Swatow and Honolulu."

"You stated that you were not going on business when you testified on March 13," accused the Inspector. He still smarted from the humiliating redress his superior, Inspector Halsey, gave him for refusing L. Ah Leong.

"Because at that time the new company did not ask me to go. But this time, they want me. They said I am an old merchant and know better than they."

Farmer submitted his formal summary.

This applicant filed his application for a Form 430 certificate on February fourth, 1919. When he came to make his statement on March thirteenth, he stated that he was going to China merely on a pleasure trip and not for business. His application was, therefore, not considered, as he would not be entitled to a passport under the present regulations. He has now requested that his case be reopened and he claims that he is going to do business. His former positive declaration that he intended to go abroad for pleasure only tends to weaken his claim that he is now going on business. On the other hand, it may be that his purpose was business in the first place and that he did not want to say so for fear he would have to reveal some of his business purposes. But as he has made his claim, his case will be considered.

He is a man of sixty-three years and has been in Hawai'i a great many years. I have known of him since some time in the 1890s. He has always been in the grocery business, one of the largest and best known businesses in Honolulu.

From the fact that Lau Ah Leong, or L. Ah Leong as he is usually called, is so well known and from the other circumstances and the evidence, documentary and otherwise, I do not think there is much doubt that this applicant is the same person who was naturalized as a citizen of the Hawaiian kingdom in 1890.

(signed) Edwin Farmer, Immigration Inspector

❧❧

Knowing he would be gone for a few months, Ah Leong brought home a young *mui tsui*, a servant girl, to assist Dai-Kam in his absence. Peony was young, pretty, quick, and obedient.

Dai-Kam knew this Peony, with her smooth white face, thick black hair, and a swing to her youthful gait, was not all she appeared to be. Her husband had brought women home before. Some he kept as wives, such as Ho Shee and the two dead ones, Chung Shee and Zane Shee. Some he kept as servants.

With Ah Leong gone, Dai-Kam and Yukmoy threw their most distasteful chores to Peony. She refused and instead sashayed around the house.

"Sell her," Dai-Kam ordered. "Quickly. Before my husband returns."

In the late afternoon as the skies threatened a Hawaiian blessing of rain, the neighbors heard pitiful shrieks from the Ah Leong house.

"No, no," Peony screamed, "I'm not for you." Her hair ribbons tossed frantically as she tried to escape out of the pig farmer's wagon.

The sun-baked farmer dragged and tugged, embarrassed and humiliated with his future wife's vehement rejection. He had come to Hawai'i at eighteen. After twenty years with his pigs, he looked forward to the companionship of a wife. He had scrubbed and bathed with meticulous attention this morning and wore his best shirt and trousers, soaked and sun-dried the day before.

Peony pulled back in repulsion. A smell clung to him like a fog of pig dung.

Dai-Kam and her allies, bathed in perfume from the upscale American stores, followed the couple out of the house.

Peony begged her former mistress for mercy. She promised to reform.

"I have no patience to fight with you," the farmer shouted with exasperation. "I give you a new life. You learn respect."

With that, he grabbed Peony's waist and tied her wrists and ankles as expertly as he lassoed his pigs. He plopped her into the back of the wagon usually reserved for slop.

"You give me trouble, you stay there. If you want to act like a lady and be nice to me, you can sit up here with me. What do you choose?" His ears were used to the mellow grunts and occasional squeals of the piglets, not the loud shrieks and cries of a woman. He threw an oiled tarpaulin over the top of the wagon bed, as he normally did to protect his slop from torrential downpours, and trotted down the road.

Chapter Sixteen
Tat-Tung's Motorcar: 1919–1920

The day after his father left for China, Tat-Tung stood at the window of his office overlooking King Street, the heart of Hawai'i's Chinatown. His eyes caressed the angular lines of the new motorcars as they maneuvered around the horse wagons in clouds of dust. Their engines gave off an efficient sound, the sound of serious movement.

On the way home, he stopped and admired the gleam of paint and chrome. He asked their drivers, "How fast can you go? How much fuel? How about care and maintenance? How do you drive it?"

The first time he rode in a motorcar he hung on tightly, grasping the sides of his seat. His friends sped down Queen Street to the wharf. A policeman yelled at them to slow down. Then they drove out toward the country, past farmers bent in half in the rice fields, children waving in front of small country stores, and the mute faces of plantation workers.

When he came home, his normally serene face was flushed. His crisp white shirt and tie were dusted with dirt. "Extraordinary, extraordinary," was all he could say. His mind was moving ahead, absorbing the experience and integrating it into future possibilities.

Most of the roadways within Honolulu were reasonably flat with the wear of horse wagons. As the number of motorcars increased, being the latest status symbol of the wealthy and privileged, the city smoothed more roads.

One afternoon, Tat-Tung hummed merrily down the stairs of his office. "Ah Wang," he called. He motioned his brother outside, evading the crowds of customers yelling orders to their clerks. The two stood on the sidewalk piled with bags of feed, rice, and vegetables. The air was rich with the smell of horses, the fresh ocean breeze from Honolulu Harbor a block away, and the occasional lei worn by passersby carrying jute and lauhala shopping bags.

"Look out there, Ah Wang. Motorcars. What do you think?" Tat-Tung pointed to the motorcars in the street.

"Those noisy things. A novelty for the rich," Ah Wang dismissed with a wave of his hand. This was a grand gesture, patterned after his father's.

"The future, Ah Wang," insisted the enthused Tat-Tung.

"Humph. Playthings."

"We should buy one of those," Tat-Tung pointed as a gleaming Model-T Ford sped by, narrowly missing a horse wagon. He laughed at the wide eyes and gritted teeth of the motorcar driver, who obviously didn't think he was going to make it past the horse. The wagon's driver now stood and shook his fist at the motorcar racing away at twenty miles an hour.

"You crazy! What for?" his brother asked incredulously.

"Look, a horse you have to feed. It needs a stable and a man to take care of it. If a horse is sick or lame, we have to get a veterinarian, right?"

Ah Wang nodded. Everyone knew you had to take good care of your horses if you expected them to carry loads all day, like they did.

"If we use a motorcar, we don't need a stable or a man to take care of it. We just park it."

"*Baba* will never go for the idea. It's too new. He has his own way of doing things. He doesn't like change."

"No hay to buy."

"Humph. A passing fad."

"Goes five times as fast. Finish all deliveries same day. We'll teach Ah Chung to drive and make him our delivery man. Also, think of the modern image it will create: 'L. Ah Leong Store delivers by motorcar.' Everyone will want to buy from us so we can drive to their store or house and deliver from our motorcar. Gives them plenty face."

Tat-Tung was inspired as he created his vision. The image of the L. Ah Leong motorcar deliveries speeding through Honolulu driven by the Lau sons was a modern view offering speed and efficiency for their customers. It could set them a step ahead of the other enterprises in town.

True, there were limits to these machines. They broke down occasionally. If an excited driver ran them off the road, they would not get right back on the path the way a horse would. They could only travel on reasonably flat roads, and definitely not through mud after a tropical storm. A bumpy road could pop a wheel or twist an axle. In the country, one could send a horse out to graze in the open land. A motorcar driver had to make sure he had a sufficient fuel supply.

Ah Wang knew his brother had researched this decision. "What will *Baba* say?"

"I'll talk to him when he gets back from China."

Tat-Tung had already checked out the feasibility of buying a motorcar for the store deliveries. He confirmed the size and model he needed, then put the word out through his network of friends. He negotiated a deal for $200 for a used Model-T with a modified delivery bed large enough to handle the volume currently managed by the horse wagons.

☜☞

The steamer bringing L. Ah Leong was sighted by the lookout at Diamond Head. The whistle from the Hawaiian Electric Company blew, announcing its impending arrival.

Tat-Tung drove down to the dock at Honolulu Harbor and joined the quickly gathering crowd already excited by the heart-thumping marches of The Royal Hawaiian Band.

The steamer tooted. The crowd cheered. When the boat docked, the greetings of friends and relatives charged the atmosphere with kisses and screams, for the Hawaiians loved the sound of their welcoming songs and the press of human hugs. Jubilant waves from the passengers met with screams of "Aloha" from the lei-bedecked greeters on the dock.

Tat-Tung, dressed nattily in a crisp white shirt, wide flowered tie, and neatly pressed slacks, leaned boldly against the motorcar. It was polished to a gleaming black sheen, reflecting the Hawaiian sun in flashing radiance. The thirty-year-old merchant acknowledged the admiring glances of the disembarking passengers and visitors who crowded the port on Boat Day. The men salivated over the dashing vehicle. The ladies oohed.

"Look at that new machine."

"Expensive, isn't it?"

"He must be some rich guy."

Tat-Tung chuckled to himself. He couldn't wait to see his father's reaction.

Soon enough, L. Ah Leong, in no-nonsense work shoes, walked down the gangplank followed by five porters bent in half under the weight of his trunks. The sixty-four-year-old merchant had packed away his elegant Chinese clothes, his long banker's coats of *dai fong chau* silk, and black pigskin-soled satin shoes in reverse appliqué. Since Hawai'i meant business, he now wore thick cotton trousers and a well-mended jacket that Wong Shee had laundered, starched, and ironed. As expected, he was the first Chinese to get through Immigration.

Tat-Tung greeted him. Then the two walked out to the street.

"And how was your voyage, *Baba?*"

"Ships are going faster nowadays. Only took two weeks to get here. Saves time. See the weight I gained? Second wife Ho Shee and Fifth wife Wong Shee insisted on serving me all my favorite foods. Your Eighth brother Lau Chen is married now. The District Governor of Kwang Tung came to his wedding banquet. We served two thousand friends and relatives! Unfortunately, the warlords are gaining more power in the cities and it cost me much silver to convince them to leave my lands alone. They're still fighting among themselves."

Tat-Tung hmm'd and nodded. He said business was good. When the men reached the car, Tat-Tung instructed the porters; he pointed to the arrangement he wanted for the trunks in the back of the motorcar. He ignored the stunned look on his father's face.

Ah Leong walked closer, paused, then paced slowly to the front of the motorcar. He paused, then walked around to the back. He looked at his son, then back at the gleaming machine. He exploded, "Hah, what's this?"

"Your new motorcar," Tat-Tung replied calmly. He motioned his father up to the passenger seat with a gallant sweep of his arm. "Get in."

Ah Leong bellowed. "Where's the horses?"

"I sold them. Come on, let's go."

"What? You sold my horses? You spent my money?"

Tat-Tung tipped the porters. They dashed back to the ship to avoid the old merchant's legendary temper.

"*Baba*, we bought this motorcar secondhand. An excellent deal. No need for horses, so we sold them."

Ah Leong stared rigidly at his son.

"It makes good business sense," Tat-Tung continued. "This car doesn't need anyone to take care of it. We don't need a stable man to brush its coat every night and make sure it has hay and water. We just park it. There is no need to buy it food. We fill it with gasoline. The motorcar is so fast we will beat up the competition. Get in. I'll show you how it works. Give me your hand."

Ignoring his son's assistance, Ah Leong heaved his body into the passenger's seat. He turned around to see all his trunks firmly in place. His son had tied them down in exactly the same way they tied down loads in the delivery wagon.

The motorcar gave Ah Leong a new perspective. He observed the way people stared in admiration and the looks of respect they gave him when Tat-Tung started up the motorcar and pulled away from the curb. He could even see, reflected on the hood, the clouds floating against a turquoise sky. Best of all, he no longer saw Honolulu from behind the trotting rump of a horse, but from behind an efficiently churning engine.

"See how people are watching you?" his son shouted over the humming chug. "Business picked up since we started motorcar deliveries. We can do more deliveries per day than with the horse wagon. Drive all day long without having to change to a fresh horse. At night, I drive it home and park in the side yard of our house. In the morning, I drive to the store for the next day's deliveries." A glance at father's expression told him the old merchant was considering this analysis.

"Going home first?" Tat-Tung asked.

"Course not."

Ah Leong watched the heads that turned his way. People stared at him in the passenger seat of the gleaming motorcar. What did his son say? They were doing more business now because people wanted others to see they were receiving their deliveries via motorcar? Via the modern L. Ah Leong Store motorcar? Ah, the focus on business and greater profits from his First son who thinks like a Chinese and a *haole*.

Tat-Tung drove his father up to the front of the store. Sons and workers dashed out to greet him and unload the trunks.

"Hey, Ah Leong," his cronies called when they saw him alight. They ran over from their businesses, waving their greetings. "How was your trip? What's the news from the village? Rode back in this new thing, huh? Can you give us a ride?"

As friends crowded around his father, Tat-Tung directed the workers to unload the trunks into the warehouse until his father unpacked and gave his instructions. In the meantime, the old man was enjoying the adulation of his colleagues. Some took turns climbing into the driver's seat to get a feel for the wheel. Others ogled the engine.

❧❧

That evening, Tat-Tung drove his father home to the mansion with the wide lanai.

There was a serious frown on the old merchant's face. He looked at his son and nodded. His son nodded back. Ah Leong slowly got out of the vehicle. He ran his fingers over the shiny polished chrome. From the shadows of the lanai, he watched his son and the motorcar chug down the road in the darkness

Chapter Seventeen
Ah Leong's Property Returns: 1920–1921

"Phoenix, *Baba* brought you a letter," my husband called.

Tat-Tung's ebullient smile when he walked through the door the night Ah Leong returned from China told me his father was pleased with his son's surprise transportation.

I clapped my hands and plucked the letter from his pocket. I wanted to rip it open as soon as I recognized the thin tissue envelope with Mama's small and timid writing. Yet, part of me wished to savor each word with as much emotion as I could. I had sent money to my grandparents, mother, and sisters with letters of how different life was in Hawai'i, but I never told them that I thought I might never see them again. So I curled up in an overstuffed chair in my high-ceilinged parlor where all I could hear was the distant barking of poi dogs and the rustle of the wind licking the leaves in the mango tree. I carefully slit open the envelope.

I cried when I read that my brother, so handsome and spoiled, sold off Grandfather's business; he felt it was his since he was the only male heir. But Grandfather had given an adopted nephew the power of attorney, intending to split the assets between nephew and grandson. Grandfather chased after my brother with a butcher knife. My brother eluded him and escaped with his ill-gotten wealth to the lands bordering the South China Sea.

I felt the sadness and desperation of my grandparents and mother. My brother ruined everything he touched.

Three of my sisters had married distant cousins. One died. The fourth was given to the Buddhist nunnery, but she ran away to Hong Kong and married a man who abandoned her and their child to marry another woman. When I read their stories, I longed to return, to care for everyone as I had done before. But my children had a better future here. Plus, my husband would never leave. He was too Western.

"These Chinese," Tat-Tung complained after spending an afternoon writing letters for laborers sending money home to China. "They think they're all going back someday. How long they've been here—thirty years or more? They yearn for their boyhood China: their village dialects and games, clan ceremonies, family weddings, birthday banquets, home-cooked meals with their parents. What's left for them to go back to? Their young wives and doting parents have died. When they go back, it will be as ashes."

"Hush," I said. "They've given up their lives to make their fortune here. They're lonely with no family to welcome them home after a hard day, no children to call them *Baba*, no wife to warm their bed and cook their favorite dishes on festival days."

"Humph. They work hard and save little," he criticized. "All they can do is work the fields. Wear their hands and back down to broken bones for what? Then they come to town to gamble or smoke opium. Soon they don't write home anymore because they have no money to send. In the meantime, their parents and wives turn to dust and their children grow up never knowing their father. The plantation owners don't care. Most throw the workers out when they can't work anymore."

I turned away and pressed my trembling fists to my face. Never to hear my family's voices or see their faces again. Never to dress gaily in fine cottons with combs and tassels in my hair and step out in satin shoes to have tea with cousins and aunts. Too late, I remembered my mother's warning that the mother's personality when she is pregnant is manifested in the child that is born.

The first time I was pregnant, I lived in China, the wife of the First son of the rich and famous Lau Ah Leong. I could have been sassy, but

I lived up to the rank in which I had been born and married. My first-born daughter was cheerful and outgoing, enchanted with her own fingers and toes. Her quick smile and rosebud lips delighted the other women in the family. I thought she knew more than we give babies credit for, watching us with her dark eyes–the eyes of an old soul.

My second child was the son we wanted. Yung Chan had brown-sugar eyes and a prominent forehead, family traits of his father and grandmother, Dai-Kam. Unlike his elder sister, he was a quiet child, overly sensitive and careful not to offend. When I was pregnant with him, we lived in the Lau Ah Leong family compound in Hawai'i, caught in the web of family conspiracies and intrigues.

How could anyone understand this hole in my heart? I didn't fit in here. My mother-in-law always found something to scold me about.

My father-in-law was different. He had homes in Hawai'i and China. In each location he had wives, children, investments, power, and prestige. His international networks and money flowed freely between two countries. How lucky, I thought.

☜☞

Ah Leong missed his servant girl Peony when he returned from China. However, pressing matters commanded his attention.

First, he agreed with Tat-Tung; motorcars allowed them to deliver five times as fast as the horse-drawn wagons and provided better service to their clients. In turn, their customers enjoyed the novelty of this latest mode of commercial delivery. So he acquired a second. Amazed locals sighted his motorcars dashing to the waterfront docks to pick up goods, wheeling through the prestigious neighborhoods of Nu'uanu, Manoa, and Makiki, and whizzing through downtown Honolulu with their horns tooting "ha-oo-ga."

Next, Ah Leong wrote to his contacts to find my brother. After selling Grandfather's Singapore business, my brother had disappeared through an underground network of smugglers. Ah Leong's overseas correspondents located him through their tongs and merchant societies in Bangkok, the port city of Siam. They "persuaded" him to return home to our village.

Most importantly, Ah Leong and Dai-Kam hosted an overflowing crowd of family and friends for our son's first birthday. Since Tat-Tung was president of the Lung Kong Kung Shaw, the Society of the Four Families cofounded in Honolulu by Ah Leong, a thousand guests presented our baby with precious jades as well as thousands of dollars. Ah Leong ordered his new grandson Yung Chan, the First son of his First son, recorded in the Great Ancestral Hall in Kew Boy as the latest asset of the Lau family.

Meanwhile, Ah Leong's Third son Ah Kong and Sixth son Ah Sang had graduated from Mainland universities. Ah Kong joined a stock brokerage in Shanghai and settled his family in a posh neighborhood. Ah Sang made plans for travel throughout Europe and Asia to further his education and play for an Asian all-star baseball team.

Finally, Ah Leong had time to ask about his servant girl.

Dai-Kam, now a stately fifty-five, sat ram-rod straight at the massive koa wood dining table straightening dollar bills into orderly stacks between her palms and heaping coins into staggered towers, her mahjongg winnings from the day before. Behind her, the morning light streamed through the lace curtains of the bay window, framing her in a delicate pattern. If she were one of his customers, he would have warmed her up with a little chitchat and said a few complimentary things about her health. But she wasn't.

So he asked bluntly, "What happened to Peony?"

"Gone," she answered without looking up. She stretched her bare feet and dug her toes into the carpet.

"Gone where?"

She looked him dead in the eye. "I sold the lazy girl to a pig farmer." She lifted her eyes and watched his face.

"What? What?" he bellowed. "What kind of woman are you? You sell my daughters. You sell my servant girls. Get her back." He raised a husky arm and stepped forward.

She stood up. "Too late," she declared. She stared down at him, pained at his shock, furiously jealous that he cared. "She's married."

Then she swept up her winnings from the table and stomped past his bulky frame on her way out. The red satin fringes across the doorway swirled angrily in her wake.

❧❧

The morning broke with multicolored shades of pastel pinks and blues over the Koʻolau Mountains as the last drifting showers washed away the dreams of the night before.

The L. Ah Leong Store buzzed with a cacophony of languages. Ah Leong had already forgotten about the loss of his servant.

Dai-Kam had not. In a comfortable cotton tunic, dark blue to accentuate her statuesque height, she walked purposefully towards the store when the showers cleared. While her husband was in China, she had gone to the store daily. Customers and friends hailed her as they had in the old days when she worked beside Ah Leong. Without her boundless energy and hard work, there would be no L. Ah Leong fortune, they said. She realized she missed their conviviality, the downtown gossip, and the excitement of commerce. Today, she would pick up her order of Chinese blue porcelains before some clumsy oaf broke her treasures or sold them by mistake.

At the same time, a disheveled pig farmer rode up King Street peering at the names of the stores. He had been up before the sun, feeding and tending his beloved pigs. He hadn't bothered to bathe or change before leaving on his early morning route to the fine Waikiki hotels where he had contracts to pick up the kitchen slop—plate cleanings and leftover food. He and his wife would then dig through the slop to take out the solid matter—bones, sterling silver forks, knives, and spoons—that waiters brushed from the plates they cleared. He drove directly to the L. Ah Leong Store and urged his horse on a little further where there was room to tie up. A pretty woman, dressed in simple trousers and tunic frayed at the seams, clung to his arm with a pleading look which he ignored with a determined expression.

He jumped down and tied up his horse. She brushed back her long black braid then stepped down, careful not to disturb the plump baby strapped to her back in a bright cotton sling. The baby sighed in her sleep. Her cheeks, as full and round as sweet pork buns, jiggled softly.

"Please, dear husband, no. Take me home, I beg you," she cried. She tugged at his arm. The man ignored her. "I have been an obedient wife. I like to work for you," she begged, wiping the tears from her pale face. She tried to keep up with his determined clomp.

He shook his arm free when she touched him. When he got to Ah Leong's store, he looked around, his face scrunched in an angry scowl. The overhead fan spun lazily above shelves crammed with tins and boxes and bulk sacks of dried mushrooms and rice. He spied Ah Leong in the back of the store arranging crates of fresh fruits and vegetables, next to a display of blue porcelain bowls.

"Hey you, Ah Leong," the farmer hollered with a voice strong, clear, and resonant from years of pig calling. "Welcome home. I have something that belongs to you." He pushed his way towards the startled merchant.

All heads turned towards the door.

The farmer grabbed his wife and pushed her forward. "Peony had your baby." She struggled, twisting and turning to release his grip.

The local people pushed forward to get a better look. They shoved and yelled for others to get out of the way.

On the street, Dai-Kam heard the agitated yells and was immediately swept along with the tide of curious locals along King and Kekaulike streets. Then she saw the pig farmer and his wife. And the baby.

"Hey, Ah Leong pulled a fast one on that country farmer," she heard behind her. "He got two for the price of one," exclaimed another. She glared at Peony.

Dai-Kam stormed through the crowd, flinging the stunned onlookers back with a ripple of her arms. "What? What did you do?" she bellowed, aiming her shoulders at both men. "You old goat, now what?"

Dai-Kam charged at Ah Leong. On impact, he flew upwards and across the aisle, splitting open a bag of rice with a resounding Thwack! The crowd gasped and leapt back.

Tat-Tung heard his mother's angry voice and flew down the stairs just as she raced towards Ah Leong with both fists.

The pig farmer, who had been so arrogant a minute ago, now crouched in a ball on the floor, his hands protecting his head from her fury.

Tat-Tung brushed the grains of rice off his stunned father. "*Baba?*" He held out his hand. His father batted it away. His brothers pushed the gawkers and amused shoppers out of the store.

"Come, come," Ah Chung coaxed his mother out through the back room. Dai-Kam bellowed loudly as he loaded her into the motorcar with her Chinese blue porcelains, even louder as he drove her home.

Tat-Tung appeased the pig farmer. The young wife left, tearful and humble, with her husband who was richer for having to support a wife and a baby that was not his. The baby, obviously content, was still asleep.

The Chinatown merchants and residents laughed with knowing smiles the rest of the day. The old men joked, the herbalists nodded, and all marveled at Ah Leong's passion for business and women.

PART IV

Chapter Eighteen

L. Ah Leong, Limited: July 1921

L. Ah Leong turned from the letter in his hand and glared out from Tat-Tung's office window. Below him, the Honolulu streets bustled with commerce. The whizzing click-clack of Tat-Tung's abacus confirmed that each year grew better than the last. Since Hawai'i's economy was dominated by the sugar cane and pineapple industries, World War I had not hurt the Islands.

He felt the cycles of his life shifting like the seasons with a new challenge. He had grown from a bankrupt shopkeeper to a shrewd businessman. His business had expanded to an international network. Now he was in his mid-sixties with thriving businesses in China and Hawai'i, four estates, three wives, ten sons, and tremendous face in both the Chinese and American communities.

In the meantime, his family demands grew more complex.

He held Ho Shee's letter to the light and reread her plea. His Second wife feared the hundreds of bandits that swarmed the mountain passes. Each time the Kuomintang army surrounded the wild horde, they melted into the tangled forests of Wong Soo Sang mountain in Fukien Province, an ominous dark peak to the north.

She and Fifth wife Wong Shee felt like prisoners. *Ming Yang Tong* was so huge that they suspected every creak was an ax at the door, every groan the step of a marauder. If they should scream, no one in Kew Boy village would hear. She wished to move to his first house, the Story of the Southern Breeze, that he had built in the village. It had forty-eight bedrooms, more than enough room. Wong Shee always kept it provisioned, just in case. But Wong Shee would never leave Ah Leong's largest estate and its treasures unguarded.

Please, Ho Shee begged, let me return to Hawai'i. She had one problem. In China, Wong Shee did her bidding. In Hawai'i, Ho Shee would be First wife Dai-Kam's subordinate. Ho Shee had not planned to return; she left Hawai'i in 1910 without an approved Form 430. She did not have permission from Immigration to reenter the United States as required by the Chinese Exclusion Act. Could he take care of it?

Ah Leong looked past Honolulu Harbor, in the direction where his estates sparkled in the hot Chinese sun far beyond the horizon. The year was 1921. After forty years of marriage to Dai-Kam, he welcomed a change. He longed for a compliant companion. He would persuade his First wife to return to China. Fiery Dai-Kam, that voluptuous hot-tempered amazon, could fight off the bandits. She would make mincemeat of them, or vice-versa.

Fifth wife Wong Shee and her son, Eighth son Ah Chen, would oversee his lands in China. Ah Chen's wife was already pregnant, ensuring a line of descendants to care for the ancestral homes he had built. In Shanghai, Dai-Kam's Third son Ah Kong had asked to manage the family's China investments, hotels, and stores. First son Tat-Tung could sail over periodically to collect the revenues and audit the accounts. Through the blood of his sons, the name of L. Ah Leong would always stand in China.

Behind him, Tat-Tung steadily sifted through the accounts, tallying invoices and profits of the L. Ah Leong empire. Ah Leong turned. Look at the way he focuses, he chuckled to himself. Tat-Tung doesn't even lift his head to daydream out the window. Yes, he'll build the Lau legacy and command the affairs of the family. After all, he alone held the respect of all the brothers. Now was the time for Ah Leong, who had manipulated his holdings into millions in real estate and investments and commanded lands and resources in two countries, to exercise his power at home.

For forty years, he and Dai-Kam had worked together to build their family and fortune in Hawai'i. Everyone recognized her as Mrs. Lau Ah Leong. But her outburst over Peony, a trifling, caused him to lose face. He resented the way his wife challenged him. He had set everything in place for a smooth transition of ownership and power. He wasn't going to let his empire dissolve if they fought. Under American rule, Dai-Kam could contend that they built the L. Ah Leong empire with her dowry after he had gone bankrupt in Kohala, and claim everything.

Ah Leong tapped Ho Shee's letter against his knuckles. He turned away from the window and walked resolutely down to his store to the pleasing staccato of Tat-Tung's abacus.

⚘⚘

Dai-Kam sat stiffly in the overstuffed high-back chair in the parlor for this talk with her husband. They had avoided each other since the morning she went to pick up her Chinese blue porcelains and confronted the pig farmer and Peony. She dabbed at her angry, jealous tears. She hoped she wouldn't have to get physical; this room held a treasure in carved Chinese chairs, fringed lamp shades painted with dream-like landscapes, thick silk rugs, and hand-painted porcelain deities.

When he strode in she watched him warily, her dark eyes guarded. His words were cajoling and kind, unlike the gruff bluntness that had crept into their conversations the past few years. He stood before the lace-trimmed windows looking out on Queen Street.

"I'm sorry for causing you so much grief and embarrassment," he said sorrowfully. "I am too old for young girls. I was stupid." He described the luxury of *Ming Yang Tong*, The Shining House Beyond the Bridge. She hadn't seen their latest and largest estate, the heavy flowering of the lychee and loquat trees in the open air atriums, and the bounty of their new farms. "I only wish to make you happy now. I will provide everything you desire in China. Stay as long as you wish and enjoy the grand life as if you were the Empress Dowager," he beseeched.

He placed his large hands on her broad shoulders and stroked the curve of her neck where he knew she would respond. "You must see it for yourself," he said, his voice as alluring as a meandering brook. "I will pay for First daughter Kai-Tai and Fourth daughter-in-law Yukmoy to accompany you." He paused with the familiar heat of his hands resting on her bountiful breasts. My dessert, he had called them years ago.

"I make this offer to you because I should know better," he said in that urgent needy voice. "I am an old man now, and should take care of the First mother of my sons. You deserve to live in luxury."

☜☞

The following week, Dai-Kam mulled over her return to China.

Her mah-jongg friends congratulated her. What a generous husband. How wonderful to have a choice of homes and countries. What wonderful cooks you can get from Canton. He will give you anything you want? Aaaah, so fortunate.

She had to agree. In America, wives had clout and power. Above the clack of mah-jongg tiles, she and her lady friends discussed how American equality was better than Chinese subservience.

Yukmoy and Kai-Tai encouraged her to go. They would like to keep her company in China, they sighed, but both were pregnant again and wanted their children to be born in Hawai'i as American citizens.

In the freshness of the mid-morning air when the humidity wakens the delicate scent of blossoms, Dai-Kam ambled towards the L. Ah Leong store greeting everyone she knew along King Street. Sheathed in a yellow tunic that complimented her tawny complexion and exotic dark eyes, she seemed to glow in the bright Hawaiian sun. She saw her husband loading the motorcars for deliveries and admired his industriousness. She greeted the loyal customers and assisted them with their purchases as she had done years ago when she worked beside her husband.

"Ah Leong," she called sweetly. He turned in surprise. She smiled. At his age, his back still rippled with muscles. "You're right. It's time I saw *Ming Yang Tong.*"

Ah Leong wiped his hands off on his pants and grasped her shoulders warmly. "We'll take care of everything. Nothing to worry about." Tat-Tung would arrange for passage and make the appointment at

Immigration for her reentry papers. "You'll need lots of money to spend. I'll take care of it," he enthused.

At the first available opportunity, Ah Leong went upstairs to confer with Tat-Tung on Dai-Kam's travel arrangements. The next available boat left next month, in August.

Then he headed towards Merchant Street with the listing of all his Hawaiian assets.

❦❦

"I don't want my business known all over town," Ah Leong told Joseph Lightfoot at their first meeting.

Lightfoot's office exuded tasteful confidence and elegance–forest green chairs in the waiting room, mahogany wainscoting, gilt frames depicting pen and ink drawings of scenic landscapes and seascapes of London. Lightfoot himself sat behind a solid mahogany desk topped by a black marble insert, highly polished to reflect the dapples of sunlight streaming through the open shutters. Polished brass lamps and certificates from a prestigious university were mounted on the wall.

Lightfoot told Ah Leong that he had his legal papers ready for his signature. These documents combined all of Ah Leong's and Dai-Kam's businesses, lands, and holdings under a new corporation, L. Ah Leong, Limited. Lightfoot placed the thick pile of documents before his client, adjusted his wire spectacles, and came around to the front of his desk. He drew up a chair upholstered to match the rich forest green of the carpet.

Together, they reviewed Ah Leong's plan. Out of a total of 6,000 shares, Ah Leong would keep 2,060 shares. Dai-Kam received 2,000 shares. Eldest sons Tat-Tung and Ah Wang received 400 shares each. The next two sons who worked at the store, Ah Chu and Ah Chung, received 200 shares. The remaining sons received one hundred shares apiece, except for the last two, who received sixty shares.

"Who are these four men who get eighty shares each?" Lightfoot asked, tapping his pen at their names.

"Chinese style, I pay low wages to these workers. They receive a share in the business. I teach, they learn. I profit, they profit."

"I see, a way for you to teach your kinsmen a trade in exchange for labor." As one of the leading immigrant rights attorneys in Hawai'i, Lightfoot tried to understand each culture's practices.

Lightfoot confirmed that he had reviewed all the real estate holdings with Tat-Tung. The merchant's son, impeccably crisp in a white tropical suit, had brought all pertinent records and documents. These included detailed descriptions of the land holdings. Twelve in all, they included downtown areas bounded by Hotel, Maunakea, King, and Kekaulike Streets, Kekihale on Pauahi Street between Maunakea and River Streets, the property along Beretania Street, lands at King and 'A'ala Streets, the makai side of School Street, lands at Kinau and Lunalilo Streets, and the Lau family compound at Punchbowl and Queen Streets: all prime locations.

Lightfoot also included Ah Leong's hundreds of shares of King Market, Honolulu Canning Co., Chinese Mutual Investment Co., Honolulu Soda-Water Works, O.K. Soda-Water Works, City Mill, and O'ahu Market. Leases for properties on King and Liliha Streets and the Hop Sing Company business location were listed, as were his two mortgages with the Bank of Honolulu on the L. Ah Leong Store and all goods in the store and warehouse, and all credit accounts and debts owed to L. Ah Leong.

"What about my wife's claim on the property?" Ah Leong asked. "The deeds have both our names on them."

"I have covered that with this statement:

And I, Fung Dai-Kam, wife of the said L. Ah Leong, in consideration of the premises, and for the further consideration of One Dollar to me in hand paid, by said L. Ah Leong, Limited, do hereby release and forever quit-claim unto the said L. Ah Leong, Limited, all my dower and right of dower in and to the above described and granted premises."

Lightfoot offered his pen.

Ah Leong bobbed the gold fountain pen on his fingertips as if assessing its weight, then signed with a grand flourish. He asked his attorney to present this to his wife for her signature and respond to her legal questions.

❧❧

"One dollar for all my property?" First wife Dai-Kam scoffed. The Articles of Incorporation crackled when she crumpled them in her fists.

Lightfoot shifted uncomfortably in the formal curved-back chair.

"L. Ah Leong Store was built with my dowry. All our lands were bought with the profits of my hard labor." She flung the wad of papers at Lightfoot, unsigned. "You insult me."

Lightfoot leaned forward. He explained to her and her companions that she was receiving 2,000 shares, or one third of all of L. Ah Leong, Limited. The dollar was a formality. Then he explained the legal advantage of putting the business and all the holdings into a corporation.

"How do I know this isn't a trick? What if he's taking our property to put into the business and he loses it all?" His former bankruptcy in Kohala had shamed them both. And taught her a lesson about the instability of business.

Lightfoot assured her that the incorporation was the modern way to do business. To her advantage, it removed their personal liability in case of bankruptcy. Her husband insisted on the incorporation of his holdings for its tax advantages and to ensure the growth of the business.

"No! He made the store with my money. I own everything equally with him. No need to change anything to modern way. Old way is working fine."

Her eldest daughter, Kai-Tai, explained to Lightfoot that her mother had put up with her father's wives and servant girls all these years, in her own house. The L. Ah Leong success owed just as much to her mother's hard work as her father's. Naturally, she was suspicious.

Yukmoy frowned, raised her painted eyebrows, and whispered to Dai-Kam that Tat-Tung must have talked Ah Leong into doing this. He was probably planning to take all the shares and leave nothing for everyone else.

"Madame, I assure you that your husband has considered this incorporation in good faith. We carefully researched the holdings with full cooperation of your son, Tat-Tung. Your husband wants to streamline operations, limit your liability, and protect you," explained Lightfoot.

"I told you Tat-Tung put *Baba* up to this. *Baba* will turn around and give his shares to his First son, who will cut everyone else out," wept Yukmoy.

Dai-Kam rose from her carved rosewood chair and headed out the parlor. She dismissed Lightfoot with a curt good-bye and shuffled barefoot across the thick Chinese carpets.

"Madame, please reconsider." Lightfoot leaned forward to stop her.

Yukmoy jumped up and waved him away with both hands as if he were a diseased dog. "Out! Get out. We don't want you here."

Dai-Kam turned and marched towards the stunned Lightfoot. "Go!" she bellowed.

"But Madame." Lightfoot raised his voice. The uncomfortable setting, the dark room, the heavy rosewood and koa furniture, the satin fringes in the doorways, the smell—was it mothballs? It was all unsettling.

Dai-Kam took another step.

The other two rushed to her side.

The attorney bolted for the door and jumped into his waiting motorcar. "Office!" he barked to his driver.

☜☜

It was July. Dai-Kam's boat to China was scheduled to leave in August. As the well-known wife of a merchant, this Immigration interview was a formality. She asked Ah Leong to be her witness, as he had done many times before, to secure her reentry permit prior to her departure. This time, L. Ah Leong told Inspector Curry that Dai-Kam was not his wife.

The inspector's jaw dropped.

The Chinese merchant insisted that this woman was an impostor. His wife was still in China and would arrive in December.

Instead of facing Dai-Kam himself, Curry sent his assistant to tell her that she could leave Hawai'i. But under the Chinese Exclusion Law,

Immigration could not approve a permit for her to return since she was not the wife of the merchant L. Ah Leong.

The assistant flew out of the room at the same time Dai-Kam stood up with a tremendous scream of "What?!"

Chapter Nineteen
Betrayal: July 1921

Ah Leong swung his arms as if to catch the afternoon trade winds with energetic pumps of his fists. He nodded to the right, to the left, caught the hails of his friends, and waved at his friends from Oʻahu Fish Market across the street. He stepped into his store with a cocky swagger.

"She was here," Tat-Tung warned. He handed his customer her purchase, folded in brown paper and knotted neatly with red string, then motioned his father to the privacy of the warehouse.

Ah Leong, delighted with the shock he had just left on Inspector Curry's face, dismissed the warning with an indifferent grunt. He imagined Dai-Kam's reaction: how she must have jumped suddenly to her feet, dark eyes flashing, hands to her heart in fear. She might even have crumbled in tears, filled with shame and embarrassment. Now she would sign. Now he had control.

Once they were alone in the dim warehouse, Tat-Tung faced him. He clasped his hands, still shaking with anger, behind his back. "*Baba*, you can't go into Immigration and swear you're not her husband when everyone in Honolulu knows otherwise. Forty years you've been married."

His father picked up the invoices for the day's deliveries and perused them. He laughed, then shrugged nonchalantly. "If she signed the incorporation papers as my attorney asked I would have said she was my wife. Since she won't, she's not. It makes no difference to me." He gloated, "The laws work for men, not women. If I say she's not my wife, she is not the wife of a merchant. When she obeys me, I will let her travel."

He shoved the invoices at his son and picked up a crowbar, grasping the cold steel with relish. Winning always made him feel like doing something physical. With unrestrained vigor, he pried open the crates of preserved vegetables and salted fish that Ah Chung had just unloaded.

Tat-Tung leaned back to avoid the flying debris. The sun streamed through the dusty windows of the warehouse and displayed its beams in the excelsior his father flung from the boxes. "*Baba*, all your legal documents are in both your names as husband and wife." He waved the floating particles away from his face and coughed. "She can use those deeds as evidence. Sue for your business. Then *you* have nothing."

"Never!" his father yelled. "I've worked seven days a week since I was nine years old. See what I've built—vast estates in China, land holdings all over Honolulu, the business you will inherit and continue to run—perpetuating the name of L. Ah Leong for generations, forever." He grinned devilishly. "All she does is play mah-jongg and gossip. When she signs the papers, I will say she is my wife. Until then, she is nobody."

"Think carefully," his son cautioned. "This could have greater ramifications than you think. You can't throw away a woman who has headed your household for forty years. She's given you four sons. She's *my* mother."

Ah Leong insisted this had nothing to do with him, only Dai-Kam. "Your loyalty belongs to me," he warned. He whipped out a rusty knife from his pocket and snapped the waxed twine that bound the lids on the jars of preserved vegetables. He inspected the contents, nodded, and turned to the next crate.

"Then think of the family. She's built your business. You may end up losing more than you bargained for if she fights back. More people would be hurt than you realize. Think of our family name and honor."

"She *will* do as I say. I want those papers signed."

Tat-Tung crumbled the invoices in his fist. Nothing he could say would sway his father now. He could look and act like a humble merchant dressed in worn work clothes, but his mind worked as cagily as a hawk's, able to analyze his prey, eliminate its options for escape, and strike swiftly. Without a word, Tat-Tung walked back to his office and left his father chortling to himself in the warehouse.

The merchant continued to unpack his inventory, creating clouds of dust and littering the floor with excelsior. He stopped when a toenail caught on a metal strap. He nonchalantly swung his rusty pocket knife to cut the offending portion of his nail off, hacking at it in the dim warehouse. He roared when he missed, then scowled at the rivulet of blood that dripped to the dirty floor.

☜☞

Dai-Kam plopped in a koa wood rocker and moaned.

First daughter Kai-Tai bent down and dabbed at her sweaty forehead with a crumpled handkerchief. She soothed, "We're home, Mother. Relax. Take a deep breath." She disappeared into the kitchen and padded back with a cup of tea.

Dai-Kam shook her head and waved the tea away. "I am his First wife. All the property's in my name as well as his. Even the federal courts said I am his wife. Twice they named me his legal wife. How can Ah Leong speak such lies?" She tore at the top button of her tunic and rubbed the small red mark where it pinched her neck.

Fourth daughter-in-law Yukmoy perched on a polished carved chair opposite Dai-Kam, nervously turning her jade and gold bracelets, expensive presents from her mother-in-law. "Mother, men are in charge of the laws. They can change their mind," she pouted. She opened her handbag, rouged her lips, and snapped her mirror case reassuringly.

"There must be laws to protect a wife if there are laws to protect a husband," Dai-Kam insisted with a shake of her head. The ruling officials believed Ah Leong because of his long history in the islands and reputation for business. How could she defend herself?

"Why was my father arrested twice for having more than one wife even though Chinese and Hawaiians accepted it as proper at that time?" mused Kai-Tai. She sipped the tea her mother had refused and paced the parlor decorated with the dark Chinese furniture her parents preferred.

"Because new American laws say he can have only one wife. We better get a *haole* attorney, too."

❧❧

A subdued Dai-Kam sat on the edge of her chair in the waiting room of Thompson, Cathcart, and Ulrich. She queried her daughter again. "You sure?" She sighed and looked to Kai-Tai for reassurance. Her First daughter had the same voluptuous figure, the same defiant snap in her large dark eyes as she had had when she married Ah Leong.

"Mother," Kai-Tai repeated patiently, "Frank E. Thompson is the attorney Queen Lili'uokalani chose to protect her claim against the United States for seizure of her personal crown lands. Princess Kawananakoa is one of his clients, too."

The formidable Thompson was well connected with the controlling Republican oligarchy in the Islands. He had served on the Supreme Court of the United States and in the U.S. District Court of Hawai'i, specializing in admiralty law. He counted among his prestigious clients Matson Navigation, President Lines, and the Royal Hawaiian Hotel.

Dai-Kam straightened in her chair. She pointed at the portraits on the opposite wall. "Look! If they can trust him, I can, too." His paternalistic affection for Hawai'i was mirrored in the pen and ink drawings of sugarcane fields amidst plantation homes and the portraits of his clients, the Hawaiian monarchy. The attorney for the powerful Hawai'i Sugar Planters Association was known for his fair interpretation of the law and ability to achieve justice from an unequal system. His office reflected power–from the solid, carved desk to the firm leather chairs.

By the time Thompson explained his strategy to the two large elegantly dressed Chinese women, they were both nodding confidently. By refusing to identify Dai-Kam as his wife, Mrs. Lau Ah Leong's husband was exerting pressure on her to sign the articles of incorporation for his business. Under the Chinese Exclusion Laws, if she wasn't his wife she could never return to Hawai'i. But Thompson could prove that Ah Leong had previously sworn, under oath, that Dai-Kam was his wife.

To substantiate Dai-Kam's position, Thompson obtained copies of Ah Leong's federal conviction in 1910 for bigamy naming "Mrs. Fung Dai-Kam Ah Leong" as his legal wife, and the deeds and legal papers with signatures of Lau Ah Leong and his wife "Fung Dai-Kam Ah Leong."

Ah Leong's attorney, Lightfoot, paid Thompson a visit a few days after Dai-Kam consulted with Thompson at his office at 214 Campbell Block, Merchant Street. Lightfoot advised Thompson that Ah Leong wished to protect his family by keeping their assets together.

Thompson replied that Dai-Kam had no desire to sign over her interest in income producing real estate in exchange for shares in a business that she had no assurance would continue to be profitable.

"Nonsense," said Lightfoot, "the merchant is a well-known businessman—the richest in Chinatown."

"Which gives him the right to tell Immigration that she is not his wife after forty years of marriage and eight children?" Thompson, the attorney of the powerful oligarchy in Hawai'i, thanked Lightfoot for coming to see him and refused the compensation that Ah Leong offered to drop the case.

A few days after Lightfoot visited Thompson, Ah Leong personally called upon his wife's prestigious attorney. "I apologize for coming barefoot. A knife accident in the warehouse," he explained, gesturing to the dirty bandage on his foot.

He sighed that his wife misunderstood the meaning of incorporation. A business matter, you understand, he explained. "I'm expanding our retail and wholesale operations. It will be worth more if it is incorporated with all our properties in the name of L. Ah Leong, Limited. You must convince my wife to sign the Deed of Conveyance so all our properties will be in one place and protected. They will be more valuable to her."

He appealed to Thompson in the most straightforward manner. He mentioned his personal relationship with members of the Chamber of Commerce of Honolulu. He paused, then held out a thick red envelope with an offer to pay for any inconvenience for having to put up with the woman pretending to be his wife. She was penniless, he said. He himself was wealthy.

Thompson declined Ah Leong's generous offer and told him he would discuss his visit with his client.

⚁⚁

"Your wife won't sign." Ah Leong and his attorney faced each other across Lightfoot's desk. Its gleaming surface reflecting the dappled late morning sun. Lightfoot looked down at the open file. "Her attorney Thompson now has copies of your bigamy conviction naming Mrs. Fung Dai-Kam Ah Leong your legal wife and all the deeds you've signed together as husband and wife. Without her cooperation, we can't proceed any further on this incorporation." He sat back and paused for Ah Leong's reaction.

The merchant watched his attorney's eyes but his focus was inward, analyzing all that had happened to thwart his ambition.

He painfully shifted his bandaged foot. Herbalist Yuen had clucked and scolded by the time Ah Leong went to see him. "Look at this! Even I can smell the poison. One more week and you would have been crossing the Seven Heavenly Bridges." Yuen swiftly slit open the wound and drained the pus. Then he applied a fresh herb poultice to the infected toe and rewrapped the entire foot in fresh bandages. The stabbing pains in Ah Leong's foot still throbbed.

Lightfoot closed the file with a slow turn of his finger and stood up. "I'm sorry," he said. He held out his hand to say good-bye.

Ah Leong waved him back down. "No!" He leaned forward, both hands planted firmly on his attorney's polished desk. "I have another wife." He grinned devilishly. "With an American marriage license."

"But Mrs. Fung Dai-Kam Ah Leong?" exclaimed Lightfoot.

"I married her Chinese style—big banquet, Chinese ceremony, exchanged Chinese papers. No American license."

Lightfoot plopped back in his chair, speechless. Prior to the American takeover, the local community marked births, marriages, and deaths with their own religious and cultural observations. Celebratory feasts and ceremonies honored marriages and births. The Christian missionaries, shocked at the "heathen practices," persuaded the monarchy to eliminate polygamous relationships and marriage within the royal family that continued the royal line. The laws regarding marriage had not changed since 1872, but the interpretation of these laws now reflected the Christian influence of the new government of the Territory of Hawai'i.

The year before, on April 6, 1920, the Supreme Court reversed a decision made in 1905 that held valid common law marriages or marriage by custom, such as Hawaiian and Chinese. The local population mistakenly believed that the new law that required a marriage license applied to future marriages, and that marriages conducted according to accepted traditions up to that time were valid.

After meeting with his attorney, Ah Leong walked directly from Lightfoot's office to the Board of Health. He explained to the clerks that he needed a duplicate copy of his marriage certificate. His wife, Ho Shee, had obtained it in 1907 for their marriage dated May 25, 1891. The clerks were happy to assist the well-known L. Ah Leong.

☞☜

Once, the L. Ah Leong store hummed with prosperous energy as sons hustled to and from the store, their delivery cars laden with orders and deliveries. Now, in 1921, it buzzed with war-like animosity. Ho Shee's sons campaigned for the incorporation of L. Ah Leong, Limited and Dai-Kam's sons defended their mother's honor.

Both camps—father, mother, and brothers on both sides—aired their strategies to Tat-Tung for confirmation and approval. He tactfully negotiated the explosive ground between them.

Ah Leong resorted to intercepting Dai-Kam's groceries. She and her children could starve, he threatened. He himself ate at the store. His toe had miraculously healed; the infection had dried up within days of Herbalist Yuen's herbal dressing. The release from pain was euphoric. Ah Leong felt invincible and powerful once again.

His wife Dai-Kam marched indignantly to the store to take what she wanted. He leapt to the entrance and barred the doorway with his arms. "You want to eat? Sign it! Sign this paper."

"Forty years and four sons I gave you, you old man," she baited him.

Ah Chung waited until his father left, then concealed his mother's groceries for delivery on his regular routes.

Tat-Tung's brothers told him that their families hid in their houses when *Baba* stormed home. Both parents were firmly dogmatic. "Lau blood," it was called–that stubborn streak and hot flaring temper.

Even Inspector-in-Charge Richard Halsey called on Ah Leong to question his refusal to identify Dai-Kam as his wife. Ah Leong confidently booked Second wife Ho Shee on the SS *Siberia Maru* to arrive in two months.

He sneaked back to his house one morning when he knew his First wife would still be home. He yanked open the wooden screen door and kicked off his shoes.

"What now, you old man?" Dai-Kam stormed forward to confront him. Yukmoy followed behind her.

"I give you one last chance to sign these papers." He thrust the Articles of Incorporation and Deed of Conveyance on the dining table with his fountain pen. "Sign now," he demanded. "I'll tell Immigration you're my wife. Then you can go to China."

"You think I don't know what you're doing?" She squared her shoulders and pulled herself up to her full six-foot height, towering a head over her husband.

"I'll leave you penniless," he warned. "You'll be out on the streets. You and your daughters begging. Hah!" His relished the image of his wife barefoot and groveling.

"I'm not turning my property over to you to lose."

"No one's losing. Everyone wins. You get 2,000 shares of my entire company." His knuckled fists turned white. Frustration and anger flushed his face.

"Shares? What do I do with shares? You think with your head

between your legs." Her voice shook the fringed lamps in the parlor and shocked all the neighbors within a block's radius.

"You old hag," he bellowed. "I'll kill you!" He leapt like a tiger to pin her shoulders against the wall. But she dodged his advance and belted him with the back of her hand.

He flew backwards against Yukmoy, the momentum carrying both to the floor with a resounding thump. Feet and arms sprawled awkwardly. He struggled to his feet. "You whore," he spat in disgust.

Yukmoy cowered and yelped, "Oh, oh, oh."

Dai-Kam screamed, her teeth bared, the whites of her eyes flaring daggers. She rose above him like a thunderhead cloud and heaved a rosewood chair at his head.

He smashed it in two with a swipe of his forearm. "I'll kill you both," he roared and flung both women back with one sweep of his muscled arm like a massive tidal wave.

Chapter Twenty

The Strategic Divorce: December 6, 1921

"Phoenix, Phoenix!" Kai-Tai's urgent knocks became the threshing of Mama's bountiful rice harvest. Farmers threw their baskets high in the wind to separate the grain from the hull. And in my dream, my men lifted my sedan chair high above their shoulders to carry me across the harvested fields of China for dinner with Mama, Papa, and my grandparents. My mouth watered when I saw their serving bowls overflowing with vegetables, dark and sweet from our garden, roast duck, and steamed pork seasoned with pungent spices. I would never be hungry again.

Stay, stay, Papa. I reached for his hands. He faded away.

I shook myself awake. Aaah, I sighed wistfully. I was not in China anymore. After washing diapers, scrubbing floors, and laying my two babies down for their mid-afternoon nap, I had fallen asleep sitting upright. In a couple of hours, Edith and Lani would be home from school. I smoothed the creases from my house coat and rushed to the door.

A huge Chinese woman, her hair pulled in a tight bun, threw her heavy shoulders back and banged on the door frame. Her pale companion, eyebrows penciled in an arched look of surprise over ruby red lips, crouched behind her. What could be so urgent to bring Kai-Tai and Yukmoy running up my front stairs in tight *cheong-sams* and high heels? I unlatched the screen door and flung it open. I looked behind them.

"Where's Mother?" I asked. They never went anywhere without her.

"She had a terrible morning," Kai-Tai answered. She wiped her flushed cheeks with a rumpled handkerchief from her handbag. "*Baba* tried to kill her..."

"And me," interjected Yukmoy patting her chest with a bejeweled hand.

Kai-Tai stared her skinny companion into silence and continued, "So her attorney wants her to file for divorce. Mother's so mad she could wring *Baba*'s neck the way she silenced that rooster we had that never shut up. You've got to tell us what to do."

"Proper Chinese women do not divorce," wailed Yukmoy. She dabbed at her swollen red-rimmed eyes. "Her lawyer says if she doesn't, Ho Shee and her sons will take our money, our house, everything!"

"Sssh!" I yanked Yukmoy inside. Kai-Tai followed.

"But why ask me? Mother says I am the renegade. The naughty one. Disobedient."

"Because you're Tat-Tung's wife," Kai-Tai answered. I stared questioningly into her eyes, dark and bottomless like her mother's. She smiled bravely, and quietly added, "And because you know the right way."

Kai-Tai walked Yukmoy to the kitchen. I put on the kettle for tea. My sisters-in-law joined me at the kitchen table as if we always met informally like this in the heart of my home. I set out the tea cups and patted Yukmoy's shaking shoulders.

"Mother's attorney, Frank Thompson, says that Second wife Ho Shee arrives in two days, on December seventh, and will try to enter as *Baba*'s legal wife," Kai-Tai began. "You know she had no intention of returning when she left eleven years ago so she has no reentry permit. Immigration will detain her. By law, she should be deported. Thompson says if Mother serves *Baba* with these divorce papers, *Baba* may drop his plan to incorporate. If he insists on trying to get rid of her, with a divorce she can claim her own property: half of what she bought with *Baba* plus her share of the business. And since he's so rich, enough money to take care of her and my two sisters still at home. You know he has that London attorney, Lightfoot."

"Is this the only way for her to keep her house and lands?" I asked.

Kai-Tai nodded. "Four months ago, *Baba* started telling everyone that 'his wife' Ho Shee was returning from China. He even went to Immigration Inspector-in-Chief Halsey. Mother's attorney discredited *Baba*'s lies by contacting Prince Kuhio in Washington D.C. Prince Kuhio contacted the Secretary of Labor. Because of that, Inspector Halsey has to inspect the Immigration records of our entire family. Prince Kuhio sent a telegram to Halsey stating that he has personally known *Baba* and Mother as husband and wife since 1883."

I heard that The Honorable J. Kuhio Kalaniana'ole delighted Washington with his convivial manner and regal bearing. Despite all the evils that progress brought to the islands, he believed sugar brought wealth to Hawai'i. He enjoyed, as heir to the throne, a powerful following in the Islands. During the days of the Republic, Queen Lili'uokalani sent him to Washington with her attorney to lobby for her interests in Congress when she was imprisoned in her home, Washington Place. The popular Prince Kuhio persuaded many former chiefs and Hawaiian leaders to run for office to gain political clout and empowerment for the Hawaiians. It was not enough to stop the Americans.

"Phoenix, Mother would like you to read the divorce papers the attorney drew up," Yukmoy pleaded. Her words oozed like dripping sap. "She wants your opinion. You're so smart when it comes to understanding words." She filled my tea cup.

Kai-Tai handed me the papers and explained that this long complaint detailed her parents' history from their marriage in Kohala, bankruptcy, hardships in Honolulu, and her father's scandalous sexual liaisons. It said that her father had forced Dai-Kam to feed and clothe his many wives and the children they bore him. He had forced her to visit China, then falsely and maliciously lied that she was not his wife, causing her mental suffering. She believed her life was in danger. The divorce complaint detailed the numerous business interests and lands they owned, and requested a divorce and an upfront settlement to protect her assets.

My hands shook when I handed the papers back. I grabbed a dish towel and wiped my tears. Ah Leong had boasted to all his cronies that he was going to get rid of his First wife. We all knew this divorce was not right. Second wife Ho Shee didn't deserve the lands and business, the legacy that Dai-Kam had worked to build.

Every day I soothed my husband's drawn face, his wrenching sorrow. His entire being was intertwined into each deal, sale, and investment L. Ah Leong touched. They drained him of his life, his energy, his *ch'i*.

I stared in Kai-Tai's eyes and said, "Tell her to sign it."

Chapter Twenty-One

The Board of Inquiry: December 7, 1921

Second wife Ho Shee, in a coarse black tunic and trousers, her hair pulled back in a severe bun, shuffled to her seat before Immigration inspectors Edwin Farmer, Louis Land, and Martha Maier. Chinese interpreter Hee Sou Hoy swore her in. She kept her eyes on her fingers which she pressed and twisted into little fists while she listened to Hee Sou Hoy interpret the Inspectors' questions. When asked, she said she wished no friends or relatives present. Her husband would get witnesses to establish her right to admission to the United States on this day, December 7, 1921.

She presented three documents: an affidavit sworn by herself before the American Consul at Hong Kong that she was the lawful wife of Lau Ah Leong, a marriage certificate stating that she and Ah Leong were married on May 24, 1891, and a new certificate from the Board of Health showing the record of the marriage signed by the Registrar General on August 5, 1921. Yes, she came to Hawai'i in 1891 when she was eighteen and returned to China in 1910 with three sons and two daughters when she was thirty-five. No, she did not have a permit to return to Hawai'i. The forty-six-year-old woman now wished entry as the wife of L. Ah Leong, merchant.

"Do you know this woman?" asked Inspector Farmer. He held up First wife Dai-Kam's photograph.

"No," she said. She dug her fingers into her palm to quell her trembling. For eleven years, Ah Leong's estate *Ming Yang Tong* had been Ho

Shee's domain. No one to serve except Ah Leong. Why did they ask about his First wife, the one whose shadow she crouched under for twenty-five years. Didn't Ah Leong tell them she, Ho Shee, was his wife now?

Farmer said, "This woman was married to your husband by Chinese custom in Hawai'i before he was married to you. Dai-Kam has been recognized as the First wife of Lau Ah Leong on various occasions in this office. The last time she returned from China on January 7, 1910, she was admitted as the lawful wife of Lau Ah Leong."

Ho Shee hung her head. "My husband said that he had arranged it with Immigration, that you would admit me as his wife." She thought back to his letter. He said that he looked forward to her return.

Inspector Farmer named each of Dai-Kam's children. She said she did not know them. The inspector tapped his pencil on the wooden desk and conferred with fellow inspectors Louis Land and Martha Maier. Maier argued that if Ho Shee did not request a permit to return to Hawai'i when she sailed to China in 1910, why did she want to be admitted now as the wife of L. Ah Leong, merchant? And why had the marriage certificate in the woman's possession been obtained only four months ago? If this woman was the same Ho Shee who lived in Hawai'i for twenty years, bearing nine children prior to going to China, why couldn't she identify her husband's family?

Farmer picked up his carbon copy of the transcript and turned back to Ho Shee. "On November 26, 1906, L. Ah Leong testified that he had three wives. Dai-Kam and Ho Shee were in Hawai'i. He named each of his children by his three wives. How could you not know about the other wives and all their children?"

"When I was married to Ah Leong I was eighteen years old and lived in a different place, far distant away."

"How do you know they lived far distant away?"

"I made my husband live far away. He went home at night."

"Is it not a fact that your husband has a wife in China?"

"I don't know. I lived in Hong Kong when I was in China," she shrugged. She said she knew her husband's store was on Queen Street near a Hawaiian church. She didn't know if that was in Kaka'ako or how far it was from where she lived. When Farmer repeated the question, she cowered and admitted it wasn't far.

Farmer threw his chair back and stood up. "You understand that you are now under oath testifying before this Board of Special Inquiry and that anything which you say which is not the truth pertaining to a material matter is perjury. You can be prosecuted and punished by fine or imprisonment."

Upon the request of Prince Kuhio, Inspector-in-Charge Richard L. Halsey had called this special board of inquiry to hear Ho Shee's application. Halsey told Farmer that the U.S. Attorney and the Supreme Court were interested in this case because it tested Federal laws against Territorial laws. Prince Kuhio had personally requested that the Department of Labor straighten out Ah Leong's family history, a history already common knowledge to the local people. This should have been a simple matter to resolve.

Farmer leaned forward, his knuckles pressed white and angry on the table stacked with the Lau Immigration files. He shook his head, capped his pen, and closed his files. "After you have said so many things contrary to evidence, things which we have every reason to believe are false, how can we believe you?" He dismissed her and called in her son.

Lau Chong entered the room and sat down on the hard wooden chair still warm from the heat of his mother. He wore a rumpled white shirt and too-tight trousers. The room was warm with the nervous smells of the interviewers and interviewees.

The Chinese interpreter, Hee Sou Hoy, instructed the boy to answer the questions of the woman and two men who were Immigration Inspectors. He would tell Lau Chong what the Inspectors asked and translate his answers into English. He placed the boy's hand on a black leather book and told him to swear to tell the truth, the whole truth, and nothing but the truth. Then Hee Sou Hoy placed his chair to the side of the Inspectors so he could see everyone clearly.

Lau Chong testified that he was twelve years old, born in Hawai'i, and had gone to China with his mother when he was two. "Yes, I lived in Kew Boy Village the whole time, except for a ten-day visit to Hong Kong. My mother, Auntie Ho Shee, says my father has three wives. My father often speaks of our Mother, Dai-Kam, although three of my brothers and I are really Auntie Ho Shee's sons." He named his nine brothers and explained that in the Chinese style, they all called First wife Dai-Kam "Mother," and his father's other wives, "Auntie."

☜☞

L. Ah Leong waved aside the Chinese translator when he entered the interview room and greeted each inspector by name. Yes, he testified, he was the same L. Ah Leong who had appeared before Immigration so many times before not only for himself, but as witness for each member of his family. "No, Dai-Kam is not my wife. She works for me," he corrected Farmer.

Farmer looked through the files before him and pulled out three tissue-thin sheets. He held them out. "When Dai-Kam arrived on the SS *Siberia* on January 6, 1910, you testified under oath that she was your lawful wife."

Ah Leong's jaw stiffened.

Farmer cocked his head and shook the papers in his hand. "You were asked, 'Well, which is your lawful wife?' and your answer was 'Fung Dai-Kam.' Here is your testimony."

Ah Leong dismissed it with a shrug. "Maybe I made a mistake in answering."

"You testified fully in that case. I will ask the interpreter to read everything you said at that time."

Hee Sou Hoy picked up the typed transcript. He adjusted his spectacles and blinked rapidly before he began. His voice wavered as he read Ah Leong's full testimony from January 7, 1910 in both English and Chinese.

Farmer leaned across his desk towards Ah Leong. "You must admit there could be no mistake. You came to this office for the express purpose of testifying on behalf of Fung Dai-Kam and securing her admission at this port as your lawful wife."

"No. I call her my wife in Chinese, but she isn't my wife in English."

"How can one thing be the truth in Chinese and a lie in English? You know that she could not be admitted at this port unless she was considered your lawful wife. You said she was. We do not care what language you use when you speak the truth," warned Farmer.

"I don't understand," Ah Leong shrugged.

Farmer jumped to his feet. "Mr. Lau, we are not going to argue with you. We are not going to listen to such foolish talk that you did not understand your own plain words and the purpose for which you actually came here. How could you live with Dai-Kam all these years, have a great number of children by her, and say she was not your wife?"

"She didn't want to marry me. She only wanted my money, so afterwards I married Ho Shee."

"You lived here in Hawai'i with two different women and had children by both of them at the same time?"

Ah Leong threw back his shoulders and exclaimed, "Yes. And yes, both women lived together with me in the same house at Punchbowl and Queen Streets for over ten years."

⁂

Fung Dai-Kam, identified as the wife of naturalized citizen Lau Ah Leong, appeared before Immigration's Board of Special Inquiry in a dark blue cotton *cheong-sam* which showed off her jade earrings, necklaces, and bracelets.

"I," she affirmed in a low voice, "am his lawful wife." She explained that she had married him thirty-eight years ago, when King Kalakaua was on the throne and Chinese were freely welcomed in Hawai'i. She and her sister had arrived with an uncle who had debts to claim in Hawai'i. Ah Leong's friend had met them at the steamer and picked her out to be Ah Leong's wife. They were married in Kohala according to Chinese custom. She was now fifty-five.

"Mrs. Lau, the laws at that time required a marriage license from an agent in Hawai'i. Do you know whether your husband secured such a license?" asked Farmer.

"I didn't know what a license was. You see, I was young, only seventeen when I came. I gave the Chinese marriage certificate that my mother gave me to my uncle who, in turn, gave it to Ah Leong. My husband had papers in his hand and there were many guests present at our wedding. My uncle asked Ah Leong if everything was settled up, and he answered, 'Yes.'"

Farmer showed her Ho Shee's marriage license.

Dai-Kam shook her head apologetically. "Maybe they were married secretly. I had four children, two sons and two daughters, before Ho Shee came to Hawai'i as my servant." She described how shocked she was when she discovered Ho Shee pregnant ten months after her arrival in Hawai'i. She scolded her husband and intended to get rid of the girl, but he pleaded and asked for her pardon. He took three more servants as wives: Zane Shee died twenty years ago, Chung Shee died ten years ago, and Wong Shee still lived in China. She didn't know if she could identify Ho Shee. It had been ten years.

Hee Sou Hoy slipped out and returned.

"That's her!" Dai-Kam jumped up and pointed to the pear-shaped woman wiggling out of Hee Sou Hoy's grasp. "I employed that woman as a servant in my house. She bore my husband's children."

Ho Shee averted her face and dashed for the door.

Farmer's eyes snapped. "Ho Shee, do you know this woman?" he demanded.

The second wife struggled out of Hee Sou Hoy's vise-like grasp and fell to the floor, twisting to get away. "This was not supposed to happen," she whimpered, Ah Leong had promised.

"You must look at her," the Inspector insisted. He motioned the translator to lift her face.

"Come, madam, you must look. Do you know her?" shouted Hee Sou Hoy. He grabbed her with both arms and twisted her face towards

Dai-Kam. "Have you seen her before? Is she Fung Dai-Kam, your husband's first wife?"

"No. No. No. I do not know." Ho Shee squeezed her eyes tight.

Dai-Kam glared down at her rival. She lifted her chin triumphantly.

The Inspectors hauled Ho Shee out of the room.

Chapter Twenty-Two

The Two Month Battle: December 1921–February 1922

"Tat-Tung!" Ah Leong strode up Circle Lane and bounded up our front steps. He knocked crisply on the door. "I'll let myself in." The unlatched screen door banged behind him. Wham! By the time my husband got up from his reading chair and I ran into the parlor from the kitchen, he was already settled in his chair next to his son.

"Good evening, Phoenix," my father-in-law waved. "Another busy day?" he asked my husband, not expecting an answer. His visits were now part of our evening routine.

Ever since his parents started to fight over the incorporation of L. Ah Leong, Limited, my husband had shortened his work days. By late afternoon, I'd hear the slam of the taxi's door. Tat-Tung would head straight for the kitchen, roll up his sleeves, and wash his hands. Scents known only to the finest chefs in Hong Kong and Canton wafted from his touch. He focused on the rhythmic chopping and perfect sizzle of each ingredient; all the better to forget the accusing eyes of his half-brothers, his customers' probing questions, and the oppressive walls of the L. Ah Leong store, the well from which his family's greed bubbled over.

And every night, his father sought his opinion about the painful issues that his son came home to avoid.

My husband leaned back and lit a cigarette. The smoke curled upwards as if taking his prayers to Heaven. These days, his father seemed to spend most of his time at his attorney's, at Immigration, or with his cronies dissecting his case.

Ah Leong unwrapped a cigar and rolled it between his fingers. "Your mother's attorney Thompson sent a letter to the Secretary of Labor in Washington D.C. testifying that my attorney and I separately approached Thompson to get 'my wife' Fung Dai-Kam Ah Leong to sign the incorporation papers for L. Ah Leong, Limited."

His son cocked his head and narrowed his eyes. "You tried to bribe her attorney?"

"I tried to talk sense," Ah Leong puffed. "So today, that hard-headed Immigration Inspector Farmer interrogated me about the two times I was arrested. He says pleading guilty means Dai-Kam is my real wife. Humph!"

❧❧

Fung Dai-Kam huffed into attorney Thompson's sedate office, her hard soles clicking angrily on the mahogany floor. Behind her, Kai-Tai and Yukmoy hurried to keep up. They continued the complaining and bickering begun when they left home.

"Mother, tell your attorney to move faster. Tell him you want this impostor wife sent back to China immediately. Ah Chung says *Baba* has already kicked out the tenants in his Palama Street house and boasted that he's moving in with his wife," whispered Yukmoy twisting her jade bracelets.

"Quiet. Thompson knows what he's doing," shushed Kai-Tai.

"How do you know? Mother's already testified and told them the truth. Ho Shee is still here," Yukmoy whined.

Dai-Kam trembled. Over the years, she had observed how the unspoken hierarchy worked: the whites over the Chinese; men first, women last. She depended on this white attorney with the influential contacts to work his magic. It was all a mystery to her how justice was settled in Hawai'i. After all, she was Chinese...and a woman. If a white Immigration officer weighed her word against her husband's, who would win? Would it be her husband, the famous merchant L. Ah Leong with his large circle of powerful acquaintants and chummy Chinese friends? Would they confirm it was up to Ah Leong whether or not she was his wife?

Thompson agreed with Kai-Tai. "Your daughters are right, Mrs. Lau. Immigration has not yet decided on the status of the woman claiming to be Ho Shee."

"Why not? Why not?" Dai-Kam cried. What more could she do? She had told the truth and still she would lose?

Kai-Tai asked Thompson to explain everything he had done so her mother could better understand and be comforted by his actions.

Thompson's deep voice soothed her frown into a smile. Queen Lili'uokalani and Princess Kawananakoa had also been inquisitive clients and insisted on knowing the details of his actions on their behalf. He understood the nature of the Chinese men he dealt with; they vastly underestimated their women. He explained that he had submitted in triplicate to Immigration and the courts certified copies of all divorce papers, motions, deeds naming Fung Dai-Kam as 'wife,' indictments against L. Ah Leong for unlawful cohabitation with Ho Shee, and the indictment against Ah Leong for bigamy.

☞☞

A few weeks later, Fourth son Ah Chung drove up Circle Lane at midday. His mother sat rigidly in the passenger seat, head high, surveying the homes of my neighbors. Ah Chung stopped at our front steps. Dai-Kam got out and motioned him off with a shoo of her fingers. I waved her up to the front porch where I rocked, the only motion that seemed to keep this baby I was carrying from pounding and kicking its way out of my belly.

"Phoenix, get me tea. Tell Tat-Tung I'm here. I'll sit in the parlor where it's cool," she beamed, resplendent in a deep purple *cheong-sam*. She claimed the best sofa.

"Tat-Tung! There you are! Come, what have you been doing this afternoon? Did you straighten out the charge accounts at the store? That's where your father loses money. Sit here." She patted the sofa next to her. "You should get more sleep. Your eyes are sagging."

My husband ignored her and sat on his favorite chair to the left of the window. I served them both, then sat in the spot Dai-Kam had patted down for my husband.

She brought him wonderful news. Immigration Inspector Martha Maier had been her champion, she exclaimed, clapping her hands to her ample bosom. Dai-Kam was declared Ah Leong's legal wife. Ho Shee would be deported on the next boat which left in a month. Mother had won.

Chapter Twenty-Three

Triumph and Appeal: August 1922

My labor pains began after Tat-Tung left for work and the children were in school. I gathered the sheets, boiled the water and knife, and waited. How I relished the afternoon trade winds, thick with cool and sweet rain that washed away the pain of childbirth. I awoke to the touch of my husband's fingers upon my face, his eyes caressing my brow.

"Phoenix, Phoenix," he whispered.

I closed my eyes and dreamt once again of the sun sparkling on his father's estate in China, *Ming Yang Tong*, its atrium filled with the laughter of all our children. I saw my sons bent diligently over scrolls unrolled across the scholar desks in Ah Leong's libraries. Servants steamed trays and trays of *dim sum* in the gigantic woks.

I opened one eye. Aaah, the smells were real. As tired as I was, I could not resist the delectable scents Tat-Tung conjured to lure me to the kitchen. Everything he cooked that night–dark, juicy, and exotically tantalizing–was to build my health and produce overflowing quantities of milk.

When Ah Leong came to our house later that night, I stepped from our bedroom wrapped in a cotton robe. I was weak, but with our growing family I had no time to rest. I had pulled my hair back and secured it in a loose bun with a long comb. Tat-Tung waited in his customary chair, head tilted, watching his father quizzically.

"What did you have?" Ah Leong asked.

I hung my head. "Only a girl, *Baba*." I shrugged apologetically.

Everyone knew Ah Leong didn't like babies. And a baby girl? A waste of rice to him.

"Let me see," he enthused. He walked past me to our bedroom and drew aside the mosquito net that covered her basket. He reached down and caressed her cheek. "Fat cheeks," he cooed. He straightened and turned to me. "I'll send you a couple chickens. You'll have plenty milk when Tat-Tung makes his wine chicken. I hear he uses a whole bottle in each pot."

"Thank you," I gasped. Two chickens was considered a generous gift for the birth of a son. What miracle had I heard? I stared at the two forms in the dim light: my daughter sighed in her sleep while her grandfather tried to nudge her awake. Tat-Tung beamed, the glow of the amber sconces reflecting his contented smile.

I followed Ah Leong back to his chair and set his whiskey on the doily-covered table between the two.

"Things look bad," he grunted to his son. "Immigration is sending Ho Shee to China on the first boat."

My husband nodded. He had his expressionless face on now, the mask he used to hide his pain and sorrow. "When's that?"

"End of this month." Ah Leong filled his whiskey glass and pulled out the work he had brought for his son. "I told my attorney to keep fighting. I will win!"

I turned and walked out before I had to hear any more.

The next day, Ah Chung delivered a bamboo cage with four fat chickens. Four chickens! He looked at me with raised eyebrows and a suspicious stare. "*Baba* says this is for you, Phoenix. For you and your baby girl!"

⚘⚘

Ah Leong shouldered his way to his attorney's office on Merchant Street. He ignored the police directing traffic and motioned motorcars crossing his path to stop.

When he arrived at Lightfoot's office, he paced the waiting room. His masters used to chide his impatience when he was younger. He had bowed humbly, then. He had learned that the Confucian "middle way" would never be his strong point. His success was due to his proclivity for action and aggressive assertion.

Lightfoot opened his door and greeted the merchant. "You know Harry Irwin, don't you?"A thick gentleman in a rumpled tropical suit had just thrown back the shutters so the sun blazed across Lightfoot's desk. His shock of white hair matched his bushy mustache.

"Hawai'i's Attorney General," exclaimed Ah Leong, extending his hand.

Lightfoot motioned both to be seated in the leather chairs and couch near the open window. "Mr. Lau, when you first came to my office you needed your wife, Fung Dai-Kam, to sign your business's incorporation papers. Since she would not, you sought to establish Ho Shee as your legal wife."

Ah Leong nodded.

Lightfoot tapped his fingers tip to tip in front of him as if in prayer and stated their obstacles. First, Fung Dai-Kam's name was on all the property deeds as his wife. Next, that Ah Leong and Dai-Kam were husband and wife was common knowledge in the Islands. Third, Ah Leong had married her before he married Ho Shee. And fourth, on a visit Ah Leong made to Dai-Kam's attorney's office, he repeatedly referred to Dai-Kam as "my wife."

Unfortunately for them, Dai-Kam had retained Frank Thompson, one of the most powerful attorneys in the Islands who had used his connections in Washington to support her claim that she was L. Ah Leong's legal wife.

Ah Leong locked his gaze on Lightfoot and narrowed his eyes. "In China, if one has 'face,' one has power. If one has money, one can change the direction of the river."

"Men of power never concede defeat," Lightfoot responded in a low voice. He smiled at Ah Leong's acknowledging nod.

He motioned to Irwin. "The Attorney General has a private practice. His name will lend more weight if we appeal the case since the courts give more credence to one of their own. We will need his clout, especially when William Carden takes office as District Attorney."

Ah Leong knew about this local boy, Carden. The press loved this "home grown" son from Honolulu who had returned after graduating from the University of California at Berkeley and receiving his law degree from Harvard. The young Republican had just won the six-year term as the first elected U.S. District Attorney for Hawai'i, unseating the Democratic political appointee whose legal opinion Lightfoot and Ah Leong had originally used to sway Immigration.

Attorney General Irwin's reputation and connections within the Territorial government were vast and he knew Judge Poindexter of the District Court. The Judge was a religious man and offended by what he considered the loose moral conduct of the Hawaiians and Chinese, regardless of their cultural justifications, a "law and order" judge who believed that the Territory should be under the jurisdiction of federal laws. A newcomer to the Islands, he felt it was the role of the ruling white class to maintain control and set the example for the "Asiatics" and the "natives." The brief drafted by Lightfoot and Attorney General Irwin would appeal to Poindexter's Christian conscience and narrow interpretation of the law.

Their strategy worked. A month later, Lightfoot and Irwin drove up to Ah Leong's store and leaned on the horn so long that everyone on King Street ran out to the street.

Ah Leong whooped when saw his attorneys' faces. He ran out to shake hands and pound shoulders.

As planned, Judge Poindexter had agreed with Ah Leong's attorney's opinion. He ruled that the Secretary of Labor used an erroneous principle of law in holding common law marriages valid in Hawai'i. He reversed Immigration's decision.

Ho Shee was now L. Ah Leong's lawful wife.

☜☞

Dai-Kam had followed me around the kitchen all afternoon waiting for her son to come home. She leaned over my shoulder, tea cup poised in her left hand. With her right finger, she criticized the way I peeled, chopped, sliced, steamed, and roasted.

I ignored her. This was my kitchen. My passion for cooking came from her son, probably because he was always hungry when he was young. Whenever Tat-Tung had a particularly delicious dish, no matter whether it was in a elegant restaurant in Hong Kong, a family stall in Shanghai, or the estate of one of his peers, he'd walk into the kitchen and pay the chef to teach him how it was prepared. He taught me the secrets he had learned, the recipes that made the air explode in scents so enticing one's mouth would water with the sheer thought of it.

At last, his taxi arrived.

His mother flung open the kitchen door. She stuck her head out and waved, "I'm here."

He stopped, startled by the sound of her voice.

Normally, my husband paused to gaze up and down Circle Lane before he hurried up the five steps to the front door. Those few seconds cleared his mind of the L. Ah Leong Store and focused his attention so when he walked through the front door, his heart was home.

But tonight, he walked briskly up the side path to the kitchen door.

I met his eyes and shrugged with a tilt of my head. I didn't need to remind him that in three hours his father would walk through our front door for his nightly visit. The table was laid with six dishes: succulent Chinese mushrooms over beds of vegetables, a whole chicken simmered in soy sauce, sweet red snapper, and more. I wanted to show Dai-Kam that I fed her son better than she ever did.

"You are late," she scolded when he had washed and sat down to eat. "How's business?"

"Very busy." A festive air permeated the store as friends clamored to hear the news of Ah Leong's victory firsthand. Ah Wang was happy for his father and mother. The store clerks were confused. What were they supposed to do when Dai-Kam came in? What to do about her groceries? Tat-Tung had stormed out the store without a word.

"What's wrong with your eyes?" The bags under his eyes had grown darker, sadder.

"I'm tired, Mother."

After Ah Leong left our house, usually at midnight, Tat-Tung would linger on the front porch and stare at the stars. One night I joined him. I wondered what he saw that so intrigued him.

"Look, Phoenix. Night after night, year after year, the stars twinkle in the sky, as they always have and always will. No matter how *Baba*'s case is resolved, no matter what happens to the L. Ah Leong Store, the heavens will always be there. We could all turn to dust. We're not that important." If it rained, he stuck his hand out to feel its power. Once he stuck his head out in a torrential rainstorm and laughed at how completely it drenched him. How petty everything else seemed compared to the power of nature and the infinite night.

When I returned after putting the babies down, Mother had gone from asking him about the business of the store to describing her latest meeting with her attorney. Immigration had asked the new District Attorney Carden to appeal Judge Poindexter's decision. "This time, we will win," she pronounced, eyes snapping. She lifted her chin triumphantly, then added, "Before I go, I want you to read me a letter." My mother-in-law opened her purse and handed my husband a much-creased envelope, still sealed. "The postman gave this to me yesterday. I didn't show it to anyone. Who would write me?"

Her son raised his eyebrows. His mother could not read or write. Who, indeed? He gasped when he saw her elegantly written address, the rounded swirls and full curves characteristic of Palmer penmanship that all St. Louis College boys practiced for an hour every morning. He inspected the stamped postal mark.

"Mailed from San Francisco. Know anyone there?"

She shook her head. I walked quickly to my husband's side and leaned over his shoulder. He slit open the envelope and pulled out a single sheet of paper. He looked at his mother, took a deep breath, and read.

I heard that *Baba* is trying to get rid of you.

Good riddance. I hope you lose.

(Signed) Ah Yin

Dai-Kam jumped up and screamed as if a ghost had grabbed her by the neck.

Tat-Tung traced his fingers over the hand of his eldest brother, lost now for over twenty years. Ah Yin, his protector. Ah Yin had taught him how to avoid Mother's tempestuous outbursts and stinging slaps, to study hard when their stomachs twisted with hunger. Ah Yin said someday they would run *Baba*'s store and never be denied the sweets that Mother lavished on their younger brothers, half-brothers, and sisters. But when he was nineteen, Ah Yin abandoned his wife and two daughters after another bitter fight with Mother. Some say he caught a steamer to Chile, others thought he sought his fortune in California. No one knew for sure.

"Ah Yin," Tat-Tung whispered, unable to stop his tears.

PART V

Chapter Twenty-Four
A Family Divided: August 1924

Before the sun set in a blaze of red and orange, my husband headed out of his father's store. His black leather shoes shone like mirrors as they clicked on the wooden sidewalk. He turned off Beretania Street and paused, then walked slowly up Circle Lane, dappled in sunlight piercing its canopy of Royal Poinciana trees. The tense furrows melted from his forehead when he inhaled the scents of dinner, each as distinctive as our neighbors' homes—the Chinese with eye-popping red walkways and eaves, the Hawaiians with mangoes for eating and overflowing flowers for leis, and the miniature worlds created by twisted bonsai in the rock gardens of the Japanese. Despite their differences, this neighborhood of diverse families shared their food, music, joys, and stories.

And his father's family? They fought, bickered, connived, and schemed. His father had successfully torn apart and divided the dynasty he had spent a lifetime creating. He squashed and humbled what displeased him, leaving in his wake the remains of a family splintered with lies and deceit, open to the scrutiny of a judgmental community. Ah Leong called it justice.

In the two years that passed, the lines had been drawn through the family and courts. No doubt, powerful underhanded agreements had been made. Three thousand miles away, the Ninth Circuit Court of Appeals in San Francisco ruled that Ho Shee was Ah Leong's lawful wife, even though his marriage to Dai-Kam had been celebrated and well known from the days of the Hawaiian monarchy. Immigration and Hawai'i's

District Attorney requested an appeal to the Supreme Court. But Attorney General Irwin, Ah Leong's attorney, advised Washington against it.

Immigration was forced to release Ho Shee.

"My husband," Ho Shee repeated for emphasis, "Why is Tat-Tung still here? How do you know he isn't stealing all our money while he's doing the books? My eldest son Ah Wang deserves to be First son now." Ah Leong waved her off and told her to leave the business alone. This infuriated Ho Shee, the personification of his victory. She walked through the store every day to acknowledge her good fortune and needle Dai-Kam's sons, waving her feather duster and stirring up clouds of dust from the boxes, bins, and cans.

Today, she prowled upstairs and rifled through the receipts. She didn't understand these markings. She had never even learned to speak English. Before she left she stuck her finger in Tat-Tung's face and said, "Make sure you check the books twice. I don't want you cheating me." Then she ambled down to Ah Wang and protested, "Watch your half-brother. Make sure he isn't taking our money."

Ah Wang waved his hands frantically. "Hush, hush," he gasped.

But Tat-Tung had already thrown back his chair and stalked home.

☙❧

"Mrs. Lau, how's your quilt coming along?" My neighbor Loretta Akana held her mu'umu'u up to her knees to clear the front steps and glided next to me on the front porch. Fresh flowers from her garden, plaited artfully in the old style called *haku*, were pinned in her thick chestnut hair. Today, white waxy trumpets of stephanotis, sending out a fragrance similar to hyacinths, framed the right side of her generous face. She settled her voluptuous body on the top stair with a sigh and wave of her lauhala fan. She inspected my stitching pattern of undulating waves and nodded her approval. After threading numerous needles, a tedious task that was easier when eyes were still fresh and sharp, she paced her quick stitches with mine.

Our Hawaiian-Chinese neighbors, Danny and Loretta Akana, barely scraped by on Danny's salary as a police officer. Despite the hardship, they presented a cheery optimism. Loretta's favorite saying was, "If you no can say something nice, no say 'em." She made everyone laugh and taught me about the easy-going gentleness of the Hawaiian way of life. Her lively brown eyes and hands animated her stories while we watched our children play in the yard below.

Whenever I needed a muscleman to lift the iron wok outside or to build an extra shelf in my house, I called Danny. His shoulders were bulky from paddling his eighty-pound hardwood surfboard off Queen's. Like the men in his family who came from Waimanalo, he was as creative with a hammer as he was magical with a ukulele.

This afternoon, I sat in the koa rocker and watched my little ones and their friends play in the shade of the flowering mango tree. Spikes of white blossoms burst between the reddening leaves. A good season. I looked forward to a month of heavy fruit. The squeals of playing children filled the neighborhood with voices–a mixture of Chinese, Japanese, Hawaiian, Portuguese, and English. They had learned to give and take, to look beyond the culture and many languages of their playmates to the honesty and fairness of the soul inside. What a contrast to our judicial courts, where people who spoke the same language fought like alley cats killing for the same piece of scrap.

These days, I looked forward to Loretta's Hawaiian quilt lessons. She stitched as quickly as she passed the neighborhood news: tirelessly, for hours on end. Loretta taught me how to trace the shadows of flowers and leaves to create my own unique patterns. Each design expressed the personal creativity of the quilter with either an intimate experience or a secret inspiration. After I had drawn my design, we laid out the pattern on folded layers of colored muslin and cut it out with the elongated German shears that Tat-Tung had honed razor-sharp on his wet stone. We unfolded the cut muslin like a paper snowflake and centered the design on a backing of contrasting cotton. The design, layers of cotton batting, and a backing were all basted together. Only then could I quilt my design with the tiny stitches that swirled and eddied like the churning surf and tumultuous sea.

Each Hawaiian quilt was a work of art and a family heirloom. When the quilt was finished, the designer destroyed her pattern. It was *kapu*, forbidden, to "borrow" another's design.

"Quilting helps me forget my family problems," I admitted to Loretta.

"I understand. Everyone's talking about your father-in-law. The *haoles* downtown say, 'Only L. Ah Leong can make Washington stop the District Attorney from appealing to the Supreme Court.' Maybe Judge Poindexter got paid-off, my husband says. You know what else?" She lowered her voice. "Ah Leong, his attorneys, and the judge could all have been in cahoots because they're all Democrats. You know the politics in this island. Everyone takes care of their own side. Money can fix the case. Especially L. Ah Leong. His name is big." Her face and eyes told the story along with her words, her melodious voice dipping and rising in the local Pidgin English. "My Danny says it wasn't right for the Attorney General to be Ah Leong's lawyer. What did he say? 'Conflict of interest' and 'conflict of laws?'"

"I thought Mother had the best attorney," I ruminated sadly.

She did, Loretta answered. "These Islands, so much politics and pay-offs. My husband says people *suspect*." Loretta dragged that word out with a meaningful nod and an arched look in her eye.

I sighed that somehow, the mah-jongg tiles of life had been stacked against us.

Loretta continued, "And when it comes time for the decision, what happens? Here comes a Chinese merchant willing to pay off these big shot Democrats. One with powerful face and plenty money. Men have the power. Some more than others. No fair for your mother-in-law."

Dai-Kam had been shattered with the decision even though she had been able to keep one-fourth of all the lands she and Ah Leong owned. Her friends came to offer their sympathy but most of the time, she brooded alone. Watching the world through the lace-covered windows of her darkened parlor, she stared out at the Hawai'i she thought she knew, a firm look about her jaw, a stern edge hiding hurt and betrayal. Still critical and judgmental, there was a vulnerability about her sadness.

Over and over, she repeated her stories about her early days in Hawai'i: how she and Ah Leong worked side by side to build their business, how it was a goal they shared, and how their friends and neighbors helped them when they were a struggling young family with a tiny storefront in Kaka'ako. And then *she* came, the second of Ah Leong's many wives. She rued how naive she had been. But then, everyone believed him, his cajoling words, his power. "I thought America was better than China. My children told me we have 'equal rights,'" I told Loretta.

She threw her head back, her shoulders shaking with laughter. "No. Some more equal. Look at us Hawaiians. You think we're equal with the *haoles*? Long ago, the businessmen and U. S. Marines took 'Iolani Palace from our beloved Queen. The Americans chose who they wanted to rule. Now American laws overrule our Hawaiian laws.

"Mrs. Lau, no worry. You have a good husband and four healthy *keikis* with one more on the way. I tell Danny we better marry American style. He said with six kids and us just making it, how we going to afford a marriage license? Plus, if no more extra money, what's to fight over? We laughed so hard we couldn't see for the tears." Loretta stretched her bare feet and readjusted her ample shoulders, stitching faster now that her mouth was at rest.

Dr. Chang, a medical doctor from Queen's Hospital, strolled towards us, headed home. He was a tall fidgety Chinese gentleman in white starched collar and tie. His long, bony fingers tapped the side of his head when he was thinking. He knew we had little money so he dressed the children's scrapes for free, and occasionally he asked Tat-Tung's advice on herbal remedies for particularly resistant ailments. Dr. Chang bought a radio when Hawai'i's first commercial radio station began broadcasting in 1922. For two years, we listened to his warbley accompaniment to the Saturday Chinese opera broadcasts.

Dr. Chang tipped his gray felt hat and paused at the bottom of the stairs to observe our progress. "Greetings, Mrs. Akana, Mrs. Lau. How's our expectant mother?"

"I have no time to be anything but perfectly healthy, Dr. Chang," I answered. "But I'm glad I have only two months more to wait."

I had delivered my own baby last year. I bled until my sheets were so soaked I thought I would run out of blood. I pushed and cried out in the hot afternoon until I felt the release of pressure. Clutching the sharpened knife, I severed the cord myself. When Tat-Tung came home from work to make me the wine chicken to build my blood, the birthing sheets were already soaking in Borax. His new son was sleeping.

"And everyone else in your family? Especially Tat-Tung?" inquired Dr. Chang. All fine, I thanked him. He waved again and continued up the front walk to where his own family lived, in a house like all the simple wooden homes on Circle Lane.

"How *is* your husband?" Loretta asked as she stitched waves of perfect tiny stitches and rethreaded her set of needles. She raised her eyebrows questioningly.

My heart fell. How could I tell her how much pain he kept bottled up inside, even from me? Each parent came to him to vent their anger against the other. For the three years that it took, from the start of their acrimonious fight to the final incredulous judgment, Tat-Tung fielded the family questions and ran the business while Ah Leong was in court or scheming with his lawyers and politician friends. Ah Wang managed the front end of the business, the retail and wholesale customers, so Tat-Tung could concentrate on the finances. Together, the brothers worked as efficiently as they always had.

The troubles Tat-Tung kept to himself erupted in a debilitating illness, eating him up from the inside out. Dark circles hung from his brooding eyes. Anxiety and exhaustion did no good to a body physically weakened by opium. His moody depressions grew as he struggled to maintain the serenity dictated by Confucian beliefs. Dr. Chang visited often to check on him. But Tat-Tung was an old-fashioned gentleman and kept the deepest pains to himself.

Business picked up in a perverse way. Curious locals stopped by the store each time new gossip surfaced. Ah Leong enjoyed his notoriety: the side-long glances from the ladies as they appraised his reputation, and the wise-cracking jokes of his cronies. In the smoky tea houses where they toasted his victory, Ah Leong was their notorious renegade. On the one hand, they congratulated him for exerting his male prerogative and outsmarting Dai-Kam. On the other, they cussed him for making them spend money to get a marriage license at the incessant nagging of their wives; they complained they didn't have his money to buy off the judge if their wives hauled them into court.

Horse carts and automobiles slowed past the store. The Lau sons put up with the townspeople, from those in dusty slacks and bare feet to the elegant in starched collars, who stopped to stare at the infamous L. Ah Leong and his "wife" Ho Shee.

His sons kept their heads to their order books. He had the power and money to influence courts and sway the law to his will. What would he do to them? Morale among Dai-Kam's sons dropped to fearful grumbling.

Tat-Tung burned with shame. His ears smarted with hurtful insinuations. Was he the First son running the Lau business, or the bastard? He wondered if he would inherit his father's business legacy or the humiliation of his mother. Meanwhile, his father expected his son's consistent focus on business. His business. If anything, Ah Leong's dependence increased as his cronies demanded he retell his story over and over again.

So on that night when Ho Shee ordered Tat-Tung to check the books twice, as if he were a common cheat, he stalked off and hailed a taxi home. Too agitated to face his family immediately, Tat-Tung got out on Beretania Street so he could unwind in the serenity of a slow walk up Circle Lane.

Chapter Twenty-Five

Entrapment and Deceit: October 1924–1926

"*Auwe!*" My neighbor Loretta Akana ran down Circle Lane clutching her basket of stripped lauhala leaves. "Did you hear the news? He's dead!"

I pushed up from the koa rocker on the front porch and leaned over the siderails. "Who?" It was October 1924. I was due in a month. My feet had swelled so I went barefoot all the time now. I was too tired to quilt so Loretta had taken to weaving lauhala while we watched the children play.

Loretta plopped on the top steps, a commotion in yellow and green floral print with yellow plumerias cascading through her hair. "You remember that young District Attorney who tried to help your husband's mother stay Mrs. Lau Ah Leong and send the Second wife back to China?"

"District Attorney Carden?"

"Yes, that one. The local boy. Only thirty-six years old. To die so young."

"What happened?"

"Natural causes, the report said." Loretta raised an eyebrow.

How could this be? Such a young man. Tat-Tung said Carden had been Immigration's counsel to deport Ho Shee and, with the authorization of the Attorney General in Washington, pursued the case all the way to the Ninth Circuit Court of Appeals. He would have appealed to the Supreme Court, but Ah Leong's well-chosen attorney convinced Washington to stop him.

"Danny just called from the police station. No one can believe it. Just four months ago the case was decided in San Francisco. Carden was only halfway through his six-year term. So unnatural–like those black clouds up there, unusual for October. You know how Danny listens to his instincts; he'd say the great sky gods are angry. Oh, times are so bad. *Auwe*," Loretta wailed, her face lifted to the sky.

⚛⚛

"No more children," Tat-Tung commanded. "I almost lost you this time. Dr. Chang didn't think you could pull through. I love my children, but they can't replace you." He avoided my eyes. A casual observer might think this Chinese gentleman, in a natty white tropical suit, with his neatly-dressed young wife, was out for a routine evening stroll with their children.

"No chance now," I answered bitterly. "You're leaving. I don't know how I'm going to manage five little ones by myself."

We continued through the gardens surrounding Queen's Hospital. Red-crested cardinals swooped from the canopy of trees overhead to pluck twigs for their nests. Cackling mynah birds argued in their kangaroo courts. Our daughter, Fung-Tai, now a coltish long-legged seven-year-old, pranced at my side. The toddlers held their father's hands. Our youngest, a daughter, slept cradled on my back. I had five babies of my own after eight years of marriage. Edith and Lani brought the total to seven children to care for.

"You'll be fine," he said. "Edith and Lani are old enough to take care of the house. The delivery men at the store will bring you all the groceries you need. If you have any problems, talk to Ah Wang personally. Loretta will keep you company and watch the babies. If the kids get sick, see Dr. Chang if your herbs don't cure them."

Despite his careful arrangements, I resented staying home alone while he sailed to China, even with stepdaughter Edith and adopted daughter Lani to run errands. But it was not my place as his wife to argue.

Even he, a Hawai'i-born Chinese well-known to the Immigration officers, had to personally appear for his background check and interrogation. Not only did he have to detail the dates of his previous trips and the ships he had traveled on, he had to recount the movements of his family including all his mothers and siblings—which to our shame, was common knowledge to the whole island.

When Immigration asked him the reason for his travel, he said he had had a nervous breakdown and his doctors had ordered him to rest. After Immigration refused his father's request to travel for pleasure in 1919, he preferred to lie and avoid their probing questions.

He left for Shanghai on the SS *Siberia Maru* on June 15, 1925.

That first night I lay alone in my bed, I gripped my fists and wept. The first time I came to Hawai'i I had cried every day. I struggled to understand L. Ah Leong's family, so different from my loving family far away in China. Now I cried bitterly because I was a twenty-six-year-old mother, homesick and alone in Hawai'i with a house full of children. I was tired of being a good wife.

I could imagine my thirty-five-year-old husband enjoying the life of a suave playboy in Shanghai, that cosmopolitan city I had read so much about. When the evenings were velvet black, men could frequent the famous international nightclubs in the swanky sections of town. There they lost themselves to the pleasures that other men only dream about in their darkest nights.

I envisioned that as dawn broke gray and cold along the Bund, Tat-Tung watched the devotees of *tai chi* and other martial arts move in synchronous harmony with the rising sun. Some rolled heavy silver balls in their hands to build strength and agility in every muscle of their fingers, or flipped their swords and staffs with disciplined choreographed control. Vendors hawked their wares from the sidewalk and peddlers pierced the air with melodic calls. Baskets of frisky soft-shelled crabs, tanks of turtle and fish, and trays of writhing eels and snakes filled the food markets of the Chinese section of Shanghai. Up and down the river, coolies loaded and unloaded ships, bent with their heads almost to the ground. With a lusty whistle, ships left for distant ports, sometimes with a crew dragged unconscious from sailor dives, to waken as unwilling seafarers.

❧❧

The children heard the L. Ah Leong delivery car chug up Circle Lane before I did. It was September 29th, 1925. By the time I ran down the stairs, Tat-Tung had the children in his arms and L. Ah Leong had flung open the door of the passenger seat.

"I did not have time to write and tell you I was returning so soon," Tat-Tung apologized. "Come, I'll tell you the details." He motioned us to follow him to the parlor.

Ah Leong fussed that he was missing work. And why was his son back so quickly from China? Did he take care of his business? What was so important that had to be discussed right now?

I brought out the tea cups and set out plates of sweet almond cakes. Ah Leong, in his dusty work clothes, took his favorite chair. Tat-Tung pulled me to his side on the sofa. He wore his hair slicked back now. I didn't recognize the cut and stitching in his cuffs, either. Newly tailored monogrammed shirts and the latest hairstyle from Shanghai, that seductive cosmopolitan port, I sniffed. How arrogant of him to sail off for three months, to return suddenly without the sad shadowed eyes and sorrowful droop in his shoulders. I felt dowdy in my handsewn cotton tunic and trousers, even if they were bright blue with black bias trim.

Earnest furrows creased his brow when he faced his father. He chose his words carefully. "*Baba*, your Fifth wife, Wong Shee, requests your permission to leave your estate, *Ming Yang Tong*."

"Who does she think will take care of my lands, my houses?" Ah Leong demanded.

Tat-Tung dismissed his protest. "If the family stays, they die. Bandits have already attacked. That's why I came straight home."

Ah Leong jolted up. "Attacked *Ming Yang Tong*? Impossible! The walls are as thick as mountains."

"*Baba*, you know that the thousands of bandits who swarm down to pillage every village, every travel route in the province, hide out in that huge mountain in Fukien named Wong Soo Sang. Those bandits know the mountainous area so well even Chiang Kai-Shek's army can't rout them."

"That mountain's in the next province!"

"And our house is so big they can see it from Wong Soo Sang, *Baba*."

Ah Leong's face clouded unhappily.

"I left Shanghai for *Ming Yang Tong* estate because Auntie Wong Shee had arranged a marriage for Sixth brother Ah Sang. He was already there with Ah Wang's wife to make the arrangements. After I got off the pole-boat at Cheung Hew I walked five hours to our village. I got to the outskirts about sunset. Auntie Wong Shee spotted me before I reached the bridge into Kew Boy.

"'Tat-Tung, is it you, or a ghost? Where did you come from? From Hawai'i?' she demanded. She started to cry and pull me away.

"'Auntie Wong Shee, what's wrong? Why are you shaking? Are you sick?' I asked. She frightened me, *Baba*. I have never seen her upset before.

"'Don't go to *Ming Yang Tong*,' she cried. 'No one should know you're here.' All the while, she pulled me along the shadows to your first house, the Story of the Southern Breeze."

Under the cover of twilight, they slipped through its massive doors and felt their way into the middle parlor so no one from the street could see the candles they lit. Once they were safely barricaded deep in the heart of the house that she always kept ready for the family's return, she collapsed. Tat-Tung carried her to a carved sofa.

"Tat-Tung, you can't stay! Go back to Hawai'i. Tell your father it's too dangerous here." Her fingers clutched at his coat.

"Tell me what happened, Auntie Wong Shee."

She said that soon after her son Ah Chen left for Hong Kong to study, Ah Leong's Sixth son Ah Sang and Ah Wang's wife and children arrived to arrange Ah Sang's wedding. The growing hordes of bandits were increasing their brazen attacks.

Meanwhile, the Kuomintang generals demanded a special tax to "protect" Ah Leong's homes and lands. They demanded an exorbitant amount based on Ah Leong's reputation and wealth–more money than she had ever seen. Wong Shee was terrified. The women and children lived in fear day and night. During the day, they kept a look-out for the Kuomintang soldiers who pounded on their doors demanding money. At night, they barricaded their doors and windows against the bandits.

Ah Sang was so frightened he abandoned his bride-to-be and fled secretly to Honolulu with Ah Wang's wife and children.

The day Tat-Tung arrived, Wong Shee and Ah Chen's wife arose as usual at 5 A.M. One woman scrubbed out the wok for breakfast and started the fire while the other fetched their cooking water from the natural spring behind the house.

"We had just finished breakfast and were getting ready to go to the fields," Wong Shee wept. "Suddenly, all the dogs barked and growled as if possessed by devils. We knew something was wrong. We peeked through the locked shutters and saw hundreds of bandits circling the house. They must have run all night from their hideout at Wong Soo Sang mountain. They knew the main doors were impenetrable, so they axed the side doors. They came so swiftly we did not have time to escape." The bandits ran up to the second and third stories.

"Most of all, we worried about the baby, Ah Chen's second son," Wong Shee wept. "What if he should cry? We whispered, Hurry! Hurry! Hide! Ah Chen's wife hid behind one of the spare doors stacked against the wall in the pantry where we keep food and the huge banquet cooking pots. She clasped the baby to her breast. We left the door ajar. My lady friend Zhang, who came to help with the harvest, hid in the banquet rice steamer. My eldest grandson and Ah Leong's sister's son, both only five, ran to the small third house on the west side, the one with the library. They scrambled under a bed in the farthest bedroom. I was the last to hide. I jumped in a kitchen cupboard. We heard the bandits running through the corridors of the house.

"'Why is the wok cleaned and filled with fresh water? Where are the people? Ah Leong's sons are supposed to be here for the wedding. They must be hiding somewhere,' they yelled. They smashed the locks on each of the 118 bedrooms. They assumed that we were hiding behind locked doors, not the doors left ajar. Oh, we trembled and prayed they would not find us.

"Meanwhile, we heard the villagers screaming. Two women who had gone to the spring at dawn had seen the bandits pouring from the hills. They sneaked back and warned the others. The lookout sounded the gong from the watchtower.

"The bandits heard the gong and the villagers yelling 'Bandits! Bandits!' They were in such a hurry they did not have enough time to completely search each room. We heard them whistle to retreat. 'Hurry up,' they yelled. They were afraid the soldiers would catch them. They didn't know that the Kuomintang keeps few soldiers in Kew Boy."

Before dawn, so early they could barely see the road, Wong Shee and Tat-Tung slipped out. For three hours, they hiked through the black night, feeling their way along the narrow mountain path to my family's home. Once he was safe, Wong Shee walked all the way back to *Ming Yang Tong* estate without telling anyone, not even her family, that she had seen Ah Leong's First son from Hawai'i. He sailed immediately to Honolulu.

My husband paused, feeling once again the panic and fear that terrorized his Fifth mother. "Auntie Wong Shee warns that the bandits planned to kidnap anyone from Hawai'i who came for the wedding. They knew you would pay dearly to have us released. Eighth brother Ah Chen is studying English in Hong Kong. His mother begs your permission to close up *Ming Yang Tong* and move to Canton, *Baba*. The estate is separated from the village by a river and too vast to fortify securely. No one can escape if it's surrounded."

Ah Leong grumbled. But he granted Wong Shee's request and arranged for her to receive $100 per month through one of his contacts in Hong Kong.

☙☙

My husband returned to China the following April.

This time, while he was gone the children and I joined the Akanas on their weekly jaunts to Waikiki. All my loneliness and frustration melted away after an afternoon of sun-swept beaches. We watched the girls leap in the waves and the boys race the tides. We marveled at how my children tanned golden-brown and their hair reflected the reddish bronze color of their grandmother, Dai-Kam, so they looked more like Akana cousins than the Chinese grandchildren of L. Ah Leong. And in the evening, after dinner on the beach, the Akana and Lau children captured sand crabs by the disappearing sunset, only to release them again when we went home.

The only time I really missed my husband was when the amber sconces reflected the emptiness of his favorite chair. And if a problem arose? I handled it myself, never once asking his brother Ah Wang for help or money. By the time he returned four months later, the children and I were so independent Tat-Tung wondered how long he really had been away.

"You're losing more than you think," my husband warned his father the first night he returned from China. The two men picked at the remains of dinner while I shooed the children to their rooms. I had become a clever cook, able to turn simple pieces of pork, chicken, fish, or beef into the delicacies of my childhood. The enthusiastic compliments and empty plates reflected my family's agreement.

Now it was time for serious talk. Tat-Tung took out a bottle of whiskey and two tall glasses from the sideboard while his father digested his last comment. Ah Leong watched his thirty-six-year-old son, anxious to hear.

Tat-Tung had secured the proper "protection" for the real estate, farmlands, fish market, stores, two hotels, and other investments. The two hundred rice farms generated a profitable harvest. But he found a discrepancy between the totals the farmers gave him and Wong Shee's brother's report. "Since he manages the estate in our absence, I calculate he's embezzled half the profits–selling the rice on the side. He's counting on your absence to protect him. Also, he's struck up unusually close friendships with key Kuomintang–his 'insurance' in case you're thinking of taking action."

Ah Leong swore under his breath. "He's family! He can't even read or write! I married his only sister." He took a large swig of whiskey and muttered angrily.

"That's why I didn't confront him directly. No one knew I was auditing each account separately. When I told him that his report did not reflect the estate's true profits, his mouth quivered liked a dried leaf. He was waiting for me to accuse him. I said nothing. I went out for a walk around the moat while he stewed. When I came back, I told him the family wanted the full profits paid by the New Year because of our legal problems. Right now, Auntie Wong Shee and Ah Chen's family can't live without the money we send them every month."

"Has he no shame? He lost face with you, but we all lose face if others find out," snarled Ah Leong.

"It's dangerous for the Laus to show any sign of weakness with the current political situation. When I returned to Shanghai, I told Ah Kong to go to Kew Boy quarterly to check on the harvest. I didn't tell him what I suspected. Instead, I told him Auntie Wong Shee's brother guaranteed triple production from now on. That may pressure him to make good," Tat-Tung concluded. The family was supposed to stick together, to be supportive.

Ah Leong shook his head. "Hah! It's getting too hard to keep everything together," he complained. "I'm seventy-one years old. If I were in China I would be considered an elder. Treated with respect. Honored. Here, people wait for me to die."

"*Baba*!" my husband grasped his father's arm. "It's bad luck to talk like that. Look how strong and healthy you are."

Ah Leong took another sip of whiskey, then leaned forward. He lowered his voice. "According to Chinese custom, I give everything I own to you, my First son. It is your birthright. But here with American laws, Ho Shee can challenge that." He slapped the table with a rough square hand for emphasis and leaned back, his forehead furrowed. Then he squared his shoulders. "My son, I have split my Hawai'i holdings in thirds. One third for you, one third for Ah Wang, and one third for Ho

Shee. It's up to you and Ah Wang to divide your shares with your brothers, if you wish."

Pinch-faced Ho Shee had demanded that she inherit Ah Leong's entire estate. She didn't like the gossip that she had taken Dai-Kam's place, that she had unfairly usurped Ah Leong's First wife, that if it were not for Ah Leong's money and power she would have been deported. A legal will stating her as his heir would legitimize her position as his legal wife. She wanted to squash the malicious rumors. Then she could clearly triumph over her rival, Dai-Kam.

Tat-Tung raised his eyebrows and shivered, visibly stunned. To the Chinese, talk about wills was akin to wishing to die. He had heard that while he was in Shanghai, Ho Shee had hosted 2,000 guests at Wo Fat Restaurant in the heart of Honolulu's Chinatown to celebrate her husband's seventy-first birthday. Although he was only seventy years old by western standards, Ah Leong was a venerable seventy-one by Chinese count, since Chinese males celebrate their major birthdays at the beginning of each decade of life. Odd numbers represent *yang,* a positive male force, so seventy-one was a most propitious birthday for Ah Leong. Dai-Kam and her sons' families were noticeably excluded from the party. Those who were invited reveled in describing the expensive foods, the profusion of fireworks, and the impressive guests who had attended.

Afterwards, Ah Leong heard the speculative gossip from his cronies. Ho Shee told everyone who would listen that since she was L. Ah Leong's legal wife as confirmed by the U. S. court, she should inherit all his businesses and lands. Of course, she would allow her sons, and only her sons, to share in her fortune.

"Ho Shee wants it all. She and her sons squabble day and night over who will get what as if I were already making my way across the Seven Heavenly Bridges. If I give you anything, Ho Shee will sue you for sure. When I went to Hawaiian Trust they said the best way was to split everything I own into thirds, one for you, one for Ah Wang, and one for Ho Shee. You and Ah Wang can share with your brothers or keep it all to yourself. I know you are fair. Ah Wang's brothers can yell at him if they want his share."

"What about Mother? You can't leave her penniless."

"Hah! Through her fancy attorney, she got one-fourth of all the lands we bought together. She collects enough rent to support her and Fourth son Ah Chung's family in her new house at Palama and Magoo Lane. She doesn't need anything."

Tat-Tung stared at the golden glow of whiskey in his glass and inhaled a slow deep breath. He mulled over his father's words. There had to have been a lot of squabbling while he was gone to force his father to make a will in the prime of his life.

"My son." Ah Leong lowered his voice, compelling Tat-Tung to turn his head. "There was no other way."

☜☞

My sister-in-law Yukmoy got worried when she heard about the will. Her husband, Fourth son Ah Chung, was not ambitious. At the mah-jongg tables, she wept that my husband Tat-Tung would take the inheritance of his brothers, leaving her and her children destitute. "Phoenix's husband will figure out how to keep the entire fortune for himself, whatever he hasn't already taken," she warbled over the mah-jongg tiles. She smiled sweetly. "L. Ah Leong will make his First son a millionaire." She accused me of influencing Ah Leong since I coveted everything she had.

I was so angry that I wanted to scream, "There's nothing you have that I really need or want. Everything I desire is here in my house on Circle Lane."

She was right, I wanted the peace of mind that money brings. But not if my heart turned black, like hers.

Chapter Twenty-Six

Storms of Devastation: 1926

By the time I was twenty-seven, I had three girls and two boys not including Edith and Lani.

Hin, our youngest son, was a non-stop whirlwind of mischievous energy. When he was one, he climbed up the walls to pull down the amber sconces. The next day, my girls screamed, "Mama! Mama!" I ran to the kitchen in time to catch him as he fell from a pillar of cushions he had built to get to the altar Tat-Tung had built in the kitchen for Kwan Yin, the Goddess of Love and Mercy. Hin had been entranced by the red hot tips of incense and the tendrils of smoke that curled upwards like dancing snakes.

When he was a year and a half, his sisters taught him how to open macadamia nuts on the front walk by peeling off the thick hulls with pliers and wedging the round nuts into a crack in the sidewalk. Then they smashed them open with Danny's framing hammer. Whack! The kids gorged themselves.

That night they all had the runs. But Hin cried, "Mac-a-nut," and pointed to his abdomen. "Ah, baby, what's that?" I soothed. I pressed the lump. It disappeared. Tat-Tung simmered herbal cloths to warm his tummy. I cradled Hin until he went to sleep.

The lump returned the next morning. I paced the porch until Dr. Chang walked by on his way to work. He probed Hin's tummy, furrowed his brow, and shook his head. A hernia, he pronounced. Anesthesia was dangerous for a baby. He would find the surgeon at

Queen's Hospital most skilled for this delicate operation.

A week later, our Portuguese neighbors left a bunch of bananas on our front step. Hin stuffed himself. That night, the lump popped out and did not go back. Hin's mouth screwed up. He gasped for air between screams. I held him close to my bosom all night, hoping the heat of my body would melt the hernia back where it belonged.

I ran to Dr. Chang's house the next morning. He probed the lump gently. "Quick, call Tat-Tung. Tell him to drive the motorcar and pick you up. Meet me at the hospital immediately," he ordered. He called his office, barked out orders for the staff, then ran to the hospital to meet the specialist, a German surgeon named Straub.

Tat-Tung and I stayed with Hin in Queen's Hospital for two days and nights. We were frightened. Never had any of us ever been in a hospital. We pulled the hard chairs close to our son's bed, helpless to do anything but listen to his tiny breaths and flag down a busy nurse when he cried. The operation cost $500, in cash.

Afterwards, Dr. Chang came to our house every evening before he went home. He held Hin on his lap and cleaned the stitches. He sang Chinese lullabies to soothe him. Two weeks after the operation, he placed Hin on the kitchen table and deftly removed the stitches while the other children ooh'd at the angry red marks they left.

☙☙

The next week, a storm blustered in with a clattering explosion. Overflowing gutters turned the streets to muddy rivers. Wooden sidewalks slipped with mud.

The skies poured rain for a solid week. Sheets and sheets of sweet cool rain. The picturesque waterfalls of Nuʻuanu became roaring brown torrents crushing the tropical forest twined below the cliffs. In town, horses whinnied their complaints against the rising waters. Motorcars stalled. Rivers and streams threatened to overflow their sides.

Fearful that the storm was a harbinger of a larger catastrophe, customers swept the shelves of every candle, every food tin, and all the fresh vegetables and fruits. Everyone, even the stock boys, worked the crowded sales floor.

Ah Leong felt particularly belligerent. Maybe it was worry about the storm or the change in barometric pressure. But whenever he and Ho Shee found an occasion to scold my husband, they brought up his two missed days of work. Especially today, the day the winds howled and the skies crackled with sheets of lighting.

Tat-Tung and Ah Wang had just leaned back, exhausted. Their white short-sleeved shirts were limp and flecked with dust. Since the shelves were bare and no customers remained they waved to Ah Chung to handle any stragglers and headed to the back where the store cook grumbled loudly, with swats of his apron, that no one had time to eat his food still steaming in the wok.

Ho Shee flung her duster across the empty shelves. "So busy, day and night. Ah Leong, things would have gone smoother if Tat-Tung had not wasted two days sitting in a hospital. Because of him we have to work five times as hard!"

The merchant grabbed the banded stack of bills that Tat-Tung had left in the money drawer and shoved them in his right pants pocket. "Humph! His wife's fault. Always calling him home," he grumbled loudly.

Tat-Tung stopped and swept back the hair that fell across his forehead. He was so tired he didn't know if it was morning or night. All that registered was that he had heard the same complaint for too long. "*Baba*, do you think I'm cheating you?" He whipped out his wallet. "If you think I am, here's $100, half my month's pay. Take it! That'll make up for two days," he growled.

Ah Wang jumped between them. "Tat-Tung, don't. *Baba* didn't mean it like that." He clutched his brother's arm and pleaded with him to put his money away.

"No, Ah Wang. Let him do what's right," his mother yelled. She snatched for the bills Tat-Tung extended.

Ah Leong stared, shocked. "I just said I want you here, that's all. Don't yell and throw money around," he bellowed. He waved the outstretched money aside. "Get back to work."

"I know what you said. You say my wife's no good. You say I listen to her too much because she asks me to help her. You bring it up often enough. Your grandson just had an operation, *Baba*. The hospital cost $500–that's more than you pay me in two months! They cut him open. He could have died."

Tat-Tung pushed aside his brother's hand. Thrusting the money in the pocket of his father's shabby work shirt, he patted the bulge of bills. "There. Happy? I pay you back."

Ah Wang reached to return the bills. Ho Shee pulled him back. "No, Ah Wang," she sputtered. He yelled and shook her off.

"Quiet, quiet!" Ah Leong hollered. He waved his thick arms over his head for silence.

"No, *Baba*," Tat-Tung answered. "No."

Ah Wang put his arm on his brother's shoulder. He pulled him away and walked with him out to the sidewalk, away from Ho Shee's and Ah Leong's escalating fight. They fought so much, the brothers wondered why their father had wanted her back. Their arguments were getting physical. Even Dai-Kam warned Ah Leong that it wasn't right to beat someone who was working for him.

Tat-Tung stood at the edge of the sidewalk. He felt the rain splatter on his face, blend with his tears, and cool the sharp pain in his chest. "I can't stand it anymore."

Ah Wang looked at his brother and nodded sympathetically. "*Baba*'s getting old," he sighed. "Their arguing gets to me, too. My mother attacks you and Dai-Kam at every opportunity. She complains that you're irresponsible for putting your family above business. Did you know your mother came in last week and bawled out *Baba* for beating my mother?"

Tat-Tung winced at the irony. "I know you cover for me."

"But I'm not as good at it as you are," Ah Wang regretted. He thrust his hands into his pockets and turned back to the rain. He preferred staying out here on the sidewalk. There had been no customers since the fury of the storm picked up in the last hour and the streets had flooded.

"Remember," Ah Wang said, "how you wouldn't let the villagers in Kew Boy give me opium? You didn't want me to get sick, like you. And when I got appendicitis in the village, you ran for the Western doctor in the next town and saved my life. You were only fourteen years old with *Baba* gone back to Hawai'i. I'll never forget how you saved my life."

The brothers stood on the sidewalk listening to the rain drown out the arguments inside. Suddenly, Tat-Tung pointed to the bags of feed and rice on the sidewalk. "Look! Everything's getting wet," he grumbled.

The rain had increased to blinding gray pellets. Most businesses hadn't even opened because of the foreboding forecast. The brothers picked up the furthest bags and heaved them into the store. Normally, the awning that covered their section of the sidewalk protected the goods. Today, the wind blew the rain in from the side. Down the street, the last of the merchants closed their doors. The sidewalks emptied as people, having bought all the provisions they could carry, hurried home. Sheets of tin, most likely unsecured roofing, flew dangerously down the street.

The police came by on their final check and ordered the store vacated and locked.

Tat-Tung ran upstairs to secure the office windows while the others closed up.

The rain pounded harder. The Hawaiian-style construction, a single wall of one-by-sixes, suited a more balmy climate than these buffeting winds that thrashed the awnings and flimsy roofs. The post and pier foundation consisted of beams sitting on level lava rocks which allowed a crawl space below the floor for ventilation and stopped ground termites from getting to the wood structure. But a tropical storm with enough strength could pick up a roof as easily as if it were a cardboard lid and suck out the contents or whip under the house and lift it up like a puff of silk.

Tat-Tung ran downstairs, caught his father's eye, and patted the folio of legal files under his arm. "Ah Chung, you drive *Baba* and Ho Shee home. I'll take Ah Wang," he ordered. The brothers locked the doors and slammed the iron gates. "This is madness. We shouldn't have opened today," Tat-Tung snarled.

☙☙

When I received the hurricane alert from Danny Akana at the police station, I called Mother and the L. Ah Leong Store. The word spread quickly from neighbor to neighbor.

I took out candles and matches from my cabinet of prayer supplies and put them on the kitchen table where I could find them easily in the dark. The older children ran into the yard to put away anything that the wind could lift, throw, or carry away. They stored toys, potted plants, my broom and rake, the piece of tin that protected my orchids from the sun, and all the shoes and slippers outside the door. They moved the koa wood rocker from the front porch to the parlor. By the time Tat-Tung got home, mangoes from the tree in the backyard were bombing the roof like missiles. Whap. Whap. Whap.

Darkness enveloped the islands. We could hear the constant drumming of the rain. The winds roared us to sleep and woke us up for the next two days.

On the third day, we looked out on a soggy city. Hurricane force winds and torrential rains had paralyzed the islands. Now, a light rain fell and the river of water down Circle Lane was reduced to a stream of rivulets coursing past the tree limbs and debris that littered the road. Tat-Tung and I picked our way over downed trees and wind-torn roofs to Beretania Street and watched the emergency crews working on the telephone and utility poles. The streets were a tangle of downed live wires and shattered timbers. The city workers motioned us back.

Danny Akana waved us down when we returned. He had just completed his shift but was too keyed up with the activity at the police department to go to sleep. High winds had sucked up tin and wooden roofs on the windward side of the island. Torrential rains completed the destruction. A twelve-foot ocean surge flooded buildings closest to the coast in the low-lying areas such as Wai'anae and had swept wooden homes right off their foundations. A few fishing boats were lost. Most had headed safely out to sea. It would take a week to clear the streets before it was safe to drive cars or ride horses again.

By the waterfront, coconut trees lay like dead soldiers, ripped out by their shallow roots. The surge had flooded the waterfront and beaches leaving behind the decay of trapped fishes and torn seaweed. Even the Portuguese man-of-wars that dotted the dirty beaches became deadly obstacles, able to inflict their stings even in death.

Ah Leong called from the store. He complained that the city crews were cleaning up the debris yet no one could get to his store. Tat-Tung assured him that he did not think anyone would go shopping today, except to City Mill to get materials to repair roofs and windows. Ah Leong fumed that his business would be ruined. Tat-Tung assured him that their customers had stocked up for two days before the hurricane, which more than made up for being closed. In fact, their warehouse was empty. There wasn't much to do until the streets were clear and new stock came in. Ah Leong grumbled that his store had been open daily including Sundays and holidays since 1903 and would continue to do so.

❧❧

A couple of nights later, when the tradewinds blew a fresh breath through the parlor and all seven children were in bed, I laid my book on my lap. I studied Tat-Tung absorbed in smoking a cigarette. By the amber lights of the wall sconces, I traced the dark shadows beneath his sunken eyes and the creases across his once-smooth forehead. He turned his weary gaze towards me, then looked away, eyes glazed with his private thoughts. He exhaled. The thin curls of smoke rose and turned with the slight breeze, trailing the scent of anise.

"How long are you going to take this?" I asked.

"I have a duty," he said, smooth and subdued. His eyes glimmered. Such sadness!

"Ah, Tat-Tung," I moaned, my heart heavy with tears fighting to tumble from my eyes. "You are a good man with fine children. I am a good wife. But I see your family destroying us. We have no privacy. They discuss, dissect, and analyze everything from what we say to what we wear to what we do to how we do it. Your mother is jealous of you and calls you 'good-for-nothing.' Your father says I am a 'no-good wife' when the children are sick and I need your help. You work sixteen hours a day, six days a week. When you are sick he calls you lazy. Yet, whenever he has a problem, he comes to you for help. When no one listens to him, he comes to you because everyone respects you and will do what you say. Meanwhile, my friends tell me that Yukmoy and Dai-Kam spread rumors all over Chinatown that when Ah Leong dies, you're going to take all his money and cut out your brothers. They say you have always been greedy.

"Why do we take on all this trouble?" I cried. "It would be better if we had nothing. We work hard so we, too, can get ahead. For what? A good name is better than an emperor's kingdom. If I were a man, I would rather be poor and happy with our pride and honor intact."

He sat speechless.

My heart pounded so hard I knew he could hear it. I had harbored my anger for a long time, never daring to tell him. These disrespectful words hurt him. But he kept everything inside to brew and stew until the shadows on his face darkened and his face wore the pain of anguish. He leaned back to collect his strength.

He finally said, "I have no time to be sick, no time to go to the doctor or dentist. I work day and night. I hear the rumors from my friends. My father wields his power like a titan. Everyone bows to him and his great face. And we, his sons, are kept behind him. Dutiful, like dogs. But I am his First son."

I rose from my chair and cradled his head between my breasts, lightly massaging his temples. He was thirty-six, an age many of his friends owned their own law practice or business. How successful he would have been if he had found a way to remain a dutiful son outside his father's grasp. "Your father could not do his business without you. But he has his own way. It is not our way."

Tat-Tung put his hands up to my fingers and held tight, as if it meant his life.

☜☞

Behind the facade of the model Chinese family, deadly storms brewed. The violence of winds whipping coconut trees up by the roots paralleled the devastation in the Lau family. Unlike a hurricane's physical destruction, our damage lay inside the soul. One could repair the house flooded by the tides of the pounding waves, but not the bitter pain of families ripped asunder. Ah Leong was caught in the web of hypocrisy as wives, sons, and daughters-in-law maneuvered for favorable positions in his will.

Ho Shee insisted that Ah Wang live above the store as their live-in manager. Someday, the store would be her son's, she had complained. Ah Wang had to take control. Ah Leong agreed, just to keep her quiet.

On the day Ah Wang and his family moved to the apartment above the L. Ah Leong Store, my husband did not go to work. I rolled out of bed to prepare breakfast for the children and let him sleep. After I sent the older ones off to school, I plucked weeds and snails from our vegetable garden behind the house, scrubbed the wash in Borax, and hung out scores of diapers. I did not smell rain, so I let the clothes flap on the line in the trade winds.

The phone rang.

"Where's my son?" Ah Leong demanded. I heard Ho Shee in the background telling him what to say. I could imagine him waving at her to be quiet.

"He is sleeping. Shall I wake him?"

"Tell him to get here now," he bellowed without a pause.

I tiptoed into our bedroom where my husband lay, his eyes closed, eyelids flickering.

"It was my father," he stated flatly, rolling over towards me.

I sat on the bed and reached out my fingers to touch his cheek.

He grabbed my hand before it got any closer and pushed it aside. "He wants me to work." He moaned wearily. "Not today."

"He was yelling."

"He's always yelling. Yelling at me, yelling at my brothers." He closed his eyes and lay motionless. "I only work for the sake of the family. For its honor and success. I'm so tired." He rolled back against the pillows with a sigh. "All my life I did my duty, sought the middle way, and obeyed my father. I have worked for him since I was thirteen. He wants me to run his empire like the Western businessmen, to compete in their world. Yet when I tell speak my mind or do the work to comply with the American laws, he and my mother berate me in public." He held his head between his hands as if to shut out their voices. He groaned, "Everything is out of balance."

The choices tore him apart, weakened his *ch'i*, his vital life force. In his youth, opium had wrecked his health so he looked and felt older than his years. He coughed too much. His fatigue was unnatural.

I stood up. "You decide what you wish to do," I said and added before I walked out, "I will support and honor you." At that, he turned and stared, wondering what I understood and what I knew.

In the late morning, Ah Chung chugged up Circle Lane in the L. Ah Leong Store delivery motorcar. He hated unloading the heavy crates and boxes, but he could bully a warehouse man or stock boy to do that chore unless he delivered to a residence and had to do it himself. At least he was out of his father's way and away from the store. Especially today.

"Phoenix, so sorry to bother you," Ah Chung apologized. "I brought your groceries today because Tat-Tung didn't come to work. I came to see if he is all right. No, I don't want to disturb him. If he feels like it, I'll visit for a little while, to see how he is."

Tat-Tung, in slacks and a short-sleeved shirt, sat in the cool darkness of the parlor reading the paper by the light filtering through the leaves of the mango tree. He was as fastidiously groomed as if he were going to work. His large dark eyes glimmered in the darkness.

I laid out their tea and disappeared into the kitchen, where the incense from my early morning prayers to Kwan Yin glowed from my altar.

Ah Chung sat close to his brother. "*Baba* is furious. Ah Wang's wife is moving in upstairs and keeps calling for Ah Wang. 'Bring up the bureau now. Carry this bed to the bedroom over there. Move those boxes.' You know how *Baba* is when you're not there. He gets anxious. Now Ho Shee is screaming that you're lazy and take advantage of him."

Tat-Tung harrumphed. Ho Shee had caused the ruckus. "I'll take you to the store now, my brother. Everything's in chaos. The stock boys are hiding in the warehouse because Ho Shee wants them upstairs to move furniture but Baba needs them to get our shipment from the docks. Ah Wang can't concentrate on the customers because his wife ordered him to watch the babies. *Baba* is handling three or four customers at once plus the wholesale lines. Mother came in when eight customers were waiting to pay and saw Ah Wang pocketing the customers' cash instead of putting it in the register. We desperately need you to put things in order. I'll drive you back home tonight whenever you wish. Early, after dinner."

Everyone was scared of the old man and cowered during his tantrums. Everyone except Tat-Tung. Ah Chung said that when he wasn't there, the business couldn't run properly.

"Tell that to Ho Shee." Tat-Tung glared at his brother. "I will not work where I'm not wanted. There can be no harmony at the store for me."

Ah Chung leaned forward, his face white with fear. "What are you saying, my brother? What do you mean?"

"Ah Wang is moving above the L. Ah Leong Store today. He will take over. He will figure out what needs to be done."

"But what will you do? You've worked for *Baba* your entire life."

"I have a good reputation in the community. My family will not starve."

Ah Chung bit his lip and hung his head. He sat in silence, too shaken to move. He begged his brother to reconsider. But Tat-Tung had made up his mind.

From herbalist Yuen's recipes, my husband brewed energy-nurturing tonics. The bitter smell permeated the house. The little ones ran around with their fingers clasped to their noses squealing, "Daddy, your medicine stinks!"

"Ho ho ho," he shouted when he caught them. They were the only ones who could bring a smile to his face these days. They screamed and ran down the hallways, their bare feet thumping across the hardwood floor. He lay down with them for their nap, letting the herbs infuse his body with their power. I smiled to see the children nestled against him, then shut the bedroom door. The swish of leaves and sway of branches from the mango tree soothed them to sleep in the warm afternoon.

All was peaceful until Ah Leong's Third wife Chung Shee rose from the grave.

Chapter Twenty-Seven
Chung Shee Reappears: 1926–1934

Ah Wang's cracked voice screamed, "Help, help, help!" His frenzied pounding on our kitchen door startled us awake.

We slipped on our bathrobes. My husband flung open the door. "Ah Wang! What are you doing here so late? It's past midnight."

"Tat-Tung, look at his face!" I gasped. Ah Wang's eyelids and lips shivered erratically as if he had been embraced by a procession of Hawaiian ghosts.

Ah Wang stumbled through the open door and grabbed my arms. "Quick, Phoenix, get your Buddhist priest to bless my apartment."

"Too late. You already moved in. You have to ask me what day to move before you do it. Why do you ask such a thing in the middle of the night?"

"You must," Ah Wang begged. He fell to his knees. His face was as white as the full moon.

Tat-Tung steered his brother towards the kitchen table. I poured him a cup of tea. Ah Wang picked it up with shaky hands and gulped it down. I poured him another.

"*Baba* was upset today because my wife made so much noise moving in," Ah Wang began, carefully choosing his words. "He yelled when he heard beds and chairs scraping across the wood floors. *Baba* kept looking towards the office stairs, waiting for you, Tat-Tung, to complain about the noise. My wife came down and told my mother that she needed help. She asked for two men to come up right away and move the stove and ice box—she couldn't move it all alone. My mother ordered two clerks to go upstairs quickly and get back before *Baba* noticed."

I imagined Ah Wang's wife, her dusty apron firmly tied around her tunic, ordering Ho Shee and the two clerks to do her bidding. She looked very much like her mother-in-law, short and plump. But her face was sculptured like a statue, with magnetic commanding eyes.

Ah Wang clasped his hands in front of him and stared earnestly in his brother's eyes. "I pretended not to notice. Moving is woman's work. I was looking forward to the short walk up to my apartment every night after work. I thought, I can sleep in every morning until everyone else comes. I could even have the store cook prepare the meals for my family. That would save even more money. You know we still have seven children at home."

"Yes, Ah Wang," my husband agreed. He motioned to his younger brother to continue.

"After our ten o'clock dinner, I asked *Baba* to come up for tea and cakes. To appease him, you know, since he was so mad at my wife. He agreed. My mother had been up and down all day helping my wife get settled. I knew she would be there now, tucking in her grandchildren.

"*Baba* had me lock the doors and padlock the iron gates. All the other businesses were closed, so the streets were quiet. I felt happy, Tat-Tung, to walk upstairs and be home. The full moon lit the alley to the stairs of our apartment. I grabbed the hand rail and started up.

"But at the top of the stairs, I saw a woman. She glowed with an unearthly sheen that gave me the shivers. Her arms opened and cascades of thick black hair rippled to her waist. The scent of fresh silk wafted from the filmy layers of her gown.

"'Aaah, you've come back to me, Ah Leong,' she called. Her voice shimmered like the glow of the moon. She glided down towards us.

"'I've never seen or heard anything like this. I opened my mouth to scream but no sounds came out. All I could say was Aaaaah....aaaa. I couldn't move. Icy fingers ran from my spine to the edges of my scalp.

"When *Baba* saw her, he froze. He reached out one hand. 'Chung Shee,' he called, 'Chung Shee, Chung Shee.'

"'My husband,' she called, her arms outstretched. The wind picked up in the alley and her hair flew back from her face. She floated closer. Her burial garments fluttered, sheer and iridescent. 'Come to me. I will be yours forever.'

"'No,' yelled *Baba*. He threw up his arms as if to protect his face. He kept yelling 'No, No, No!' He shut his eyes and turned away.

"She called him by name. 'I need you,' she wailed. She reached for him, her thick hair flying behind her, reflecting the moonlight like a shining mane. 'You promised.' She stretched out her fingers and floated towards us.

"*Baba* whispered, 'No, you're dead. You're dead.'

"I covered my ears with my hands and fell to the stairs when she howled. Her cries turned my bones to ice. Her voice faded into echoing shimmers, 'You will be mine forever.'

"Then the wind died. There was a terrible stillness. *Baba* leaned against the building, his arms still thrown up in front of his face.

"'Who was that?' I demanded. When *Baba* put his arms down, he looked around and asked where she went. Again, I asked, 'Who was that?' *Baba* said, 'A long time ago she was my Third wife, your Auntie Chung Shee.' I asked why she was here tonight. He said she died here.

"'Here?' I asked him. 'Here?' *Baba* nodded. 'You want me to live where she died?' I moved my jaw up and down but no words came out. Then he barked, 'Tell Phoenix to bring her Buddhist priest to bless your apartment and appease your Third mother's spirit.' He turned and walked out the alley. His final words were, 'I can't go up there with you.'

"I tell you, as long as I live, I will always see her gliding down the stairs towards me, her arms open wide and her hair flowing back in the gusts of wind that puff through the alley."

❦❦

Ah Wang, driven by the economics of free lodging above the store, convinced himself that Chung Shee's ghost was a dream. The next morning I asked the Kwan Yin Temple priests to bless every dusty inch of his lodgings, including the alley and stairs. The customers remarked how devout Ah Wang must be, for every morning the hefty scent of incense sticks, indicative of many prayers carried aloft by spirals of perfumed smoke, drifted down from his apartments.

☜☞

My husband never returned to the confines of his father's store.

Every night for the next eight years, when the only sounds we heard at night were the rustle of palm fronds in the tradewinds and the call of wild boar in the Koʻolau mountains, Ah Leong came to see his First son.

After Tat-Tung quit working for him, Ah Leong's hair turned snow white. But the merchant's distinctive footsteps up Circle Lane were as crisp as ever.

On warm summer evenings, the men sat on the front porch. Ah Leong, now in his early seventies, smoked fat Havanas, slugged teacups of whiskey, and talked business. Always business. Sometimes he asked for strategic advice and plans for expansion. Often he requested help with his other sons who refused their father but obeyed Tat-Tung. Many discussions revolved around potential investments. What would you do under these circumstances? he would ask. Tat-Tung would explain his options.

"Come back to work," Ah Leong ordered.

His son refused. Both were too much alike. Two stubborn, hard-headed, strong-willed Dragons. They jeopardized what mattered the most to themselves.

During the cooler evenings when the trade winds picked up and the temperature dropped, the men talked by the light of the amber sconces in the parlor. The children and I moved like flower petals when their grandfather was here. They greeted him graciously and politely as they were taught, but preferred to stay out of his way. He could be gruff when he was in a terrible mood.

On the Mainland, the Depression changed life for many. But for my family, used to just getting by, life was unchanged. I made the children's clothes from bleached flour sacks. Out of my husband's monthly salary of $200 when Tat-Tung last worked for his father, I had allotted him forty dollars, kept sixty for the household and children, and saved a hundred to buy land and buildings. Now we lived off these rents. Our house was filled with growing children racing in and out with their friends. The boys went to St. Louis College and the girls walked to nearby public schools: Central Intermediate and McKinley High.

After Ah Leong and Dai-Kam sold the family compound at Queen and Punchbowl Streets, Ah Leong and Ho Shee moved to one of his bungalows in Palama. Dai-Kam had moved to a large mansion in Kamakela with enough bedrooms for Fourth son Ah Chung, Yukmoy, and their eleven children.

I had no time for self-pity. I hid my jade, gold, diamonds, and pearls for a future time. I had seven children to feed, clothe, and educate, and a husband to nurse back to health. Meanwhile, I saw Dai-Kam gift my sisters-in-law and her daughters with gold and jade jewelry. Dai-Kam continued to buy toys and clothes for her other grandchildren, but never for Tat-Tung's children.

I was struck speechless when grocers would stop me and compliment my children's manners. "Mrs. Lau, your mother-in-law came today with her grandchildren. She bought ice cream for all the children, except yours. But your children have such beautiful manners. Do they beg, whine, or stare at those who have what they want? No, your children turn around and go home. So polite and pleasant." I thanked them graciously. But her prejudice turned my heart ice cold.

Dai-Kam knew we struggled. But when she took Ah Leong's advice and asked Tat-Tung to develop her vacant lands with cottages that gave her a handsome income, she would not pay him for his work.

Sometimes, he lapsed into dark moods that no one could reach. He yearned for the euphoria of opium, to sink into its abyss. That had been his escape when he was a teenager. Now, whiskey eased his pain. Even the laughter of the children failed to draw him out, then. He sat in the shadows brooding over the merciless twists of fate and the burdens of his family. He developed an ugly cough.

Many afternoons, he would stare at the formal portrait of his father that Ho Shee had given each of his sons in honor of Ah Leong's big seventy-first birthday, the party we had not been invited to. He felt torn with love and resignation when he stared at his father posed regally on a rattan chair, one hand firmly grasping the armrest, the other confidently placed on his crossed knees. How unlike Ah Leong–to be still. Although he wore the simple blue Chinese work clothes he preferred, the portrait captured his proud gaze. A bull of a man. Thick and sturdy. Direct and determined.

On the koa wood rocker on the front porch, Tat-Tung smoked endless cigarettes until his children came home from school. They were the lights that blazed his soul. In turn, he was their strong hand of authority and discipline gloved in love. His eyes spoke volumes; one stern glare could wither any teenager's foolhardy arrogance.

❧❧

I heard my two sons whispering in their room after school. Usually, they raced out to play with the Akanas as soon as they came home. I peeked in. Yung Chan sat on his bed reading. Hin lay on his belly next to him.

"Boys, homework done?" I asked. "If so, you can rake up the leaves in the backyard."

Hin kicked Yung Chan and whispered, "You tell her."

I raised my eyebrow and sat next to them on the bed. I patted Hin's butt. "Tell me what?"

"We need bus fare to go to school, Mom," he said. "Yung and I have decided to take the bus to school from now on." He turned to his older brother. "Right?" My eldest nodded.

I frowned at the boys. "Your Uncle Ah Chung's job is to drive all the Lau grandsons to school and back every day in your grandmother's big car."

"But Mom, every time we get in, he complains that Circle Lane is too narrow for Grandmother's car. Too crowded, he says. Too many boys. Complain, complain. Then our cousins moan and groan. They don't want to hear him, either. So today, we said, 'Stop the car, Uncle Chung. From now on we'll take the bus.' We got out and walked home." Hin looked up at me and shrugged his shoulders. "We don't want to listen to Uncle Ah Chung complain any more."

I agreed. I had seen how Ah Chung drove Dai-Kam's big black Studebaker through Circle Lane and how his sons grumbled about moving over when my boys got in, even though there was plenty of room. "You boys go outside and play," I told them.

My sons bounced off the bed and scrambled out to find the Akanas. I knew I would hear from Dai-Kam soon enough, asking for something.

Two months later, Dai-Kam commanded all her sons and daughters-in-law to her new house. An emergency, she said. She gathered us around the dining table. Fourth son Ah Chung and Yukmoy flanked her sides. She had borrowed $4,000, she said, eyeing each of us. But the bank repossessed her car because she forgot to repay the loan.

"Tat-Tung," she ordered, "Since you're the oldest you borrow $4,000 to pay the bank so I can get my car back. After all, Ah Chung uses the car to take your sons to school."

We didn't ask why she had borrowed the money. But we had all seen the extravagant new furniture and clothes Yukmoy bought, now that she was pregnant with her twelfth.

My husband hemmed and hawed.

I stood up. "Mother," I demanded, "your car doesn't hold my children. I had to reimburse Ah Chung four dollars a week for gas and he scolded my children all the way to school and back. What's so good about that? If it's so good for Yukmoy's children, have her borrow $4,000."

Yukmoy screwed her face angrily at me.

I held my ground. I would get my own car.

❧❧

On the weekends, Dr. Chang piled his family into his open-top Studebaker to go to church or for rides to the country.

"Sell it to me," I teased when he thought of buying a new car. What did I need a car for? he asked. My girls walked to school and the boys caught the bus to St. Louis College. My husband did accounting in Chinatown and hired a taxi to take him to see his clients. But on rainy days when the boys got soaked waiting for the bus or the taxi was late, even Tat-Tung agreed that a car might be convenient.

"My car's too old," Dr. Chang protested.

"Good enough for me to take my children to school," I decided.

A few years later, I sold the Studebaker and paid $200 for a used Hudson that had doors that locked. The only problem was that it took all my weight on a well-timed swing to close the car doors.

Later, I bought a larger used Packard for $800.

One day, Danny Akana stopped me near Central Intermediate School. "Mrs. Lau, all the police know you as the little girl with the biggest car."

"Little girl, indeed," I blushed. I pointed to the seven children packed elbow to elbow. "That's why I need a big car. When it rains, I can take all of them to school in one trip instead of two."

During these lean times, I resolved to never sell my jade and gold jewelry the way Yukmoy did. We were poor, but I still possessed my family's legacy. I hid everything–flowered hair-ornaments with natural pearls and emerald green jades from when I was a young girl, solid gold bracelets from the finest Hong Kong artisans, ruby flower pins, even Tat-Tung's buttons from his mandarin gowns, one set in carved jade and another in pure gold. These I could never replace.

Chapter Twenty-Eight

The Ghosts Return for Ah Leong: 1934

It was just a little cut.

Within a week, the cut on L. Ah Leong's toe sent needle-sharp pains up his leg. The flesh on his toe around the open wound turned black and exuded the odor of decayed flesh.

"Junk toe," he complained to Tat-Tung. That's why he couldn't get to Circle Lane to see him. The last time he chopped his toe like this, herbalist Yuen had applied an herb poultice. Cured within days. Yuen had retired now, and anyway Ah Leong knew his body could cure itself.

At first, Ah Leong took to working barefoot. He limped on feet toasted brown by the sun and soiled with worn-in dirt. Eventually, he could not manage short distances. Fourth son Ah Chung chauffeured his seventy-eight-year-old father everywhere in the delivery motorcar.

Then Ho Shee, now fifty-nine, refused to crawl into bed with him. She complained about the stench of the putrid pus that oozed from the growing sore.

By the time Tat-Tung found out, it was too late for his Chinese roots and herbs. His father paid Chinese doctors to administer poultices to draw the poison out of his body. Acupuncturists twirled their needles in designated spots to improve his circulation and speed the removal of toxins.

When the blackness spread from the toe to the foot, Ah Wang brought a Western doctor. The Western doctor shook his head. "How did this happen?" he asked when confronted by the black, decaying flesh. The jagged cut reminded him of the infections he had treated on the battlefields of the Great War where hygiene and first aid were scarce. He would have to amputate the toe, maybe the whole foot. It was the only way to save his life. If Ah Leong waited too long to decide, he would have to cut off the whole leg. Left untreated, gangrene would spread. The merchant would die.

"No cutting!" Ah Leong roared. He ordered Ah Wang to take the Western doctor away. A little cut was of no concern, he fumed.

Except for this one.

※※

Yuen the Herbalist tapped his way up the steps of the modest two-bedroom bungalow on Palama Street where Ah Leong and Ho Shee lived. Painted white with generous eaves and an inviting front porch, the little house was one of ten identical bungalows Ah Leong had built decades ago to house families who left the plantations to seek their fortune in Honolulu. The front yard was mainly scrubby dirt with bedraggled ti plants on either side of the front steps.

My husband and I guided Yuen, one hand on his back and the other on the elbow of the wispy-haired healer.

"You are kind, Tat-Tung and Phoenix, to an old blind man," he said. His voice cracked but it was strong and confident.

"Thank you, my teacher," answered Tat-Tung. "You are the one who is gracious to see my father. You are busy with sons and grandchildren now."

We paced our steps, allowing Yuen time to place each slippered foot. Still lean and wiry, the high-cheekboned healer climbed surefootedly.

"I don't know how much I can help him now. But I try, I try," Yuen said.

Tat-Tung opened the front door and guided Yuen into the parlor where his father rested. The offending foot was propped upon a rattan ottoman, its pad worn shiny and bare in spots. My husband seated Yuen in the high-back rattan chair facing his father. When both men were comfortable, I called for tea. Ho Shee brought it, then disappeared in the shadows as she always did when we came.

Ah Leong welcomed Yuen, his friend from the days of old Hawai'i.

Yuen leaned forward and clasped the merchant's hand. "I live in never-ending nights now, but I have many sons and grandsons to keep me happy." He heard his family's voices around him at all times, his cloudy eyes seeing nothing but knowing everything.

"You are strong. At least you can still get around," Ah Leong grumbled.

"That's because I must walk everywhere I want to go. From my eldest son's house where I live now, I walk to Chinatown. And all the way up to the farms of Manoa. My grandchildren guide me. Every day we walk miles to do our errands."

Ah Leong complained that he lived alone with his wife. And his toe would not heal.

"So your First son tells me. He describes a blackness from your foot sending needle pains up your leg." Yuen sniffed the odor of death and shook his head. "The medicines I gave him for you will not work. Why didn't you call me earlier?"

"It will heal. They make a big fuss over nothing," Ah Leong said with a cursory wave of his hand.

Yuen sat back. "Tell me how you got this cut."

"Hah! So stupid." Ah Leong lowered his voice. He leaned back and wiped the sweat from his temples. "I was in this very room. Cutting my toenails with my knife. I do it all the time. Trouble was the light. I only have the one light bulb, you see, hanging from the string. I missed. Cut my toe. Chopped out the flesh."

Ah Leong winced at the memory of the bloody mess. He had wrapped his chopped toe up in a towel and went to bed. He was convinced by morning it would heal the way it did the last time. It didn't. "Something's wrong. It gets worse," he grumbled.

"Aaaah, my friend. Always so impatient." Yuen leaned forward. He nodded as Ah Leong described the various poultices from the Chinese doctors and the efforts of the acupuncturists. They discussed the results. When Ah Leong told him the verdict of the Western doctors, the herbalist listened carefully.

"And what will you do?" asked Yuen, cocking his head towards the old merchant. Ah Leong told him what the herbalist already knew he would say.

The two men reminisced. They talked-story of Hawai'i in the 1880s and how they had made their mark in the Islands. They recalled the colorful days of the Hawaiian Monarchy and the difficulties of being Chinese under American rule. They complained about the laws that had told them what kind of work they could do, where they could work, and if they could travel.

When the sun set lower over the ocean and the afternoon trade winds picked up in anticipation of twilight, both men sat in the waning light, silent for once.

"Yuen," Ah Leong asked, "will it be painful?"

"If you wish to live, the Western doctors will have to amputate, as they say. But we Chinese believe in being buried whole. Yes, you will suffer." Yuen held Ah Leong's heavily callused hands between his own fingers, to aid the *ch'i* of his suffering friend. They were all getting old. Hawai'i had changed. The vanguards who had made Hawai'i a unique culture were dying. Perhaps it was better to die before one became obsolete.

"Ah Leong, I wish you well. I will be by your side whenever your First son comes for me," Yuen promised. He squeezed his friend's hands, imprinting in his memory the feel of his weathered palms and fingers. He had fewer of these old friends now. "I can do no more."

"To see you has made me better than a thousand Western doctors and their medicine," protested Ah Leong. He struggled to get up. "You see me as I am."

Yuen turned his cloudy eyes towards him. "I see through the face to your heart."

☜☞

Tat-Tung and Ah Chung moved their father's bed out of his small bedroom and repositioned it in the bungalow's parlor to accommodate the doctors and friends who came every day. This room was simple and undecorated, not at all like Dai-Kam's Victorian mansion filled with rosewood furniture and koa wood tables, fringed painted silk lamps, and gilded figurines from China, nor like the magnificent grandeur of his estates in China. When Ah Leong's visitors came through the screen front door, they crossed a woven Chinese carpet centered on the small parlor's hardwood floor. Opposite his bed, his seventy-first birthday portrait hung on a nail. Overhead, a single light bulb cast a harsh glow on the cotton curtains which Ho Shee now kept closed, even during the day.

Ah Leong's face softened with the painkillers he needed. He drifted in and out of lucidity. Sometimes he spoke as another Ah Leong, from a time before money, power, and success.

The Western doctors warned that unless they amputated his infected toe, gangrene would spread through his body. Eventually, the toxins would reach his heart and kill him.

No amputation, Ah Leong insisted. He held firm to the teachings of his masters. Chinese believe that their ancestors have given each person their body; it is a sacred gift that should not to be violated.

Every day, Tat-Tung changed the bandages that wrapped his father's black flesh. He applied painkilling herbs while I chanted prayers for his father's spirit. The merchant clung to his son and remembered. "The village laughed when they threw us out of our house. My foolish, weak father begged for mercy when they hauled away our blankets and pillows. All we had was the clothes we wore."

Grasping his son's sleeve, Ah Leong relived the humiliation. "No one saved me when I fell off the bridge. I was a poor beggar boy, invisible, not worth saving. I showed them, didn't I? I came back fat and rich with five wives and ten sons. They didn't turn away when I built the new temple or gave jobs to everyone. I fed their children. Every New Year when the rivers flooded the farmlands with rich silt for the new crops, I sent the money to feed the flood victims. They gave me the most honorable Five-Star Name!"

He sunk back on his pillow and gazed at his son with regret. "Fifteen years it's been since I last smelled the scent of the pak-lan trees at *Ming*

Yang Tong. Fifteen years since I last saw Fifth wife Wong Shee and Eighth son Ah Chen," he groaned. He imagined entering Kew Boy Village dressed in the robes of a fine Chinese scholar, villagers clambering after him, and passing under the village gates carved with his name. Ah, to feel the hot China winds again, to see its broad blue skies stretched over his endless rice paddies.

His other sons came but left quickly. He grilled Ah Wang about the store and customers, worried that he couldn't keep the business going with the same momentum and vigor. Even Ho Shee stomped out to the small kitchen to get away from the oppressiveness of death, slamming the door shut behind her.

One day Ah Leong moaned so pitifully that Tat-Tung and I jumped up. No one else was here. Had gangrene finally reached his heart? Was he going now? Ah Leong opened his eyes wide. He gripped his son's arm and pulled him closer.

"Tat-Tung, I made a terrible mistake," he roared. "All this time, only you come to see me every day. Only you care about how I feel, about my comfort. You are the only one concerned about my business while I lie here too pained to move. I look back and see all these years it was you! You watched out for me, took care of my business, took care of me." His eyes, now faded yellowish brown, widened in anguish.

Tat-Tung bowed his head. "I'm your son."

"But I gave it all away. Your shares. Ho Shee told me you were unfilial when you wouldn't work for me anymore. She said you were a bad son; greedy, only wanting my money. I believed her. I changed my will and gave her everything, the way she wanted. Now you have nothing. Nothing!" The old man reared up and grabbed Tat-Tung's shirt so they were face to face. "I made a mistake. I was blinded by their lies. I see it now." His eyes burned with regret. He moaned.

My hands flew to my mouth. I did not know if the tears in my husband's eyes were from hurt or sorrow. He turned away, stung by his father's betrayal.

"My son, call the attorney to come now. Bring me pen and paper.

Now. I will change my will and give it all to you." The old merchant gasped and sank back on his bed. "I must, before I die."

Tat-Tung turned to me, his face wracked with anguish. "Phoenix, if I get the attorney to do as he wishes, *Baba* dies happy and you and my family are secure. But my brothers and Ho Shee will rip us apart."

Ah Leong apologized for his mistake and promised us his fortune. We listened to his regrets as we changed his bandages and washed the pus from his sores.

Tat-Tung vacillated. Should we fulfill his dying father's last wish? How the others would scorn us, berate us for tending to *Baba* for greed, for his great fortune. We would never let money alone guide us. I knew that if we didn't say anything soon, Ah Leong would continue to badger my husband until Tat-Tung's pain sunk him into depression.

Finally, I propped Ah Leong comfortably on enough pillows so he could sit up and face us. I spoke slowly and deliberately. "If we call the attorney now, Ho Shee and everyone else will say we took care of you because we wanted your money. Your heart knows that isn't true. Your son has always loved you, no matter what happened in the past. When you recover, you can change your will and protect Tat-Tung's good name." I told Ah Leong that we loved him whether we were rich or poor.

His breath was labored, but the fire in his eyes blazed as powerfully as ever. He reached out his hand and grasped mine. His grip was firm, hard, and dry.

"Phoenix, I regret that I have been a foolish man," Ah Leong repeated, his voice strong and determined. He stared at his son, breathing heavily, willing him to do his bidding. "I gave away what is rightfully yours. I promise to correct my mistake." ·

"When you recover," my husband assured him, "we'll call your attorney." He fought back his tears. Tears of sorrow for the fights, the humiliation, for all the past wrongs, the past mistakes.

Ah Leong's grip relaxed. I caressed his hands so he could feel our sincerity.

"You have promised, so it will be." His voice relaxed, softened. "My First son...knows the honorable way."

☜☞

Ah Leong trembled when he saw the ancient specters waiting for him. They stood like sentinels in the corners of the parlor dressed in Chinese robes of the past twenty generations. They gestured and called his name. Their shapes shimmered and glowed independently of the single light bulb that lit the parlor where he lay.

The ghost of Third wife Chung Shee returned, as she had promised. The scent of fresh silk filled the room when she rushed to Ah Leong and ran her fingers along his face. His eyes opened wide with longing and he remembered how wonderful she felt when she lay naked on her bed, her long hair wrapped around his body.

"You will be mine forever," she promised, shimmering with a translucent glow.

"Forever," he promised, his voice barely audible. He felt her touch, now very real upon his cheeks. Her eyes glowed more vividly than those of his family who were very much alive.

The heavy koa wood chairs and end tables had been moved far against the walls to make room for the family that sat vigil. The spirits did not bother the humans. They came for the dying merchant.

"Look, look. There they are, can you see? So many children calling to me. They surround my bed," Ah Leong cried to Tat-Tung. His son held his hands and wiped his face with towels scented with jasmine water.

Ah Leong asked if he brought the attorney yet to change his will. Tat-Tung told him the attorney would come later.

His father clung to his hands and rasped, "I promise you my entire fortune. You'll never have to worry again."

One night when Ah Chung joined us, Ah Leong screamed, "A boy! Tat-Tung, Ah Chung, I saw a boy, only twelve years old. He pointed a gun in my face. He said, 'I don't like the way you treated my mother and father.' Quick, call the police."

"Hush, *Baba*," Ah Chung soothed. "The police will never come to chase a ghost." He turned to his brother. "You tell him, Tat-Tung." But my husband was already on the phone. The Honolulu Police hurried to Ah Leong's modest bungalow and stationed armed officers at his bedside.

"There he goes. Get him!" Ah Leong struggled up from his bed. He pointed out the ghosts as he saw them dash across the room. The officers brandished their guns and yelled at the spirits to leave L. Ah Leong alone.

But only the merchant could see them. The spirits danced. They leered at the old man, taunting and making faces. Ah Leong clutched Tat-Tung's hand and described each one.

I bowed my head, burned incense, and prayed to the deities to protect my father-in-law from the demons that tormented him.

❧❧

The smell of rotting flesh mixed with the thick scent of incense as the family prayed for his next life. The drawn drapes kept the life-giving breezes out, concentrating the oppressiveness of the death house. The Honolulu Police stood guard at his bedside with their guns drawn to chase his devils.

All his wives, sons, daughters, and families added their moaning and crying to the cacophony of the droning priests. The younger children, put to bed in the back bedroom, were so terrified that they sat up, wide-eyed. If they did fall asleep, they woke up screaming with nightmares of black figures, dark looming faces, and death.

Dai-Kam sobbed, slumped against the shoulders of her First daughter Kai-Tai. She tried to remember the eager young man she had married in Kohala where lush deep valleys were kissed by the soft breezes rushing between the islands. Now he lay gasping in the middle of the parlor.

Shoulder to shoulder, nine sons and their wives sat in hierarchical order with the older grandchildren, three deep around their patriarch. We were hypnotized by the droning priests and the tinkle of prayer bells. Smoke burned our eyes. Through the haze we heard hushed voices and shuffling feet, the rustle of cotton and an occasional satin skirt. Doors opened and closed all night as families came and left, drifting in and out of the dark scene. The death smells hung heavily like a thick fog, an oppressive stench that made the women lightheaded.

It was hot. Not only because it was a warm summer evening, but because of the press of people summoned to this small cottage by death.

As the sky turned purple-gray with the rising sun, the blackness of Ah Leong's rotting flesh reached his heart.

The seventy-eight-year-old merchant gasped. He saw his First son's face close to his. "The lawyer?"

"When you get well, *Baba*," Tat-Tung answered tenderly. He wiped his father's forehead with a cloth soaked in pomelo leaf water so he would enter the next world clean and sweet. "Then, I promise you."

Ah Leong's eyes closed. His lips trembled. Then he exhaled slowly. "You're right, my son. I'm getting better already. I feel...no pain..."

Tat-Tung clasped his father's hands in his and ran his fingers over his calluses as he cleansed them with pomelo leaves. Millions of Chinese and American dollars had flowed through these hands, drawn by the power of the Money Dragon.

Ah Leong's face relaxed into a smile. "Time, my son. No pain. We have time."

I sprang tearfully to Ah Leong's side and put my lips to his ear. "*Baba*, when you get to the other side, watch over my children. Protect them! You owe us that."

He gazed once more at me, eyes shimmering wet. Then his mouth opened and closed as if he were drowning. He could not escape death a second time.

I turned to my husband and opened my palm. Our eyes met. Tat-Tung placed the two natural pearls I offered on his father's tongue, to be the eyes of his soul as it rose from earth.

Chapter Twenty-Nine
Funeral of Honor and Dishonor: May 1934

L. Ah Leong's funeral site was chosen for its auspicious location. It was on the highest hill in Manoa Cemetery, on a gentle slope backed by the mountains. He had an uninterrupted view of the city in which he had made his fortune. He could see all the lands he had owned and watch the ships coming into Honolulu Harbor as he had done so often when he was alive. But the squabbling of a lifetime did not end with his death. It continued with vigor during the weeks of ritual and planning.

By Chinese custom, the proper rituals in mourning and burial reflect one's understanding of each person's responsibilities attached to their position. Everyone is ruled by their hierarchical standing: younger sons were subordinate to elder sons, female family members to the males. These rituals dictated not only where each family member sat during the all-night vigil with the open casket, but in what order they walked in the funeral cortege the next morning.

Fifty professional mourners were hired to reflect L. Ah Leong's great status. They would wail loudly with vociferous anguish whenever visitors entered the funeral parlor to pay their respects to the dead. Taoist priests would conduct the all-night ceremony to the accompaniment of Chinese musicians. As visitors entered, they were given a piece of candy to sweeten their sorrow and a nickel wrapped in red paper to bring them good luck and happiness. At the end of the all-night vigil and service, all the visitors, followed by the family, would walk around the coffin for their final goodbye. Then we would turn away. The priest would summon Ah Leong's soul to accompany his body to the grave and the coffin would be closed.

Accordingly, Tat-Tung, his brothers, and uncles would lead the funeral procession from Nuʻuanu Mortuary, through Chinatown, to Manoa Cemetery. The men would bear lanterns inscribed with our family name, Lau. The hearse would bear L. Ah Leong's portrait. As eldest son, Tat-Tung would walk ahead of the coffin carrying a wooden staff and burning incense. His mother, First wife Dai-Kam, would follow immediately behind the hearse with the brothers, sons, daughters-in-law, daughters, and all other Lau relatives in hierarchical order.

Along the way, an attendant would throw funerary money in the hearse's path to placate the malevolent spirits so they would not harm Ah Leong.

Five marching bands, including the prestigious Royal Hawaiian Band and the Saint Louis College Band, offered their services for what would be the largest funeral procession in Honolulu.

The Honolulu Police called in all reserve officers for the Sunday funeral, for they anticipated that the sidewalks from Nuʻuanu Mortuary to Manoa Cemetery would be lined five deep with viewers, not to mention the hundreds who would be marching.

Two nights before the funeral, I was still sewing white dresses for my girls. For the funeral, the women would wear white, the traditional mourning color for the Chinese, and the men, my sons included, would wear dark Western suits and white shirts. My husband came home late that night. I heard him pour a whiskey in the dining room. When he did not answer my call, I hurried into the darkened parlor. He slumped in his favorite high-backed chair pretending to be absorbed in his drink.

"Tat-Tung?"

His hair limped over his forehead. His short-sleeved shirt was rumpled and pulled to one side. He had heard the crisp clip of the sewing machine and the clatter of my shears on the kitchen table, but didn't want to face me. He saw my worried frown. "They argue and bicker about everything from who stands where to where each person will sit to what food they will serve," he said reluctantly.

I stood behind his chair and massaged his temples. My fingers were ugly now, worn with cooking and cleaning, but they remembered the vital spots that needed to be touched. "Tell me what they finally decided," I coaxed. I knew the proper funeral etiquette, but since his family did not ask, I had not volunteered any advice. I knew his family considered me outspoken when I did speak, and stupid when I held my tongue. As he described each detail of the funeral, the Chinese service, and the procession, I imagined how it would appear. Each segment of the funeral reflected Ah Leong's power and prestige. Organizations he belonged to were invited to march in the funeral procession, in hierarchical position behind the families and dignitaries.

"My husband, you reminded them that the First wife must walk behind the coffin and the First son must carry the lighted incense?" I had stressed that these traditions would be obvious to everyone. Hundreds, maybe thousands would observe the long funeral procession that would wind from Nuʻuanu Mortuary, through Chinatown, and up to the Chinese cemetery deep in Manoa valley.

"We fought about it all week. Ho Shee insists she is his legal wife by American law, despite Chinese custom. Ah Wang is her eldest son. He will walk behind the coffin." For the first time in his life, Tat-Tung's brothers had defied him. Because of the will, Ho Shee controlled Ah Leong's estate now. Ah Leong's sons feared angering her and losing what assets she might dole out. Tat-Tung had pleaded for reason, for family honor, to follow the Confucian rituals for their father's funeral.

"But this is a Chinese funeral. You have always been considered the First son. Dai-Kam is his First wife. Everyone in Hawaiʻi knows this." I stiffened and stepped away from him. My face flushed hot. I believed in family loyalty despite all the past hurts. But I could not tolerate their brash arrogance in full view of the entire town. What humiliating shame. Harmony would be disrupted if Second wife Ho Shee and her son Ah Wang took First wife Dai-Kam's and First son Tat-Tung's places.

My husband could never walk behind his younger brother. It was not right. The whole family would lose face.

When I was a little girl, my Grandfather sent me to the Buddhist nuns in the next village for my education. There I learned the teachings of Lao Tzu, Buddha, and Confucius that guided me, that gave me the strength and courage I needed every day.

"If I were a man, I would have fought for my rights," I said in a slow, measured voice. From the troubled look in my husband's eyes, I knew he was waiting for me to say what he couldn't. So I did.

"We will join your family for tonight's vigil as is the custom. We will take our place, as the family of the First son. You men will sit on chairs at your father's feet. The girls and I will sit on the lauhala mats on the floor at your father's head. If the family does not concede to give you and your mother your proper places in the funeral procession, we will not join the cortege in the morning. We will not lose face. I will not bring the anger of our ancestors upon my children. I will prepare food for the day and we will mourn here in private, with dignity and humility."

"We can't," he argued. "That would be even more disrespectful to my father. The whole town will notice we're missing from the funeral procession."

All my anger against the Laus for mistreating my family rose from the well deep in my heart where I hid my ugliest secrets. They would never hurt us again. I snatched up his whiskey glass and smashed it against the wall. "What you have agreed to is worse. It is dishonorable to the name of Lau Ah Leong. Before he died he recognized that you were his loyal First son, the one who should have been his heir. Will you go against his wishes? He wanted you to carry his legacy forward. I will not bring evil and bad luck to our family. Think of your children! It is better to pray respectfully here in our own home than to march behind Ho Shee and Ah Wang and incur the wrath of our ancestors."

He buried his face in his arms. I did not know if my husband could bear to abandon his filial duty on the day of his father's funeral.

But my mind was made up. No matter how much distress my disobedience caused, I was determined to return home with my children before the funeral if Ah Wang and Ho Shee did not observe the proper hierarchy.

All of Honolulu would be watching.

❧❧

Ah Leong, dressed in a new Chinese coat buttoned with mandarin knots and sharply creased trousers, seemed to sleep peacefully. "Goodbye," I whispered when the family walked past him for the last time. "Do not forget your promise to watch over my children, *Baba*. Your protection is all you can give them now." My hands trembled. "Please forgive us for not honoring you in your procession. Please, let us mourn you our own way, with dignity."

After dawn seared the sky, the entire clan emerged from our all-night vigil exhausted and numb. Everyone stumbled out of the mortuary worn from the droning of the priests and wailing of the professional mourners. Our eyes burnt from the thick heavy clouds of incense that had burned all night. With hundreds of relatives sitting vigil, and hundreds of carnation wreaths lining the walls, the funeral parlor had become nauseatingly clammy. The youngest grandchildren slept fitfully and occasionally cried out with horrifying nightmares.

Nu'uanu Mortuary carried Ah Leong's casket to the black hearse gleaming brilliantly in the steaming sun. His portrait was already mounted on the hood, draped in black satin. Behind the hearse, Second wife Ho Shee walked to her position as the First wife. Her eldest son, Ah Wang, followed holding the lighted incense in memory of his father. Behind them, the sons and wives would march. And behind them, the grandchildren. The rest of the extended family had designated places behind the immediate family.

Five brass bands, led by the Royal Hawaiian Band and the St. Louis College Band behind the Lau family, lined up in the funeral procession, one of the largest in Hawai'i's history. Hundreds of people of all ethnicities–politicians, businessmen, customers, friends, farmers–joined the procession honoring Ah Leong's last ride through Honolulu.

Just before the bands began, Ah Wang noticed that Dai-Kam and Tat-Tung were missing. Ah Wang sent his brothers to check the grounds of the mortuary and scout up and down the street. Meanwhile, hundreds of mourners milled about, fanning themselves as the morning sun rose. The bands, the civic organizations, and the family associations swayed impatiently. The funeral director asked if they could please start.

Ah Wang turned as pale as the white carnations topping the hearse. Sweat coated his forehead and the back of his neck. "No. My brother's not here." His mother Ho Shee and his wife looked angry. His brothers shifted their weight from foot to foot. The rest of the marchers wilted in the melting heat.

☜☞

Tat-Tung answered the phone when Ah Wang called.

I heard the screams of brothers, wives, and children in the background.

Within minutes, carloads of Laus arrived at our house on Circle Lane. The mourners clamored up the porch steps.

The black wreath on our front door bounced with Ah Wang's frantic tapping. "Come now, Tat-Tung, hurry," he pleaded.

Behind him, the brothers and their wives grumbled. "Think of what everyone will say if you're not there. Everyone will talk about us if the family doesn't appear together. We will be shamed. You dishonor our father."

When Tat-Tung opened the door, the Laus spilled into our parlor. My husband stepped back with his hands in his pockets and stared at them with a glare grown colder over the past ten years.

"You talk about dishonor. How about the dishonor you bring our First mother and my family? Dishonor indeed. Here is our father's First wife who should walk behind her husband. You know she was his First wife and the first to bear him sons." He gestured to Dai-Kam sitting rigidly in a wing-backed chair, glaring angrily at the intruders.

Tat-Tung turned to Ah Wang and placed his hands on his shoulders.

"My dearest brother, how can you walk in my place as his eldest son? How disrespectful you are of the customs we were all brought up to follow. Has this world turned your head so much that you think only of yourself? I have heard all of you argue and fight among yourselves for money and prestige. I do not fight for the same things. I honor my family and keep the traditions." He walked to his mother's side and faced his brothers.

"What do you want?" Ah Wang asked, waving back the brothers and wives pushing behind him.

"Protocol and honor. Mother walks behind our father as his First wife. I lead the family as the First son."

"Naw," ridiculed Fourth brother Ah Chung. He stuck his hands in his pockets and turned to the others. "This is America. What difference does it make where you walk in a funeral?" Ho Shee's sons agreed with him. Tat-Tung glared at his traitorous brother.

"Ah Wang," bellowed Dai-Kam. She pointed an accusing finger. "It's all your fault. You should fight for what is right. You agreed earlier this week that we were going to do it the right way." Her dark eyes blazed.

Ah Wang flushed and tried to defer the confrontation. "My mother and brothers made the decision. I am not dishonoring you. I want you all there at *Baba*'s funeral. Hundreds are waiting."

Tat-Tung lowered his voice. "You didn't do anything about correcting the arrangements whenever I brought it up. You sided with your mother against me. I've always protected you, Ah Wang, kept you from making mistakes. How many times I have saved your life. Don't betray me now."

"Ah Wang, you weakling," Dai-Kam added to the argument. "If you want us to come, you fix everything the way it's supposed to be. Twenty generations of Chinese ancestors are waiting for your father to be buried correctly. Honor him."

"What's done is done. We are late," he pleaded again.

"Will Mother walk behind *Baba*?" asked Tat-Tung.

"It's already set," Ah Wang answered meekly.

"Then go to *Baba*'s funeral. Let everyone see what fools you are and what dishonor you bring to our family and ancestors. We will honor him with dignity and respect here." Tat-Tung opened the front door to let them out.

His brothers stepped back. They were confused. They looked to both Tat-Tung and Ah Wang for direction.

Ah Wang hung his head and apologized. Then he turned to the others. "Come, let's go. We should not have questioned Tat-Tung. There's nothing we can do now. He'll come when he's ready. *Baba* must be buried." He turned to his elder brother. His eyes softened. "You'll come, won't you?"

Tat-Tung stood silently and motioned him out.

"Yes, yes, Ah Wang." The brothers turned with embarrassment towards the door. "Sorry, Tat-Tung. We'll leave. Good-bye, Mother, we'll see you when you get to the funeral."

Dai-Kam glared at her sons and daughters-in-law. They jumped in their cars and zoomed out of Circle Lane leaving hot swirls of dust in their haste.

The children and I sat through the entire performance in stunned and embarrassed silence. I was alarmed by the growing pallor of my husband's face.

"Lie down for a while," I coaxed.

"No, I'll sit here," he answered. He straightened his shoulders, stretched his back, and lowered himself stiffly in his high-backed reading chair.

That day reminded Dai-Kam why she was so afraid of her son.

☜☞

I saved L. Ah Leong's obituary from the *Honolulu Star-Bulletin*. There were many legends about L. Ah Leong, so many tales, some true. I hoped someday my children would know he was held in high esteem by the white Americans.

The Americans called him the Merchant Prince of Hawaii. His obituary recounted his fifty-eight-year history in the islands starting with his arrival in 1876. The Americans considered his life a Horatio Alger tale. They touted that he was a poor beggar from Kew Boy Village in China who, through his own industry and thrift, accumulated a vast fortune in Hawai'i. They say he was worth over a million dollars a few years ago. That he owned real estate, stocks, bonds, and businesses.

Tat-Tung crumpled up the obituary when it appeared in the American papers the day after his father died. I know it contained lies, that it did not name Dai-Kam as his wife, that the sons were listed in the wrong order. But someday my children and their children will want to know the truth.

And we must learn from lies as well as truth.

Chapter Thirty

Where the Wind Was as Sweet as Wild Gingers:

May 1935

I whizzed around the bend of Circle Lane to our house with a carload of children. I passed my neighbor Loretta Akana's house and motioned that I would be right back.

Loretta nodded, her hands busily stringing the leis for the visitors due on the next ship. Giant Catalaya orchids framed one side of her face. Their deep violet colors matched her mu'umu'u, reminiscent of an overflowing garden. Lauhala baskets of fresh blooms, rich with the scent of dew on perfect petals, surrounded her ample figure on the front porch.

I shooed my brood into the house to change to their play clothes, then put out fruits for their afternoon snacks. Manners, please, I reminded them before they walked to the Akana's. They were the picture of decorum until they caught sight of the Akanas in the backyard with the other neighborhood children. Off they ran.

I changed to a blue cotton *cheong-sam*. I traced the pattern of flowers with my fingers and marveled at how lighthearted it made me feel. It had been a year since I wore anything but black or white. The night L. Ah Leong died, all the women had to strip off their jewelry, even saw off their solid gold bracelets. I hadn't worn jewelry since Ah Leong died, and had missed their bobbing movement. As I walked to Loretta's, I twirled my wedding ring awkwardly and reached up to touch the comfortable weight of my jade and diamond earrings.

"You look nice. New dress?" Loretta kidded me when I saw her.

"One whole year you never come see me. That's a long time to stay home and go no place."

"It's just our custom. It's for respect," I answered. We had not visited anyone except family for a whole year following Ah Leong's death, and could not go to any parties or celebrations during the long mourning period. We could not wear jewelry or brightly colored clothing, especially red. I knew these were old customs, but who knew what ghosts clung to us during this time? We did not want to be the ones to spread bad luck or death.

"Speaking of respect, you know the new governor who was appointed by the President?" Loretta asked without a pause in lei-making.

I shook my head.

"Well, Danny said that our new Governor Poindexter is the same Judge Poindexter who decided against your mother-in-law over ten years ago. You know, the one when L. Ah Leong said the first Mrs. Lau was not his wife. Then your husband got mad and quit work at the store because the second Mrs. Lau was making trouble for him because he was the son of the first Mrs. Lau..."

"Yes, yes, yes," I nodded finally. "Governor Poindexter was the Judge?"

"Not only that, but District Attorney Huber, who was the D.A. on Ah Leong's side before Carden was elected D.A., just got appointed to the U.S. District Court of Hawai'i. My husband said he was talking to the guys at the police station about how the Democrats are taking over. When they started naming all the big shots in government, Danny realized they were the ones who were so cozy with your father-in-law. That's how business and politics work here." Loretta nodded with affirmation. "All in the hands of a few, and their friends."

One of Loretta's daughters, with the same sweet gentle ways and generous mane of chestnut hair, gathered up the finished leis in large lauhala baskets to store in the coolest part of the house. She brought more baskets of flowers. Her mother continued as nimbly as before, stringing them into intricate leis.

"Have you heard from your husband's family in China?" asked Loretta. She handed her daughter a dozen strung leis.

"They had to move back to *Ming Yang Tong*, Ah Leong's estate, to observe the year of mourning. Yukmoy and I sent them money for the funeral rituals. Every day for three months they had to have a different ceremony or banquet to honor Ah Leong, with auspicious seafood imported from the coast, to ease my father-in-law's path through the Seven Heavens."

Wong Shee had been diligent in her preparations, as usual. Now that she was back in Kew Boy with her daughter-in-law and her six grandchildren, she looked after all of Ah Leong's homes and lands by herself. Her son Ah Chen was an attorney in Canton. But even with his income, there was never enough money to maintain all of Ah Leong's grand estates in the style that he had envisioned.

Loretta ooh'd and aah'd as I described the elaborate ceremonies attended by thousands of mourners in China. "They must have thought he was a god," she exclaimed.

"The Money Dragon, they called him," I agreed. "He left his China family three homes that must seem like palaces to the villagers. I hear they still talk about his banquets when he fed two thousand people a day." I sighed, remembering the hot winds that kissed the trees in the open-air atriums of *Ming Yang Tong*, and how softly my footsteps floated on the thick silk carpets. I hoped to return, someday.

"You don't see your mother-in-law anymore?" Loretta asked.

I flushed. "She calls Tat-Tung when she needs something. But you know she never cared for us or our children." I wiped a sudden tear, prompted by the long-ago image of Ah Leong bent over our newborn daughter, tenderly stroking her cheek.

Dr. Chang roared past in his new convertible and waved. By his lighthearted attitude, we could tell that today was his day off. He said he would be moving soon, to a bigger house in stylish Makiki Heights. We congratulated him though we would miss him as our neighbor and family doctor.

Loretta spied Tat-Tung stroll up the lane dressed casually in a light-weight suit with a packet of papers, tax work from this morning's client, tucked under an arm. "Mr. Lau. Yoo hoo! Over here!" she called, flailing a lei over her head.

He turned and joined us on Loretta's front porch. The cocky strut of his younger days was now a dignified pace. Drawn and skinny, he had never recovered from the sixteen-hours-a-day pace of running the L. Ah Leong Store. Fortunately, he was in demand as an accountant.

We talked in the shade until the Hawaiian Electric whistle announced the imminent arrival of a steam ship. Loretta and her daughter gathered up their baskets of leis. I rounded up my children and sent them home with their father. When Loretta's aunties drove up in a hustle of dust, I helped the women add Loretta's baskets to their stack. Then I blew kisses for good luck and called "*Aloha, Aloha, Aloha,*" until they turned onto Beretania Street.

"Hey, Mom, let's go for a ride!"

I turned swiftly and smiled at the sight of Tat-Tung and our five children calling through the open windows of the Packard. They threw open the passenger door. I slid in next to my husband. His eyes danced now, so bright and lively. I wondered if he knew they creased into smiles at the corners when he was with us.

He dodged the heavy traffic and parked by the pier where we could watch the approach of the arriving ship in Honolulu Harbor. For all the years we had lived in Hawai'i, we had never come down to Boat Day just for fun. In fact, we had not had any money to do anything just for fun.

"Come on, let's get closer," Tat-Tung suggested. I laughed, surprised by his unusual spontaneity. We strolled along the pier enjoying the press of warm bodies and fragrant flowers. As we stood surrounded by the swell of the Royal Hawaiian Band and the scent of leis carried aloft by the lei sellers, he leaned down and whispered in my ear, "Someday, I'll send you home on a ship like this to visit your mother."

I stopped his lips with my fingers. "We don't have the money. We barely get by now." What was wrong with him, I fumed. I hated his teasing about money; I was the one who worried about stretching the meager dollars to feed and clothe our family.

With absolute seriousness, he announced, "Mrs. Lau Tat-Tung, we are now the owners of Lusitana Market, grocery and general merchandise."

"What nonsense!" I huffed.

"L. Ah Low's son, Lau Chip Quon, is going back to China. He wants me to take over his store," he said as if it were the most logical thing to do. Ah Leong and Dai-Kam had worked for L. Ah Low when they moved to Honolulu from Kohala more than fifty years ago.

"For free?" I asked. Amazement lifted my voice. It was a small store in a good residential neighborhood in Honolulu. But it took money to run a store. We had nothing extra.

"Ah Wang is giving me credit to stock it at wholesale prices. A family deal between the two of us. Lau Chip Quon leaves for Shanghai for good, so the store is ours."

So Ah Wang had found a way to help his brother around the confines of their father's will. When Ah Leong died, Ah Wang had taken over the L. Ah Leong Store. Their father's vast land holdings were sold and the proceeds went to Ho Shee and her sons. We heard they fought each other for larger shares. Acrimonious suits and countersuits were filed, brother against brother. We did not know who won. This was not what L. Ah Leong would have wanted; he had built three homes, the largest a 118-bedroom estate for all his wives, sons, and grandchildren to live together in China with two hundred farms and businesses in Hawai'i and China to support them all.

We felt that this was the bitter part of the family history best forgotten.

I looked at my husband, wanting him to continue. Instead, he pointed to the local boys calling to the passengers to throw quarters and silver dollars into the sea. The boys dove for the coins with neat tucks and surfaced waving their bounty above their heads. We cheered for these audacious young men risking all for a few cents, bravado, and a demonstration of masculinity. We were going to take a chance, like them, and dive into the unknown. For those who took the risk, there was the opportunity to succeed.

Loretta Akana sashayed over with a bountiful smile. "*Aloha*," she beamed and handed Tat-Tung an orchid lei. "You have given your wife some good news. Now you give her your *Aloha* Hawaiian-style, right?"

Tat-Tung reached for his wallet.

Loretta stopped him with a shake of her head. "Don't offend me. I'm your friend. It's time for some love and good luck in your life." She tossed us a smile and sauntered towards the disembarking passengers, singing a Hawaiian melody.

❦❦

From the gaiety of the dock, Tat-Tung drove up the winding two-lane road to Manoa Valley. We passed wooden homes, mom-and-pop groceries, and the last of the taro and chicken farms that had once dominated this picturesque valley of waterfalls and streams. He followed Manoa Road to the top of the Chinese cemetery and parked under the banyan tree at the highest point of the graveyard. Here, the winds were as sweet as the wild gingers. He led us along the maze of ornate marble tombstones, carved statues, and mausoleums, to his father's grave.

Ah Leong's grandiose monument was high on the hill, on a prestigious site overlooking the lush valley. I suspected my husband visited his father when he knew no other Laus were going to be here, when the two could be alone.

I bit my lip when I saw that today, on the first anniversary of Ah Leong's death, there were no flowers, no incense sticks, no offerings of food to feed his hungry spirit. "Oh, *Baba*, how hungry and lonely you must be," I whispered. I knelt sorrowfully before his tombstone and traced his name carved deep in the black marble.

While Tat-Tung cupped his hands and lit the candles and incense, our children cleared away the dried leaves and pulled the weeds from the grave. My husband placed the white carnation lei that Loretta made for this occasion so that his father's carved name was circled with blossoms. Below it, he laid out platters of Ah Leong's favorite dishes that we had prepared that morning. He clasped his hands and bowed three times, saying his private prayers. The children and I took our turns, one by one.

Eat, *Baba*, I prayed. Enjoy. We're here to honor you.

At the foot of the grave, I grasped Tat-Tung's hand and looked deep into the dark eyes that had seen so much pain. I thought back to the very first time I met my husband's father, how profusely I thanked him for rescuing me. He had paid my passage to Hawai'i and forced Immigration to release me.

I leaned against my husband's shoulder. "I remember many things about *Baba*," I said. "But my fondest memory is the sound of his horses, 'clop-a, clop-a, clop-a,' as they carried me away from the boat, to my new life under the protection of L. Ah Leong, the Money Dragon." The warmth of Tat-Tung's arm around my shoulders when he pulled me closer felt like a protective shield.

He stared at the sharp red glow of the incense sticks bobbing in the breeze that whirled around the edges of the food. "Seventeen years ago," he reminisced. His voice surged with passion. "I thought the carriage wheels would fly off when *Baba* raced his horses to get you."

With each tear that fell in his memory, we released the sorrow, the struggles and his ruthless ambition.

L. Ah Leong left us a legacy. Never again would the streets of Honolulu hear the charm of his glib banter or the legends of how he amassed his great fortune.

He may be forgotten in time, the memory of this extraordinary merchant as obscure as his grave. But his legend lives on in the bustle of Chinatown, the dust of old stories, and his seed scattered to the wind.

Glossary

H = Hawaiian   C = Chinese

‘A‘ala. Section of Honolulu near Nu‘uanu River emptying into Honolulu Harbor. (H)

Ah Bahk. Uncle. (C)

Ah moy. Little sister. (C)

Ahuna. Hawaiian nickname for Lau Kong Yin. (H)

ai-yah. Alas! (C)

aku. Bonito, skipjack. (H)

ali‘i. Nobility. (H)

Aloha. Love, kindness, hello, good-bye, farewell, alas! (H)

‘ama’ama. Mullet, a choice indigenous fish. (H)

amah. A child's maid. (C)

auwe. Alas! (H)

‘awapuhi melemele. The fragrant yellow ginger flower popularly used for leis. (C)

Baba. Father. (C)

Bodhisattva. In Mahayana Buddhism, a saintly being who remains on earth to help other humans.

bok choy. A familiar Chinese vegetable with fleshy stems and green leaves. (H)

bow-lei tea. A rich black tea reputed to have medicinal properties. (C)

Chang-An (Xi'an). Ancient capital of China under the rein of the First Emperor of the Qin Dynasty, Shihuangdi (403–221 B.C.). (C)

char siu. Chinese roast pork. (C)

cheong-sam. Fitted, mandarin-collared Chinese dress. (C)

ch'i. Human spirit, energy, or cosmic breath. (C)

Confucius. The Chinese sage (551–479 BC) born of a poor but aristocratic family in Shantung province. Throughout his life, he was best known as a teacher. When he died at the age of seventy-two, he had taught a total of three thousand disciples who carried on his teaching. Three doctrines of Confucius are particularly important. The first is benevolence. Confucius considered benevolence as something people cultivate within themselves before it can affect their relations with others. The second doctrine concerns the superior man. The superior man is one who practices benevolence regardless of family background. Ritual propriety is the third doctrine. Confucius emphasized right behavior in one's relations; man should act in accordance with propriety.

dim sum. "Heart's delight," Chinese tea cakes.(C)

Do-jei. Thank you. (C)

face. One's respect and honor within the community.

feng shui. Traditional Chinese technique which aims to ensure that all things are in harmony with their surroundings. (C)

Fukien Province (Fujian). A province in southeastern China which lies on the Formosa Strait across from Taiwan.

Galicians. People from Galicia, a historic region of Eastern Europe, located north of the Carpathian Mountains and extending from the area around Krakow in Poland as far east as Ternopol in Ukraine.

Great Mahele. Upon the urging of his foreign advisors, King Kamehameha III divided all the Hawaiian lands into three parts in 1848: one part for himself and his heirs, one third for the government, and a final third to be distributed among the common people. This land division and its laws, known as the Great Mahele, allowed ordinary native Hawaiians to own property for the first time.

Gum Sahn Yun. "Gold Mountain Men." Chinese who went to San Francisco. (C)

Hankow. One of the three towns which make up Wuhan (Wu-han), the capital of Hubei (Hupei) province and the major industrial, cultural, and transportation center of central China, at the confluence of the Chang Jiang (Yangtze) and Han rivers.

Hakoko. Ancient type of sitting wrestling. The objective is to topple the opponent. (H)

Hakka. Chinese who were "newcomers" or "guest people," not the earliest settlers. Hakka are found not only in Kwantung Province but throughout other provinces in China and in foreign countries. (C)

haku. Braided lei. (H)

haole. Caucasian: American, English, any foreigner. (H)

Havanas. Cigars from Havana, Cuba.

heiaus. Pre-Christian place of worship ranging from elaborately constructed stone platforms to simple earth terraces. (H)

herbalists. Chinese healer who uses herbs as a key element of treatment which also encompasses the philosophy of well-being of body and soul.

Heungshan District. West River delta area lying west of the Pearl River estuary, named for the fragrant flowers growing there, renamed Chungshan to honor its native son Dr. Sun Yat-sen. (C)

holoku. Loose, seamed long dress with a yoke and train. (H)

Hop Mian Lau. The third of Lau Ah Leong's homes in Kew Boy, built as a place to study. It has eighteen bedrooms. (H)

Horatio Alger. Author of heroic characters who rise to prominence from poor childhoods by performing a daring brave deed to win the support and patronage of a benefactor.

Jiaoling. River city in the mountainous Mei Hsien district. (C)

jing. The creative force inside the body. (C)

jook. Chinese rice gruel. (C)

Kahuku. Northern part of Oʻahu. Site of sugar plantations. (H)

Kaimuki. Section of Honolulu between Ala Wai and Kahala, and St. Louis Heights and Diamond Head. (H)

Kamaʻaina. Native born. (H)

Kamakela. Archaic Hawaiian designation of the area between ʻAʻala and Nuʻuanu. (H)

kapu. Taboo, forbidden, sacred. (H)

keiki. Child, offspring, descendant. (H)

Kew Boy. Small mountainous village in Mei Hsien district of Canton near its northernmost border adjacent to Fukien Province. (C)

Koʻolau. Windward mountain range of Oʻahu. (H)

koa. Fine red wood formerly used for canoes, surfboards, calabashes, now for furniture and ukuleles. (H)

Kowloon (Zhoulong, Chiou-lung). A town on the west shore of Kowloon Peninsula, southeastern China, in the British crown colony of Hong Kong.

Kuomintang. Organized in 1912 to succeed the society founded in 1905 by Sun Yat-Sen to overthrow the Qing (Chʼing, or Manchu) dynasty. Although Sun had been elected (1911) provisional president of the new Chinese republic, he reluctantly yielded the presidency to the north China military leader Yuan Shih-kʼai. Sun Yat-sen became director of the Kuomintang, which was organized as a political party advocating a system of parliamentary government. After the first KMT election victory, however, Yuan had all Kuomintang members, including Sun, expelled from the assembly. Many fled the country, and Yuan became virtual dictator by 1914. Not until Yuanʼs death, in 1916, did the exiles dare to resume political leadership. Sunʼs Kuomintang government assumed control at Guangzhou (Canton) in 1917. (C)

Kwan Yin. Chinese Bodhisattva of Mercy and Compassion. (C)

Kwang Tung (Guangdong, Kwantung). Province in South China, ancestral home of the early migrants to Hawai'i (C)

Kwangzhou. Guangzhou, Canton. (C)

Kweilin (Gweilin, Gui Lin). area in central China noted for its peculiar topography of majestic limestone hills perforated with caverns in weird shapes.

Lao Tzu. Laozi (Lao-tzu), or Master Lao, is the name of the supposed author of the Taoist classic Tao-te Ching. An older contemporary of Confucius (551–479 BC), he was keeper of the archives at the imperial court. In his eightieth year, he set out for the western border of China, toward what is now Tibet, saddened and disillusioned that men were unwilling to follow his path to natural goodness. At the border, the guard requested that he record his teachings before he left, whereupon he composed in five thousand words *The Way and Its Power.* The essential teaching is the way of the universe exemplified in nature. The harmony of opposites is achieved through a blend of the yin (feminine force) and the yang (masculine force); this harmony can be cultivated through creative quietude, an effortless action whose power maintains equanimity and balance. (C)

lauhala. Pandanus leaf used in plaiting. (H)

lei. Necklace of flowers, leaves, shells, ivory, feathers, or paper given as a symbol of affection. (H)

li-see. Chinese good-luck money wrapped in red paper. (C)

lokelani. The common small red rose. (H)

loongan. A Chinese fruit. (C)

loquat. An orange-yellow skinned Chinese fruit. (C)

luna. Foreman, overseer. (H)

mah-jongg. Chinese game played with tiles. (C)

mahimahi. Dolphin. (H)

Makai. In the direction of the ocean. (H)

Makiki. Residential area of Honolulu near Punchbowl. (H)

manapua. Chinese pork buns. (H)

Manoa. Residential area in the cool Manoa valley inland from Waikiki. (H)

Mei Hsien. Primarily Hakka district (Kayingchow) in northern section of Kwang Tung Province. (C)

min nap. Elegant quilted jacket with mandarin collar and knotted buttons. (C)

Ming Yang Tong. "The Shining House Beyond the Bridge," Lau Ah Leong's largest house with bedrooms for 118 descendants. (C)

monkeypod. A fine Hawaiian wood used for furniture, calabashes, and utensils.

moonharp. Chinese stringed instrument played with fine bamboo slivers.

mui tsui. servant (C)

Nam Nong. Cantonese dialect spoken by many Chinese in Hawai'i. (C)

Nam Shun Lau. "The Story of the Southern Breeze," Lau Ah Leong's second largest house with bedrooms for forty-eight descendants. (C)

Nu'uanu. Cool valley above Honolulu, once the summer home of the ali'i, legendary home of the mythical Hawaiian menehunes. (H)

'ohana. Extended family, clan. (H)

Okoleha'o. Liquor distilled from ti root and later, a gin made of rice or pineapples. (H)

opihi. Limpets. (H)

pak-lan. Flower tree valued by the Chinese for its delicate fragrance. (C)

pakalana. The Chinese violet with yellowish-green flowers. (H)

Pake. Chinese. (H)

pomelo. Chinese grapefruit.

saimin. Local-style noodles.

Shee. "Wife." Married Chinese women were known by their last name followed by "Shee" to denote they were married. (C)

Shenzhen. A city in Guangdong (Kwangtung) province, China, is located near Hong Kong on the east side of the Pearl River Delta. (C)

Tai Tong Mee. The Chong family home of Phoenix (Chong Fung-Yin) in Mei Hsien. (C)

Tan Heung Shan. "Fragrant Sandalwood Mountains," Hawai'i. (C)

Tientsin rug. Rug from the famed Tientsin rug-making area of China.

tilapia. Perch-like freshwater fish that used to be farmed on O'ahu.

ulua. Certain species of jack or pompano. (H)

wah kiu. "Overseas Chinese." (C)

Wai'anae. Coast area of O'ahu between Ka'ena and Barbers Point. (H)

Waikiki. Famed beach in central Honolulu. (H)

Waimanalo. Coastal area designated primarily as Hawaiian Homestead lands, a quiet country area inhabited primarily by native Hawaiians and their descendants. (H)

Photographs and
Documents

THE HAWAIIAN KINGDOM

RECORD OF NATURALIZATION.

In the Department of the Interior,

In the Matter of the Naturalization of

L. Ah Leong

Be it Remembered that on this____ day of ___October___ A.D. 189 0, L. Ah Leong _____ an alien and late a subject or citizen of ___Canton, Kwang Tung, China___ applied in writing to the Minister of the Interior to be admitted a Citizen of the Hawaiian Kingdom pursuant to the acts of the Hawaiian Legislature in relation thereto, and it appearing by his said application and by other satisfactory proofs that he has resided within the Kingdom for ten years next preceding said application, and that he intends to become a permanent resident of this Kingdom, and that he is not a party nor a refugee from the justice of some other country, and his said application having been approved by the Minister of the Interior, and the said L. Ah Leong _____ having on the 12th day of November A.D. 189 0, taken and subscribed the Oath of Allegiance required by law before J.A.Hassinger Chief Clerk.Int.Dept. therefore I do admit said L. Ah Leong - - - - - - - and declare him to be a Citizen of the Hawaiian Kingdom.

(sgd) C. N. Spencer,

Minister of the Interior

3. L. Ah Leong's Record of Naturalization
November 12, 1890. (National Archives. San Bruno)

1. L. Ah Leong's Record of Naturalization: Kingdom of Hawaiʻi. November 12, 1890.
Only one hundred Chinese men were naturalized and thus allowed to vote under the Hawaiian monarchy. Ah Leong's guarantors are indicative of his influential connections. U.S. Immigration interviews in 1903, 1910, 1915, and 1919 note that L. Ah Leong presented this certified copy of his Record of Naturalization each time he applied for a passport to travel to China.
(National Archives, San Bruno)

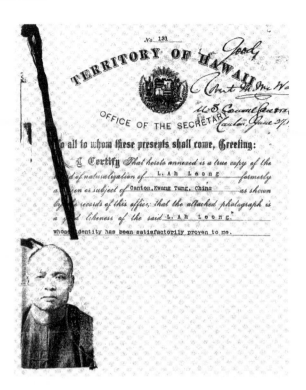

2. L. Ah Leong's Certificate of Naturalization: Territory of Hawai'i. June 2, 1902.

The provisions of the "Bayonet Constitution" that King Kalakaua was forced to sign in 1887 offended the established Chinese who considered themselves Hawaiian residents. Article 59 specifically gave Caucasian male residents who met certain property qualifications the right to vote. Naturalized Asians were denied the right to vote, but Caucasians could qualify without becoming citizens of Hawai'i. Following annexation to the United States, Chinese and others who had become naturalized subjects of Hawai'i were considered American citizens. The Organic Act in 1900 made all U.S. laws applicable in Hawai'i including the Chinese Exclusion Act of 1882 that prohibited Chinese from becoming naturalized citizens. Since L. Ah Leong was a naturalized citizen of the Kingdom of Hawai'i, he was classified as a naturalized citizen of the Territory of Hawai'i. However, Chinese born in Hawai'i were classified as nonresident citizens by U.S. Immigration.

(National Archives, San Bruno)

3. L. Ah Leong.
In 1902, L. Ah Leong was forty-six years old, a Chinese merchant respected for his conservative approach to business. He lived with his four wives in Honolulu and owned L. Ah Leong Store in the newly rebuilt Chinatown.
(National Archives, San Bruno)

4. The First wife, Fung Dai-Kam.

Fung Dai-Kam married L. Ah Leong in Kohala, on the island of Hawai'i, in 1881. She was seventeen. After his business went bankrupt, the couple moved to Honolulu where he worked for L. Ah Low as a clerk and she cooked for the L. Ah Low family. After ten months they had saved eighty dollars. They used this savings and her $200 dowry to open a grocery and general merchandise store in Kaka'ako across from 'Iolani Palace and Kawaiaha'o Church.

(National Archives, San Bruno, undated.)

5. L. Ah Leong's first estate, *Nam Shun Lau,* in Kew Boy.

L. Ah Leong built *Nam Shun Lau,* "The Story of the Southern Breeze," in 1903 when he and his sons Tat-Tung and Ah Wang returned to his village, Kew Boy, in the Mei Hsien district of Kwang Tung Province. Within its walls are two to three open-air courts, a small garden, and forty-eight bedrooms. Ah Leong married Wong Shee to care for his homes in China, the farms around it, and his families. At age thirteen, Tat-Tung was expected to monitor its construction and pay the workmen and building suppliers. Wong Shee had one son who became an attorney in Canton.

(Author's private collection)

6. L. Ah Leong's estate *Ming Yang Tong*.

Once surrounded by three hundred acres of farmland, *Ming Yang Tong*, The Shining House Beyond the Bridge, contains 118 bedrooms. An unusually high wall encloses the house and gardens which were planted with lychee, loongan, star fruit, grapefruit, and tangerine trees. On the grounds, Ah Leong built a third house with eighteen bedrooms that was to be used by the family while they were studying. Wong Shee managed all three homes as well as the surrounding farms. Lau Ah Leong boasted that the exorbitant price he paid for the land for this house was equal to layering every inch of earth with precious Chinese silver coins. Wong Shee died in 1949. The Communists killed her only son in 1950 for being an intellectual and a land owner. They took all L. Ah Leong's property and his attorney son's three-story house in Canton. Ah Chen's wife and twelve children were driven out of their homes which stand vacant today. The villagers say the homes are haunted.

(Author's private collection)

7. Tat-Tung and Phoenix Chong Fung-Yin Lau with their first-born daughter Fung Tai.

Twenty-eight-year-old Tat-Tung and his eighteen-year-old wife Phoenix arrived in Honolulu, Hawai'i, in 1918. U.S. Immigration admitted Tat-Tung as a native-born citizen. Like all Chinese born in Hawai'i, he was considered a nonresident. As his wife, Phoenix was assigned her husband's status. Immigration found the only discrepancy in the testimonies between Tat-Tung and Phoenix was that he claimed two men carried her in the sedan chair from her father's house to her husband's, and she claimed there were four. The Chinese interpreter stated that it was customary to have four men when the first wife is married and two when a concubine is taken, but that among the Hakka people they are as apt to have two men for a genuine wife as for a concubine. Phoenix did not assume that the Americans knew the difference between Hakka and Punti marriage customs. She wanted to be sure they knew she came as Tat-Tung's wife.

(1918. Author's private collection)

8. Dai-Kam's three daughters-in-law.

(Left to right) Ah Chung's wife Yukmoy, Tat-Tung's wife Phoenix Chong Fung-Yin, Ah Kong's wife Ho Fun Chew.

Fung Dai-Kam considered Yukmoy, wife of Fourth son Ah Chung, the most beautiful and her favorite daughter-in-law. Phoenix should have ranked higher than Yukmoy, but Dai-Kam regarded her as a renegade, the naughty one. Third son Ah Kong and his wife shared the same small bungalow with Tat-Tung and his family before Phoenix bought the house on Circle Lane and moved her family out.

(Approximately 1919. Author's private collection)

9. L. Ah Leong's Immigration Form 430 with photo. 1919.

L. Ah Leong submitted an application for a passport with a dollar bill and a loose photograph of himself as required under the Chinese Exclusion Act, along with his Citizen Identity card number 1932 and a certified copy of his record of naturalization as a citizen of Hawai'i on November 12, 1890. U.S. Immigration Inspector-in-Charge Halsey denied his request because he did not show "an absolute necessity for traveling abroad." The Chamber of Commerce of Honolulu interceded on L. Ah Leong's behalf. Halsey granted L. Ah Leong the right to go to China for business purposes. This was the last time Ah Leong saw his homes and family in China.

(National Archives, San Bruno)

10. Phoenix with daughter Fung-Tai and son Yung Chan.

Phoenix's status rose with the birth of her son, Yung Chan. Phoenix, carrying her infant son, is now twenty and her daughter Fung-Tai is two.

(1919. Author's private collection)

11. Tat-Tung's children.

(Left to right) daughter Fung-Tai is four, Edith (daughter of his first wife Wong Pin) is fifteen, daughter Ah Hin is less than one, and his First son Yung Chan is three.

(1922. Author's private collection)

12. Family picture.
Phoenix and Tat-Tung with their natural-born and adopted children.
(Left to right) Fung-Tai, Lani (Ah Wang's daughter), Phoenix, Ah Hin, Ah Gin,
Tat-Tung carries their last daughter Ah Fung, Edith (daughter of his first wife
Wong Pin), and his eldest son Yung Chan. Edith is nineteen and Lani is eleven.
(1925. Author's private collection)

13. Tat-Tung with his brother Ah Kong's family in Shanghai.
Tat-Tung managed his father's business interests in China and Hawai'i. In 1925 and 1926, he visited his brother Ah Kong in Shanghai to check on his stock-brokerage business, which he found never existed. On the 1926 visit, Tat-Tung was stopped by his father's Fifth wife Wong Shee from entering Kew Boy. That morning, their largest estate had been surrounded and attacked by hundreds of bandits who hoped to kidnap one of L. Ah Leong's American sons, who they anticipated would come for Ah Sang's wedding celebrations.
(1926. Author's private collection)

14. Kew Boy Village, Kwang Tung Province, China.
In 1926, bandits from Wong Soo Sang mountains in Fukien swept down on
Ming Yang Tong, Ah Leong's largest estate. Tat-Tung arrived that afternoon. L.
Ah Leong's Fifth wife Wong Shee hid him in *Nam Shun Lau*, the second largest
estate within the town of Kew Boy. *Nam Shun Lau* is the large rectangular complex of tiled roofed buildings in the lower right corner of the village, next to the
arched bridge. Lau Ah Leong built this bridge for access across the river to his
largest estate, *Ming Yang Tong*.
(Author's private collection)

15. L. Ah Leong's seventy-first birthday photo.

For the Chinese, one's seventy-first birthday is most auspicious. Second wife Ho Shee threw a large party at Wo Fat Restaurant in Honolulu, Hawai'i to celebrate the occasion. All sons received a copy of L. Ah Leong's portrait.

(1926. Author's private collection)

16. The herbalist Yuen Gnew-Nam.

Yuen Gnew-Nam was born in 1856, the same year as L. Ah Leong. He left his Punti village of Chuck Hum in the Pearl River Delta at thirteen with his uncle to raise chickens in New Zealand. He returned to Chuck Hum, married, then left immediately for Hawai'i. He returned nine years later for his wife and nine-year-old daughter, Sun Mui. Yuen operated a laundry in Chinatown until it was destroyed in the Chinatown fire of 1900. He moved to Manoa Valley and earned a living as a woodcutter and taro grower. He was known as a healer. He could be found in the heart of Chinatown sitting on a wooden crate surrounded by his clientele of both Punti and Hakka Chinese. He was popular with the Hakka because unlike most Punti, he understood and spoke Hakka. In his later years, Yuen lived with his elder sons and their families. Although by then he was totally blind, he would sit in the parlor and whenever anyone came through the front door, he would turn his head and call out their name.

(Author's private collection)

50 PAGES—HONOLULU, TERRITORY OF HAWAII, SATURDAY, M

TWO TO PRISON IN MA

L. AH LEONG, 'MERCHANT PRINCE' OF HAWAII, DIES

LARGE FAMILY SURVIVES HIM IN TERRITORY

Dies Here Today

BULGAR ARMY ESTABLISHES A DICTATORSHIP

DARROW'S AID IS SEEN FOR 'INSULL TRIAL

CHINA IN FEAR OF NEW MOVE BY NIPPONESE

End Comes Early Today At School St. Home; Had Been Here Since '76

Funeral Plans Await Arrival of Son From China; Had Many Holdings Here

Lau Fat Leong, known in business circles as L. Ah Leong, wealthy Chinese merchant, died at 6:35 a. m. today at his home at 435 N. School St. after an illness of two months.

Ah Leong, who was 78, had been a resident of the islands for 58 years, coming to Hawaii in 1876 from his native village of Kayin, Kwantung, China.

During this time he amassed a large fortune in business and real estate transactions.

He is survived by his widow, Mrs. Ah Keea, 10 sons, three daughters and 56 grandchildren.

The sons are Ah Yin, Ah Wong, Ah Tung, Ah Kong, Ah Chung, Ah Beng, Ah Chew, Ah Ping, Ah Chen and Ah Bheong.

The daughters are Mrs. C. F. Zane, Mrs. Ah Leh Liau and Mrs. Gladys Chung.

The body is now at the Nuuanu mortuary. Funeral arrangements will be announced later upon the arrival of a son, Ah Bang, from China.

The story of Ah Leong's rise from a cook to a merchant prince reads like a Horatio Alger tale.

He came to the islands at the age of 20 first going to Kohala to become a cook for a man named Lau Keng Yin Ahulu.

Later he went into partnership with Ahuna and others in a store doing business in groceries and dry goods.

The "Kohala business failing he moved to Honolulu, serving as a clerk in a store owned by L. Ahin and later starting a small store of his own in Kaakako.

L. Ah Leong, widely known merchant of Hawaii, who died at his home here today at the age of

NOTED MAORIS WILL COME TO SESSION HERE

Arts of New Zealand Aborigines Will Be Shown At Pan-Pacific Conference

Maori leaders of New Zealand will take an active part in the Third Pan-Pacific Women's conference here August 9.

Among those who will be here are Mrs. Haruta Te Maiharoa and Mrs. H. S. Bennett, who will bring samples of Maori handicraft including some of her own weaving. Mrs. Cowell is the daughter of one of New Zealand's early settlers, the late Hon. William Rennett. She is a chieftess of the Ngati-Kahungunu tribe.

Mrs. Cowan Fraer

Zealand's outstanding

Government Is Overthrown In Sofia As Troops Join In Swift Coup

Failure of Party System Is Blamed For Action In Official Manifesto

(Associated Press by Wireless)
SOFIA, Bulgaria, May 19.—The Bulgarian army overthrew the government today in a swift coup d'etat, but whether King Boris engineered the coup was not known although he signed 20 decrees for reorganization.

Following closely a cabinet crisis, a military dictatorship was established and troops were rushed from the Sofia barracks, occupied all public buildings and had taken positions at strategic points in the capital.

Reinforcements of troops in provincial cities thronged similar maneuvers. Strong detachments of soldiers and police patrolled the streets and kept the public indoors.

While members of the outgoing cabinet were arraigned and kept under military and petty guard, King Boris dissolved parliament.

A manifesto addressed to the nation attributed the change of government to failure of the system of party government, due to political reasons.

"The cooperation of the army" in assisting the new government was attributed to the manifesto to the general collapse of the entire machine of state, and the present evolution of the times.

This regime and consciousness of the necessity of ending the dangerous situation.

Austria Is Tense

VIENNA, May 19.—While another session burgeois government in Bulgaria, led to be surmounted by military dictatorship today, travelled episodes during the night marred a warning of the seizure of the Austrian government.

J. W. GARRETT QUITS POST AS O. T. A. CHIEF

To Devote Time To Executive Position For Teachers; Spencer Assumes Duties

The resignation of John W. Garrett as president of Oahu Teachers association as of August 1 was accepted with regrets at the reported monthly assembly of the organization at its meeting at the Y. W. C. A. Friday evening.

The step was taken at his request of order that he may concentrate his efforts upon his new duty as executive secretary of the Hawaii Education association.

Formal announcement of Mr. Garrett's appointment will be made in the forthcoming issue of the Hawaii Educational Review. The post of executive, to be filled for a two year period becoming August 1.

Robert Spencer, vice president will serve out the unexpired term of O. T. A. head, it was announced. Attorney O. P. Soares, a member of the board.

Mr. Garrett has been in the islands since 1924, and has taught in rural studies at the Kamehameha school for boys. Liliuokalani and industrial school and McKinley high school. He will resign from the department of public instruction in order to take the new position.

Officials Say Simon's Talk Invitation To Japan For More Aggression

Hint British Lining Up With Tokyo Against Russia-U. S. Alliance

(Associated Press by Wireless)
TOKYO, May 19.—It was learned authoritatively today that Japan plans to strengthen its air forces along the coast near Siberia.

It was understood that the plans to establish air squads at the Majuro naval base at western Honshu and the Chinkai naval base at southern Korea.

The naval aviation program is designed to provide 128 squadrons by March, 1937.

LONDON, May 19. — An official in high Chinese quarters told The Associated Press today that Sir John Simon's declaration Friday "constitutes an open invitation to Japanese militarists to bite off another chunk of China."

Sir John, the British foreign secretary, told the house of commons Friday that Great Britain "never signed any treaty to preserve the territorial integrity of China."

"Claim is now in direct danger as a result of Great Britain's statement of policy. The Chinese official looks as though Great Britain if making in the direction of allying itself with Japan to counterbalance the Russo-American preponderant. Chinese hope this really is not true, for Great Britain should line up with the United States and thus hold the balance of China."

15. Obituary from The

(Reprinted by permission of the *Honolulu Star-Bulletin.*)

17. Obituary from *The Honolulu Star-Bulletin*. May 19, 1934.

Headlines announce the death of "L. Ah Leong, 'Merchant Prince' of Hawaii, Dies." Obituary in the Caucasian-owned newspaper reads, "Lau Fat Leong, known in business circles as L. Ah Leong, wealthy Chinese merchant, died at 6:35 a.m. today at his home at 435 N. School Street after an illness of two months. Ah Leong, who was 78, had been a resident of the islands for 58 years, coming to Hawaii in 1876 from his native village of Kew Boy, Kwang Tung, China. During this time he amassed a large fortune in business and real estate transactions.

"He is survived by his widow Ho Ah Keau, 10 sons, three daughters and 56 grandchildren. The sons are Ah Yin, Ah Wang, Ah Tung, Ah Kong, Ah Chung, Ah Sang, Ah Chew, Ah Ping, Ah Chen and Ah Sheong.

"The story of Ah Leong's rise from a cook to a merchant prince reads like a Horatio Alger tale. He came to the islands at the age of 20 first going to Kohala to become a cook for a man named Lau Kong Yin Ahuna. Later he went into partnership with Ahuna and others in a store dealing in groceries and dry goods. The Kohala business failing he moved to Honolulu, serving as a clerk in a store owned by L. Ahlo and later starting a small store of his own in Kakaʻako.

"By dint of industry and thrift he accumulated his holdings. The Ah Leong fortune was estimated to be in the neighborhood of $1,000,000 a few years ago and is composed of real estate, stocks, bonds, and other assets. The beginning of this fortune was laid at the time the store at its present site at 11 N. King St. near the fish market, was opened. This store does a large volume of wholesale and retail business in general merchandise and has been under the personal management of Ah Leong from the beginning.

"Last September, the Hatch trust property at King and Maunakea Sts., in which the Ah Leong store is located, was purchased through the Bishop Trust Co. for a consideration of $140,000. Previously, the site of the store was held on lease."

18. Photo of Fung Dai-Kam. Seventy years old in 1934.
L. Ah Leong testified in 1910 in U.S. Immigration that Fung Dai-Kam was his only wife. This was important because wives of merchants were exempt from the Chinese Exclusion Act. Testimony from U.S. Immigration officers during the Board of Special Inquiry in 1921 states that they had known Lau Ah Leong from the 1890s. "He has always been in the grocery business and done a very large business, one of the largest and best known in Honolulu." They state that it was common knowledge that Fung Dai-Kam was considered his legal wife, and the other women were Ah Leong's Second, Third, Fourth, and Fifth wives in the Chinese custom. In the opinion of the Immigration officers, Dai-Kam should be considered Ah Leong's lawful wife; "she had been living with him and had a large number of children by him and has given him material assistance to amass a large fortune, but from the opinion of the United States Attorney," Ho Shee was held as Ah Leong's lawful wife. Fung Dai-Kam was awarded one-fourth of Ah Leong's real estate since she had signed numerous deeds as Fung Shee (her "wife name"), wife of L. Ah Leong, while she and her husband were building their real estate holdings.
(Author's private collection)

19. Picture of the building and sign, "1909 L. Ah Leong Block."
L. Ah Leong's name still stands above Honolulu's Chinatown at the corner of
King and Kekaulike Streets.
(Author's private collection)

20. Pam Chun with her grandmother, Lau Fung Yin, the Phoenix, at age 102.
(Author's private collection)

21. Divorce Complaint filed in the Circuit Court of the First Judicial Circuit, Territory of Hawai'i. Fung Dai-Kam Ah Leong, Libellant, vs. L. Ah Leong, Libellee. December 5, 1921. Divorce was considered scandalous in 1921, an embarrassment that reflected upon on the entire family.

In the Circuit Court of the First Judicial Circuit,
Territory of Hawai'i
December 6, 1921
FUNG DAI-KAM AH LEONG, Libellant
vs.
L. AH LEONG, Libellee

COMPLAINT
Now comes Fung Dai-Kam Ah Leong, of the City and County of Honolulu, Territory of Hawai'i, and complains of L. Ah Leong in an action of divorce and says:

I.
That they have lived together for more than thirty-eight years as husband and wife; that during all of said thirty-eight years they have been residents of the now Territory of Hawai'i; that they now reside in the City and County of Honolulu, Territory of Hawai'i.

II.
That they are now living separate and apart.

III.
That there have been issue of said marriage fourteen children, all past the age of minority except Myrtle, a daughter, aged seventeen years, and Mew Len, a daughter, aged sixteen years.

IV.

That for over twenty-nine years, L. Ah Leong lived in open and notorious adultery with numerous women including Ho Shee, a union which produced five children. That during this period he also lived in open notorious adultery with Chung Shee, and as a result of said adulterous relation, three daughters were born to the said Chung Shee. That during the said period he lived in open notorious adultery with one Zane Shee. And that during the same period he lived in open and notorious adultery with one Wong Shee, and that, as a result of their adulterous relation, a son was born to the said Wong Shee.

V.

That on April 12, 1907, the Grand Jury of the United States District Court of the Territory of Hawai'i charged L. Ah Leong with cohabiting with more than one woman: Fung Dai-Kam (being the libellant herein), Ho Shee, and Chung Shee.

That on April 17, Ah Leong pleaded guilty to said charge and was sentenced to pay a fine of Three Hundred Dollars, which said sentence and said libellee thereupon did duly perform.

VI.

That on March 1, 1910, in the District Court of the United States for the Territory of Hawai'i an indictment charging the said libellee with Bigamy in that he did unlawfully and feloniously marry and take for his wife one Ho Shee when he was already married to Fung Dai-Kam. He pleaded nolo contendere, was found guilty of Bigamy, and sentenced to imprisonment for one hour and to pay a fine of $500, all of which sentence said libellee thereafter performed.

VII.

That for more than twenty-nine years, L. Ah Leong treated Fung Dai-Kam with extreme cruelty in that he forced her to associate and consort with the women by whom he has had nine illegitimate children. He forced her to occupy a position of servility to each of the women as they ascended in his affection, forced her to cook their meals, make and mend their clothes, and attend to the illegitimate children born thereof. He has professed a preference for each of these women over Dai-Kam and exhibited to the illegitimate children greater affection than towards his lawfully begotten children.

VIII.

In July 1921, L. Ah Leong suggested that she, Fung Dai-Kam, pay a visit to China. When she went to the Inspector of the Port of Honolulu to have a pre-investigation of her status under the Chinese Exclusion Act so she could return without difficulty, she requested L. Ah Leong to give testimony to the effect that she was the wife of a merchant and therefore entitled to travel. He refused to give such testimony, that well knowing such statement to be false, and for the purpose of causing her mental suffering and pain, he stated that she was not his wife, had never been his wife, and he recognized no wife other than Ho Shee, whom he was bringing to the United States as his wife.

Thereupon, Fung Dai-Kam informed L. Ah Leong that she refused to live and cohabit with him until he rescinded his false and malicious statement. That ever since the last mentioned date, Fung Dai-Kam has refused to live with L. Ah Leong; that L. Ah Leong has falsely and maliciously, and for the purpose of inhumanely and cruelly subjecting Fung Dai-Kam to mental suffering and pain, repeated to her and to many other people his statement that Fung Dai-Kam is not and never has been his wife.

IX.

On October 5, 1921, at Honolulu, L. Ah Leong called Fung Dai-Kam, in the presence of numerous people, violent and opprobrious names including "Song Lee Ma," a Chinese expression which he intended to mean "a married woman who cohabits with men younger than her husband." He then and there told her to get out of the house or he would

kill her, raised his hand to assault her, and was restrained by the inter-
ference of her lady friend. He turned to the lady friend and called her a
whore and said she, like his wife, was looking for outside intercourse.

X.

Because of this extremely cruel treatment, Fung Dai-Kam has become
nervous and distraught and believes her life is in danger from L. Ah
Leong.

XI.

Fung Dai-Kam alleges that L. Ah Leong has property and effects worth
$750,000 in excess of his liabilities. All this property was acquired by
him through the joint efforts of L. Ah Leong and Fung Dai-Kam. At the
time of their marriage, they lived in Kohala on the Island of Hawai'i
where he was a storekeeper in partnership with Liu Kon Yen. The partnership went bankrupt at the time of their marriage, so they moved to
Honolulu were he was a clerk in L. Ah Low's store and she was a cook
in the house of L. Ah Low. They continued this employment for ten
months, during which they saved $80. Fung Dai-Kam had $200, her
dowry, given to her on the date of her marriage. They used this money
to open a grocery and general merchandise store in Kaka'ako which was
the nucleus of their fortune. This store was called "Wing Fung Kee."
"Fung" was her family name, and "Wing" and "Kee" are Chinese "store
names."

Over a successive period up to ten years from this date, the business
of L. Ah Leong and Fung Dai-Kam continued to progress, additional
stores were purchased out of the moneys jointly earned by L. Ah Leong
and Fung Dai-Kam. Fung Dai-Kam worked watch for watch with him
in the stores, sold and delivered groceries and merchandise, in addition
to doing all the housework and taking care of their children. Fung Dai-
Kam worked by hand, and thereafter by sewing machine making
blouses, jumpers, overalls, petticoats, underwear, muumuus and holokus
for sale to customers of their stores. She delivered goods and wares to

customers. As the deliveries became heavier, she used a wheelbarrow and subsequently a two-wheeled go-cart for the purpose of transporting merchandise purchased from the store.

Fung Dai-Kam says that in 1892, under the pretext of having her work as a servant in the house and store, L. Ah Leong brought Ho Shee into Dai-Kam's house. It came to Dai-Kam's attention that L. Ah Leong and Ho Shee were having sexual intercourse. When Fung Dai-Kam protested and demanded that Ho Shee be removed from the house, L. Ah Leong refused to do so. Fung Dai-Kam took her minor children and left home. She had to leave the house on four different occasions because of such conduct. Each time L. Ah Leong would bring home a new woman and she protested against his successive unlawful sexual intercourse, he would state that if she didn't like the conditions she could leave. Which she did. And each time she returned upon the earnest solicitation of L. Ah Leong and the promise that he would reform.

L. Ah Leong is a general merchant with a store situated in Honolulu. Part of his property consists of stocks and bonds and other negotiable instruments transferable by delivery. L. Ah Leong threatens to give to his illegitimate offspring of the women herein above mentioned all of his property in so far as he can do so. To that end, he has prepared Articles of Incorporation incorporating all of his business under the laws of the Territory of Hawai'i. He begged, then cajoled, and then threatened Dai-kam regarding the signing of a conveyance conveying all of the real property into said corporation. Upon Dai-Kam's refusal, he entirely cut off his support of her and told her to get out of the house.

XII.

Fung Dai-Kam says that unless protected by a Decree awarding her alimony in gross, that L. Ah Leong will dispose of his property and leave for China for the purpose of avoiding payment of any monthly stipend awarded by this Court.

WHEREFORE, libellant (Fung Dai-Kam) prays that she be granted an absolute divorce from said libellee (L. Ah Leong); that she be awarded custody of said minor children; that the Court do award her alimony in gross in such amount as may seem meet and just and a reasonable sum for the education and maintenance of said minors; that she be awarded costs, expenses, and attorneys' fees in this behalf.

Dated at Honolulu, T.H. December 5, 1921

(signed) Fung Dai-Kam Ah Leong

Maps

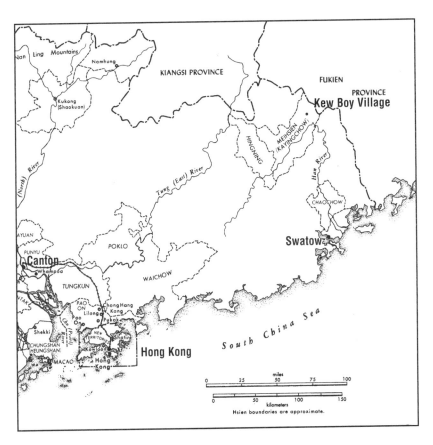

1. Southern China showing location of L. Ah Leong's village of Kew Boy located in the Meishan (Kayingchow) district which is primarily Hakka. Travelers sailed to Swatow and took the boat up the Han river to Meishan, then walked or rode a carriage to Kew Boy. Most of the Chinese in Hawai'i came from the Pearl River Delta area of Cheung Shan (Heung Shan).

(©1975 *The Sandalwood Mountains*, The University Press of Hawaii. Reprinted with permission.)

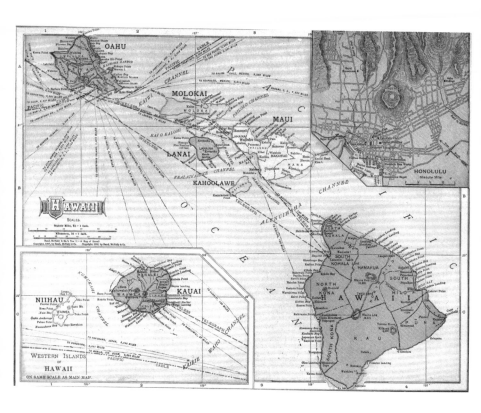

2. The Islands of the Kingdom of Hawai'i.

The United States annexed the islands in 1898. L. Ah Leong and Fung Dai-Kam married in Kohala in 1881. His grocery went bankrupt so they moved to Honolulu where he made his fortune.

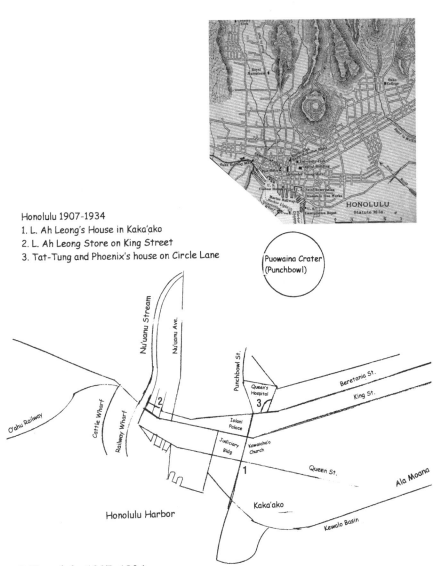

Honolulu 1907-1934
1. L. Ah Leong's House in Kaka'ako
2. L. Ah Leong Store on King Street
3. Tat-Tung and Phoenix's house on Circle Lane

3.Honolulu 1907–1934.

L. Ah Leong and Fung Dai-Kam first lived in Kaka'ako across from Kawaiaha'o Church and within sight of 'Iolani Palace. The L. Ah Leong Store is located at the corner of King and Kekaulike Streets in the heart of Chinatown. In those days, he could see the pier at Honolulu Harbor clearly from his store. First son Tat-Tung and Phoenix bought a house on Circle Lane next to Queen's Hospital to get away from his family.

About the Author

Pam Chun is a novelist who first learned about Ah Leong and her family relationship to him from former U.S. Senator Hiram L. Fong. Born and raised in Hawai'i, Pam Chun attended Punahou Academy and the University of Hawai'i and graduated with honors from the University of California at Berkeley. She lives in Alameda, California.

The Money Dragon

Reading Group Guide

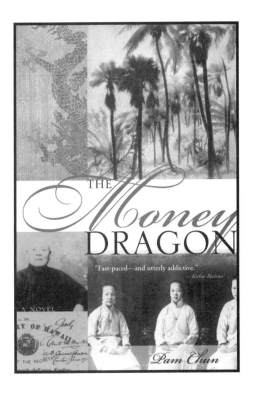

These questions were developed for readers of *The Money Dragon*
by the author.

For Discussion

1. The family and social structure of traditional Chinese culture is defined by Confucian standards, which preach that harmony comes from order. Therefore, family and social positions were highly structured, and people's worth was defined by how well they lived up to these standards. Since family order was seen as the basis of social order, maintaining a harmonious and orderly family was vital to the Chinese. Parents had authority over children throughout life, husbands over wives, First sons over Second sons and so on, and First wives over Second wives. In *The Money Dragon*, were family members of lower rank always obedient? How did they get around the rules?

2. Lau Ah Leong's life mission is to become an honorable Chinese man, admired by his neighbors and esteemed by the country's officials. How did Lau Ah Leong display his success in Hawai'i's society? How did this differ from the ways he chose to display his success in China? What does this tell us about which country he felt was his true "homeland"?

3. Lau Ah Leong believes he has reached success according to Confucian ethics. What makes him employ American laws to disrupt this hierarchy in his family? How was his ploy both a success and a failure?

4. In the Chinese culture depicted in *The Money Dragon*, men and women hold different views of family. This may be attributed to their "roles" within the family structure. We see these beliefs questioned by the younger generation. How does Lau Ah Leong's view of "family" differ from his son Tat-Tung's? How does Fung Dai-Kam's view of family differ from Phoenix's?

5. How does Fung Dai-Kam's attitude towards her rights as a Chinese woman in the 1800s compare to her attitude toward her rights as a woman in the 1900s? Why do you think she decided to divorce Lau Ah Leong despite the social stigma? What does this reflect about her? About her understanding of society? How has her concept of a wife's duties changed from 1880, when she was married, to the 1920s, when she filed for divorce?

6. Phoenix was raised with Confucian beliefs. Does her attitude change as she confronts life in Hawaiʻi? How does she adapt her Confucian beliefs to survive in the Western world?

7. What romantic notions of family and marriage does Phoenix have as a young girl? How do they change after as she marries and matures? How does Phoenix's attitude toward marriage and her in-laws change over time?

8. Is Phoenix a "good wife"? How do her husband, father-in-law, and mother-in-law view her?

9. What is more difficult for Phoenix, the physical demands of running a household or the emotional problems of being Lau Ah Leong's First daughter-in-law?

10. How do the Confucian ethics of honor and hierarchy conflict with American beliefs of the 1920s? How does Lau Ah Leong use Confucian ethics to his advantage?

11. Tat-Tung was raised with Confucian beliefs as well as Western beliefs. Does he hold to these Confucian beliefs? How do his beliefs change? How does his understanding of both Chinese and Western beliefs help him in his family, in his business, and in maintaining his honor?

12. Lau Ah Leong strove for success in both the Western world and the Chinese world. What are the measures of success in the Chinese world? What are the measures of success in the Western world? How do they conflict? How does this knowledge help Tat-Tung in his personal and business life? Does this make it easier or more difficult to maintain his "honor"?

13. Why does Tat-Tung continue to work for Lau Ah Leong's store even though he does not agree with his father and the wages are low? What does this demonstrate about his concept of a "dutiful son"?

14. Who is your favorite character in *The Money Dragon* and why?

15. The overthrow of the Hawaiian monarchy changed the lives of the Chinese who lived under the laws of the Hawaiian Kingdom. Under the Hawaiian monarchy, Lau Ah Leong could have up to seven wives. Under American law, he could have only one spouse, and that marriage had to be conducted according to American law. How could the Americans have fairly handled the situation when one had more than one wife, which was allowable under one government but illegal under the conquering government?

16. One of Lau Ah Leong's attorneys was also the attorney general for Hawai'i. Did this give him an unfair advantage in the judicial system? Should this have been allowed?

17. Although the Americans consider Second wife Ho Shee L. Ah Leong's legal wife, the Lau family has the opportunity to demonstrate Confucian harmony by allowing Dai-Kam to march as First wife. How does the final outcome bode for the future of the family? Is there honor and social harmony? If not, what do you surmise will happen?

Pam Chun